BOOK 5

CLEAVE BOURBON

FURY OF THE LICH

SHADOWS OF THE FIRST TRINE

Seer of Shadows

Contact info: cleavebourbon@gmail.com

Front Cover Design by Oliviaprodesign

Print Cover Design by Oliviaprodesign

Editor: Courtney Umphress www.courtneyumphress.com

This book contains material previously published as the Sacred Land Saga by Mark E Tyson.

FIRST EDITION : June 2023

10 9 8 7 6 5 4 3 2 1

Join in on the fun!

My newsletter has free books, sales on books, exclusive deals, and more. You can also get the latest news on my new releases! Just scan the QR code below.

FURY OF THE LICH

CLEAVE BOURBON

SHADESILVER PUBLISHING

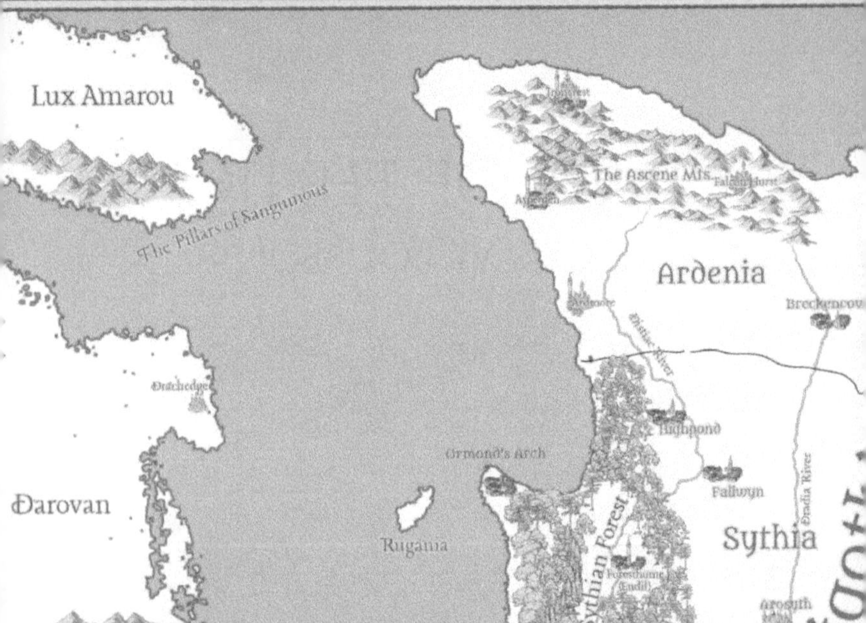
Lux Amarou
The Pillars of Sanguinous
The Ascene Mts.
Ardenia
Đarovan
Ormond's Arch
Highpond
Fallwyn
Sythia
Rugania
The Great Sythian Forest
Arosyth
Ostley
Crystal Mill
Port Arovan

Frostmere
Widow's peak
Kragador
Ishrak
Draegodor
The Plain of Storms
Ishva
Fondast
The Jagged Mountains
Trigoth
Symboria
The Strait of Adracoria
Gateway
The Southern Pass
Scarovia
The Black Forest
Wytchmore
Lake Wolfsbane
The Nightmare lands
Castle Black
The Sacred Land
Adracore
Aril
Arillia
Willow's Run

CONTENTS

CHAPTER ONE

THE ARMY OF THE WEST

Ganas Nashe, the scout from Symboria, who was lifted to the location of the lost army of the west, made a point to talk to each of the eighteen men left in the camp who were loyal to the High Lord's throne. Each one was a fierce veteran unafraid to rush into battle against abysmal odds if needed. He had been worried when he first arrived because it seemed like they were hiding from the rest of the army, self-proclaimed General Jac Wills in particular. He had discovered that Jac Wills had murdered the original commander of the army and had taken over the foreign port city of Anisport with the help of Drasmyd Duil and Dramyds. Conveniently Theosus, the one who sent him with the Lora Daine to find the army, neglected to mention the presence of the beasts. Ganas' job to rally the army and ready them for battle back in the Sacred Land was proving to be a difficult one at best. Most of the army appeared to be under some kind of control and stationed inside the port city. The highest-ranking soldier, Colonel Semten Tru, was willing enough to help Ganas recover the army, but he was not keen on dying in a suicide mission in a failed attempt to do so. Ganas needed a plan, and he needed help.

"I can't say I am surprised the dragon king sent only one man to retrieve us. What are they expecting you to do? Carry us one by one across the ocean." Colonel Tru asked.

Ganas tried to hide his annoyance, "Well, the army is a military outfit. It wasn't supposed to be scattered into two factions like this and my job was simply to gather everyone up into one place. There is a plan for extraction. I am not sure what it is yet, But I know there is a plan to get you home as fast as possible. You are sorely missed and desperately needed back home."

"Well, it's nice to know we are not forgotten."

"A change of subject, was there anything unusual or did anyone unusual show up and talk to Jac? Anything you can think of?"

Colonel Tru thought for a moment, "No, not here in camp, but my scouts tell me there is a mysterious man often seen with Wills. He is tall with dark hair and deep scars on his face and left arm."

"Is he a local?"

"How should I know? I assume so."

"I mean does he appear to be local. Does he have any characteristics that place him as a Densoian?"

"He looks like an ugly, scarred man. That's all I can tell you."

"I guess it's time I go scout for myself. I don't suppose there is a volunteer who would escort me to the city."

"I'm sure one or two would go if you asked."

Ganas spent the next hour preparing his gear for the journey to the city. As it turned out, there was one volunteer, another scout named Denten Nafere who liked to be called Den, who agreed to show him the way. The city was farther away from the camp than Ganas expected. In fact, it was a few days journey. He had assumed it was closer from the way the men talked about it. Supplies from the camp were scarce, but he had brought enough with him to feed himself and Den the entire trip. They could supplement their diet with game on the way. Den said there were plenty of cotton tail rabbits, deer, and wild vegetation on the way across the arid plains. Deer might be a difficult game to skin and prepare, but cotton tails would be quick and easy.

Ganas and Den set out at first light the following morning for the city of Anisport. Ganas tried to think of a plan to convince Jac Wills to let the army return to Symboria. Surly, once he explained they could return home, the men at least would rally to him. It was the spell the Colonel insisted the men were under that worried him. How was such a spell even possible and who would cast it, the scarred man?

The first day was uneventful. They traveled across a vast plain of prairie grass, cacti, mesquite trees, and scattered yucca plants. He could see as far as the horizon. There were no trees taller than he nor were there any discernable rock formations or landmarks to speak of on the trail. He was thankful it was arid grassland and not hot, scorching desert.

"How do you know where you are headed?" Ganas asked Den.

Den, a tall thin man with unkept sandy brown hair, lazy hazel eyes, and a hooked nose, cleared his dry throat, "We just follow the sun west."

Ganas knew to follow the sun west but that didn't mean they were going to run directly into the city, "So, the city is directly west of the camp?"

"More or less." Den said.

At dusk Den found a clump of mesquite trees to set up camp. Ganas began to gather up mesquite wood for a fire after he sat aside his pack. He combed the base of the trees looking for rattlesnakes, true to his survival training.

"You might want to make that fire as big as you can. There are many creatures on the plains, and they all seem to be afraid of fire." It was the most Den had said since they left camp. "Coyotes, rattlesnakes, dogmen, and other wild animals."

"I have already looked for rattlesnakes in the brush at the base of the mesquite trees, and I am familiar with Coyotes, but what are dogmen?"

"Wolfmen roam around here. I have seen them. They hunt deer and other animals. They don't usually come up to a camp with a roaring fire, but they are out there, I promise you that."

"They look like men?"

"They run sometimes on hind legs, and sometimes on all fours. They have the upper body of a man and the face of a dog or wolf. They have sharp claws on the end of their muscular arms they use to swipe at prey. I wouldn't go getting into any fights with them if I were you."

"You are messing with me. They're not real."

"Oh no, they're real all right. You will most likely see one before we reach the city. You'll probably see one tonight. If you don't threaten them, they will most likely leave us alone."

"That's terrifying!"

"None of them have attacked any of us thus far and we have been to the city quite a few times."

Uneasily, Ganas bed down underneath one of the mesquite trees for the night. Den bed down near the fire and as he slipped underneath his blanket, he glanced back at him.

"I would get closer to the fire if I were you. The rattlesnakes like to get in the grass around the base of those mesquite trees. You might end up with a visitor in middle of the night if you stay there like that."

Even though he had already checked for snakes, Ganas hastily moved his bedding closer to the fire. "It's autumn. When do the snakes go hibernate?"

"They won't do that until winter. They love spring and autumn the most. They don't like the cold or the extreme hot of summer."

"Good to know." Ganas said as he got comfortable in his new spot. "I never got to train much on the arid plains. It's very different than what I'm used to scouting."

"You'll catch on. There isn't that much to look out for, really."

There was a rustling near where Ganas had moved from near the mesquite tree. At first, he ignored it as nothing but his imagination, but when it happened again, he opened his eyes and slowly turned to see what was making the noise while palming his sword. He squinted to get a better look in the fading light of the fire. It took his eyes a moment to adjust, but when they did, they focused on a face lodged inside the mesquite tree. He carefully raised his sword, moving as slowly as he could. The face moved further into the light and Ganas realized it was the face of a wolf, but it was too high up in the tree to be a normal-sized wolf. It had to be one of the wolfmen.

"Don't make any sudden moves." Den whispered. Ganas was going to say something, but Den interrupted, "and keep quiet. Don't spook it."

The face moved closer to him and then left the tree getting almost close enough to touch. It began to sniff the air and Ganas realized he had some dried beef in his saddle bag not far from where the beast was aiming its nose. Its fur was greyish white with flecks of brown. Its eyes, yellowish green and focused on the saddle bag. Ganas heard the ground crunch behind him, and he realized Den was moving toward him. Then he noticed the sharp arrow point above his head as Den aimed at the creature's head.

"No! stop! He's not what you think!" came a female voice out of the darkness. "Don't shoot him!"

The beast lifted the saddle bag flap and helped himself to some of the dried meat. A young woman rushed over to the beast, "Get out of that, Verel. That isn't for you." She pushed the creature away from the saddle bags and he rushed into the field with his stolen beef to chew on it. The young woman stepped into the firelight. She was brown skinned with big brown eyes and plain brown clothing. Her face was pleasing and pretty with a ruggedness to it.

"I'm so sorry. He must have caught the scent of your pack. Sometimes they can be more wolf than man."

"Obviously, Den said."

"Now, don't be rude, Den." Ganas scolded. "You'll have to forgive my friend."

"All is forgiven." She glared at Den. "You're one of the soldiers."

"Yes."

"Why are you not in the city with the rest of your kind?" Her voice sounded unsteady now and a bit angry.

"I am not one of *those* soldiers." Den said. "I am one of the soldiers who left the city."

"Oh." She examined Ganas closely, "You are even more different. You don't smell like you have been on the plains for long. You smell like you belong in the forest."

"I do. I mean, I am more at home in the forest." He was leaning on his arm, but it was beginning to ache, so he righted himself, "I am from Symboria, across the ocean." He said it expecting her to be impressed that he come from somewhere so far away.

"So are the rest of you," she said.

"Oh yes, that's right." He held out his hand, "I am called Ganas."

She just stared at his hand with a perplexed look on her face. She didn't know what to do.

"They don't shake hands here." Den said.

"Oh," Ganas said sheepishly withdrawing his hand.

"I am Azura." She said, and the manwolf is called..."

"Verel, Yes, I heard." Ganas interrupted. "What are you doing out here in the middle of nowhere?"

"Hunting game." She said, "What are you doing out here in the middle of nowhere?"

"We are traveling to the city."

"Why?"

"I was sent here to retrieve the army and take it back to Symboria."

"Umm, should you be telling a stranger all this?" Den grumbled.

Azura's face lit up, "You are here to take the soldiers away?"

"Aye, I am."

She shook with glee she could barely contain, "If that's your purpose, how can I help?"

"What?" Ganas was taken aback.

"The soldiers are ruining my city. It's dark and dangerous now. My people and I would love to see them leave our home once and for all! I'll help you in any way I can to rid the city of the invaders."

"Well, I'm not sure what you could do to help me."

"I can get you inside the walls past the centuries to the palace where the soldiers are. I know of a couple of secret ways to get there. I can get you in without being seen."

Den shook his head, "wait a second, where did you come from and who are you? I also know how to get into the palace. Why should we trust you? You would have us believe you're someone we just happened to meet in the middle of nowhere that happens to know exactly how to get into the one place we need to go. The odds of you showing up are astronomical." He turned to Ganas, "It's too easy. Something is not quite right here.

Ganas sighed, "I hate to admit it but he's right. That is some coincidence you just happening upon us on these vast plains like this."

"So much for that tactic." Verel said.

"The wolfman talks!" Den said.

"I do," Verel said. "We were supposed to find you and offer our assistance, but it was feared you might not accept our help face to face."

"It seems silly now." Azura said, "we should have known they would be suspicious of strangers."

"Maybe this will help, we were sent to offer you our assistance by the city council. They want you to be successful in ridding the city of the soldiers and dark creatures."

"How did they know I was coming?"

"Your dragon. She sent word to us. She thought you might need assistance too."

Ganas glanced at Den who was obviously not buying it. Ganas subtly shook his head to let Den know he was not completely buying it either. "All right. I will accept your help, but first we need to get some sleep." He decided to see where this was all going. "And we need some assurances you are who you say you are. We would feel more comfortable if you made your camp nearby away from us until we can be sure of your intentions."

"Understood. I will keep watch for you, sir." Azura said, "a gesture of our good faith."

Ganas nodded, "All right, but not too close."

"Naturally." Azura grinned and then bounded off followed by Verel.

Chapter Two

Across the Plain

Ganas had a rather restless sleep, but he did get a few hours of rest. He was not sure if he could trust his new friends and that worry made for difficult sleeping. When he awoke, Azura was tending to the fire and cooking something that smelled delicious. He looked around but Verel was nowhere in sight.

"Where is Verel."

Azura looked up from her cooking, "He is around. He likes to stalk around in the morning. His people, the Indu, can be paranoid sometimes. He is just checking that nothing or no one is encroaching on his territory."

"Indu?" Ganas asked.

"Wolfmen are the closest thing I can use to explain them, but they are obviously not actually wolves or men. They are their own unique thing."

"I have never heard of them."

"They live in relatively small numbers and are loners within their own people, another difference between them and wolves who move in packs and shun loners."

Den finished packing up his bedding and was just joining them at fire. "We have seen them about, but they kept to themselves, so we did too." He sniffed, "That smell is making my stomach is growl."

"It's almost ready. It's rabbit meat with a few wild herbs from the area."

"It smells wonderful." Ganas said, "What kind of herbs grow out here?"

"Wild onion, wild garlic, and a few others. The plains have a lot to offer if you know where to look." She portioned out the meat on a couple of tin plates and handed them over to the men. I would make some flatbread, but I don't have a grinding stone for the grain to make flour. Maybe I will find one when we get closer to Anisport."

"Oh no, that sounds like a lot of work. We are fine with the herb rabbit." Ganas said.

Now that it was daylight, Ganas had a chance to really see Azura. She did have darker skin, but it appeared more tanned brown now in the sunlight than natural brown like Sanmir. She had dark hair pulled back and big brown, welcoming eyes. Her smile almost made Ganas' heart flutter with her dimpled cheeks and pearl white teeth.

"Did you save some for me?" Verel almost appeared out of thin air. He was a frightening sight in the daylight. His hind legs bowed backward, and he seemed to bounce on them. His arms were covered in thick greyish brown fur and his face and mouth were so strange looking, like a wolf but with a man's voice coming out of it. His clothing was made of woven strands of fabric and leather.

"Of course, I saved the hunter his share," she said as she handed him a plate with a slightly bigger portion. He devoured it, bones and all, in almost two bites of his powerful jaws.

"Verel, where are your manners." Azura asked. Ganas realized he must have been making a face while watching the Indu eat.

"Sorry, I am not used to fine company."

Ganas put on his best smile, "Don't worry about it. I have seen fine folk do worse." He decided to change the subject, "How far are we from the city?"

"A couple of days still." Verel answered, "if we hurry. I spotted a patrol from the city not far from here, but I will steer us clear of such nuisances. They will never see us coming. I also have some of my kin looking out for us. We will sneak into the city before anyone is the wiser."

"I really appreciate your help." Ganas said.

Azura cleared the dishes from the fire so they could cool before packing them away. "We are happy to help if it means we get our city back. No offence, but the sooner you get those soldiers out of there the better. What is your plan to get them out anyway?"

Ganas almost choked on his rabbit, "Before I answer that, let me say that I was sent here by some powerful wizards of the west and their dragon allies. It is they who have the plan to get them home. My job is to rally everyone together and assess the situation."

"Ah, so no plan then." Verel said.

"Well, yes, the plan is to convince them all to return to the camp or some other suitable spot as long as they are together so the wizards can get them back home. They can't do anything if the whole of the army is scattered about like they are right now."

Verel handed his plate to Azura and glanced at the sky, "We are burning daylight. We had best be on our way. I have scouted our route.

We will leave as soon as everyone is packed." He raised his head and let out a half growl, half howl and three other members of his kind came out from behind some mesquite trees, "Do not be alarmed, these friends are here to hide our camp once we're gone. It is Indu tradition to leave a bed down spot as it was before found."

"Not a bad idea." Den said.

The small party traveled west in a zig zag pattern devised by Verel. It was strange having his route scouted out for him. At least now he understood the trust the generals must have had in him because not knowing what was ahead was a bit unnerving. Trusting someone else to scout out and plan your route was a bit like giving up a modicum of power somehow. Still, he did seem to be doing a good job from the observations of one scout to another.

The second night, he noticed the Indu slept as soon as they set up camp and was out hunting as soon as the last light of the sun faded. He wasn't gone for an hour when he returned with supper, a few more cotton tails and a couple of Pheasants from the looks of the hunt. He also brought a few ears of corn, which explained the Pheasants.

"Are we close to a farm?" Ganas asked.

"Fairly close." Verel said. "I had to do some sneaking, but I didn't take much. I don't think the farmer will mind."

"We have Pheasants in Symboria. They are abundant around harvest time especially near corn fields. There are a few good things about the autumn season!"

"Naturally. I don't suppose you would like to help me prepare the birds for cooking then, since you have experience." Verel asked.

"Of course." Ganas went to his pack for his good hunting knife.

"Tonight, we feast!" Azura quipped.

"Absolutely!" Ganas grinned and met Den's gaze expecting him to also be smiling. He was not. In fact, Den said less and less as they got closer to Anisport. Ganas intended to have a talk with him to see if there was something bothering him once they started off in the morning.

On the final day of the journey, Ganas tried a few times to get Den off alone so he could talk to him, but the task proved difficult. There were interruptions and it seemed the soldier would move away from him each time he found an opportunity to talk to him. Being a scout, Ganas was no stranger to different customs, and he wondered briefly if he had offended Den. After all, he did take to Azura and Verel quite easily and quickly to the point where Den might have felt left out or neglected. Ganas was not a fan of men with delicate dispositions, but he had known a few before, and Den very well seemed to be one of them.

"Hey," Ganas said when he finally was able to catch up to Den.

"Hey," Den repeated.

"Is there something the matter. You have been awfully quiet the past day or so."

Den gave him a sharp, haggard look, I am just a bit tired. I do not trust easily and not only do I have to keep an eye on you, who I do not know well, I also must watch the two others now. My sleep has been uneasy."

"That was certainly an honest answer."

"What, did you expect me to lie?"

"No, I just figured you might've decided to trust me after a couple of days."

"Trust is earned, not given."

"Well, I certainly hope I have the opportunity to earn yours."

"Perhaps, we will see."

Ganas moved ahead of Den. *Well, at least he's not sensitive enough to get hurt feelings*. He thought to himself. *A true soldier*.

As the day wore on, Verel's convoluted trail straightened out a bit. They had entered into some low hills about midday. They stopped in a nice meadow for a meal. The leaves still on the trees were yellow and red. The ground was covered with dead brown foliage. As a scout, dead leaves made Ganas cringe. It was very difficult to scout around with loud, crunching leaves beneath your feet.

"The city is a few hours away from here." Verel announced. "It would be a good thing if we moved into the shade of the trees and waited for nightfall before we try to sneak inside the gates." He gazed into the sun and squinted, "A couple of hours from now, we can start that way."

Ganas walked behind Den to the tree line. As he walked, he noticed something odd protruding from the soldier's belt. It was a small scabbard with the hilt of a dagger sticking out from under his shirt. At first, he thought it might be something Den picked up since they had been marooned in Denosia because the dagger was not standard army issue. The hilt was of a strange pattern with a small hand reaching out as the pommel. As he thought about it, he became unsettled. What did he know about this soldier? Could this man be leading him into a trap? Perhaps a trap thwarted by the chance meeting of Azura and Verel. Maybe Den was acting upset and strange because he had not anticipated the two newcomers. One thing Ganas did know was that if Den was going to try something it would be a time where he had a clear advantage. He would not try anything until they reached the city. It would be too dangerous three against one. He would wait until inside the city now to give him away. Maybe he had a few buddies waiting for them?

"All right, rest here by the trees." Verel said. "I will scout around the area to make sure we are safe and undiscovered. When the evening sun appears just above the horizon, we will move toward the city and nightfall."

Ganas nodded and Verel scooted away. Azura sat and leaned against a big tree. Den also found him a spot by a tree and lowered himself, pack and all. Ganas cautiously found a spot where he could watch both of them and anyone else wandering up before he allowed himself to fully relax.

Chapter Three

The City of Anisport

Ganas wondered if he might be getting paranoid, but he kept a close eye on both Den and Azura. Verel was often scouting, but he watched him for signs that he too might be leading them in the wrong direction. He just had an uneasy feeling. When they reached the city gates, he found a possible source for his worry. He didn't know how the city of Anisport looked before, but it was definitely dark and foreboding now.

The gate they were to sneak through was made of wrought iron, but a section of it had been torn away from some long ago incident and had never been repaired. Beyond the gate was a high stone wall. They all managed to slip through the gate and scale the stone wall to drop onto one of the side roads inside the city. The first assault Ganas dealt with was the stench. The city smelled of death and decay. The walls of the nearby houses and buildings appeared to be covered in a black mold or some other nasty fungus. After the smell of death, the decay part was most likely the fungus smell. It was like mildew and rotten mushrooms mixed. The streets on this side of the city had a coating of slime from decay and disuse.

"How do you get used to this smell?" Ganas asked.

"Imagine what I smell." Verel said pointing to his sensitive canine nose. "You think you have it bad?"

"I guess I shouldn't complain." Ganas said.

Verel smiled, or Ganas thought he smiled. It was difficult to tell. A moment later, Verel stopped them and sniffed a few times into the air. "We might have company. It smells like a shadow lurker is nearby." He motioned for them to retreat into the nearest shadow.

Ganas hoped they were not moving into the shadow occupied by the lurker, but Verel's nose would most likely detect it if they were. He watched as Den entered the shadow last. They exchanged an uneasy gaze and Ganas felt a twinge of dread. He suddenly trusted the soldier even less than he did before. Azura squeezed in next him so close he could smell the herbs and flowers she used to cleanse her hair. It was subtle and cloaked largely by the horrible stench of the city, but it was there.

Verel swept his arm back over the group to make sure they were all against the wall as a shadow moved across the opposite building. The shadow lurkers' nickname was apt, for they were extremely difficult to spot. Ganas squinted at the slight movement. The shadow moved like flowing smoke from one darkened area to the next, barely perceptible, then it stopped. Ganas saw the slight outline of a spiked face peering from the darkness directly at them. His heart began to pound. He closed his eyes and tried to calm himself. There was a rumor that shadow lurkers could feel your heartbeat.

"I think he can see us." Den said in a low whisper. As soon as the soldier uttered the first word, the Drasmyd Duil unwound its hideous wings and leaped across the street with a screech.

"Nice going!" Verel said to Den. "You brought it right to us!" Verel used his immense claws to knock the creature to the wayside as soon as it got close enough.

Ganas pulled his sword, "There will be more coming after a screech like that."

"It's likely," Azura agreed.

The creature found its footing and Verel went in for the attack, claw to claw. They were moving so fast, there was not a place for Ganas or Azura to help so they scanned the alleyway for others to join in the fight. They did not have to wait long. Two Dramyds flew into the alleyway followed by another Drasmyd Duil. Ganas looked for Den, but he was not in sight. Ganas' sword found the first airborne Dramyd's chest as he thrust his sword through it. It slid down to the hilt by momentum and was almost able to bite him with its revolting, toothy mouth. Ganas pushed it back off his blade. He noticed out of the corner of his eye that the Drasmyd Duil had knocked Azura to the side and forced her to engage with the two other Dramyds. She was holding her own, but the Drasmyd Duil was now closing in on her position. Ganas jumped in front of the creature and began fighting it off with his sword. Sprays of acid were coming from the Dramyd blood behind him as Azura dispatched the creatures. The acid was burning his hands, but he kept fighting. The Drasmyd Duil's claws fought off his sword as if the creature were wielding daggers. He was about to run the creature through when he heard a muffled scream from Azura. He looked in her direction and that's when the claws from the creature he was fighting sliced through his leather armor and made a gash in his chest. Before he could feel the wound's pain, he made a last-ditch effort to force his blade into the creature. His maneuver paid off as he forced his blade through the creature's neck.

It gurgled and then spun down to the ground bleeding out. Ganas fell to his knees, blood oozing from his chest wound.

"Ganas is injured!" He heard Azura say to Verel.

Ganas, still griping his sword, leaned forward as he saw Den charging him from the shadows. The soldier had his sword drawn and was thrusting it directly at him. *The coward waited until I was exhausted and injured to attack!* He thought. He deflected the first blow with a burst of strength he didn't know he had, and he forced himself to his feet. He ignored the pain from his chest and now, he realized, his abdomen, and swung his sword at the soldier. His burst of strength was short lived, and he went down losing his sword in the process. He was just too exhausted to fight off Den. He braced for the final blow. He saw Den raise his sword.

"I fight for Jac, and I kill you in the name of my master Ezra Bannon!" Den began his blow, but it never landed on its intended target. Azura deflected it as Verel decapitated Den with his mighty, sharp claws from behind. Ganas finally let out the stiff tension he held to keep the pain at bay and collapsed. Verel and Azura were at his side in a mere moment.

"Quickly, get him into one of these houses." Verel said. "They are mostly abandoned on this side of the city."

Ganas blinked slowly as the pain came in throbbing rounds. He watched as Azura used lockpicks to gain entrance into one of the houses. Verel picked him up in his arms and carried him into the house. He placed him down on a bed in the corner of the one room dwelling.

The wolfman went to the window and pulled back the tattered curtain, "I don't see any more of the creatures. You tend to Ganas' wounds while I get rid of the carcasses. If we leave them out there like this, we will be found out in no time."

"Is there any way you could get us some water from one of the city wells? I don't want to waste our drinking water."

"Aye, give me a moment." He disappeared out the door. A few moments later he brought in two wooden buckets of water, and some cloth to tear into strips. He gave them to Azura and then went about the task of clearing the area outside. Azura began using her dagger to cut the edge of the fabric and then tear it into strips.

"Who is Ezra Bannon?" he asked.

Azura began dipping one of the strips in the water and cleaning his wounds. Ganas winced. Azura dabbed the wound once she realized she was being a little rough, "I have no idea. Try not to talk or move around too much."

"I knew Den was not what he appeared."

"Shh, I told you not to talk. We will discuss it all when Verel returns."

Azura had Ganas' wounds cleaned and field dressed by the time Verel returned.

"I got everything cleared but the blood. I hope the decay and darkness will keep away any prying eyes or curious Drasmyd Duil." He glanced out the glazed glass window. "I think it will storm. That will clear it away for us."

"Do you have any idea who Ezra Bannon is?" Azura asked.

"No, I assume it is the older gentleman I have seen with Jac Wills. He is always there whispering in his ear." Verel answered.

A crash of thunder made Azura jump. "There's your storm."

Ganas moved to sit up and immediately flatted back when the pain would not allow it.

"Easy," I said. What am I going to have to do to keep you still?"

"Sorry, Azura." Ganas said. "I thought I heard something outside."

Verel nodded, "I heard it too. Someone stirs outside the house." He perked up his pointed canine ears, "It's not a Dramyd or Drasmyd Duil. It's a man of average build." He listened more intently, "He is armed with a sword and shield." He sniffed the air and then went to the door and opened it to let the man inside. The rain had begun to fall, and the man wore his cloak tight. He entered the room while Verel shut the door behind him. "He smells of dragon." Verel explained.

The man lowered his cloak to reveal a pleasant, bearded face with silver in his temples and highlighted throughout his facial hair. "That's because I had to ride one all the way from Symboria." He placed his cloak over a chair and pointed to the fireplace. The half-burned wood inside it burst into flames. He turned to the door, raised his hand, and spoke a few words while moving his hand in a circular motion. "There, we are warded against the shadow. They will not disturb us or detect us."

"You look familiar." Ganas said. "Did Morgoran or Ianthill send you?"

"I do not believe we have met officially, Ganas Nashe, but I am aware of you and of your mission here. Aye, I am here to lend you a hand in rounding up this army and getting them home into the fight."

"Who are you, then?"

"Oh, allow me to introduce myself. I am the father of Lady Shey. Veric Namear, at your service." He bowed.

CHAPTER FOUR

MASTER OF LIES

Veric glanced uncomfortably around the one room house, "We thought you might need some help considering what you are facing."

"Morgoran knows about the city and the army?" Ganas asked.

"Not so much, but since you are still here and there has been no word, we thought maybe you had hit a snag." He examined the field bandage Azura fashioned for him, "and we appear to be right."

Verel went for the door, "I will scout out the way to the temple where Jac Wills and this Bannon have been seen."

"Uh, no need." Veric said, "I have just come from there. Both men are in the temple with about twenty men or so."

"Where is the rest of the army?" Ganas asked.

"In makeshift barracks nearby. They gutted out some shops and houses. Most of the army is still intact. What we will need to do is free them from Bannon's influence and they will all want to return home."

"Do you know this Ezra Bannon fellow?" Ganas asked.

"Aye, he is a mindwielder of Toborne's. Your friend, Tatrice, wounded him when she freed herself from his influence. It was thought she killed him in the attack, but I can see from the large scar he wears across his face that she just severely wounded him. Toborne must have had his dark clerics restore him as best they could."

"So, Toborne is behind all this? To what purpose, I wonder."

"Well, Ganas. Denosia is unconquered lands. I would imagine having an entire army here already would be tempting. All that would be required is a way to rule that army, hence the reason for Bannon's control over the commander, Jac Wills. It's a perfect setup for one who has the ambitions of Toborne."

Ganas moved uncomfortably making pain moans.

"Are there not any clerics about?" Veric asked.

Azura gave him a quizzical look, "Are you serious?"

"Yes, not everyone is under the thumb of Bannon, Wills, and their army, are they?"

"Well, no but no one is going to willingly lend a hand to an outsider, especially one from the lands of their oppressors."

Veric helped Ganas to his feet, "Are you able to get around? I know you can't fight in this condition, but can you at least return to the camp?"

"The camp is days away." Ganas said, "I'm not sure you understand the situation we are in around here, sir."

Veric cleared his throat. "I can't heal any better than your friend here did, unfortunately, but I am an expert at stealth and hiding in the shadows. I will go out into the city and find a temple of Loracia. I am not without means. Once I find someone willing to take my coin, I will return. We can't move forward with you injured like this."

"I will go with you," Verel said, "I would get too restless cooped up in here and I am also an expert at staying hidden."

Veric gave him a disproving glance and then seemed to change his mind, "All right. You might come in handy. I assume you know where a temple may be located?"

He shook his head, "I am not from the city." He looked to Azura for guidance.

"There is one across the city near the far gate. You can't miss it. There is a statute of Loracia with her healing arms outstretched on a stone dais in middle of the front steps. How you two are going to sneak a cleric all the way here is beyond me."

"You leave that to us." Verel said.

"Do not open the door for anyone. I will knock twice like this, he made a knocking noise on a nearby table, when we return." Veric said.

"Good luck. Try not to get yourselves caught or worse, killed." Ganas said.

Veric liked to work alone, the presence in the back of his mind excluded. The voice sometimes helped with decisions. He checked over his shoulder for Verel and found him also adept at moving though the shadows, but he still didn't like him tagging along.

The city was dark, dank, and damp as if it had been raining and the water had not yet evaporated. The only issue is that Veric did not see any rain. The city was just humid. They both moved through the mostly deserted streets undetected, both of nearly equal skill at stealth. The only beings lurking around the city were Dramyds and the occasional Drasmyd Duil, although they were much rarer.

Verel made a sharp hissing sound to garner Veric's attention. He stopped in his tracks as he saw what Verel was warning about. Ahead, just before the steps of the temple of Loracia, just a few steps from the statue giving away whose temple they had found, was a creature Veric had never seen before. It was like a larger Drasmyd Duil complete with wings wrapped around its rotund body. Drasmyd Duil were essentially humanoid dragons not much larger than their human counterparts, but this one was something special. *Humans come in all shapes and sizes so why not Drasmyd Duil?* He thought.

He stealthily made his way back to where Verel hid in the shadows and whispered, "What? It's only a bigger Drasmyd Duil. We should be able to overpower him."

Verel shook his head, "No, this one is different. His acid spit is much more powerful and plentiful. Even if we could overpower him and even defeat him, his acid would get on us and continually burn us to death."

"Does it cling in some way or something?"

"Aye, it's sticky. At first, it doesn't do much. You forget about it, and it moves to cover your entire body, then it starts eating away at you. Water or anything else you use to try and wash it off makes it work faster. We need to find a way around him or find another cleric."

"Is there somewhere with another cleric?"

"Fawlsbane Vex's temple is not far."

"Vex? His clerics can heal now?"

"What an odd question. Surely, you know they can."

"Where I come from, there were few temples devoted to the father of the gods and very few clerics in those. The men and women who worshiped him were fierce fighters and warriors. There were no clerics. They left all the healing to Clerics of the goddess mother."

"I didn't say they were particularly good healers, but one would be better than nothing. Ganas' wounds are bad, but not so bad one of the Vex clerics couldn't help him."

Veric weighed the options, fight the acid creature, or divert to find a lesser healer, "Is there a way around this thing into the temple, you think? What if I run out there in the street and get it to chase me so you can get into the temple?"

"Aye, that may work, but it would never stop chasing you, and if it caught you..."

"Aye, I know. I do have a few tricks up my sleeve. I might be able to lose it in the city."

"Not if you run into other Drasmyd Duil in the meantime. You could have an entire mob chasing you if you aren't careful."

"You let me worry about that. Here's the plan: I will run out and get its attention and then you go into the temple and find a cleric that will help us and head back to the house. I will lose the creature in the city and meet you back there when I'm able."

"I can't say I agree with this plan."

"Regardless, wish me luck!" He ran out into the street before Verel could answer. The creature had one other feature Verel either didn't know about or forgot to mention, it snorted, and smoke and fire bellowed out of its nostrils. This Drasmyd Duil was a firebreather. It focused on Veric and charged. As Veric had hoped, it was alone. Whoever stationed it there at the temple thought it would be enough and didn't bother to station any others, and to be honest, it would have been enough for most. Veric scanned the alleyway to make sure Verel sprinted and made it to the temple before he turned and ran down an empty street. He wanted to get the creature away from the temple and out of sight for what he had planned for it. To his dismay, he ran directly into a horde of Dramyds along with two Drasmyd Duil. He tried to avoid them seeing him by ducking down a small alley which led to another broad, this time empty, street. All the creatures followed.

He traversed the perimeter of the area and enchanted a blue circle that whooshed out from his position to magically seal off the street as he let the creatures in to confront him. He turned to the largest Drasmyd Duil just as it was breathing fire on him. The flames did nothing. Veric snapped his fingers, and all the creatures froze in place, unable to move. He examined the large creature, slowly strolling around it as it stood frozen before him. Its eyes followed him as best they could until he was behind it.

"Hmm? Impressive. Who made you big fella? You don't look like one of the Drasmyd Duil Toborne or Morgoran made, and you breath fire!" He addressed the others frozen behind him, "You may go." He waved his hand and the Dramyds and Drasmyd Duil became animated again. They stood around for a moment confused. Veric felt a twinge of anger well up in him, "Go!" The creatures scattered. He returned his attention to the large one once more, "Such good work. Bannon couldn't do this, nor anyone in the army. Perhaps no one made you and you are simply an abnormality, a Drasmyd Duil born different. It was bound to happen with all your brothers' eggs being manipulated, prodded with, and tampered with. It is of no matter now." He touched the snout of the creature and stroked it. The creature's eyes were red with fury. "I may have a use for you later. You are completely being wasted here under the control of Bannon. I need you where the real fighting will be very shortly." He waved his hand, pulled out a small jade statuette from beneath his robes, and held it toward the creature. The Drasmyd Duil began to disintegrate, and the particles sparkled and entered the statuette. Once it was done, he put the figurine away where he got it.

From the corner of his eye, Veric saw an old man poking at the blue barrier he had made earlier as he put away the statuette.

"I can't let you take that." The old man said.

Veric let the barrier drop, "Be on your way old man."

The old man's hands began to glow in a blue tint, "I said I can't let you have that creature, Return it to me."

"Fawlsbane Vex, is that you? Did you make this creature? Why would you do that and trap the army here in Denosia."

The old man let out a beam of blue light from his hands and Veric blocked it with a wave of his. "No, you are not Fawlsbane Vex. Who are you wizard?"

Another attack hit him this time, Only, it was much stronger this time, "I didn't make the creature. I don't really care about it. I just don't want *you* to have it or use it. I want you to leave this place and to stop your meddling. You know we are not supposed to interfere."

"Who do you think I am? I am simply Veric Namear. A humble servant of..."

Another bolt hit him and knocked him onto his back this time, "Give me the statuette, Aedreagnon!"

Veric got to his feet, "Aedreagnon? Who are you?"

The old man facade dropped to reveal a handsome man with short golden hair wearing a plain, dark earthen cloak and black boots. He stood with his hands bathed in a blue tinted light.

"Xeian! Go back to Mount Venifyre to your father. You can't do anything here."

"You first!" Xeian said. "I am sure Father would love to hear what you've been up to of late."

"Brother, I don't want to fight you. You know what's at stake. You know what I must do."

"Sorry, Aedreagnon. I can't let you go through with it. Let go of this man, Veric, you possess and fight me deity to deity, brother to brother. You know I am stronger than you when you exist this way, and I can defeat you easily in this weakened form you take. I do not wish to harm the innocent man you harbor. Show your true self."

Veric fumbled in his pockets and removed from one of them what looked like a Lora Daine, "Sorry, Xeian, perhaps we could argue about this some other time. Right now, I have work to do." As Veric faded out he saw Xeian drop his blue attack spell and watch him helplessly as he dissipated out of sight.

CHAPTER FIVE

FELL NIGHT

Dorenn was exhausted. All he wanted to do was return to his bedchamber and sleep. Forming an army when half the kingdom still didn't want to recognize the king was a monumental task. To make things worse, there was talk of a civil war between the Trigothian kingdoms. Dorenn had no idea where Seandara had gone, or where his friends were. If they wanted him, they could search for him. If they did search, his chambers were probably the last place they would look, ironically. He put on his bedclothes and crawled into his luxurious bed, ready for a good night's sleep that would probably never come. Instead, he would dream. They would begin almost immediately. The chief among the intrusive dreams would be that of Toborne. Not the Toborne who had occupied the personage of Drakkius, but the original Toborne who was ripped from his body by Sylvalora while she was in the form of the Silver Drake. Dorenn bolted upright when the dream came and went. He glanced around the room and then closed his eyes, still feeling tired. He heard rustling and then the dull sound of someone plopping down on one of his plush chairs. He opened his eyes to see Toborne sitting in a chair next to his bedside.

"What do you want?" Dorenn asked. He was not frightened. He knew Toborne was all in his head. He had absorbed his essence in Lux Amarou.

"Dear boy, it's time to part ways. I thank you for not letting me parish and for keeping me here close, but I must go now."

"Oh, no. I am not having you running about thwarting my plans. You will stay where I can keep an eye on you."

"Your plans? I have never gone against you. It's all in your flawed perception of me. I have actually been trying to help you. Don't worry, I will leave something of myself behind. I have a gift for you to aid in your struggle in the new coming war."

Dorenn tried to get out of bed but found he could not move, "What have you done to me?"

"Nothing, this is a dream. You are only bound by your own limitations."

"How are you in my dream? You're manipulating it in some way."

Toborne sighed, "Dorenn, I am not a nice man. I don't mince words. I don't play nice with others, and I hold steadfast to my own plans regardless of how my brothers or others think about me. Perhaps that was a mistake on my part. I forgot that others might need to trust me sometimes and that doing my own thing for so long might undermine that trust. I admit it. I am not very personable. But this time I am pleading with you to trust me. Let me go willingly. I don't want to tear myself away from you and potentially cause you harm. Not now that we have come so far."

"This is just a dream. That means you are not real. I don't have to let you go."

"Good for you!" The voice was familiar, "don't let him manipulate you." Esperdahl appeared from out of thin air, glowing in essence."

"Esperdahl is right. Toborne cannot be trusted." Now the essence of Ianthill appeared.

Toborne grumbled, "You still have all these essences in your head from your trials. You need to suppress them, or they will all show up in this dream."

Morgoran's essence appeared, "Listen to him. Suppress the others. This isn't helpful. I trust Toborne, Dorenn. I have never led you astray. Look at how I have conducted myself since my curse was lifted. I have not disparaged Toborne when I clearly could have. Did you ever consider that?"

Dorenn concentrated and suppressed the other essences. He didn't need a parade of all the wielders in history cluttering his thoughts right now. "I'm sorry, Toborne. I am not convinced your heart is on our side. You have done too many things that were either against us or appeared to be against us. I simply do not trust you."

"What of the jade statuette? Surely you realized that old man was Fawlsbane Vex. He gave you the statuette with my essence to free me for a purpose."

"And you very nearly killed Ianthill with Dragon's fire as I recall."

"Did I. Morgoran came and rescued him at that precise moment, didn't he."

"Are you saying you knew Morgoran would show up at that particular moment?"

"You are not getting it. Fawlsbane Vex, the father of the gods, wanted me to take my place through Drakkius. Why would he do that? Ask yourself!"

"I have thought about it. You and Morgoran have been kept at bay for a thousand years for a reason. You were manipulating dragon eggs and creating abominations. You were the reason the Oracle wanted to outlaw magic! You have done nothing but damage this realm and now you're trying to convince me you want to save it? You want to save it from the damage *you* have done!"

"There is more to the world than your puny view, boy."

"Ah, there's the Toborne I know!"

"Man and Dragon used to be connected. They are not anymore. It took me a while to convince Sylvalora I was right. She fights by my side now because she realized I was not trying to control her to take over. I was trying to get her to help me put things right. I may not have done it the way I should have. In a way to gain trust, but I did it my way."

"Your way gets people killed."

"What are a few deaths compared to hundreds or thousands of deaths? Drakkius sacrificed himself willingly for the cause, and others did the same. I *need* to go."

"No, I will not allow it." Dorenn was firm in his conviction.

"All right. So be it. I had hoped to avoid this, but you leave me no choice."

"You can't do anything to me, Toborne. I control you not the other way around. It would take the act of one of the gods to free you from me."

Toborne's anger filled his face, "I don't have the ear of a god. What I am proposing will allow me to help you, and it will also allow you to live. Normally, you would have to die to release my essence from you."

Dorenn sighed. "You are putting me into a bad situation. I want to believe you, but you do have a terrible habit of lying and betraying those who believe you." He thought it over for a moment, "But, since you are a part of me and I do not detect any insincerity, I think I can trust you this one time. Besides, I don't want you in my head. I will warn you, though. If you step out of line, I will hunt you down and it will not end well for you!"

"I will honor you and respect this decision." He waved his hand to the side of the bed and Sylvalora came through the door."

"Is this still a dream?" Dorenn asked.

"Not for much longer...awaken Dorenn Adair!" Sylvalora said.

Dorenn's eyes opened, "What? What are you doing."

Sylvalora stood there looking very much like and older version of Lady Shey, "I'll try not to hurt you."

"Wait! What? This will hurt?"

"I am basically severing an essence from you by force. It's not going to be pleasant. It's going to hurt."

"Did you have to use the word sever?"

Sylvalora grabbed the sides of his head with both hands and Dorenn felt the essence, or whatever it was Sylvalora used, flow into his mind. It wormed its way uncomfortably touching each essence within him. He could hear the essences plead with her to free them each time she touched them, but she let them go until she reached Toborne. "Brace yourself, Dorenn. Clench down if you must. I will try not to hurt you too much. I'm sorry for this."

Dorenn felt her tugging on Toborne's essence. It was like she was trying to tear skin from his bones. He could tell Toborne also felt the pain. He involuntarily screamed as the essence or Toborne ripped from him. He felt wetness run down his neck as if he were bleeding. When she released him, he checked himself but there was no blood even though the sensation was still present. He could feel it trickle down his neck and he could feel the wetness of his bed clothes. He began to draw in essence.

"Oh, I would not try to draw essence just yet, Dorenn. Your mind is wounded. It could kill you." Sylvalora cautioned.

He ignored her until he could feel the essence enter him and then leak out of the mental tear she had created. “How long until I can wield again?”

“A few days. I would say you need to find a cleric. Preferably a cleric of Fawlsbane. One of them might be able to heal your mind faster.” She raised her hands into the air and the essence of Toborne began to swirl in front of her. A few moments later and the body of Toborne returned and his essence returned to it. A thousand years ago she had taken his body away from him, and now she returned it to him as only she could.

Toborne clenched his fists and then rotated his neck, popping it in several places. When he was fully returned to his normal self, he focused on Dorenn. “I promised you a gift. I said I would leave behind a part of me. He reached for Dorenn, and he tried to pull away from the newly restored wielder. He didn’t want a gift from Toborne.

Toborne took his head into his hand, “I will leave you a part of me so that you will be recognized when the time comes. I thank you, Dorenn. My brothers did pick wisely, and I can see you are going to be the one they hoped you would be for the tough times still ahead.” He smiled a rare, warm smile. Dorenn felt what seemed like a soft breeze in his mind. Toborne and Sylvalora went to the balcony where Dorenn could see Sylvalora shift into her large dragon form. Toborne joined her and together they flew away into the night air.

The door flew open and two guards along with King Lourn and Seandara burst in. Seandara rushed to Dorenn.

“Are you all right?” She asked. “We heard you cry out in pain.”

He tried to speak, and the dryness of his voice made it difficult for a moment until he at last rasped, “Cleric, I need a cleric of Fawlsbane Vex.”

Lourn pointed a finger at one of the guards, "Fetch a cleric of Fawlsbane Vex at once!"

The guard nodded, bowed, and disappeared back out the chamber door.

Chapter Six

Liberation

Ganas startled awake when the door opened and Verel rushed in followed by a lovely young woman dressed in the gold and white of the clerics of Loracia. He didn't use the signal or the knock, he just burst into the room. He shut the door and latched it. "Have you two no sense? Why was the door left unbolted?"

"I unbolted it. Azura said. We are in a nondescript house. No one knows to look for us here and I knew you and Veric would be returning soon."

"Well, it's not being responsible. You should keep it bolted out of a pure need for safety."

"Sometimes the safest places to hide are right under the enemy's nose. My father taught me that." Azura said.

"No offense to your honored father, but that's nonsense!" Verel shot back.

"You two stop bickering." Ganas said, "Where is Veric? He didn't return with you?"

"No. When we got to the temple, it was being guarded by a behemoth of a Drasmyd Duil. We contemplated going for help at a Fawlsbane Vex temple, but Veric decided to distract the beast while I went inside the temple for help. He ran off down an empty street and the creature followed." He indicated the cleric with a hairy claw, "This is Xarelda, a cleric of Loracia. She agreed to come with me after a bit of persuasion. I almost had to fight my way into the temple, being that I am...different."

"Coming with him and getting out of the temple was preferable after he convinced us he was honest and friendly. He recited the covenant of Loracia to prove his worth." She grinned at him and Ganas imagined he blushed under his fur. "That's all I needed to hear to trust he was being earnest." She bowed, "Pleased to meet you both."

"Likewise." Ganas said.

"The pleasure is ours." Azura said.

The cleric made her way to Ganas, "Let me see these wounds of yours." She began tugging at his bandages and he winced. "Sorry, I'll be more delicate." She helped him sit up and then she removed the bandages revealing his wounds. "This is bad. It's a good thing you brought me here." She placed her healing hands on Ganas and began her channeling. She stopped and addressed the others since they were starting, "This may take a while. Why don't you two find something to keep yourselves occupied while I work."

"Oh, sorry. We are starting aren't we. Come along, Verel. Let's go through the provisions and see if we can find something for dinner."

"I think I will go back out and see if I can locate Veric. He may need my help. That beast is probably still chasing him."

Azura nodded, "Just be careful out there."

"Always." He pointed to the bolt on the door, "and bolt this after I leave and *leave* it bolted until you hear our voice after we knock."

Azura nodded and went to the door to secure the bolt after Verel exited.

Ganas fell asleep from the warm healing chants and healing fingers massaging him and alleviating his pain. When he awoke Veric and Verel had returned, and they were munching on whatever provisions Azura had prepared.

"Ah, you're awake." Xarelda said. "Your body has been working hard to heal you. Here, eat this." She brought him a bowl of some kind of sweet-smelling soup. "We don't have spoons unfortunately." Ganas sat up and found no pain plagued him. He took the bowl and drank from it. It was delicious and he didn't know how hungry he was until the liquid touched his lips. He gulped it down.

"Whoa, slow down. I made plenty." Xarelda said.

Veric took a drink of what looked like bittering tea, "I'm glad you're awake. After I foiled the beast chasing after me from the temple, I found myself near where Jac Wills and Bannon are housed. I scouted around the place, and I think I found a way to enter undetected. From what I understand, Bannon has a mindwielder hold on Jac. All we must do is kill Bannon and we are done. Jac will be freed from the spell and I'm sure he and the rest are more than ready to return home."

Ganas coughed on his soup, "Kill Bannon? There is no negotiation?"

Veric snickered, "What kind of negotiation did you have in mind? You think he will listen to reason and say sure, here take all the men I have under my control? This is war, we are warriors, and Bannon is the enemy." Veric pulled out one of his daggers and twirled it, "I don't even need any of you. I can just slip in and end him on my own."

"It just seems a bit harsh, don't you think?" Ganas asked.

"Time is of the essence, is it not. We need to get this taken care of as soon as we are able." He pointed his dagger nonchalantly toward

Verel, "They want their city back." He pointed the dagger to his chest, "We want our army back." He pointed the dagger to the eastern wall, "And Bannon is the only obstacle. It's time for action."

"If you were planning on just waltzing in and killing him, why bother even finding a healer for me?" Ganas asked.

"Simple, I didn't want you to die. You are needed to lead the army back to camp so we can get them back to Symboria."

"No, we may have to kill Bannon, but I want to try to reason with him before we just assassinate him on the spot. I want to know what he's up to here in Denosia. We will all..." He looked at the cleric and Azura, "We will all go to palace unless of course anyone wants to wait here out of danger or return home. I won't kill until we deem it absolutely necessary." Ganas said.

Veric sighed, "Why must you people always do everything the hard way? It's a simple sneak and thrust. It would be merciful. He would be dead in seconds. Then you could talk to Jac Wills and muster the army here and lead them back to camp. The Dramyds and Drasmyd Duil would most likely flee once he's dead."

"I said no, Veric. Why are you in such a rush? What did you find out there on the streets of Anisport?"

"It's the fact that this army has been here in Denosia for far too long. Things have gotten out of hand and discipline must be restored or they will be useless to fight. They need to be re-trained and re-directed. Do you believe there is adequate time for this? They will be slaughtered on the battlefield if we don't allow them time to recuperate from Bannon's influence. To put it more plainly, they are soft and no longer ready for a fight on the scale of what's ahead."

"I don't care. I'm more worried about getting them home. We can assess their training once they're safely in Symboria."

"Suit yourself."

Ganas finally recuperated enough strength to proceed with the mission. He eyed Veric with trepidation, "Are you ready for this? I mean, are you ready to follow my lead and not run off on your own?"

"Naturally, why would you ask me such a thing?"

"You have managed to do your own thing ever since you have arrived. You talk as though you want to follow me but then you follow your own agenda. At some point, I need to stop trusting you will do as I ask."

"Nonsense! You say you want Bannon to live to talk and I shall honor that."

Ganas nodded, "All right, Verel, you and Azura prepare yourselves to leave at nightfall. We will proceed under the cover of darkness and travel amongst the shadows. Bannon will no doubt detect us if we get too close. Do we have a way to mask ourselves from him?"

Verel sniffed, "Azura and I can blend into the surrounding peoples. You and Veric are the two I worry about. Bannon may not be looking for indigenous people, but he will be looking for the likes of you two."

"That's right, but I may have a solution. Veric, do you have that Lora Daine with you? The one you traveled to Denosia with?"

"I arrived by dragon, remember."

"Aye, I remember, but I saw you with it. I know you have a dragon stone."

"Yes, I have...something like a dragon stone."

"Something like? What does that mean?" Ganas asked.

"All right, yes, I have a dragon stone."

"Verel, you and Azura can get in close within an open area near Bannon and Veric and I will travel to you via the stone. By the time Bannon senses us, it will be too late."

"Excellent plan!" Verel said.

“How long do you think it will take you to reach Bannon’s chamber?”

Verel stroked his chin while thinking, “About half an hour, give or take.”

“Can you be more precise? We need to time this right or Veric and I may end up face to face with Bannon alone, or worse, we may end up in a wall or something.”

“The dragon magic doesn’t work that way. That is a myth. A Lora Daine will not allow one to appear in a wall.” Veric said. He chuckled mockingly.

“Give us one hour after nightfall and we will be in position.” Verel assured him.

“All right. One hour it is. As soon as you two are prepared and the sun sets beyond the horizon, move out.”

Once Verel and Azura left, Ganas once again turned to the cleric of Loracia, “Is there anything you can do for my headache?”

Xarelda became concerned because her face wrinkled into a frown, and she felt his forehead with the back of her hand. “You have a headache? You should not be feeling anything of the sort. Is it behind your eyes or all over your head?”

“All over like a dull ache.”

Xarelda channeled some more divine healing to Ganas before he finally reported the headache had gone. During the healing session, neither had been aware of Veric’s departure. Ganas shot up from his chair where Xarelda had been tending to him, “Did you see Veric leave?”

“No, I didn’t.” Xarelda said.

“He left me here!” Ganas said in a panic as he gathered his things and bolted out the door. He had to catch up with him before he reached Bannon. He carefully, but quickly, slipped into the shadows.

Several Drasmyd Duil and Dramyds would be on the prowl, and he had to be careful to avoid them since he was alone. He deftly maneuvered through the dark, dirty streets, searching for signs of where to go. He used his common sense and knowledge of how a city might be laid out to guide him, but the place was too unfamiliar, and he soon found himself lost. Thoughts of giving up and accepting what may come began to seep into his mind. He slid into a shadow in an alleyway off the main street when he saw an old man creeping along the opposite side. He sunk deeper into his hiding spot letting the man pa ss.

Someone or something tapped Ganas on the shoulder and he almost cried out in surprise. "Don't let him find you." It was Veric. "He is a pretentious old man, and he will not approve of you helping me."

Ganas could feel the heat of anger cover his face, "What are you going on about?" He asked. "You left me!"

"The old man is what I am going on about. I would be confronting Bannon right now if not for him."

"Who?" Ganas asked.

"The old man." Veric said. "He is not who he seems."

"What?"

"Oh, never mind. Forget the old man and stay still. I will get us to Bannon."

Ganas swallowed his anger as Veric drew out the stone from his pocket. He spoke a few words Ganas did not understand and in an instant, they were standing in a room lined with soldiers and weapons. A man with white hair, a wicked fascial scar, and a gnarled staff dressed in blue robes at the front of the room stood and pointed to them, "Get those men!" he shouted.

The guards began to move in on them.

Before Ganas had a chance to draw his sword or get into a defensive stance, he saw Veric's dagger whiz by his face. It sailed through the air faster than Bannon could cast a protection spell and landed blade first in his throat. Bannon gasped and clutched his hands to his throat in vain as the blood gushed out. In an instant two more daggers flew from Veric's hands, both finding their targets in Bannon's body, one in the heart just under his upraised arm, and the other in his left, widened eye socket.

"I wanted to..." Ganas trailed off as he found his words repetitive. Veric knew full well he wanted to interrogate Bannon.

Veric didn't hesitate, "I know what you wanted. I wanted him to be gone without a shadow of a doubt this time. He survived before, but he'll not survive me!"

Ganas took a deep, deliberate breath trying to calm himself. Jac had gone to the aid of Bannon. The soldiers stood around dumbfounded as if they had come out of a fog. One of them recognized Ganas.

"Ganas, is that you? What are you doing here?"

"What are *we* doing here?" the soldier next to him said.

Ganas nodded at the soldier who recognized him before rushing over to Jac. He put his hand on the soldier's shoulder and the man met his gaze with terrified eyes.

"Ganas Nashe? The scout?"

"Aye, I'm here."

Jac lowered his head. His eyes remained fixed on the bleeding Bannon, "Ganas, what have I done?"

"What do you remember?"

Jac gave him a pitiful gaze, his lower lip quivering, "Everything. I remember everything."

CHAPTER SEVEN

RECLAMATION

Ganas patted the distraught man on the back trying to comfort him. He thought Veric would be by his side but when he turned to see where he had gone, the man who slew Bannon was nowhere to be seen. The men were milling around, and some were grumbling about being hungry. Others were complaining of headaches. How had Bannon been in all their heads at once?

"Ganas, Bannon was not alone. He had help controlling us. He used something to strengthen his power. It's in the chamber there." Jac pointed to a door behind the throne Bannon had been using as his own.

Ganas motioned for the nearest officer to join them. "Jac, tell your officer to take the men to the streets and liberate the city. The people will be grateful and most likely feed them too. Clear every Drasmyd Duil and Dramyd from every corner."

Jac rose from his prone position to address his nearest officer, "You heard the scout! Rally the men and liberate the city of that filth. You have permission to confiscate any rations they might have been guarding or hording."

"Aye, sir!" The officer said. He hurried to the men, shouting for them to take up arms and follow him into the city. Ganas could see in the men's eyes they remembered their captivity, and he could also hear it in their shouts and angry cries as they clambered to get at the monsters. Driven by anger, hunger, and adrenaline they filtered out of the building.

Ganas again searched for Veric but did not find him. Verel and Azura wandered up. They were both happy and excited to see the men rushing out to fight off the filth who had taken their city. Ganas nodded when he realized they were staring at him with pleading eyes. They both smiled and rushed to go join in the fight.

Jac Wills took out a handkerchief and wiped his brow, "I will submit myself for disciplinary action to whomever is in charge at the camp when we return."

"We will deal with all that when the time comes, for now, we need to make sure the city is secured, the men are fed, rested, and ready to return to the main camp. As soon as I send word by the means the dragons left me, they will come for us."

Jac made an attempt at a smile, "You should not be a scout. I will make sure you are recommended for promotion with whatever influence I have left."

"I am just doing my job and my duty, sir. That's thanks enough."

"Oh no you don't soldier. You have done far more than could ever be asked of you at your station. You deserve more. Now, come with me to the chamber so we can figure out what to do with that artifact Bannon was using."

"What about Bannon? Should we bury him or something."

Jac looked at the corpse with disgust, "Let him rot where he fell."

Ganas took one last look. The daggers Veric had thrown were gone. The man had disappeared on purpose. He knew exactly what he was doing in killing Bannon so fast, "That dirty bastard."

"Aye he was." Jac said. "He had all of us under his sinister spell."

Ganas let Jac think he was taking about Bannon as he led him into the room with the artifact. It was a blue crystal. Ganas reached out for it, but the thing shocked him. The electricity arched from the artifact to his hand just like how pulling apart a woolen blanket arched and crackled on a dry night.

"Careful," Jac said. He found the wooden box Bannon carried the thing in and tipped it over onto it. He slid it to the edge of the table and rounded it off the edge so as the box turned on the edge of the table, it would brace the artifact inside until the box was upright with the artifact fell safely inside. He shut the lid of the box and latched it. "There, we can carry it this way."

"We will need to lock it away and give it to either Ianthill or Morgoran. They will know what it is and what to do with it." Ganas said.

Jac nodded, "I'm sure they will. All I know about such things is they are dangerous and almost impossible to destroy by practical means. One of the wizards will have to deal with it."

Again, Ganas nodded.

"Come now, we will go see how the men are faring in the liberation of the city."

Ganas could tell Jac was trying to put his best face forward, but the truth of the matter weighed heavy on the man's brow.

Later near the town hall, Ganas left Verel and Azura with a group of townsfolk to debate on who to install as the next leader of the city.

Once the people saw the soldiers fighting off the creatures infesting their city, they joined in the struggle. The whole ordeal took only a few hours. The Dramyds and Drasmyd Duil who were not killed had now left the city. The debate took up most of the night and some of the following morning. The entirety of the next day was filled with modest feasting and celebration. The townsfolk did not have much, but what they did have made for a lively meal. Ganas was thankful the city was short on ale and spirits. It made the trek back to camp much easier.

Over the next few days it took to return to camp, Ganas found he missed his new friends more and more, especially Azura. She was on his mind more than he personally found necessary. After all, he had only met her a few weeks ago and she had given him no indication she might be interested in him. For all he knew, she was betrothed to someone already. The customs of this land were different. How could he be sure of anything when he was so ignorant about how things worked on this side of the sea? *Focusing on getting this army back to Symboria is my priority, nothing else matters.*

When they saw the smoke of campfires wafting over the treetops, Ganas knew some of the army had already returned to their military lifestyles. Several scouts and anxious men had already rushed to the camp within hours after the liberation. They did not care to stay and celebrate the victory. Once Ganas had freed them, hope had returned. He wisely waved off any of the men who tried to praise him for freeing their minds from the mindwielder. It was Veric's impetuous daggers not his careful sword that freed them from their trance. Veric's hasty attack was to hide something; he was sure of it. Why else would he have disappeared before the man's final drop of blood hit the floor? He had an agenda Ganas was not privy to. At any rate, it was all over now.

"You are deep in thought." Jac Wills said.

Ganas nodded.

"Something bothering you?"

Ganas shook his head, "No, just replaying the death of Bannon in my mind."

"Why?"

"Did you happen to see a tall man with greying hair standing beside me when Bannon went down?"

"I remember seeing Bannon go down, but I didn't see who felled him. I remember focusing on you briefly, and then looking down to see Bannon taking his final breaths. Come to think of it, it looked to me like you were the one throwing the daggers. There was no one else there I could see."

"I didn't throw any daggers. It wasn't me who killed Bannon. I wanted to talk to him and try to negotiate."

"Then it's a good thing he died. He would have gotten onto you head the moment you let your guard down. If you didn't throw the daggers, who did?"

"I wasn't alone. There was another man who came to the chamber with me. It was he who threw the daggers and killed Bannon on sight. He didn't hesitate or waver. He strolled in, cast his deadly daggers, killed Bannon, and then vanished."

"I saw no one else enter the room other than you. As I said, I'm glad he's dead. He didn't wait to hear any pleas or words from the townsfolk. Anyone who opposed him, he used the artifact on and drew them into his fold. He would not have wasted words with you either. The element of surprise is what saved you and us."

"How did Veric know that?"

"Maybe he didn't."

Ganas nodded again, “Perhaps you’re right. Look, the camp is already thriving.” He pointed ahead to the opening in the trees where the tents were once again in neat rows and no longer blowing in the wind in disrepair.

“Who did you say was in charge?”

“Colonel Tru.”

“Colonel!” He lowered his head. “All the ranks above colonel are gone, I guess. There will have to be some field promotions and a lot of training before we can return and fight.”

“Yes, Veric reminded me of that very notion. I’m sure you and your officers are up to the task.”

Jac nodded, “We will have to be.”

Ganas turned to survey the army marching behind him, “I would say we still have a formattable force all things considered.”

Two men exited the big tent in the distance and made their way toward Ganas and Jac, “See the two men headed this way?”

Jac squinted, “Aye. I do.”

“That’s Colonel Tru and his second.”

A few minutes more and the two men confronted them, “Hail Ganas. I see you did it. Above all odds you have liberated the army. I am truly impressed. His eyes fell upon Jac. Jac bowed his head in shame.

“I give myself to you, Colonel, for disciplinary action. I have acted against the army and my fellow man. I will except whatever punishment you decide. May I remind the colonel that punishment for brutally killing a superior offer is death. I do not need a tribunal. I accept the standard punishment.”

Tru stood motionless for an uncomfortable amount of time before speaking, “General, you were not acting on your own recognizance. You were being manipulated. I don’t see how any of this was your fault.”

Jac's voice wavered, "I could have resisted...harder."

Tru put his hand on the general's shoulder, "Nonsense, sir. I saw what that man did to the army."

"Then how did you resist? I should have been better."

"I don't know how I and the others with me resisted him." He sighed, "We have more important matters now. I can't let you hang for this. The men would have my head on a pike before your body was cold. I don't understand what happened to you because it didn't happen to me, but the men who were under the spell understand and they would not take it well. So, sir, what are your orders?"

"You are a wise commander, Tru. My first point of order is to officially field promote you to general with all the privileges there in." He pointed to Tru's second, "You witness that and write it down." The man nodded. "Now that you are a general, Tru, I hereby relinquish command of the Army of the West to you General Semten Tru." He pointed to the man again, "Witness that too." He looked at Ganas, "But before I completely turn over command, I wish to promote Scout Ganas to Captain Ganas Nashe and recommend him for a command."

"So be it. I accept your decree, general, and hereby pledge to do my duty to the best of my ability. However, I will not let you off the hook that easily. You will have your own garrison. Captain Nashe will be the first officer under your command."

"I know you will do us proud, Tru. Should this army run a foul of another mindwielder, I know we will be safe. Come now, we should inspect the army and shore up the rankings. We have a lot of training to do in a short amount of time. Oh, and one other thing," he gestured toward the artifact box, "General Tru, please have that box taken somewhere defensible and post guards around it. I will explain it to you when we get a moment alone."

"I will see it done," he said.

Chapter Eight

Wings of Fire

Ganas left the box with the artifact with the chosen guards after he was certain it was safe as night began to descend on the camp. The plains before the great Kastian Mountains got cold at night and he wanted to get to his tent so he could signal Andelwyre. She must have returned to Denosia otherwise his dragon stone would not have been glowing periodically. Morgoran must have sent her to check on him. When he got to his tent, he took the Lora Daine and sent the signal. The day had been long, so afterwards he crawled into bed and fell asleep. It was a ritual he would repeat for another full two months.

On the second day of the third month since the reclamation of the army, Ganas awoke a to a rustling at his tent flap, "Yes, what is it?"

An army regular stood just outside the tent, "Sorry to disturb you sir, but the generals request your presence on the field."

"All right, tell them I am on my way."

"Aye, sir," and the man was gone.

Ganas moved to the edge of his wooden cot, the straw, make-shift, mattress made a crunching noise as he did. *The generals? More like general.* Tru, despite being officially promoted and having General Wills at his constant side, did not fully trust the man. Ganas found himself as the go between quite a bit. General Tru must have felt the fate of General Rellagorn would not befall him should Ganas be present. At any rate, Ganas dressed himself in his new uniform, which come from the tent of a soldier killed in one of the battles before he arrived and adapted to fit him and left for the field where the newly ranked army was practicing maneuvers.

The camp was buzzing with activity now; a sharp contrast to the camp he found when he first arrived four months earlier. There were cook fires burning, hunting parties bringing in game and wild vegetables to feed the men, archers fletching bows and arrows from trees and saplings cut and brought in from the nearby forest, and three rotations of field training. To Ganas, the army looked to be in fine form, probably the best he had seen since the beginnings of his enlistment. He made his way to the training field dreading the question he knew he was about to be asked. When were the ships arriving to take them home? Never mind the fact that the nearest inlet into a cove was a half day's march from the camp. The generals planned to move the army closer to the cove once the men's training was completed, but they were reluctant to move too soon due to the area around the cove being not suitable for camp or training.

"Any word on when the ships will arrive?" General Tru asked as soon as Ganas was in earshot.

"Not yet."

"Any communication at all?" General Wills wanted to know.

"Not in a few days. After I sent word the army was ready to return, Master Gondrial sent word that he was working on a plan to get everyone home at once. Andelwyre flew off that day with the men's letters and that's the last I heard. We'll be on ships soon enough."

"I don't see how. I don't think there will be enough ships in the Trigothian or Symborian navies together to bring us all home at once." Tru said.

"Regardless, I think we are ready to move the camp toward the cove to the west." Wills said.

"Are you certain?" Ganas asked, "what if the ships take another month to arrive. All the training and conditioning you have done would be in jeopardy." Ganas said.

"It's a risk we have to take. The men are getting antsy waiting, and frankly so am I. At least if we tear down the camp and get on the move the moral will improve."

General Tru cupped his hand under his chin, "Send another missive. Tell this Gondrial fellow we will be headed toward the largest cove in the Denosian western coast. He will find us there before spring becomes summer. We will be waiting for him."

Ganas stroked his beard, "I don't think we have anymore carrier pigeons in the coop, sir."

"I'm sure you'll find a way. You have gotten us all this far. Finding a bloody pigeon to send a message shouldn't be too difficult for you."

"Aye, sir. I will see it done."

"Good, dismissed." General Tru said.

Ganas left the field grumbling. Now that the ranks and discipline had been restored, he was once again just another soldier.

He scratched his beard, "I will be glad to shave this thing off."

"I think it looks nice on you."

"Azura!" Ganas said. "What are you doing here?"

"Looking for you, of course. Some of the men said they saw you headed this way."

"Is there something wrong in the city?"

"No, of course not. Anisport is strong once again."

"Any word on acquiring ships?"

"The new docks are still under construction. They were utterly destroyed when Bannon was in power. He really didn't want an attack by sea to thwart his plans. Only one or two ships can dock at a time."

"I'm sure we could figure something out. The ships could still anchor along the coast and we could ferry the men to them."

"Great idea, if we had the number of ships you require, but I'm afraid we don't. we don't even have enough ships or men to sail them. That has been the problem since your army arrived. You will have to send your armada to come get them. Even that makes the elders anxious. An invasion force of ships arriving at our shores with benevolent intent is rare."

"So, what brings you this far inland then?"

"I just wanted to check on you. Things are going well in the city, and I needed to get out and get some fresh air. Plus, my old homestead is nearby, remember. I need to run by and get a few things." There was an awkward pause between them, "So, when do you think you will be leaving Denosia? I mean when and how if you don't have enough ships."

"I wish I knew. That question comes up a lot."

"My people have asked me many times why you don't go back the way you came?"

"The army was moved here unnaturally. Not only does no one here know how to do something like that on such a large scale, it's doubtful the most powerful wielders at home could pull it off. Naneden clearly amplified the spell somehow."

"Wielders?"

"Those among us who can use magical essence."

"Oh, Wizards."

"You have wizards here?" He had not considered the wielders of Denosia might have the ability to get them home.

"We do, but I don't think they would help you if that's what you're asking. They are serious, reclusive, and scary. Most people would not want to come across one if they could avoid it." She shifted; didn't you say you had a magical amplification artifact?"

"It's for mindwielders. It doesn't work on essence wielders. Can you contact these wizards?

"Uh, no, but I might know someone who can. I will talk to him and get back to you."

"I would appreciate it if you would."

"I can't make any promises."

"I know. Say, how is Verel?"

"I wondered if you were going to ask, He's fine."

"Good, good." He had run out of things to say. "Well, nice to see you again. Let me know about the wizard."

"I will."

Surprisingly, she came close for a hug and Ganas embraced her. She smelled of lilacs. He held her close. She gently released him. He stumbled back.

"I will stop back by after I get done at the homestead," she said as she backed away from him.

"I'll be here."

She turned away toward the direction of her homestead. Ganas watched her until she disappeared in the distance.

The rest of the day the men moved the entire packed up camp into position so in the morning they could move out at first light. The final structures like the tents they needed to sleep in and the cook's nook where all that remained. Ganas thought about what he said to

Azura and suddenly realized he had told her he would be here when she returned. *Stupid, stupid man*, he thought. *Well, surely, she would have the brains to follow their trail.* He settled down in his tent for the night. Scenarios of what Azura might do if she returned and found the camp abandoned played in his head as he drifted off to sleep.

Morning came fast. He had barely shut his eyes when the sunlight and noise of men preparing to leave woke him up. He peered out of the tent. There were only a few men stirring in the still dark of the morning. He dressed, went to the cook's enclosure, bittering tea cup in hand, to see if the cook had started the morning brew. He was pleasantly surprised to see he had. More of the early to rise soldiers also began to pour into the enclosure. All the chairs and collapsible tables had already been packed away so he found a stump to sit on. By the time the sun was fully ensconced in the sky, the cook's area was overrun and the preparations of the day were in full swing. The men were getting the final few odds and ends ready for the move.

He left the enclosure and trekked back to his tent. Before he entered, he stretched and looked up to the heavens. A glint of something shiny reflected the sunlight from way up above. He put his hand up to his forehead to block out the brightness of the sun, and squinted to see what it was. The land began to darken as hundreds of dragons filled the skies. At the head of the first column was a great silvery one. He went back to his tent and found his bow. He pointed the arrow up into the air and fired it. The tip was made of a silvery, mirrored pinwheel that spun wildly as it soared up into the air, catching the attention of the lead dragon, who swooped down to his position. Silver and white shimmered and changed into a beautiful woman with white hair and steel blue eyes. She elegantly strolled up to him as the other dragons began landing and depositing hollowed crates resembling boats all over the grass and rocky terrain nearby.

"What is your name?" the woman asked.

He bowed. "I am Ganas Nashe of Brookhaven." He returned her gaze. "Are you the Silver Drake? We were about to lose hope."

She signaled to the others who were all taking on the guise of humanoids. "Aye, I am she. We have brought provisions and equipment, but most importantly, we have come to take you home, lost sons of the Sacred Land."

Ganas gazed over the area as hundreds of men began to shout out in glee. Some went to greet the dragons and others, excited they were finally being rescued, began hastily tearing down their tents.

Ganas smiled at the woman before him, "Well, it's about time."

Chapter Nine

Mount Venifyre

Within the great hall of Draegodor, dimly lit in the dead of night, sat King Amarantus, dragon lord of the realm. He busied himself pouring over maps of the Mountains of Madness where the so-called bad dragons resided in Kragodor. The black, brown, and green dragons had long ago rebelled against guarding mankind and were exiled to the mountains to make a new colony for themselves or die. Dragons are resilient, so a new great city was built and the dragons who reside there have been rivals to the dragons of Draegodor ever since. King Amarantus also had a few black dragons from his ranks, which he wisely used as spies, providing him with the intelligence before him. He peered up from his work when he heard the familiar creak of the great double doors to the chamber. One of his spies, a great black dragon named Char, entered the room and shape-shifted into his humanoid form. A dark elf with deep set eyes, a wary sharp-featured face, and a hooked nose.

He walked up to Amarantus and bowed, "Forgive me, your majesty, I do not mean to seek your council at so late an hour."

"Yet here you are."

"Aye, your majesty. I have urgent news."

Amarantus nodded, "Very well, give me your news."

"Your majesty, it's the Garden of Bones. I have seen with my own eyes how the bones have been disturbed. Someone or something is disturbing the ancient dragon skeletons and remains."

"That's unsettling. Who would do such a horrendous thing?"

"I do not know, your majesty, but the rumor is that necromancers may be to blame."

"Necromancers! You must be joking." Amarantus went from disgusted to concerned, " Although, some of our ancestors would be formidable weapons in the hands of a skilled necromancer who could control one of them." He wringed his hands, "You have done me a great service. I will see you are compensated for your work."

"Thank you, your majesty. I know it isn't my place, but I am curious. Do you have a plan?"

"You're right, it isn't your place. There is only one course of action for something such as this and I'll not discuss it with even my most trusted advisor. Forgive me, Char, it's nothing personal. I trust you, but this is something I dare not let our enemies discover."

"I understand, your majesty. I worry is all."

"As you should. But rest easy, my friend, I do have a course of action in mind. It turns out there is a protocol set in place for this sort of thing. Kings of old used to have to deal with monsters meddling with the dead in the days of old."

"That is good to hear, sire. I shall take my leave." Char bowed and exited the room.

Amarantus rushed to the antechamber adjacent to the great hall where the great Lora Daine sat covered in the darkness. He stopped before entering the room to grab a fire crystal off the wall to illuminate the chamber. Once he had the cover off the enormous stone, he pressed something at the base and a hidden chamber door popped open to his left. He slithered through the tight opening into a small room with a portal ring at its center. He placed the fire crystal in a holder attached to the wall and cleared away the cobwebs from his path. The portal ring, made from carefully sung marble by the stone singers of the Noanas, was covered in golden symbols and accented with gems.

"I hope the old man is in a good mood. I have not showed up unannounced in thousands of years." Amarantus mumbled.

He took a deep breath and activated the portal. The ring began to swirl and then the realm of Venifyre appeared within. He stepped through. The air was crisp and clean. The sun was shining, birds were singing, and just up ahead was the glistening white towers and gold trimmed marble city of the gods. He decided to shift into his dragon form because it would be easier to get past the golden dragon guards into the city. He made his way to the city gates and the two huge dragons guarding them. They immediately opened the golden gates to admit him without an issue. Once inside he shifted back into his smaller, human form, to honor Fawlsbane Vex the father of all humankind, and made his way to the throne room.

"Ah, Amarantus, what brings you to Venifyre unannounced on this fine day?" Fawlsbane Vex asked when Amarantus was admitted. The father of the gods was dressed in pristine white, but he wore the familiar countenance of an old man. He was tending to some pink and red flowers beside the throne as he puffed on a clay pipe.

"I come to speak with you and to enter a plea." Amarantus bowed.

"It must be grave indeed for you to enter the realm of the gods. I will hear it."

"It's confirmed, my lord. My scouts near the Garden of Bones have seen signs the barrows and final resting sites of my ancestors have been disturbed."

Fawlsbane took the pipe from his lips and considered the king of dragons' words intently, "What does that mean, signs? Are your ancestors being dug up, or desecrated in some way? Signs of disturbance doesn't seem like much in the way of evidence, certainly not confirmation."

The king of the dragons wringed his hands nervously, "You know that valley is difficult to get to. If my scouts say there is evidence someone has been there, other than dragons, I believe it. You're a god, can't you tell or go there and do something?"

"Now, you know better than to ask me that, Amarantus." Fawlsbane took another puff from his pipe. "Everything has a consequence, take away one brick and the whole wall may come crashing down around you, I should think you would understand that, being a king yourself."

"Aye," Amarantus said reluctantly. "I realize you have had your hand in this, guiding and maneuvering events carefully."

"Aye, I have. Sometimes over centuries, which reminds me. It occurred to me just now how I can help you with this problem. The protocol your ancestors put in place."

"Yes, that is why I have come. What is the protocol?"

"Simple, we use the sword. It's already in position. We just need to activate it."

"In position? Are you speaking of the sword, *Dranmalin*?" Amarantus asked.

"Aye. Dorenn also has the Tome of Enlightenment and the Myradon Codex of the dragons. I think the time is right."

Amarantus took a deep breath. "*Dranmalin.*" He shook his head. "I hope you have considered all the possibilities. That sword's power can easily backfire on us. No dragon can stand against the dragon hammer when it is truly unleashed. If the problem is necromancy, wouldn't the answer be not to let the dragons be resurrected in the first place?"

"Aye, and I will see what I can do about that. I will summon Aedreagnon. I believe that is his area of expertise. I can have him stop it, however, should anything fall through the cracks I should think *Dranmalin* would be the answer."

"The sword is dangerous, my lord, surely it is better kept as it is now docile in the hands of a novice. He truly believes it's powerful enough as it is."

"I didn't have your kind create it so many years ago just to be a glorified, glowing boomerang."

"What's a boomerang, my lord?" Amarantus asked.

"It's a curved stick you throw, and it returns to you." He looked at Amarantus as if he should understand, "The elves of Darovan use them to hunt."

"*Dranmalin* is not curved."

"Never mind, I was attempting to use a metaphor. Dorenn calls the sword back to his hand and...um...oh, forget it. Can you still activate the sword or not?"

"Of course, I can. But I will need the help of the goddess Ageanna to do it."

Fawlsbane coughed on his next puff of pipe smoke. "I discovered recently that my mischievous daughter is flittering about as a Kylerie elf named Kyrie. She has been meddling in all this too, but she doesn't know I know about it."

"I thought you decreed the lesser gods not to interfere."

"Aye, I did." He smiled. "That was to mitigate the interference. Surely you didn't believe they would stand by and do nothing at my request. No, I expected at least one or two of them to intervene. I don't want to call Ageanna out on this issue yet. She has actually been doing some good with her meddling. What about Xeian? He is the co-creator of the elves."

"Perhaps, *if* he will allow it to be activated. You know how Xeian feels about such things."

"I will convince him. If not, I will find Ageanna."

"Will the chosen one be able to understand what to do with *Dranmalin* once it's active?

Fawlshbane scoffed, "There's no such thing as a chosen one. Dorenn is just my way around the noninterference order I gave to the other gods."

"You choose him, did you not?"

"Aye, I suppose you are correct in that, but he was not prophesied or any of that nonsense. He can succeed or fail just like any other. I don't want the outcome of this to be attributed to anything we gods did *this* time. I want it understood he had free will to succeed or fail." He thought for a moment. "Although, he has not been without his surprises. I would never have thought he could do some of the things he's done. I suppose he is the chosen one if you look at it that way." He took another puff on his pipe, "I will send word for Xeian to go to Draegodor at once."

The dragon king hesitated. "Dorenn will not like what *Dranmalin* will do to him."

"He will adapt. He always does." Fawlsbane said undeterred. "It's the only way. It's the sword's ultimate purpose."

"The sword is still somewhat unpredictable. Its magic makes it seem as if it has a mind of its own. There is no way to know exactly how this is going to play out. *Dranmalin* may not be the solution you hope for."

Fawlsbane Vex put his hand on Amarantus' shoulder. "You dragons are Ageanna's greatest creations, and *Dranmalin* is your greatest creation. The dragons will aid and protect man once again! I will send word at once to Aedreagnon. We will try to nip this in the bud before it gets out of hand but rest assured should the dragons of old return to the realms as abominations, *Dranmalin* may be the very weapon you require. I will have you make it ready should we be faced with the prospect. It is better to be prepared than to be caught unawares."

Amarantus nodded. "I will make sure it is as long as Xeian agrees to do his part."

"You leave Xeian to me. I will convince him. Go back to Draegodor and await his arrival."

Amarantus bowed, "Yes, my lord." He left the throne room, passed through the gates and beyond the great dragon protectors to the spot where the portal would whisk him home. In the chamber he looked back through the portal as it closed, "He is mad. Who will save the realm from him?" He took the fire crystal and returned to the Lora Daine room. "Still, it's the plan my ancestors put in place for a reason." He covered the stone and left the room to go back to his maps.

Chapter Ten

At the Southern Pass

Fayne stood, rolling the damp soil between her fingers. "I don't know. I can't be sure which way she went. The rain makes it tougher for me to track her."

"Yes, but are you *able* to track her anyway? Did she go this way?" Tatrice asked.

"I said it was tougher, but yes, I can still track her. Aye, she went this way." Fayne answered.

"Are you sure? "You have lost her trail twice before."

Fayne clinched her fist, "I am certain."

Deylia noticed the clinched fist. "Sisters, sisters!" She stepped over to the spot where Fayne was just standing. "Bickering isn't getting us any closer to finding your mother."

"Don't call us that!" Tatrice said.

"Aye, I agree," Fayne said. "I would rather be sister to a pig."

"Oh, well, I am a sister to a pig."

"Then I'll show you what a pig can do!" Fayne lunged toward Tatrice, sword drawn, and then she abruptly let the sword fall to the ground before she could use it. She sighed and clenched her teeth, "Let me go, Deylia. I have warned you about getting in my head!"

"I won't let you fight one another especially not with swords!" She pushed Fayne back away from her, letting her hold on her mind drop. "I'm sick of it, all this fighting and posturing. You two *are* sisters, whether you want to admit to yourselves or not. What happened to the sentiment you two were sharing back at Cedar Falls? You were both talking about men and love and..."

"It must have been the corn liquor," Fayne interrupted.

Tatrice regained her composure. "Well, which way since you're so sure."

"East," Fayne replied.

Tatrice looked to the sky. "East, through the Southern Pass. She is heading into Scarovia?"

"It appears that way," Fayne answered. "She has picked up her pace since she doubled back in Symbor."

"I still want to know what made her turn back east," Tatrice said.

Fayne continued to examine the ground. "There may not be a reason. She isn't in her rational mind from what I've gathered from the people who have sighted her."

"We should try to catch her before she crosses the border. If she goes into Scarovia we might lose her." Deylia said.

"Not necessarily." Tatrice countered, "We used to go into Scarovia to trade for goods when I worked at the Tiger's Head. The Scarovians aren't as vicious and bloodthirsty as we were raised to believe, and I am familiar with many of their customs. I think we can pass through if you both do as I say."

Fayne cleared her throat, mostly for effect, "My people live on the Scarovian side of the Jagged Mountains. I was raised side by side with Scarovian children. I think I know a thing or two about them."

"All right, you've both had dealings in Scarovia. This isn't a contest." Deylia said. "Gather up and let's get going while there is still light out."

"There is a waypoint station on the Scarovian side of the border. If we can make it there by nightfall, the accommodations are comfortable." Tatrice said. "Mount up." She moved toward her horse.

No one acknowledged Tatrice though. Deylia was watching Fayne who was intently examining something near Kimala's footfalls. Snow had begun to fall hastening Fayne's movements."

"Did you two hear me?" Tatrice asked. "Mount up!"

"There!" Fayne pointed to the ground. "And there!" She pointed to another spot. "They are faint as if the person leaving them is hiding them."

"Not well enough," Deylia said, admiring Fayne's skill at tracking.

"What? Who is it?" Tatrice asked.

"I would say by the impression and depth of the footprint, probably an elf."

"No elf would be foolish enough to cross the southern pass into Scarovia." Tatrice scoffed at the very idea. "Besides, they have dainty little feet and would never leave tracks in the snow unless they meant to."

Fayne stood, a grim expression fell across her face. "I know one; a half elf."

"Trendan! But how could he get here ahead of us?" Tatrice asked.

"Aye, how?" Deylia looked at the footprints. "It can't be him. The last I heard he was still in Ardenia with Dorenn."

"How would you know that?" Tatrice asked with growing suspicion.

"Rennon and I are connected. It's difficult to explain but we can hear each other."

"You can what?" Tatrice's face curled up in an expression of disbelief.

Deylia waved her off. "I just know, all right! Trust me."

"Is there a way to tell if those footprints belong to Trendan?" Tatrice asked Fayne.

"Uh, No, how would that even be possible?"

"Something unique about his shoes or something, I don't know."

"I can barely see them as they are. Even if there was some unique feature, I doubt it would be visible enough to see. Whoever this is, they have covered their tracks pretty well." She held her hand out to catch a snowflake. "And in an hour or so they'll be covered with snow."

Deylia gazed at the sky to the west, "I think that's a blizzard brewing, and it's headed our way."

"Are you sure it's a blizzard and not just a snowstorm?" Tatrice asked.

"Is there a difference? A big snowstorm is a blizzard."

"I would say a blizzard is more intense."

"I used to live next to the Plain of Storms remember? I have seen enough storms in my lifetime. If we travel long enough, we might come across a fencepost you can argue with."

"Funny," Tatrice fixed a stirrup and swung her weight up onto her horse, "Keep sharp then until we get to the waypoint. We will have to pick up our pace too if we want to stay ahead of that storm. I don't want to get caught in a blizzard."

"Wait, there is another set of prints. Someone tried to hide them too. They are bigger than the other set and a bit deeper I think." Fayne said.

Deylia pulled herself into the saddle, "Bren?"

"It could be anybody." Tatrice's tone downplayed Deylia's guess. "We are just speculating wildly, perhaps in hopes that our men are trying to gallantly find us out here. Next, you will find Rennon's footfalls."

Deylia's face crinkled, "I never said I had any ties with Rennon other than both of us being mindwielders."

"Oh please!" Fayne said as she climbed onto her horse. "I have seen the way you both look at each other."

Deylia brow crumpled like the rest of her face, "I assure you, Fayne, there is nothing between the two of us other than a strong friendship."

"Suit yourself. Its none of my business." Fayne giggled when she met Tatrice's eyes, and the other woman returned the smirk in kind.

"Stop it, you two! I think I prefer you fighting with each other over focusing on me."

Deylia noticed after they rode awhile it didn't take long for the weather to take a turn for the worse. The already cold temperature continued its steady decline after the trio resumed riding. Snow began to fall in larger, heavier flakes, but worst of all, the wind began to pick up from the west. Blizzard conditions would overtake them as feared, and sooner rather than later.

Deylia was happy and somewhat relieved to see the three buildings that comprised the Southern Pass waypoint rise over the eastern horizon. The main building was a large single-story structure with a large, inviting wraparound front porch. The two outlying buildings were the stables and a smaller building of unknown function to her.

The three young women rode to the stables first. Deylia was surprised when no stable hand emerged to greet them. The place was well lit, and the horses stabled there were eating from buckets suspended over the stable gates. Each one of the beasts had a horse blanket secured over it to ward off the cold.

Deylia was the first to dismount. She wandered around the stable and looked outdoors. The weather conditions continue to decline. Snow had begun to fall quite heavily. "I guess we will stable our horses ourselves. It looks as if we're stuck here for a bit regardless, at least until the weather blows over."

"Nonsense, I will go to the main building and get the stable hand. If the horses here are still being fed maybe they all went inside to eat as well, after all, it is close to suppertime." Tatrice said.

"You can go on ahead," Fayne said. "I'm used to tending to my horse alone. I'll get started with the unloading."

Delia and Fayne began to remove the saddlebags as Tatrice traipsed across the snow-covered grounds to the main building. A few minutes later she returned with a grim expression. "There's no one here. I didn't check every room, but the common room and kitchen were empty. A pot of fresh bittering tea is boiling on the wood stove in the common room, and something in a large pot is still cooking within the hearth, but there is no sign of a living soul."

Deylia walked the length of the stables and looked in each stall. "Full up." She said when she was done. "No one left on horseback."

"Mother?" Fayne asked.

Tatrice shook her head. "I don't think so. It isn't like the other places we've gone to where she's been. There was no blood I could see and there are no signs of a struggle."

"Maybe they are out doing something and will return momentarily," Deylia said trying to sound hopeful.

"That may be. But just in case they don't return, would you two mind stabling the horses while I go back and secure the kitchen? I don't want that bittering tea to burn, and I'll finish up the cooking. We'll leave some coin behind if no one returns."

"I don't mind. I'm ready for some food!" Deylia replied.

The snow fell even harder as the hour progressed, and the wind blew it all around by the time Deylia and Fayne made their way to the main dwelling. Deylia suppressed the feeling of irritation creeping up her spine. "I swear, if Tatrice is sitting at a table sipping bittering tea when you open that door, I will have a few strong, choice words to say."

"You and me both," Fayne said.

Fayne opened the side door that led into the kitchen. Both women rushed in and secured the door behind them. Deylia immediately looked to the hearth and found a pot of something cooking there. They left the kitchen and walked into the common room. There was a huge fireplace in the center of the back wall with a roaring fire. Around the fireplace were divans and chairs draped with bearskins and other animal pelts. Lining the walls were the heads of trophies of past hunts, elk, bear, deer. mountain lion, and the like. Closer to the front door and skewed toward the kitchen sat four large tables complete with benches. Two wood stoves, one in each of the two front corners, burned with an orange glow from behind iron grates where the wood supplied the fire to the iron burners on top. Tatrice was at the eastern stove attending the pot of bittering tea. Three cups sat on the table beside her along with a pot of honey.

"Ah, there you are. I made a fresh pot after I put on the soup in the kitchen. I had no idea what was cooking in that pot before, so I took it upon myself to cook something else." Tatrice said. "I found some cornmeal, so the cornbread should be ready in a few minutes and then we can eat."

"It's nice to travel with a skilled cook." Deylia said.

Fayne nodded.

Tatrice spent years in Dellah Adair's kitchen at the Tiger's Head Inn in Brookhaven and her cooking was the best Deylia could remember ever having in her life. She followed Fayne to where Tatrice poured the aromatic bittering tea. "Ah, that smells so good."

"Here," Tatrice handed Deylia the first cup. She sat it down next to the honey and pulled the spoon out of it letting the thick, golden liquid cascade down into her cup. She returned the spoon and stirred the tea with the stirring spoon from the table. She carefully let the hot tea pass her lips. The sweet, slightly bitter taste tickled her taste buds. At once, she felt dizzy, taking a step back. She looked at the tea and then at Tatrice. Tatrice reached out and took her by the arm leading her to the bench to sit down. The dizziness subsided.

"Here, sit," Tatrice said. "What is it?" She took her own cup and sniffed the bittering tea. She took a sip and then several. "The tea is fine."

"I don't know," Deylia said. "For a moment I felt like something was wrong."

Fayne put her hand over her cup of tea and whispered a few magical sounding words. "You're right, Tat, it isn't the tea."

"Maybe you are just dizzy from the cold. Go warm yourself by the fire." Tatrice suggested. "I stoked it earlier."

Deylia took her bittering tea and went to one of the divans facing the huge fireplace. The heat felt good on her face. She sunk down in the soft cushions and let the heat penetrate her outer clothing. Fayne came and sat on the adjoining divan. She smiled at Deylia as she kicked off her wet boots and laid back letting her feet get closer to the hot stones on the floor, which was inlaid outward in a mosaic from the stones lining the fireplace.

"Good idea," Deylia said, also kicking off her boots and pointing her toes to the heated stones.

"I'll check on supper," Tatrice said, bounding off to the kitchen, almost merrily.

Deylia jolted, "What are we forgetting?"

"What do you mean?" Fayne asked.

"This waypoint. Where are the people? How easy is it for us to forget we are alone here and that's not natural. Where is the proprietor?"

"You worry too much. Listen to that whistling outside. It's the wind blowing snow. Anyone that wasn't close enough to get here when the blizzard struck took cover elsewhere. Have you ever been to a waypoint in the Jagged Mountains before?"

"No, not that I recall," Deylia answered.

"Well, I have. Plenty of times. It isn't unusual for the proprietor to allow the use of their waypoint, especially during storms and blizzards, without them being around. They just expect you to drop some coin on the counter for any provisions you use. More than likely, the proprietor and his wife are snug in their home nearby, waiting out the blizzard."

Deylia sank back into the divan and let her feet stretch out toward the fireplace again, "If that's the case then I feel a lot better."

Fayne sat up straight. "Wait, you're not getting some mindwielder sense, are you? This place isn't an illusion or something, is it?" Fayne asked.

Deylia looked around as if she were assessing the place. "No, not that I can tell. I was just concerned why it was abandoned."

"Oh, good." Fayne sank back into the cushions of her divan. "There's nothing to worry about then."

Fayne's words trailed off as the sound of scraping came from the front doorway. Deylia looked at Fayne. Tatrice bolted from the kitchen, her sword drawn. A big man stepped through the doorway and struggled against the wind to close the doors against the blowing snow. He reached to the edge of one door and found the wooden plank used to bolt the doors shut and placed it in the hooks and slid it into its place, securing and locking the doors tight. He turned to face the fireplace and then he unwrapped his face from the woolen scarves he had wound tightly to ward off the cold. Next, he took his gloves off and stomped the snow from his boots on the receiving rug. He glanced at Tatrice and seemed amused by her sword.

"Who are you?" Tatrice asked.

"Can you actually use that bear-sticker, girl?" He asked.

"This is a dragon fang!" she said, her voice escalating.

"Oh, so it is. The sword of a dragon knight. Duly noted."

"What's that supposed to mean?"

"You went out of your way to tell me it is the sword of a dragon knight for a reason, I'd wager. I'm simply acknowledging you., but without the knight, the sword means little."

"*I* am the knight!" Tatrice said.

The big man laughed and removed the rest of the scarf coving his face, revealing a thick black beard." There are no female dragon knights."

"I am the first."

He studied her for a moment. "Aye, of course you are." He moved toward the roaring fire. "Good, you have a good-sized fire burning. I am chilled to the bone. The blizzard is much worse than it seems from inside here."

"You can't stay here!" Tatrice said.

The man gave her an amused grin, "This is the southern waypoint, all are welcome."

"Not tonight." Tatrice's tone became even more forceful.

"Aye, every night. This is my waypoint and I say all are welcome."

"You are the proprietor?" Deylia asked.

"Heavens no, but he is my brother. Tomas and his wife are cozy in their cottage about a mile down the pass. I just came from there. Tomas asked me to come up here and keep an eye on things. The missus thought she forgot some bittering tea boiling. Looks like you have already taken care of it."

"Oh, was he expecting company?" Fayne asked.

The man had an inquisitive expression as he studied Fayne's face for a moment, "No, not patrons anyway. But one never knows who might show up in a blizzard." he rubbed his hands over the fireplace, "Say, you look familiar. What is your name?"

"Annabeth," Fayne lied. "What's yours?"

"Erick. Erick Bashir." He rubbed his hands over the fire to warm them again.

Deylia opened her mouth to speak, but Tatrice quickly shook her head for her to remain silent.

"What's your business, Erick?" Tatrice asked instead. She motioned for Deylia to be alert and Deylia got the signal.

"Hmm?"

"What are you doing up here. Do you live with your brother? You don't seem like the type."

"Aye, you're right. I am not from around here. I am hunting an abomination running wild through these parts. A woman creature with claws and fangs who is killing livestock and villagers alike. I followed her trail here to the pass."

"That sounds dreadful. What will you do with her when you find her?" Tatrice asked.

"I will take her head of course."

Tatrice's eyes narrowed, "Do it, Deylia. Do it now! Find out who and what this man really is."

The man took a step back as Deylia faced him with determination. "What the..."

Deylia focused in on his mind and before he could finish his sentence or go for his weapons, he was sprawled out on the bearskin rug, unconscious.

Chapter Eleven

BEHIND THE LINES

“Well, what are you getting? Anything?” Tatrice asked.

Deylia wrinkled her nose, “Shush, this is difficult enough to do without your constant questioning.”

Fayne rummaged through the pack the man had brought into the waypoint with him. “All this gear is consistent with one traveling. A spade, some rope, some kind of jerky, waters skins, yep, nothing out of the ordinary I can see.”

“Deylia, he’s coming around,” Tatrice warned.

“I can see that. I am allowing him to. He’s not coming across to me as a lair.”

The man began to grumble and grab his forehead, “What, I said my name was Erick Bashir. My brother’s name is Tomas Bashir, the proprietor of this place. They are safe and sound nearby.”

"Then where are the stablemen? Why was there food cooking and bittering tea boiling with no one around? Tatrice asked. "It looked as if everyone left in a hurry."

The man got to his feet. "That's because they did. The blizzard was coming in and everyone wanted to rush home before they ended up trapped here. Before Tomas and I left, his wife put on a pot expecting us to come back inside, but Tomas and his wife decided to stay in their cabin where it was cozy and warm. I came to get the bittering tea off the stove and to save the stew." He sat at one of the tables and rubbed his forehead, "You three are very distrusting."

"You have to admit it looked suspicious." Fayne said.

Deylia chimed in, "We are being thorough. If we are going to sleep here tonight, we want to feel safe."

"Safe? You are nearly on the Scarovian side of the pass. I would bet you haven't been to Scarovia is quite some time, if ever, if you think it's safe here."

"We know where we are," Tatrice said. "I have been to Scarovia many times."

"Recently? Since the King left?"

"You mean Naneden? Was he ever actually a king?" Tatrice asked.

"He was the protector of the realm if not king in spirit. The regular folk didn't know any different. He left the kingdom in the hands of a terrible tyrant and scoundrel and has not returned. Over the course of the past year or so people who travel through the pass to Scarovia have been seeing things and hearing things. Trade has all but halted from the west. Come to think of it, I'm surprised you're here. What business do you have on the Southern Pass?"

He's not lying, but he knows what this menace he speaks of is, and I just heard part of a thought where he is trying to hide that he plans to hunt the creature he is chasing in Scarovia. Tatrice heard Deylia speaking in her mind.

It still rattles me you learned how to talk in my head! Tatrice responded. *And please be careful, the last time you talked in my head I got a terrible nosebleed. I'm not a mindwielder.*

Deylia studied the man's rough face. She decided to see if she could get him to speak more of Scarovia. Maybe she could get him to tell her what the dangers in Scarovia are. "We are on a trade mission ourselves. I have been sent to the villages to procure spices."

Tatrice immediately gave her an odd, slightly irritated look but she said nothing.

The man gave a sneer of derision and then pointed to the door, "The villages to the east? Out there? Didn't you understand me?"

"I understood you perfectly."

"Apparently not. Let me try this again. The villages out there from this pass to Witchmoor are abandoned, people have fled to the cities for protection. There are things out there now, in the darkness, terrible things. Some have seen flying creatures and other bloodsucking ghouls. People left to the cities so fast they didn't bother to pack their belongings so there are bandits and cutthroats also roaming around making the daytime just as dangerous as the night!"

"Then why are you still traveling around these parts?" Fayne asked.

"I have no choice. I have obligations to my brother, and I have debts to pay. But I will tell you this, I don't move about in the night at all if I can help it and I stay off the main roads in the daytime. I also stay close to this waypoint. The folks along the western end of the pass, near Symboria, report the occasional abnormality but maintain that nothing unnatural passes through. Scarovia is more dangerous than it has ever been."

"We don't scare easily, my friend," Deylia said. "I think you know what hunts in the night in Scarovia and you are avoiding telling us."

"I am avoiding it because it is too unbelievable, but if you insist on hearing the story, I will tell you. There are necromancers cropping up in Scarovia and they have done more than raise the dead, they are creating creatures of the night unseen in all our days. There are vampires out there beyond the pass and they are thirsty for blood!"

"Vampires!" Fayne let out an unintended chortle. "There is no such thing."

"You can laugh at me, but I bet you won't be laughing if you travel into Scarovia and meet one face to face."

"I think we'll take our chances." Fayne said.

"Suit yourselves, but if you are planning on going into Scarovia, you best think again."

Deylia was about to respond when she happened upon Tatrice's face. Her friend's forehead wrinkled in thought. It dawned on Deylia what her friend was thinking about. *Tatrice, think about what you're planning for a moment.*

She shot Deylia an even more irritated look, *Stay out of my thoughts.*

I don't have to be in your head to see the look on your face.

"Erick," Tatrice began and Deylia suddenly felt her anxiety shoot up. "You are hunting one of these so-called creatures are you not? The creature you spoke of when you first arrived."

"Well, strictly speaking, no. I am hunting something else that happened to travel into the area. I wouldn't go back into Scarovia if I didn't have to." He suddenly pulled a handkerchief from inside his coat. "Forgive me, but your nose is trickling with blood."

Tatrice almost yanked the handkerchief from Erick's hand and touched it to her nose. She pulled it back to reveal a circle of blood. She gave Deylia a hard gaze.

"All right, but you *are* going back in. Right?" Tatrice asked.

"Aye, I only doubled back here to spend the night and restock my packs."

"You say you know the area and you don't travel by the main roads. I will pay you to be our guide."

"Um, Tatrice, might I have a word with you?" Fayne said. "In private." She waved Deylia to her as she got up from her seat, "You too, Deylia."

Tatrice and Deylia followed Fayne into the far eastern corner of the room. "What he is describing, what he is hunting, we are hunting the same thing. If we throw in our lot with him, how will we handle...things when we find her?"

"Deylia can put him to sleep or something, I don't know, I haven't thought that far ahead yet. All I know is he is our best chance of moving quickly through Scarovia."

"Aye, if what he's saying is actually true," Fayne said. "We haven't been to Scarovia yet, he might be telling us all lies. I already know he's hiding something."

"Why? Why would he?" Tatrice asked, "I get the feeling he is on the up and up. Look, I was Naneden's prisoner for a time, remember? The longer Kimala is out there under whatever it is Naneden did to her, the harder it will be to bring her back to reality. You told me you wanted to find her and help her, right?"

Fayne nodded.

"And you said you didn't want any harm to come to her. If we are with Erick, we can make certain he doesn't get to her before we do. We will hire him to take us to Witchmoor and then we can search on our own if we don't find her by the time we arrive."

"I hope you're right," Fayne said. "This could end up being a huge mistake."

Deylia felt a cold breeze blow across her neck. "Why do you think Kimala would go to Scarovia if she's under Naneden's spells? I would think he would send her to terrorize the west."

Tatrice looked grim, "She is going after something specific; I can tell you that. Something is drawing her here, something we can't yet understand, maybe something Naneden left behind and now wants, but whatever it is, it has her full attention."

"How can you be sure?" Fayne asked.

Tatrice gave her a blank stare, "Because when he, that is Naneden, was in my mind, something was drawing my attention to Scarovia too. All I can remember now is it felt like a hunger I couldn't satiate, the kind of hunger that makes your stomach ache. It was gone as soon as I was out of his influence."

Fayne clasped her hands together, "I'm in, we can hire him to be our guide. Just please promise me you two will think this plan through and come up with something should we find Kimala."

"You mean a plan to subdue Erick when the time comes?" Deylia asked.

"Aye, that is exactly what I mean."

Deylia and Tatrice nodded before Tatrice turned to Erick. "As I was saying, I will pay you to guide us through to Witchmoor."

The man rubbed his chin, "I shouldn't even entertain the idea. It's much too dangerous to travel though Scarovia alone, much less with three women. But seeing my refusal will not stop you from going there anyhow, I will accept your proposal and I will guide you, provided you pay me enough. Oh, and I require half the sum up front and half when we get to Witchmoor. Shall we talk gold now?"

"You were awfully quick to agree." Fayne said.

Erick shrugged, “like I said. You will go anyway. I might as well take your gold now and save the trouble of taking it off your rotting corpses.”

CHAPTER TWELVE

THE NIGHT OF LIES

Erick Bashir had been right, the people of the smaller villages along the road to Witchmoor had been abandoned, and the people had moved on to the bigger cities. Scarovians were not welcome on the other side of the Jagged Mountains so migration there was highly unlikely. The persecution they would find in the west would be every bit as devastating for them as whatever drove them from their homes. A couple of hours before dusk, Tatrice led the trio to the most prominent structure in the latest village they were passing through, a place known as Delve Crossing according to a sign they saw. The wooden and stone structures of the village were ugly to Deylia's eye. They appeared as if someone had covered them with mud and then only half washed it off. The wood, where there was wood, was weatherworn and hued grey. Deylia also found it strange that not even a slight breeze blew but she still felt the chill as if it did. They entered the great hall to find a long table at the rear, chairs, and divans along the length, and tapestries covering the thin walls to ward off the cold from outside. At the center of the hall was an elongated, rectangular fire pit, large enough to heat the entire structure.

"Are we going to build a fire?" Deylia asked. "Please say we are building a fire!"

Tatrice examined the fire pit, "I don't see why not."

"We might want to scout out the village first and make sure there is no one around," Fayne suggested.

"You can if you wish. I don't think there is any need." Tatrice said. "We can handle one or two stragglers if anyone is still residing in this horrible little hamlet.

"I would not venture out of this building after dark," Erick said in his booming, masculine voice. "And, aye, we are building a roaring fire and heating the end of those firebrands." He pointed to some iron firewood pokers. "If you are going to do any scouting, you best be on with it, you don't have much time before nightfall."

"Just after I get settled," Fayne said. She gazed around the large room. The floor was covered in dust. "This place looks as though it had been abandoned years ago. How do Scarovians live in such filth?"

Deylia couldn't help but snicker. "It *is* a horrible little place isn't it."

"I've seen worse," Fayne said defensibly. "I'm certain Symboria has places just as horrible. I've just never had to stay overnight in any of them."

Erick opened an antechamber door and dusted away the cobwebs, "Good the wood stores are full. We can get that fire going without having to venture out to gather any. We will be much safer in the company of red-hot flames should any uninvited guests come around."

Tatrice rubbed her finger along one of the tables and flittered the dirt away from between her fingers, "Aye, Scarovians are a filthy people with dirty cities and even dirtier minds. If we meet any, you'll find out."

"I'm not sure I want to find out," Fayne said.

"Why did Kimala come here? There is nothing here." Deylia asked.

Fayne immediately gave Erick a quick glance. He was rummaging through what looked to be kitchen wares and not paying any attention to them. "Careful, using her name. Erick might hear you."

Deylia nodded. "What do you think about it Tatrice?"

Tatrice had already been to the firewood store and had begun tossing firewood haphazardly on the fire pit, "Who knows. We just need to find her and get out of here. The real question on my mind is what could be so bad that the people of Scarovia are abandoning their villages, and don't tell me it's vampires or such nonsense."

"I agree," Fayne said. "And why the hallucinations? Why are they seeing strange things and happenings across their lands?"

"Magic of course," Deylia said.

"What did you say?" Fayne asked, "Did you say magic?"

Deylia cleared her throat, "It's dark magic. Can't you two feel it? The air is thick with it."

Fayne took a moment to pause. "Do you mean the eerie foreboding feeling? I thought that was just because this place is just downright spooky."

"Well, aye, it's a feeling, but can't you feel the oppressive power of dark magic weighing you down?"

"I have no idea what you're talking about," Fayne said. "I don't feel any different. It's just our surroundings."

"You don't have a spooky, foreign place feeling, then." Deylia said.

"Well, yes, I mean, we *are* in a spooky, foreign place. None of us are used to being in such places and the stories told to us as children always warn us of places like this. Adults tell them so children don't wonder off and get hurt."

"I remember those spooky stories." Deylia glanced around, "They sure did work on me," she said as she unconsciously moved closer to the fire pit.

"Maybe you'll feel better once we get this fire going," Tatrice said. "If you move any closer to it, we will have to light *you* on fire. Make yourself useful and help me stack the wood and light it."

"I will help you with the fire, but the dark magic will linger, I'm afraid."

"You're a funny young woman, do you know that?" Tatrice said.

"So I've heard."

"What was that sound?" Fayne said. "Did you hear that?"

Deylia had not heard anything. "What did you hear?"

There was a faint knocking as if something wooden was being blown repeatedly against the stone walls of the hall.

"Like a window shutter?" Deylia asked.

"There it is again," Tatrice followed the sound to a window and peered outside. "It *is* a shutter loose in the wind. Good call, Deylia."

"What wind?" Fayne asked. "There wasn't so much as a breeze before."

Tatrice brazenly moved to the front entrance to the hall and opened the door. A strong wind blew in with snow. "There's wind now, and the snow is falling again!" So that she didn't let in anymore cold, Tatrice quickly stepped out of the hall and closed the door behind her. A few moments later the shutter banging noise stopped. When Tatrice reentered the hall, she searched for and found the stout, wood beam that bolted the doors and securely slotted it into place. "There, that should do it. No more banging."

Deylia resumed stacking the wood for the fire. Fayne began to work on the bedrolls, putting them in close proximity to the fire pit.

"Don't put my bedroll too close to the fire side. I got too hot last night." Tatrice said. Fayne moved Tatrice's bedroll farthest from the pit. "I don't see how you could get hot when it's so cold. I liked to have never warmed up last night, and I'm from the mountains where it's always cold."

Tatrice shrugged. "I'm hot natured. By the way, I am also from the mountains, remember? Just the other side."

"Aye, the warmer side." Fayne muttered.

Once the fire was going, Fayne unpacked the food and water. It was just hard biscuits and dried meats but to Deylia, it tasted like a banquet meal. "It's funny how food tastes so much better when you're hungry. If we were at an inn, we wouldn't dream of ordering dried meat and hard biscuits, but out here, after hours of travel, I can think of nothing tastier."

"Tatrice is right," Fayne said, "You are an odd one."

After the meal, they stoked the fire and settled down on their bedrolls for a night of rest. Erick put the pokers in the fire. He said they would make good weapons, better than swords, if they needed them in the night. Deylia didn't understand but humored the man anyway and helped him.

Afterwards, Deylia had no trouble drifting off to sleep, but she woke to the sound of creaking coming from somewhere up above in the rafters. She squinted to see. The shadows danced in the flickering light of the fire obscuring anyone or anything that might be hiding. She decided to reach out with her mind instead. She closed her eyes and let her mind wander along the rafters. It didn't take long before her mind touched the tainted, fearful mind of someone hiding. It was a sickly mind with chaotic thoughts of finding the others. At first, Deylia thought the person was thinking about the other inhabitants of the village, but it was clear after a moment that the urgency was to find others of her kind and not other people. Deylia subtly pushed to probe the mind more. She was careful not to alert the person to her mental presence. The person or creature was staring down at them. Deylia leaned back, trying to appear asleep. She still kept her eyes closed even though she could feel the presence getting closer. The mind had left the rafters and was closing in on them. Deylia squinted one eye open to see the face of a woman with dark, somewhat matted hair and a pleasant face. She was on her hands and knees approaching Fayne. The woman reached out to touch her friend. Deylia reacted. She snapped a hold of the woman's mind and froze her in place. When she opened her eyes to confront the intruder, she saw it was Kimala. In that moment of startled realization, Deylia let the woman's mind go. Kimala grabbed her and pulled her from her bedroll sending her cascading across the wooden floor.

"Mother?" Fayne said, "Is that you at last?"

Tatrice was also now awake with sword in hand.

Kimala curled up in the corner holding her knees tightly to her chest. She did not speak.

Deylia's eyes darted to where Erick was sleeping. He was waking so she made him sleep again. She made sure he stayed asleep.

Fayne went to her mother and tried to give her a hug. The woman did not react to her.

From behind the embrace, Kimala's eyes found Tatrice, and a weak grin formed upon her lips. Deylia could see that Tatrice didn't know how to take the grin, was it out of recognition or malice?

"Careful Fayne, she isn't herself, remember." Tatrice cautioned.

Kimala wiggled out of the awkward embrace, "Tatrice? Her voice was hoarse and weak."

Deylia expected Tatrice to embrace her mother, or do something, but instead, she stood there looking at the older woman stoically.

"What are you planning to do?" Deylia finally asked Tatrice.

"You left me," Tatrice said. "What kind of mother runs out on her daughter?"

"Aye, I did." Kimala swallowed repeatedly as she spoke trying to moisten her throat so she could get the words out without the parched rasp. "I regret it every day. No, not just that. I have regretted it every day since I parted from you."

"Where are you going? We've been trying to catch up with you. Why are you going deeper into Scarovia?" Fayne asked.

Kimala eyes darted away. She stared blankly into the distance with a far off, hysterical look, "I have to find them. I must stop all this."

"How did you find us? How did you know we were here?" Fayne asked.

"He did something to me, something horrible." Kimala was apparently ignoring Fayne. "None of you are safe from me. I must go now. I have to...make more."

"Who Naneden?" Tatrice asked. "Make more of what?"

"Aye, he did something to me, Naneden."

"We can help you. We brought Deylia. She's a mindwielder. She can heal your mind. Nothing can resist a mindwielder." Fayne said.

"No, it's a lie. He has mindwielders now too, powerful ones. He can resist the wild magic now. They're coming, they're out there. Thousands of them. He has come to claim them." Kimala pushed away from Fayne.

"Her mind is slipping," Deylia said. "She's genuinely frightened, and there is something else, an unbalance I can't quite pinpoint."

"What does that mean? Can't you help her?" Fayne asked.

"I will try." Deylia reached out to Kimala's mind. The woman screamed and squirmed as she fixated on Deylia. The mindwielder could feel the dark essence filling Kimala and she desperately tried to stop her from gaining too much of it before she had enough for an attack, but she wasn't fast enough. Kimala sent a torrent of power at her knocking her back.

"Deylia!" Tatrice said rushing to her friend.

"I'm all right," Deylia said when Tatrice made it to her.

Kimala started unbolting the door. Fayne rushed to stop her. "No, you can't leave us, mother. We must take you with us."

Kimala rounded on her; her face had gone ashen. Her lower jaw protruded, and fangs elongated from her mouth. "You cannot stay near me. He changed me. Naneden made me into something else. You must stop them."

"We must stop who?" Fayne asked. "Are they here in Scarovia?"

"Stand back!" The gruff voice of Erick reverberated in the hall. He had one of the pokers in his hands. "I told you this place was dangerous. One of the fiends has found us." He thrusted the poker toward Kimala.

"Drat, I must have lost control of the sleep spell when I was attacked," Deylia said.

"I have to get to Veric." Kimala tossed aside the wooden beam that held the door bolted shut and she pulled the door to the hall open. Outside the wind howled and snow blew over and around figures walking slowly through the village street. They sauntered, dragging their feet. They were the dead of Scarovia heading west to the Southern Pass.

"Stop her!" Tatrice said, lurching forward. A strong hand seized her as she tried to leave. Tatrice fought to get loose.

"Don't go out there." Erick had Tatrice by her nightclothes. He pulled her in and held her with his forearm around her neck.

Deylia felt the presence of other men approaching. She turned to Fayne, "Run! We are betrayed. There are more men out there and they mean to capture us! They are right outside the door!"

Fayne, who was nearest to a window, dived through it splashing glass and wooden shards inside and out. Deylia tried to follow but a hand grabbed hold of her.

"Where do you think you're going?" Her captor had a rough, guttural accent.

Deylia spun to face him and attacked his mind. The man fell in agony, clutching his head. She turned to jump through the window once again but a sharp pain in the back of her head made her fall. She reached and touched the wounded spot on her head. Her fingers were red with blood. She spun around to see a dark figure holding a club.

"You clubbed me in the head!" She said as her capture's ugly Scarovian face came into view and his mouth twisted into a sinister smile. He put the club on his shoulder right before everything went dark.

Chapter Thirteen

Kyrie's Gambit

Ianthill paced the floor of Morgoran's study while the other wielder wrote something on a piece of parchment. The longer Ianthill was ignored the angrier the old elf became. "What the fire are you scribbling so intently?"

Morgoran did not look up when he spoke, "We were in Ardenia for quite some time. I am obliged to catch up on some business here in the Vale, or did you forget this tower and surrounding village is also my source of income?"

Ianthill scoffed, "You're rich. We have both been around for thousands of years. You have vaults of gold up in the mountains just as I do."

"And in the mountains is where my gold will stay. There are still people who depend on the income here besides me, of course." He said, still concentrating on his writing.

"Would you stop writing and look at me?"

Morgoran put down his quill and intertwined his fingers, "All right, what is it?"

"Finally, I have your attention."

"Aye, you do. So, what is it you want from me?"

"We shouldn't be here. we should go back to Ardenia and lend Dorenn our council. Why did you talk me into coming back here to the Tower?"

"We have given our council to Dorenn. He will follow it to the best of his ability, You and I can do no more there. In fact, we should leave him be. Dorenn needs to make his own decisions and I am confident he will make them well. We will be there for him when he needs us."

"We can fight!"

"We will when the time comes."

"We are master wielders after all."

"So are Gondrial and Shey, and they are much younger than you and me, Ianthill."

"Speak for yourself!"

"Well, what would you have me do? Do you want to go back then?"

Ianthill eyed Morgoran suspiciously, "Wait, it would be that easy. I just say I want to go back, and we go back?"

"*You* can certainly go back," Morgoran said, picking up his quill and dipping it in the nearby ink well.

"Wait a moment, something isn't right here. What are you keeping from me?"

"Nothing. Why are you being so suspicious? I said we can part company, that's all, I'm not keeping anything hidden or being nefarious. If you want to go, then go." He gestured for Ianthill to move along with the feather of the quill pointed to the door.

"Oh, well..." Ianthill stood there a moment and then turned to leave, "All right." He headed for the doorway.

"Of course, if I should I get any visits from unexpected visitors or word from unexpected sources, I shall not be calling you back to hear them or talk about them."

Ianthill spun around on his heels and pointed a bony finger at Morgoran, "Ah ha! You do know something. Something you saw while you were Morgoran Cleareyes no doubt. I wondered why we would come back here while war preparations were to be made."

"Don't be so dramatic, Ianthill. It's more a feeling than anything I once saw. You know I don't remember much about the time I spent seeing the future. So many images passed before my eyes, I couldn't hope to keep them all straight."

"Aye, and I know you lie about that too."

Morgoran looked up from his work, "Do you now."

"Oh stop, I knew you before you became Cleareyes. I know you tells and I know you have lied about seeing the future."

"Do tell."

"All right, first of all, you have seen a lot of the future and while the scribes were sitting there taking down dictation, hoping to find some tidbit of prophesy, you were still in your head enough to know it. You purposefully spewed nonsense knowing the truth all the while. Your actions tell me you have been carefully making plans ever since the curse was lifted based on what you saw."

Morgoran smiled, "Well done. Perhaps I misjudged you. You might have bungled along while I was incapacitated, but I see your mind is still sharp."

Ianthill took a seat on the chair nearest Morgoran's desk. "What kind of a feeling?"

"I'm sorry?"

"You said you had a feeling more than acting upon anything you saw. What kind of a feeling?"

"Oh, you know, a pull to be here. Nothing substantial, more like a want to be home, really."

"A want or a need?"

Morgoran became irritated again, "Why are you trying to pinpoint it so? I don't know, a want. In fact, I just a want to be home." He grumbled under his breath.

"What is that you just said?"

Morgoran clicked his teeth, "I said, being cursed all those years was a burden."

"Oh?"

"All those people hanging on my every word while I tried to make sense of it all on my own. It was overwhelming some days. Some days the possible future was nonsense."

Ianthill leaned back, "I'll take it by your irritation that it's even more substantial than you let on."

"You are exasperating. I am trying to open up to you."

"I know you. Now that I have tipped my hand, you will back pedal to get me all confused. I'm not going to allow it this time. I am going to stay and keep an eye on you."

"If you must." Morgoran waved the quill again, "I give up."

Ianthill tried to lighten the mood, "You do realize I have been around you for thousands of years and I know all of your mannerisms."

"Aye, if you say so," Morgoran said getting back to writing on the parchment. Ianthill ignored his telling smirk.

Ianthill was about to retort when it became apparent why Morgoran's manner had returned calm. Ianthill sensed a powerful presence. He turned back toward the doorway to see Kyrie, the Kylerie elf standing there. He was puzzled as to why he sensed a great power from the familiar small elf, Ianthill greeted Kyrie none the less, "Welcome, friend. Don't mind us, come in, come in." He ushered the elf into Morgoran's study and shut the door behind him.

Morgoran sighed and finally stopped writing. He looked up at the Kylerie elf and smiled feebly. Ianthill had not seen his friend with this melancholy expression since before the first War of the Oracle.

"Don't tell me the time has come already?" Morgoran said in a low hushed tone. Kyrie nodded and then glanced at Ianthill. "I don't think he has figured it *all* out yet."

"What?" Ianthill felt an overwhelming sadness emanating from Kyrie as his eyes stayed fixed on his. "You're not a Kylerie are you." Ianthill didn't know where the revelation had come from, other than the presence he was feeling.

Kyrie shook his head and let the illusion of the Kylerie elf fall. He began to grow, and his clothes cascaded out into a dress. The elf's hair grew long as his stature grew taller. A faint glow began to outline a feminine form. When it was done, Ianthill recognized Ageanna, the goddess of dragonkind standing before him. At once, he took a knee and bowed. He noticed Morgoran had come out from behind his desk to do the same.

"Rise wise elf of Breannan and Xeian; rise exalted man of my beloved father Fawlsbane Vex. Be seated so I may have your council." Ageanna said.

Morgoran did not go back to his desk. Instead, he sat on one of the divans that faced a high back chair. Ageanna waited for Ianthill to sit opposite the chair before she took her seat. Ianthill began to feel very uneasy, but he tried to hide the feeling from his guest.

"I do not have much time. I know my father's retribution will be upon me soon, for I have disobeyed his direct orders and meddled in the affairs of this world." A single tear rolled down her cheek and she wiped it off. "I just love it so. I cannot bear to see it blighted."

Morgoran produced a handkerchief, but Ageanna waved it away. "I will be fine."

"What is it?" Ianthill asked, making his voice as sympathetic and melodic as he could.

Morgoran took a deep breath, "Before you answer him, great goddess, may I ask that he be spared. Send him away. Don't ask him to help me."

"You have seen too much, I think, friend Morgoran." Ageanna began, "And you know your visions have always been subject to change. It may not come to pass as you have foreseen."

"He's not ready." Morgoran insisted.

"He is more ready than you realize." She countered.

"I'm not ready," Morgoran said.

"It is time, nothing lasts forever, not even old wielders."

"Somebody want to tell me what's going on? Because it's beginning to sound a lot like you two are talking about death!"

Ageanna smiled at him, "Nothing is as it seems, friend elf. Enemies are allies, what was thought to be evil is really for the greater good. Nothing in the world is so black and white, or cut and dried as it seems."

"Oh, and you think that after five thousand years walking round in this world, I don't know this?"

Morgoran cleared his throat at Ianthill in disapproval.

Ageanna startled Ianthill with a girlish giggle, "I would not presume it to be so, no. I realize you are wise and worldly." She returned to Morgoran. "I would really like some bittering tea if you please."

"Oh my," Morgoran looked horrified, "I have taken leave of my manners!" Morgoran leaped up from the divan and rushed out the door, letting it slam behind him. A few moments later he returned.

"The servants will bring a tray presently. I apologize for my lack of decorum."

"Think nothing of it." Ageanna said, "You would be surprised at how many believe gods don't eat or drink. I have become very fond of bittering tea."

Ianthill realized the diversion had calmed him. Ageanna was a crafty one. "Back to the matter at hand, shall we?"

"Aye," Ageanna said. "Back to the matter." She appeared to be gathering her thoughts. "I'm not asking you to die, either of you, but what you must do, only wielders of your significance would stand a chance, Although I do not ask it and I do not wish it, I am afraid death is a possibility. In fact, it is likely you will succumb to death."

Ianthill could feel the blood drain from his face, and he leaned back into the divan, "Oh delightful!"

"So, it's true, my vision of Aedreagnon then?" Morgoran asked.

Ianthill wanted to shout out ah ha you did have a vision as I expected, but he refrained.

"He is unleashed." She confirmed.

Morgoran clenched his fist and rose from the divan. "It's our fault. Golvashala had him trapped in the library and we let him out."

"Wait, Veric?" Ianthill asked.

"Aye," Morgoran nodded, "Veric is the mortal vessel of Aedreagnon. I had not believed it, or I didn't want to believe it."

Ianthill already knew the answer but asked the question anyway. "So, he is using Veric to get around Fawlsbane Vex's ban of him returning to this world?"

"He is, but it isn't how you think," Ageanna said, "Fawlsbane Vex never banned him from this world as was believed. He was only temporarily exiled. Vex knows he is roaming the world and has even called upon him a time or two."

"So, what is it you want? You want Morgoran and me to go up against a god. Why don't you do it?"

"You know I cannot. Magic was gifted to this world through the Tome of Enlightenment, and it was gifted to the dragons directly by Fawlsbane Vex. The magic of the gods works differently. Only father and mother have the ability to kill a child of the gods and neither of them will kill their own offspring. If I battled my brother, the war would last all eternity with no victor. Besides, I don't want my brother to die either. I am not asking for a murder." She looked at Ianthill apprehensively. "As I indicated, it isn't how you think, there's more. Aedreagnon did not take over Veric. Aedreagnon's wish to be as successful and powerful as us siblings has made him weak. Veric has found a way to bend Aedreagnon to his will. Veric is the controlling entity."

"What? That's impossible. How did a man defeat the will of a god?"

"Because the god let him, of course," Morgoran answered. "He is using Veric as much as Veric is using him. They are feeding off each other and sharing one mind."

"What do you want us to do? You want us to defeat Veric and imprison him again." Ianthill scratched his forehead.

"No, only the magic of my dragons can contain a god such as Aedreagnon."

Ianthill suddenly understood and he stood up abruptly. "The sword?"

There was a knock at the door and a servant walked in with a tray of silver cups and a porcelain pot. He poured the bittering tea and placed a lump of sugar in each one.

"Excuse me, but I don't want any sugar." Morgoran protested.

"Aye, you do." The servant handed the cup to him. "You love sugar." He turned to Ianthill and handed him his cup of bittering tea, "And so do you."

Ianthill was startled at the servant's impertinence until he noticed that Ageanna had gone rigid.

The servant handed Ageanna her bittering tea and then made some for himself. He took a sip, "Ah, delicious! Did you all know that Kellegarn, the dwarven god, created the bittering tea bean and made it grow high up in the mountains for his dwarves? He needed a powerful stimulant so his dwarves could mine around the clock without getting tired. Everyone loved it so much it spread throughout the world." He took another sip. "Sugar was my idea, I'm afraid. Loracia protested. She said it would make men fat, but I didn't listen." He took another sip. "I must admit, she was right. Some men did get fat, very fat indeed." He stopped and gave Ianthill a hard gaze, "Aye, you were right."

"I was?"

"Of course, it's the sword. Why did you think I had Ageanna take it with her to Signal Hill?"

"I took it on my own, father. That was me."

"Was it daughter? Was it you? You took it upon yourself to bond our sword?" He looked thoughtful, "What was your story again? You were stuck there, trapped with a spectre, were you? Kyrie Keeperstone!"

"Father! You knew?"

"How could I not?"

Morgoran and Ianthill slipped out of the divan and onto one knee.

"Oh, do get up before I smite you both," Fawlsbane Vex said. The two returned to their seats. Fawlsbane refocused on Ageanna. "You are good, my daughter, but your manipulations need not point in the wrong directions any longer, that time has now passed. We will tell them the truth." He took his cup of bittering tea and sat down on a nearby wooden chair. "Aedreagnon is a concern but not your concern. I have a plan for him well in hand. It's what Veric and Aedreagnon managed to do together that has me concerned. You see, when the undead, unlife, or whatever you call them here in the vale first appeared I wanted them destroyed. However, my dear wife, even though she thought them to be abominations, was horrified that I might be destroying a new kind of life. She stayed my hand. She wanted to study them. I capitulated for a while. Then, I couldn't allow them to roam the world any longer, so I wiped them away, only they didn't go away. No, we didn't create them and for the life of me I can't figure out why they only respond to the light of Loracia, my wife."

"And father, go on." Ageanna urged.

"And dragon magic." Fawlsbane Vex finished before he took another sip.

Ianthill put two and two together. "*Dranmalin* is the key to defeating him."

Fawlsbane grinned, "Ah, no. No, it isn't. *Dranmalin* certainly plays a role. I have seen to it that *Dranmalin* be activated. Some may believe it will do the job alone, I saw to that. You see, I planned long ago to spread the power. It isn't wise to have it all in one place."

"For the love of all that's holy, what is it then?" Ianthill had lost his patience and Morgoran almost coughed up his bittering tea at his elven brother's outburst. These were gods after all."

Ageanna set her teacup on a nearby end table. "There were two swords forged. *Dranmalin*, the dragon's hammer and *Cyrodel*, the heart's will. They are twin dragon swords. *Dranmalin* bonds with its master and eventually bestows its dragon magic upon its wielder. It happens gradually. We anticipated it might be in the hands of a non-dragon such as a dragon knight and they would not be able to wield it at its true potential unless they were a dragon so the sword...well, the sword transforms non-dragons into dragons, of a sort."

"It actually bestows the power of the dragons to the other races gradually, so the transformation doesn't kill them," Fawlsbane added. "They do not actually turn into a dragon."

"Unless they duel wield both *Dranmalin* and *Cyrodel*," Ageanna said.

"Well, they also have to have the will for the change to occur. That's why *Cyrodel* is named the heart's will. It doesn't just happen."

"You gave *Dranmalin* to Dorenn, why?" Morgoran asked.

"Surely you realize there is a balance that must be maintained. This isn't a matter of good versus evil anymore, Morgoran. You can't have one without the other. I can't allow one to destroy the other."

"That's why you can't get rid of the unlife," Ianthill said. "They tip the scales and if you destroy them the balance is tilted, and the world destroys itself."

"A bit simplistic but accurate. I can allow one to dominate the other. I must give both sides of the coin equal footing. For example, I gave Dorenn the jade statuette with Toborne's essence back in Cedar Falls, knowing the consequences of my actions."

Morgoran contemplated for a moment. "You forbade the other gods from interfering with worldly affairs but if what you say is true there would have to be constant manipulation to keep the balances."

Fawlsbane looked at Ageanna, "I did a good job with this one, didn't I. Very good, indeed, Morgoran. But it's a bit more complicated than you realize and I should be the one to do the manipulating. I realize my offspring will interfere too in small ways." He looked at Ageanna. "You have nothing to fear, dear." He turned back to Morgoran. "It's complicated because all the races have free will and both good and evil tendencies. The scales constantly sway back and forth second by second. It's the sweeping changes I worry about most. I can allow good to triumph, and in turn, I can allow evil to triumph. The scales teeter back and forth throughout eternity. I usually keep this knowledge to myself."

"All right, enough philosophy. As if you and I can think on the level of gods, Morgoran! Let's get down to it. Where is *Cyrodel*? What and why do we need it?" Ianthill asked.

"You know," Morgoran began. "I now, at this moment, understand Gondrial." He glared at Ianthill.

"*Cyrodel* is in the hands of the first and only dragon to ever wield it, Amakros," Fawlsbane said.

"Amakros, the black dragon!" Ianthill said. "He's a dragon from Kragodor."

"Aye, he is, and I believe he is the second in line to the throne there now. You and Morgoran must go to Kragodor and convince him to give you *Cyrodel*."

"That's out of the question. We would have to pry it from his cold dead claws." Ianthill said.

"Then do so." Fawlsbane insisted.

"Easy for a god to say."

"If Dorenn has a hope of defeating Aedreagnon and the other great threats to the Sacred Land he will have to wield both swords, or he will fall short. He can't go for the sword. He must march south to meet up with Naneden and I can't send Shey and Gondrial. It's up to you two. I would think members of the fabled first trine would be up to the task."

"Dravenclaw would burn us to a crisp if we got anywhere near his dragon throne," Morgoran said.

"Dorenn forged a weak alliance with the Kragodor dragons not too long ago, Dravenclaw may still remember," Fawlsbane said.

"Perhaps if you bestowed some godly gift upon us, we could..."

"Oh no, let me cut you off there. I already bestowed a godly gift on you with the Tome of Enlightenment. You are wielders of essence; you are *the* wielders of essence. Surely you aren't afraid of a couple of dragons?"

"Giant, iron-scaled, fire breathing lizards with razor sharp claws and needle-sharp teeth who are almost completely immune to essence magic. Creatures possessing the command of an ancient and powerful magic given to them directly by the father of the gods. What's to be afraid of?" Ianthill said.

CHAPTER FOURTEEN

AT THE MOUNTAINS OF MADNESS

"I think I should come clean with you, Ianthill," Morgoran said as he closed down the Migarath Portal on the By'temog, Ishrak side. "You should know this meeting with the Kragodor dragons might not turn out amicably."

Ianthill stepped onto the first stair toward the open covering of the chamber. "Oh, and why do you say this? Have you foreseen it?"

Morgoran coughed to clear his throat. In reality, he was trying to hide his concern. "There you go with that premonition foolery again. You just can't believe me, can you? You do realize I had many images pass before my eyes over the course of the thousand years I was cursed. Can you fathom how many different scenarios played out time after time over the same incident? You already know I saw a lot more than I let on, but did you stop to think that out of all the possible futures, I could never be sure which one would come to pass?"

Ianthill thought for a moment. "I suppose not. Come to think of it, I would say it would be difficult to discern the future out of so many possibilities."

"Aye, it's near impossible." He took a deep breath before he spoke again, "The fact is that I have seen this meeting play out over and over and I worry about it. There is no use in hiding my concern is there. You already have a sense of it, or you wouldn't question me."

"I do have a sense of it. Why do you worry? What outcome did you see?"

"As I recall, it always turned out badly. Don't forget that you and I are guilty of killing a couple of Kragodor dragons at Brightonhold."

"It was self-defense."

"Pray, Dravenclaw shares your assessment. Don't forget that Toborne and I experimented on quite a few dragon eggs too."

"I'm sure Dravenclaw hasn't forgotten it." Ianthill stopped, "Wait a moment. I think we should use this covering to close up the chamber. It's beginning to rain. We may need to get back this way and I don't want the chamber flooded."

Morgoran reached down and helped Ianthill close the semi-heavy covering over the portal chamber. "If this meeting goes badly, we need a plan."

"Might be a wise course of action. What do you propose?"

"We must agree to get *Cyrodel* to Dorenn at all costs. We will steal it if need be."

"I can agree with that," Ianthill said.

"Remember, Fawlsbane nor any of the other gods will save us. We need to do this on our own."

"I have always wondered why gods only guide but never directly take control of situations like this one. Couldn't Fawlsbane just swoop in and take the sword, or command Dravenclaw to release the sword?"

"Fawlsbane explained it to me once. He said that if he interfered with everything how would that be free will for us? He also said that there must be a balance to all things, and he can adjust the scales back and forth but if he is too heavy handed the scales will tip and everything will be for naught."

"I was there. I heard him talk about balances and whatnot. Seems a bit ridiculous to me, but what do I know about it. I'm not a god."

"How is it ridiculous?"

"Well, true free will would tip the scales farthest from the center depending on the will of the people. They would have to face the consequences of their actions. The world is equally divided so that if one people's will tipped the balance too far to one side the others on the opposite side would cry oppression and immediately began their crusade to tip it their way. No god need be involved. Eventually, there would be balance based on compromise because neither side liked it when the other had all the control."

"Interesting. What if the balance stayed to one side?"

"It wouldn't stay that way forever. People are too fickle. If they have it too good they get complacent and start seeing hardships where there are none, and then end up ruining it for everyone. Eventually the scale would tip back on its own. Men and elves forget too easily. The balance would return in time without any divine help. Look at the War of the Oracle for example. Now that enough time has passed, they have forgotten why they fought it in the first place. I doubt people know why the Sacred Land is even called sacred anymore. In their minds, it has always existed. It will be a shock to them when it finishes this regeneration cycle. The whole area will look and feel completely different."

"Ah, I see. It's like apprentices. I can give them access to all the knowledge and direct them as best I can but to be a good master, I must be able to let go and let them find their own way, even if it might hurt them."

"Aye, but you still don't allow them to hurt themselves too badly. You will step in if you need to."

"Interesting theory."

"It's funny and a bit ironic," Ianthill said sidestepping some debris.

"What is?"

"We have lived for all these hundreds and thousands of years and are just now having this conversation."

"We never had the need for it before. Besides, a thousand of those years we couldn't talk about anything, at least not coherently."

Ianthill bowed his head, "Certainly true."

"Come now, the ranchman I talked to said the stables and a few other buildings have been rebuilt already," Morgoran said.

"Look at this place. The Ishraki people are sparing no time in reclaiming the city," Ianthill observed.

"They have a long way to go but the stables are a good start. I hope the stableman can spare a couple of horses or this may be a quite a long journey."

"King Dravenclaw got your word that we were coming, and he agreed to see us. Surely, he would send an escort."

"I wouldn't count on it," Morgoran said. "He might have agreed to see us but that doesn't mean he is eager to see us."

"What is it you saw about this meeting that goes south?"

Morgoran flinched, "I'm sorry. I can't say. If I tell you too much, it might change your actions."

"What about your actions?"

"All right. All I can tell you is the king of the exiled dragons is not going to be friendly no matter what we do or say so be as amiable as possible. If things do go too far against us, don't hesitate to run for cover. Dragons are unpredictable in the best of situations, and this is one of the worst situations."

"I guess we will find out what happens the old fashion way," Ianthill said, "We will just have to wait and see what unfolds."

Chapter Fifteen

Kragodor

Inside the chamber was every bit as large as King Amarantus' throne room in Draegodor, something that Morgoran knew was by design. There is no way the king of Kragodor would allow his throne room to be smaller than the king of Draegodor. Even though the chamber was called the throne room it didn't technically contain a throne. Instead, it had a huge crevice carved into the rear of the chamber where the king could fit his considerable hide into comfortably, along with favorite treasures, dragons were very fond of their personal treasures.

Along with King Dravenclaw, another black dragon stood at attention to his left and to his right, Morgoran recognized the black dragon called Amakros. The sword, *Cyrodel*, was on a display rack a few feet in front of Dravenclaw.

Dravenclaw allowed Morgoran and Ianthill to get within a few feet of the sword before he held up his massive claw for them to halt. Morgoran wondered if the king was even going to bother with a welcome.

"Kragodor welcomes the remaining members of the First Trine," The king said. The other two dragons bowed their enormous heads, which looked even larger while standing this close to them. Morgoran and Ianthill bowed in response.

"What brings you to Kragodor?" The king asked.

Ianthill gave Morgoran a confused glance and Morgoran responded with a slight nod hoping Ianthill would pick up on it. *Don't look at me!* he thought. *Look at the king!* Ianthill must have gotten the meaning of the nod because his eyes darted back to the dragon.

"Glorious leader of dragonkind, We have come to implore you to allow the dragon sword *Cyrodel* to be rejoined with its twin, *Dranmalin*," Morgoran said.

Dravenclaw examined a piece of parchment, "Your message here both requests the sword and my help." He turned the parchment over as if he might find writing on the back. "But I see no apology, I see no request that the sword's rightful owner, Amakros, accompany the sword. I see nothing in the way of compensation." He looked directly at Morgoran.

"Your majesty, I'm sure you are aware of the fact the world is in peril," Morgoran responded.

"So, what am to do about it? The peril of *your* world is hardly a concern of mine. It's always in peril from one thing or another. No harm will come to us here in the Mountains of Madness. The very mention of our home sends most sensible people running." Morgoran knew that was meant as an insult as if he and Ianthill did not have sense enough to fear him.

"No one is truly safe, your grace. Not even the king of the dragons of Kragodor."

Dravenclaw stirred and became ridged at Morgoran's words. "Was that a threat, wielder?"

"Not at all, your grace, it was a prediction based on an observation."

"What observation?"

"I was called Morgoran Cleareyes for the past one thousand years. I have foreseen a good many things in that space of time."

"Hmph," he said as he relaxed once more. "I have heard that none of the predictions the scribes wrote down from your ramblings have come to pass, not one of them."

"That's because there are many possible outcomes, and I didn't speak to all of them. I kept some of the predictions to myself."

"How convenient for you. Am I supposed to believe this nonsense."

"You may believe what you wish, your grace."

"Aye, and I do. Now, about the apology I spoke of earlier."

"Aye, your grace?"

"I believe you and master Ianthill killed two of my subjects in cold blood and still go unpunished."

"Excuse me, your grace, but it was in self-defense. I acted against your subjects to preserve my own life and the life of others nearby. It was kill or be killed." Ianthill said.

"You have evidence of this fact?" Dravenclaw asked.

"What sort of evidence, your grace? The dragons in question were bearing down on me breathing fire."

Dravenclaw lifted his head took two steps toward Ianthill before he shot plumes of fire into the air. Ianthill recoiled from the sudden display and from the heat of the blast. "I have now walked toward you and breathed fire. Do I now deserve to die? Would you claim self-defense?

"Well, no but the situation was different," Ianthill said. "You do not show the intent to kill me with your fire like your subject did."

"No!" Dravenclaw bellowed. "It is the same. You had no idea whether the dragons in question were coming directly at you or not." He lifted his claw and pointed to them. "Seize them and charge them with the murders of Dardrake and Florendel." The black dragon at Dravenclaw's left stepped forward.

"Wait a moment." Morgoran pleaded. "Think this through, Dravenclaw."

The dragon stared at Morgoran. "Naturally, do you seriously believe I am acting on impulse?"

"Think of the world outside this fortress. There is a lich leading an army of undead out there. We have heard from Draegodor that he has already visited the Garden of Bones. Those are your ancestors buried there too. It would not be unheard of if he has called your undead dragon fathers to his side. We suspect he has plans to attack Draegodor. Do you really believe he will leave you and Kragodor alone?"

Ianthill gasped. "What did you just say?"

Morgoran whispered out of the side of his mouth to Ianthill. "I have not had the chance to tell you everything I foresaw."

"Obviously!" Ianthill said.

"More speculation, Morgoran?" Dravenclaw asked.

"Perhaps, or maybe it in the dead-on truth. Can you afford to risk it?"

Dravenclaw let out a mighty laugh. "Of course I can risk it. This is all too thin, Morgoran, entirely too thin. However, I admire your spirit. I tell you what. I will allow all the murder charges to be dropped and I will allow you to take *Cyrodel* if you can prevail in single combat."

"A trial by combat? I don't wish to shed any more dragon's blood, your grace."

"And you shall not. Your combat will be against Ianthill to the death. I have always wondered who among you was the strongest. If you win, Morgoran, the sword is yours. If Ianthill wins, the sword stays, and he goes on trial for the murder of my kin." His scaly face curled up in a smile. "If I suspect for a moment that either of you is not giving his best, or if I feel Ianthill is sacrificing himself so you can have the sword I will simply kill you both. Your lives for the lives of my ki n."

"Preposterous! You can't expect me to kill my brother." Morgoran said.

"Wait a moment brother." Ianthill protested.

"Seriously, Ianthill. You have been on a steady decline for one thousand years and I am as good as I was the moment I was cursed. You have no chance of defeating me."

"That's not true at all!"

"Look at how you directed the affairs of Dorenn and his companions up until I showed up and saved you."

"Saved me! Look at how I trained Gondrial and Sheyna while you were stuck in that tower of yours. They are both exceptional."

"Only because I trained them first. They both had good foundations for you to work with."

Ianthill began to draw essence followed by Morgoran.

Dravenclaw leaned back into his crevice. "Ah, here we go."

Ianthill struck first and Morgoran easily blocked the plume of essence before sending his own back. He was careful to pull back enough not to hurt Ianthill but to make it believable. He was a little surprised when Ianthill subverted the blast and raised his hands to bring the solid rock tiles out of the floor around him. Chunks of stone slammed into his arms and scraped his legs beneath his robe. Surely Ianthill had not taken all this fight to death nonsense seriously. Morgoran had thought it clear they would pretend to go at each other long enough to steal the sword and run, or something. He had no intention of fighting Ianthill to the death. He abandoned his light blocks and attacks for something more substantial when Ianthill began his next attack and so prevented more of the stone from lacerating him. Then Morgoran tried to move in closer to his wielder brother so he could get the message to him to lighten up, this wasn't a real battle. But as soon as Morgoran took a step forward, Ianthill took a step back and executed a lighting attack that Morgoran felt very solidly.

Morgoran decided to take another approach. Perhaps one of the dragons had managed to gain a measure of control over him. "Ianthill, do they have you under their spell?" It sounded silly to say but he could think of nothing better.

Ianthill stopped and stood from his attack posture. "What? What did you say?"

At that moment, Morgoran knew that the dragons were doing nothing to control Ianthill's actions. If they were somehow controlling him, he wouldn't have stopped to question. *He's taking this seriously!* Morgoran took the pause as an opportunity to slip in an attack designed to restrict Ianthill's movements. The ribbons of blue essence wrapped tightly around Ianthill's entire body. Morgoran became concerned when Ianthill's eyes went wide with fear. He spun to see Amakros picking up *Cyrodel*. When the dragon made his move toward the sword, Morgoran saw what spooked Ianthill. This dragon was not Amakros at all, but a black dragon that looked very similar to him. he moved as if he were about to attack Morgoran.

"No interference!" Dravenclaw shouted and the dragon halted. "Let them fight it out as I commanded."

Finally, Ianthill must have caught on to Morgoran's ruse because he repeatedly darted his eyes toward the sword. Morgoran let the ribbons of essence drop from Ianthill and the elf bolted for the dragon with the sword. He issued forth tiny shards of solid essence at the dragon; it dropped the sword as soon as the stinging shards embedded themselves under its scales. He caught the sword as it fell. Morgoran could see the clear wisps of essence flowing through the sword. "Are you mad?"

Ianthill's eyes met his with a wild gaze. Morgoran, for the first time, could not read his brother's intent. There was a brief pause and then he grabbed a hold of the pummel with both hands. "Stay back, Morgoran. This isn't going to be pretty."

"Stop, Ianthill, if you're trying to do what I think you're trying to do, remember, you have to have *Dranmalin* present."

"You're right!" Ianthill said as he threw the sword with all his might at Dravenclaw. The dragon was caught off guard and the sword sailed right into the dragon's left eye. He released a torrent of essence into it as the dragon clawed at it. "Burn! Explode!" The sword called Heart's Will, *Cyrodel* in dragon tongue, turned red hot and then exploded into flames, searing off half of Dravenclaw's face. The dragon screamed in agony. Morgoran immediately attacked the nearest black dragon with the most essence he could muster in such a short time. The other dragon, the one who had tried to grab the sword earlier, sank his right claw into Ianthill's neck, dragging the wielder to him. Ianthill, who still had a magical hold on *Cyrodel*, directed the sword to fly out of Dravenclaw's skull towards the attacking dragon. "Burn!" He shouted and again the sword ignored scales to embed itself in the dragon's chest and shortly thereafter erupt into an explosion of flames. Ianthill rebounded, holding his chest as the price of using the sword without its companion *Dranmalin* to burst into flames reflected back on him.

Morgoran managed to get to Ianthill, who had collapsed from the pain of his wound. "We have to get out of here before the other dragons see what we've done." He looked at the flaming sword. "So much for diplomacy."

Ianthill laughed and it turned into a bloody cough. "We have never been good at diplomacy."

He reached his hand out and *Cyrodel* came to him.

"How did you get the sword to work for you?" Morgoran asked.

"It was just instinct, I guess. I didn't know it was going to react. I had to do something. You thought we were really fighting, and you were about to kill me."

"I thought the same thing about you. The floor stones hurt a bit."

"I had to be convincing. I thought you would catch on."

"I did after you changed tactics, but at first I thought you were serious." He examined Ianthill's claw wound. "This looks serious. We will never make it out of here on foot before you bleed out. Of all the places to puncture you, the neck is just about the worst. I'm going to try bending us to safety."

"You still remember how to bend?" Ianthill asked.

"Mostly, but don't worry, I can do it better than Kyrie."

"Wait, get us to the Vale of Morgoran. Envision the tower."

"I know how it works. Just hold on."

Morgoran grabbed a hold of Ianthill's arm and began the spell. The stretching and folding of space pulled at them both. Ianthill screamed when the bending began on his wound. Blood oozed out but Morgoran didn't dare stop the spell. He caught the image of Dravenclaw stirring. The Dragon, half its face burnt beyond healing, leaped after them, its wings beat back in a thrust to propel it forward faster.

"Stop, for the love of the gods, stop," Ianthill yelled. But it was too late. Morgoran had already executed the spell.

Morgoran heard the awful sound of punctured flesh, the same gushing and swooshing sound he had heard many times before when someone had been stabbed with a blade. At the last moment, he had forgotten what the Tower of Morgoran had looked like and his mind focused on the most recent and familiar place he could remember vividly, the throne room in the palace of Ardenia. The two wielders cascaded into the throne room with *Cyrodel* clanking wildly on the granite and marble floor. Morgoran came to a stop still holding onto Ianthill who had come through the bending portal with part of Dravenclaw's talon stuck through his back culminating in the sharp claw at the end of the severed talon protruding from Ianthill's chest.

Chapter Sixteen

The Visit

Lady Shey stepped out of the Migarath Portal into the darkness of the chamber. When the portal closed, she was in total darkness. *I should have lighted this before I stepped through*, she thought. The torch she carried burst into orange and yellow flame illuminating the chamber. She examined the covering at the top of the stairs. It was closed. The chamber was damp, and the sound of trickling water made the place particularly eerie, as if she was somewhere she shouldn't be. "I don't remember this portal door being closed." She pushed the covering open to a rush of cool night air and surveyed her surroundings. "Who am I talking to?" She shivered and made her way to the nearest street corner. She followed the street down a hill as it snaked through the ruins and debris of the lost city of By'temog, Ishrak. The breeze occasionally blew an old shutter or dead tree branch against a stone building causing some unnerving creaking noise or cracking sound, but Shey knew she was safe. Not even the scavenger animals, birds, or rodents had returned to the formerly cursed city.

As she made her way, Shey found her thoughts kept returning to Gondrial and his insistence on accompanying her. She had been pretty harsh with her words to him, refusing his help, but it was the only way she could be sure he wouldn't follow her through the portal. She wasn't at all certain he wouldn't follow her anyway, given his legendary stubbornness. She huffed at the thought of him and gazed up at the full moon. At least the light from the moon eased her passage through the perilous streets. She felt the crunch of broken glass more than once, which made her painfully aware that all it would take was a thick piece propped up on end to easily cut through the leather soles of her shoes and into her feet.

After carefully navigated the moonlit streets to at last arrive at the great library of By'temog; the very spot where they had discovered her father, Veric, trapped inside. She pushed through the broken double doors and entered the receiving chamber. She could still see the footprints in the dust where she and her companions had visited the place before. She continued on into the first chamber where the smell of musty books and rotting wood assaulted her senses. The shelves around the library were still filled with books and thick parchment scrolls, although some had fallen and spilled all over the floor. She examined the spot where her father had been trapped. There was no magic there now and the spot appeared to be nothing more than an archway and broken trim.

"I'm here," She listened as her voice bounced off the high ceiling and walls. "Are you here?"

"I am." A high, melodic feminine voice said.

"Where are you?"

"Here." a blonde girl of about seventeen stepped out from behind a shelf of books. She wore a white gown. She carried a book in her right hand and held a wooden staff with a green crystal inlaid on the top in her left.

"This is a strange place for us to meet Oria, wouldn't you agree?" Shey said.

Oria looked round, "No, not particularly. I do have my reasons for choosing this place."

"You are aware of what we found here then?"

Oria briefly appeared puzzled as to whom Shey was referring, "Of course, how insensitive of me. I'm certain I had all that in the back of my mind but there is something of far more importance hidden here. I believe you will see what I have to give you outweighs your return to your father's prison." She gazed at Shey thoughtfully, "Curious, that you should hold any ill feelings toward this place. I would think you would be happy to have liberated him."

"So, you're saying I should find this a cheerful place since it's where we found my father and where we brought him back into our world?"

"Precisely."

"Well, I don't. He was kept from me for all those years, locked away here. I could have had a father looking after me, but this place had him instead."

"Ah, I see."

There was a long pause while Oria presumably contemplated Shey's words.

"Get on with it Oria, if you please." Shey insisted.

"Of course," Oria said. She took the book she carried to a nearby table and opened it. "Do you know the story of the Amar?"

"Some of it. They were the first men created by Fawlsbane Vex. They nearly destroyed Lux Amarou before some of them moved east to establish kingdoms like Trigothia and Symboria."

"Aye, I was in Lux Amarou lately," Oria said. "I found the place to be...unsettling."

"Your sessions in the woods with Dorenn? I am aware you met with him."

Oria nodded, "The Amar were the first men Fawlsbane Vex entrusted with the Tome of Enlightenment. They were the first to draw upon essence and the first to realize magic in this world."

"Aye, and the first to abuse it."

"Certainly, being men, they experimented with magic, molding and shaping it as their intellects allowed. They made a good number of magical items and enchantments at the time. They studied magic for thousands of years. They did better with it than you, perhaps, realize."

"So did the dragons, make your point please."

"Very well," Oria said. "Dragons didn't invent the Lora Daine, Drasmyd Duil are not the only shapeshifting creatures, and the undead have walked long before you were aware of them."

"All right, the Amar influenced our culture. I'm fairly certain that all men are descendants of the Amar, in fact. It stands to reason later generations blurred the exact origins of some inventions of ancient Amar culture."

"No doubt about that. I'm not recapping or disputing cultural influence."

"Oh, then what are you trying to say?"

Oria sighed, "I'm not one to get angry, my lady, but if you keep interrupting me and pushing me along to rush my point, I might make an exception."

Shey's first instinct was to take offense, but she also had the intelligence to realize that Oria was correct, she was being a tad bit impatient. She decided to relent. "Forgive me, Oria. There is much happening out there, and this feels like a diversion."

"Ah, it's Gondrial, isn't it?"

"What do you know of Gondrial?" Shey was suddenly very uncomfortable.

"You fear him becoming restless. You want to get back to him so you can keep your eye on him."

"When he becomes restless, he makes bad choices," Shey said defensively. "You're a seer, you have probably seen some of the foolishness he has gotten up over the years."

"Would it help you to know you have nothing to worry about at the moment? You only just left him and he is helping Dorenn, I'm sure you can trust him for a few hours."

"What does it have to do with trust? I have been away from him for months and years before. I trust him with my life."

"But not with all the pretty handmaidens running around King Lourn's palace."

"He wouldn't dare!"

"What would it matter to you if he did, my lady?"

"I don't like where this conversation has gone. You wanted me here and I'm here."

"As you wish. As I was saying, the Amar used essence and other magic to make items of unspeakable power. This book has some of that ancient knowledge. Sylvalora asked that I give it to you. She says it will become useful to you in the days ahead."

Shey examined the book, it was opened to a page describing a talisman to return the dead to their eternal rest. "This was why you wanted me to come here?"

"Partly." She went to a nearby shelf and removed a metal box. "This box contains the talisman described in the book." She held the box up for Shey to take it.

"Just set it down there." Shey pointed to the stone table where the book lay opened. She knew better than to touch ancient talismans of the Amar without first understanding them. Oria set the box down. "I have seen markings like the ones etched into that box before," Shey said. "You say my mother wanted you to bring me here?" She inspected Oria's face, but the girl was looking past her at something behind. Shey turned to see what it was and was surprised, or perhaps not surprised, to see Gondrial coming through the receiving hall into the library. "Gondrial! I told you specifically not to come here!"

Gondrial threw his hands up. "It's not my idea. It seems I am summoned."

Shey rounded on Oria. "You summoned him here? Why? I thought you said he was helping Dorenn?"

"Forgive my subterfuge."

"I was suspicious as to why you were a bit too interested in our earlier conversation."

"Forgive me Shey, but this is for your own good." Oria pointed the staff at Gondrial, and the green crystal began to glow. A blinding green light penetrated Gondrial's chest and he dropped to his knees.

"No, what are you doing?" Shey went to catch Gondrial as he fell.

He looked into her eyes, hurt, and saddened. "What a stupid girl."

"Me?" Shey asked. "Why would you say that."

"No, of course not you. Why would I call you stupid? Although, you don't seem too bright right now." He slumped over into her arms.

"Gondrial? Gondrial wake up you great fool!" She let his body fall to the floor.

"It had to be done. He was too distracting. You need to focus, and he is just in your way." Oria said. "At least that's what you keep telling yourself, is it not?"

Shey's initial shock subsided and was replaced by anger. "You had no right. He isn't dead. You can't kill him!"

"Only, I have, haven't I. Now you are free. You can concentrate on the talisman and what needs to be done to Naneden. You are free to help Dorenn, untethered by the constraints of your feelings for that scoundrel. After all, he just holds you back. Have you not thought so on many occasions? It is what your mother wants. It is what I want. It is necessary. It is done."

"Who gives a care about what you want?" Shey could feel the anger taking over and she began to slip. She told herself not to give into it, but her heart was beginning to embrace it and she finally let go, the anger filled her, and it felt good! The rage escalated, taking her over in waves. She stood up from Gondrial's lifeless body and pulled essence forcibly onto her rather than drawing it in as she normally did. Surprised, Oria took a step back. Shey released the essence into a torrent of pure force. Oria tried in vain to block the onslaught with a wave of her staff. Hit point blank, the young woman flew backwards through a bookshelf, destroying it, and then she continued on through another behind it.

Shey's face burned hot with rage. She could feel it burning up from her soul. She knew if the first blast didn't kill, the second one would. She drew in essence so fast and forcefully it was visible, throwing dust from the floor into the room as a fine mist. Her jet-black hair blew back as if she stood in a great wind. Books and parchment began to be sucked off the shelves; the weaker and more ancient ones crumbled to dust as they mingled in with the torrents of essence.

"Stop, please." Oria's voice was weak and faint.

"Too late for all that. You must be stopped." Shey said as she released the essence at the direction of Oria's voice.

In a great flash of light, Sylvalora appeared and absorbed the blast into the palm of her hand and then deflected it into a crumbling outer wall, which exploded outward into a million pieces. "Enough! This is why you will not and cannot inherit your birthright and become the Silver Drake when I am gone, Sheyna! When it comes to that rogue, your loyalty is absolute, your love is absolute."

Shey was dumbfounded at her mother's sudden appearance. "I don't understand." Shey looked for the body of Gondrial, but it was nowhere to be found. She looked at her mother with a combination of hurt, shame, and anger. "A test? Really! You are testing me, now?"

"It's not a test. It's an intercession to show you the truth of the matter." Sylvalora said as she helped Oria up. "And it's as I feared, worse than I feared!" Oria appeared to not be permanently damaged and Shey knew the girl had Sylvalora to thank for that. "Your mind is all cluttered up with feelings you can't suppress. In fact, you can no longer afford to try and suppress them. It's time to face them or you will never be able to do what needs to be done."

"Wait, I thought you were across the sea." Shey began to assume a defensive posture as she realized she might still be involved within a trick.

"A gift of the sea god Malantis at the time of my birth. I can travel instantly to any body of water."

"The trickling water I heard when I arrived."

Sylvalora nodded.

"What is all this for? Surely not to prove I have a terrible temper. You should know my temper well by now."

"It appeared the rogue's inappropriate behavior has begun to rub off on you." Sylvalora went to the box containing the talisman and opened it. She took the disk-shaped symbol from the box and cupped her hands around it. A chain appeared and attached to it, making it a necklace. "Here, she handed the necklace to Shey. "Wear this. Gondrial stole one like it from a corpse in Lux Amarou." Shey took the necklace from her mother and put it on. "You must realize as my only daughter, I care deeply for you, but your destiny is not to follow in my footsteps. My powers and gifts will pass to another."

"Mother, you make it sound as if you are planning to die."

"Do I? Well, I'm not dying. However, I am not going to be the Silver Drake forever. Each god bestowed a gift on me and I have not used them all. My final gift is a choice. I can choose to leave the Silver Drake persona behind and live out a mortal life and I plan to do just that at some point."

"I see. What a terrible thing to do to someone."

"I don't think so. I can..."

"I don't mean you. I mean what you just did to me!"

"Oh, was it. Your heart wants what it wants, and I had to be certain. You certainly weren't. Now, I think, you will finally see."

"So, what now? Do you want me to profess my love for him? I can't be with Gondrial! He is a notorious womanizer! I have caught him on numerous occasions. I once even caught him with the queen of Symboria when we were on a task for Ianthill together. He has no shame, for the love of the gods."

"His heart belongs to you, trust me. I am your mother."

"His heart belongs to himself and that's all he thinks about."

"The only way you will survive the days to come is to come to some sort of grips with this Sheyna. Whether I like it or not, you are both stronger together."

"I am not going to devote myself to him. If he wants me so much, he can come to me."

"My foolish Sheyna. He holds himself back when he is around you and you deny your heart when you are with him. It makes you both weak. I had Oria to bring you here to either prove that you are stronger with him or better off without him. You made your position clear. You were about to end this poor girl's life, the very life you once saved!" She waved her daughter off. "Now go to him and show him your true heart and become what you are both supposed to be or remain the way you are and face your utter defeat."

"I don't need some man by my side to make me stronger! That's a ridiculous notion. I'm not some waif who needs a man to make her a whole woman."

Sylvalora studied her daughter. "You just don't get it, do you. You make him stronger, not the other way around, dear. He is not a whole man without you. He is of both the Amar and of the elf kind, yet he is a mere shadow of who he can be. You are of the Amar and of the dragonkind, and too stubborn to see that your actions have made him who is, this womanizer. His unrequited love for you is what makes his heart stray. He is searching to fill the hole in his heart *you* made. He loved you when you married Naneden, he loves you still."

Shey had not thought of that. She thought Gondrial had pushed her away all those years ago. He was denying himself for what he thought would make her happy.

"Ah, I can see it on your face. Now, your eyes are finally open, my daughter."

"You could have just said this before. You didn't have to stage this elaborate farce. What is it with you and Enowene? She thought putting me on the streets when I was a little girl would somehow make me stronger and you believed killing the one man I love will make me see how much I love him."

"In both instances, the illusions worked, didn't they."

"Aye, they worked. I still maintain there are other, better ways."

"Maybe, but I do not know any other ways. You are far too stubborn to be merely told and you are far too intelligent to be goaded, that leaves only for you to be tricked." She helped Oria limp to the forefront. "I think you owe Oria an apology."

"For what? I thought she killed him. How was I to know it wasn't real?"

"Sheyna!"

"All right. Oria, I am sorry you thought killing Gondrial was a good idea."

"Sheyna!"

"All right. Oria, I am sorry you fell for my mother's tricks."

"Sheyna Namear! I am still your mother, and I can still make your life miserable."

"I'm sorry I planned to kill you."

"It's understandable," Oria said.

"Get out of here, the both of you. You each have work to do and the hour is late."

"Are you going back across the sea, mother?"

"Aye, I will fulfill my task. When you see Dorenn, tell him I am coming back with the lost army. If he can wait for me, I will see to it they join him.

"Aye, I will."

Shey watched as her mother disappeared within a puddle of standing water trickling in through the broken library ceiling. When her eyes fell upon Oria, the young woman was tearful.

"What's wrong with you, now? I said I was sorry."

"It's not that."

"What then?"

"Your story, your love of Gondrial is admirable. I'm afraid I will never have a love like that."

"Oh, brother," Shey said rolling her eyes. "Spare me."

"You know, you are kind of a mean person."

Shey instantly felt bad for her comment. “I’ll tell you what. When all this is over, and when we have some time. I know several young men I can set you up with. Would you like that?”

Oria’s face lit up. “Aye, I would like that very much.”

“Just promise me you won’t be party to anymore tests or intercessions, or whatever, like this one, especially if my mother asks it of you.”

“I promise,” Oria said. “Are you still angry?”

Shey curled her lips. “What do you think?”

“I promise never to be party to something like this again.”

Shey spoke before she thought it through, “A promise I doubt you will ever be able to keep.”

Chapter Seventeen

Beware the Dragon's Hammer

Dorenn watched with curious admiration as Seandara flitted from one tree to the next examining the leaves and brushing her hands lovingly upon the bark. The trees responded by bending branches to her like an adult reaching down for a child. Dorenn wondered how the trees outside of Trigoth were any different than the trees of the Great Forest and Endil. As the two ventured deeper into the woods and moved farther away from the city, the brush and trees became increasingly dense, but Dorenn wasn't worried in the slightest. He was with Seandara. The likelihood of her getting lost in a forest was nil. She peered back at him as she met an ancient, knarled tree with thick leaves and she smiled at him sweetly. It was a rare moment of serenity among the chaos of their lives. He rested his left hand on the pommel of *Dranmalin* as he followed her. Even though he felt safe, there was something even more comforting about keeping in physical touch with his sword. Lost in thought it took him a moment to notice Seandara was talking and waving at him.

"Did you hear that, my lord?" She asked.

There was a mournful howl accompanied by the yipping of a wounded animal. "A dog, a wolf maybe?" He answered. "It sounds like it's hurt."

Seandara took off through the trees in pursuit of the sound. Dorenn watched as she darted deftly in between the close-knit tree trucks. He instinctively followed her. She was quick, too quick for him to follow closely but he kept her in sight up ahead. His face met a few low, thin branches in his hasty pursuit stinging his face. He could feel the welts when he rubbed the hurt from his skin with his hand. He found if he rubbed the sting fast enough it abated almost as quickly.

"Here, my lord, here is the animal," Seandara said when Dorenn emerged from the tree line into a small clearing with a stream running through it. She was kneeling about two foot lengths from it. It had blueish-grey fur fading into black paws, but that's the only part of the beast he could see around Seandara.

"What is it? Don't get too close. It may be frightened." He cautioned.

"It's a silver fox! I have only seen one other in my entire life."

Dorenn moved next to Seandara and studied the silver fox. The occasional beam of sunlight through the treetops danced and sparkled on its fur and it went from a dull grey to a brilliant silver when it did. Now that he could see the whole of it, he noticed it had a tuft of white at the end of its bushy tail. He gasped at the beauty of the animal. Half of an arrow shaft protruded from one of the fox's hind quarters and blood streaked from the wound. The animal had run away fast from its attacker, but the wound appeared to have caught up with it now. It whimpered at Seandara and gazed apprehensively at Dorenn a few times. A lump from being helpless formed in Dorenn's throat. He pulled *Dranmalin* from its sheath.

Seandara saw him remove his sword and was horrified, "What are you doing!"

"It's suffering, Seandara. I need to put it down. It's done for."

"Put your butcher's knife away," she said, "I can ease it's passing." Dorenn sheathed *Dranmalin* as Seandara began to mumble some words over the animal that rhymed, whenever Dorenn could hear them, she spoke so low. The arrow backed its way slowly out of the fox, and she put her hand over the wound. A few moments later she broke out in tears. He knew the animal had passed. He put his hand on her back to comfort her. She craned her neck to look up at him, tears running down her face. "You are a wielder. Can't you do something? What's the use of all that power if you are helpless in the schemes of nature?"

Dorenn was somewhat surprised she was even asking him such a thing. He shook his head, "I can't bring back the dead."

"But it's not dead, not really. Its body has ceased but the animal is still there for a time."

"Your magic is nature based, isn't it? If your nature magic can't bring it back what makes you think my essence magic can?"

"Isn't essence the power from everything living and nonliving? Are you saying your magic isn't as natural as mine? You can draw essence from the living, can't you give it back? Draw essence from my life and give it back to the fox."

"It's only a fox, Seandara. Death is part of life; death *is* natural."

"Tell that to Naneden the lich and his army! Won't you at least try? Draw it from me."

Dorenn hesitated but he could see by the look in her eyes that she was adamant, and he knew he had better try something. Even if it didn't work, he could say he tried at least, so what was the harm? "All right, but I'm not drawing anything from you. I can better gage how much I am taking if I can feel it coming from myself. He readied himself.

This is ridiculous, he thought. He absently put his left hand on the pommel of *Dranmalin*, like he had done so many other times to steady himself on one knee, and he began to draw in essence from his own body. He could draw it in from around him, he knew, but if he was to convince Seandara, he had to make sure she knew it came from him, from his life force. Almost immediately he felt a burning sensation on the palm of his left hand where it touched *Dranmalin*. Something was different, the sword felt increasingly hot as he drew in essence. Briefly, he tried to remember if he had tried to draw essence from himself with *Dranmalin* present, but he couldn't remember. He didn't believe he had ever tried it before. When he felt he had enough essence drawn he released it into the silver fox, and for effect more than necessity, he spoke the word, "live." The burning sensation from *Dranmalin* intensified as soon as he released the power. *What is thy heart's will?* Dorenn heard the words in his head, and it startled him, He took a step backwards removing his hand from *Dranmalin*. The burning sensation dissipated, and he shook his head to regain his composure.

Seandara's face suddenly lit up and he put his hand over his mouth in surprise as the animal stirred and then bolted upright. Tinges of red streaked through its silver fur. It hopped around where it was resurrected and then began to lap up water from the stream as if it had died of thirst and not from blood loss due to an arrow to the hindquarter. Seandara leaped up from her crouched position and gave Dorenn a tight hug. She pulled away and stared worriedly into his eyes.

"What's wrong?" He asked her. He could see the worry on her face.

"You are burning hot. You have a fever."

"I do? I feel fine." He touched his hand to his forehead and felt nothing.

"No, you can't feel it yourself, but you are burning up with fever. Quickly!" Before he knew what was happening, she had him by the shoulders and was pushing him into the cold stream.

"Wait, what? Seandara! How are you so strong?"

The little silver fox squeaked as he lost his footing and crashed into the water. A sizzling sound followed by steam boiling up from the water to his left made him flinch. Either he or his sword was hot enough to flash boil water.

"What's happening to me?" Was all he could think to say.

"Maybe bringing the fox back did something to you. I'm sorry I asked you to do it!"

"I don't think that's it. Essence doesn't burn unless you make it burn, at least not that I've ever seen. I mean, I've never seen essence do something like this before." He reached into the water and spooned it over himself. He felt the urge to cough and when he did smoke bellowed out. He coughed again and flames licked out from between his lips. He quickly filled his mouth with water from the stream.

"Dorenn!" He heard Seandara say and then everything went black.

What is thy heart's will? He heard the words in his head again. "My heart's will is for this to end and to be as I was before I brought the fox back from death."

He opened his eyes to see Seandara kneeling over him. The silver fox yipped happily beside him. He coughed again but this time without smoke or flames. "Are you feeling better now?"

"Aye, I am." He said, "What was all that about?"

"I'm sure I don't know but it gave me a fright. I won't be asking you to do such a heavy task again any time soon."

"I really don't think it was the essence or the fox. I mean you can burn yourself out with drawing too much essence, but I don't think that expression means you literally burn." He looked at the sword strapped to his side. "Could it have been *Dranmalin*?"

"Your sword? Have you had anything like this happen with it before?"

"No, hut I have never tried to resurrect anything before either."

Fayne used all her ability to stalk as near to the captors as possible without being seen. It was not an easy task, especially when there was so much snow on the ground accentuating every footprint. She surveyed the skies and concluded that the snow would still fall for some time, but she couldn't be absolutely certain so she kept stepping into the men's snowy footprints where she could and dusting hers away when there was no footprint to use. She spied on the men taking Deylia and Tatrice. Of course, they rendered Deylia unconscious, or she would have made them believe some wild illusion she conjured up in their heads.

"Where's the other one? Do we have someone after her?" It was Bashir's voice.

"She's gone out the window. We looked for her but there aren't even footprints in the snow."

"So, no one's gone after her, then."

Fayne watched as the large, dark faced Scarovian fidgeted.

"Sans, answer me!" Bashir demanded.

"No sir, no one has gone after her because there are no footprints." He repeated. "We even looked up on the roof, but the snow was undisturbed. She's vanished."

"Preposterous, she's out there. You just need to outwit her."

"How do I do that?" Sans said with a dumbfounded expression.

Bashir's eyes scanned the man up and down. "Good point." The insult completely went over the henchman's head. "I will send the Drasmyd Duil after her when we get these two to the master. We can't afford to wait. If the mindwielder awakens before we get home, there's no telling what she might do to us."

"Wild magic!" Sans shuttered at the thought. "I once saw a man claw his own eyes out because he was unable to stop the visions. I never thought I'd see a day when someone had control over it."

Fayne concluded that there were only three men. A fourth might be out on the road. She could hear the faint sound of horses whinnying in the distance. She stalked through the trees, wending her way through them to confuse the trail, and followed the sounds. She watched from a crouched position as Bashir loaded Deylia on a covered, box wagon. They forced Tatrice into the same. There were two men at the wagon for a total of five including Bashir. Two more horses were led to where Bashir stood, and he mounted one of them. As soon as all the men were ready, they slowly lumbered along a snow-covered road. Fayne prepared to follow them. She didn't know exactly what she was going to do, but she had to try and rescue her friends before they reached their destination.

"Sans, as soon as we get to the keep, send for the Drasmyd Duil. The more I think about it, the more I worry about the other one getting away. It'll go better for us if we can tell the master we have the situation in hand."

Sans nodded. "I will send for one immediately after we enter the gates."

Fayne began to move to follow the wagon. She knew they would eventually move faster than she, but fortunately the snow made the wagon slow and unsteady. Stalking behind a party of alert men was no easy feat and Fayne had to be always aware of every man's position, as well as be sure of her steps. She concentrated intently. The night was dark. The only source of light came from the torches on the corners of the box wagon. *If only there was a moon out to reflect off the snow*! She thought. *I could use magic to illuminate my way.* But if any of those men are wielders they will hear the spell, and also, the Drasmyd Duil would have a nice trail to follow once they sent one out after her. She decided to rely on her better-than-average night vision to guide her. It might not be as good as an elf in the outdoors, but the evolution of her vision from underground dwelling peoples still enabled her to see quite well.

She followed the wagon at a distance, through the rough terrain of brush she could not see beneath the snow and trees that were sometimes so thick she had to go a ways around them to stay with her quarry. Finally, some thick vines beneath the snow found their way around her left ankle and she couldn't easily pull free. She was too close to the wagon party to pull on the vines too hard or they might hear her struggling. She reached down and freed one of her knives and began to cut away the vine when she heard something or someone sneaking up behind her. She slowly and cautiously moved the knife into an attack position and rounded on the intruder when she felt they were close enough to her. A shadowy figure darted out of the way of her attack and rallied behind her. She felt the soft palm of a hand cover her mouth and she instinctively reached to grab a hold. The fingertips were calloused, a sharp contrast to the soft palm. She watched the wagon move away. She went limp, deciding not to struggle. The person who had her was an archer.

Chapter Eighteen

Unexpected

Trendan removed his hand from Fayne's mouth as soon as he knew she realized who had captured her.

"Trendan! She said, the last I heard you were in Ardenia."

"I was, I was in Ardenia. After you and the others left, we tried to follow you and ended up elsewhere. When we got back to Ardenia, Lady Shey and I had a...well... a disagreement."

"A disagreement? With Lady Shey, over what?"

"Fayne, I have some potentially bad news to tell you."

"Go on. What is it?"

"Vesperin is missing. He stayed behind in the Sacred Land when we left."

"You had better start from the beginning." She looked at the covered wagon fading into the night. "Wait, you can track the wagon in deep snow, can't you? Can you track even when new snow covers the tracks?"

He gave her a sly grin, "Of course I can. Look how I just found you."

"Make your story fast. I don't want them to reach their destination without us."

"All right, when we tried to follow you and the others with Bren's Lora Daine, we ended up deeper in the Sacred Land. We managed to get back to Ardenia, but Vesperin opted to stay behind to find a way to defeat Naneden against Gondrial and Lady Shey's wishes. It almost seemed like he had a death wish or something. Lady Shey seemed to think I sanctioned Vesperin's decision to stay behind."

"Did you?"

"What? No, his decision was all on his own. He said if he must die than Loracia willed it, and he will be with her."

"I know Vesperin, and he is strong in his faith. If he felt he needed to stay behind, I'm sure he had his reasons. He can take care of himself."

"You are surprisingly calm. I thought you would react differently. You don't think he stayed behind out of guilt?"

"I'm sure guilt is part of it, but now that he has been fooled once he won't let it happen again so easily. He would not stay behind on a whim. He has some specific plan in mind. I am calm because I trust him to know what he's doing." She put her hand on Trendan's chest. "Just as I trust you to know what you're doing."

"Well, tracking in snow, even deep snow, is pretty easy."

"Even when it's still snowing like this? Every footprint is covered up again after only a few minutes."

"Aye, there are still subtle impressions and..." He looked at her smiling face. "Never mind, you know all this already. You're just giving me trouble."

She nodded. "How long have you been following us? How did you pick up our trail?"

"I left Ardenia right after Lady Shey and I had words. I thought you might be following after Kimala, so I went to taverns and listened for anything relevant. I followed Kimala's trail of chaos to you. I wish I had been here a few hours earlier. I might have been able to keep Deylia and Tatrice from being captured."

"Or you might have been killed trying or you might have even been captured yourself. At least now, you and I can track them and find a way to free them."

"Speaking of that, we should get back on their trail. Visibility is poor now, but it will be nearly impossible in this darkness if the storm continues, even with the subtle impressions." He looked out between the trees. "And it doesn't seem to be letting up. Once we rescue the girls, we need to find a hiding spot rather than make a break for it, maybe a cave or something nearby."

"You don't think we are safe here in these dense woods?"

"Do you have any idea what kinds of things live in the deep woods? No, I prefer a deep rock impression or a cave."

"How are we going to find a cave?" she asked.

"Sarcasm?"

"Well, caves can be pretty hard to come by."

"When I was coming down the slope after you, the weather cleared just enough for me to see a rock face near here. I thought I saw some caves higher up on the face."

"How far?"

"Far enough, but not so far we can't get to them quickly."

"Trendan, Bashir, the man who took Deylia and Tatrice, he will probably be searching for me too. He knows I'm out here somewhere. He mentioned sending a Drasmyd Duil after me."

"You think he will send one out here in this blizzard at night? I say good luck to that! Not even a Drasmyd Duil would venture out in weather like this."

"I don't know. They might if they felt it was matter of life or death if they didn't. What if they can see in the dark. We shouldn't rule anything out."

"Right, I am pretty sure they *can* see in the dark come to think of it. We will just have to hide well and make sure we position ourselves in a good defensible spot. Come on, we can't linger here any longer if we want to catch up with them."

Shey turned to leave the library, careful not to look at the spot where her father had been held prisoner. It still made her angry he was prevented from being near her. She was robbed of being next to her father for all those years, and for what?

"Will you return to Ardenia?" Oria asked.

Shey stopped. "Aye, I thought I would."

"There is something..." Oria had an air of hesitation in her voice.

Shey turned around to face the youg woman again. "What is it?"

Oria nervously rubbed the palms of her hands on her white dress. "I'm not certain I should tell you but you have been so kind to me and..."

"What? I just tried to destory you with essence a few minutes ago! I would hardly say I was kind to you."

Oria waved off Shey's comment. "I was never in any danger. I was provoking you and I knew exactly what to say to get you all riled up."

"Oh, how's that?"

"I have spoken to your mother and I have studied you since you rescued me as a child."

"You're still a child."

"That may be so, but it doesn't detract from the fact that I know you, perhaps better than you know yourself."

Shey became dismissive, obviously finding the direction the conversation was taking to be tiresome. "All right, if that's all, I will be going."

"Your father was safe here." Oria blurted out. "Safer than he is now."

Shey stopped in her tracks again but did not turn around yet. "You mean trapped here? He was safer as a prisoner?"

"Aye. When he was here, he was suspended. He has the soul of a lost god within him and it's killing him. Here, the god was suspended too, but now, it's all happening again. He will go mad."

Shey turned to face the girl once more. "You know what I think? I think *you* are mad. Why would you say such a thing? How is there the soul of a god within my father?"

"I don't know, how is your mother what she is?"

Shey wanted to be angry at Oria's last statement but she realized the girl was right. She stormed away back toward the entrance. "I don't have time for this. I have to get back to Ardenia."

Oria sighed, "Farewell, Lady Shey. Remember, I did try to tell you."

Shey spun around, "It's a vision! What do you see? What will my father do? But, when she turned Oria had already gone.

Lady Shey returned to the court of Lourn, King of Ardenia, feeling a mixture of excitement, anger, and fear. Excitement because she finally, with the help of Oria, had found the courage to forgive herself and Gondrial. Anger, because of what Oria had told her about her father. Fear, because she was finally owning up to being in love with Gondrial. In fact, she could leave the whole Rikard, Naneden business behind her now and give Gondrial a good solid chance. Oria and her mother had just illuminated what Shey already knew. Deep in her heart, she knew Gondrial loved her just as much as she loved him. It felt good for her to admit that to herself finally, she loved Gondrial. She decided to find him and make a date for dinner to discuss it with him. By dinnertime, she should be able to come up with a plausible plan, so it won't be so awkward.

Since it was almost time for breakfast, she first looked for him in the kitchen. The kitchen staff told her he had not been down pestering them for food yet. Next, she went to the throne room but there wasn't a soul stirring around in that room either. Giving up, she decided to go back to her bedchamber. *Gondrial has waited this long, he can wait a little longer.* Giving up on finding him didn't mean she wouldn't keep an eye out for him as she wandered the halls. She decided she would try harder to find him later. It was time to bathe and treat herself to a bit of pampering before bedtime. The royal bathhouses were said to be some of the best in all the world and she had not had a chance to try them out yet.

Still seething about the possibility of her father going mad, which she found to be preposterous, she forced herself to put the matter out of her head and focus on happy thoughts instead. "I deserve to be happy!" She told herself as she grabbed a bath towel and her bathing robe. She peered out a nearby window and saw it was still very early, earlier than she had thought when she visited the kitchens. *Gondrial will still be in bed. I can bathe and make myself appealing before I talk to him.* She thought.

She found the bathhouses and entered one of them. An attendant showed her to the private pools, she definitely wanted to avoid the public side of the baths for modesty reasons and closed the door behind her. She was just about to disrobe and enter the bath when she heard voices coming from the hall. She thought one of the voices sounded familiar. She cracked open the door and looked to see who it was. Gondrial, wrapped in a bathrobe, was helping a young woman out of the private bath next door. The young woman was wrapped not in a bathrobe, but a large towel. While still holding the door open with one hand, Gondrial ushered the young woman out of the private bath entryway, snapping a small towel after her playfully with his free hand. The young lady started with a giggle.

Without forethought, Shey spoke the dragon word for fire and Gondrial's robe flashed into white, brilliant flame and was gone in an instant. He quickly rushed back into the private bath, leaving the young woman behind. Shey heard a splash. She smiled and let her door close. *He won't have any permanent burns or injury.* She thought. *But after he gets his wits back, he will be looking for the source of that spell.* She quickly let her robe fall and she entered the private bath. *It's times like these I wish I could shapeshift!* She absently rubbed her forehead in thought. Trickles of warm water rolled down her face. *I wonder?* Apprehensively, because she had never tried or even considered that she might be able to alter her appearance, Shey considered the prospect of looking like someone else again. Illusions were the magical skill of the mindwielders, something she knew she couldn't do, but actual shifting was dragon magic. She wouldn't need to change everything, just her face. She spoke the words and tried her dragon magic, but nothing happened as far as she could tell. She rubbed her face, and everything felt the same. *Maybe I need to have a specific face in mind.* She thought. *Funny, I don't remember mother or any other dragons saying anything about the specifics of shifting.* It just wasn't something she thought she could do, but things have changed of late. Shey heard a knock at the door and the knob began to rattle. She thought of the most recent face she had seen and spoke the words, the door flew open, and she let out a curt scream, half acting, half serious. Gondrial stood there in a white robe with a horrified expression plain on his now reddening face.

"Oh, pardon me miss," Gondrial said as he hastily closed the door.

Curiosity got the better of her and She bolted up from the bath searching for a reflection glass. She found a small one near the wash-basin. She wiped the moisture from the steam away to reveal the face of Oria.

CHAPTER NINETEEN

TIES THAT BIND

Lady Shey panicked. The dragon magic she used to change her face did not work the same in reverse. She had tried it several times more to no avail. On the second try, her hair turned as blonde as Oria's, almost identical in fact. On the third try, Shey's voice matched the young blonde she was mimicking. Looking anxiously into the mirrored glass, Shey tried once more to reverse the magic and once more she failed, almost transferring completely into the visage and figure of Oria. *It was time to get help*. She thought. Morgoran wouldn't know what to do, and her mother was across the sea with the lost army by now. She needed a dragon. Dorenn might know what to do. He seemed to have a grasp on the dragon magic from the Myradon Codex. That's it! The codex might have the reversal spell. She had to find Dorenn. The young prince of Ardenia knew Oria from his interaction with her in Lux Amarou. It might be a bit difficult to explain what happened, but given the options, Shey was willing to try.

She set aside the mirror and got dressed. To her dismay, her clothes were too big for the body of Oria. She sighed and put them on anyway, holding the robe up from the floor. Shey was not only wider than Oria but taller too. She left the bath chamber, careful to look for Gondrial. She was not certain why she worried about running into him now, he wouldn't know who she was, but she avoided him anyway. He was nowhere to be seen as she stalked down the corridor and into a lounge area. On the other side of the room was the hall that led to the private baths. This area had divans and stuffed chairs with attendants serving the guests refreshments and offerings of soaps and perfumes for those who waited to enter the private baths. Gondrial and his guest sat on one of the divans. The young woman was giggling at every stupid joke he made.

"I think I will be sick," Shey said.

"What was that you said?" Gondrial asked. "If you are going to be sick, point yourself in the other direction," The young woman giggled.

Damn his elven hearing! She thought. "I thought public displays of affection were frowned upon here in Ardenia," Shey said.

"Are they?" Gondrial said, with a sense of mischief in his eyes. "Then it's a good thing I'm not from Ardenia." The young woman chortled sweetly as he tickled her ribs just under her left arm.

Incensed, Shey rolled her eyes. She genuinely felt ill to her stomach now. *How could she have let Oria talk her into excepting her feelings for this man? He is a pig!*

"Forgive me, but I have to go now," Shey said, hastening away from the divan.

Gondrial leaped from his chair and grabbed her by the arm. "Oh, don't be that way. I was just having a bit of fun with you. Don't go. Stay here and relax with us."

"I will not! I bid you good day, sir." She said, still trying to leave. He held her arm fast. "Sir, I have some urgent business to attend to unhand me!"

Gondrial let her arm go. "I know what you're thinking. You think I'm a pig or a womanizer or worse, am I right?"

Shey stopped dead in her tracks and spun to face him. "Now that you mention it, Aye! That is exactly what I am thinking."

"Then would it surprise you to know that I am more of a fool than a cad?" He reached to find his stemmed glass. He downed the last bit of liquid from it. Shey thought it might be mead by the golden color.

"You're drunk," Shey said. "That figures!"

"Drunk? Merely tipsy." He smiled at the young woman, and she giggled again.

"If you please, I will be going." Shey turned to leave once more.

"Go then, but I'll not have you walking away believing I'm a cad. I have grown a bit tired of that moniker of late."

Shey sighed. *He seemed to be fixated on telling a stranger his drunken life story.* She stopped and turned to face him once more. "All right, since you won't let me be, what is so important that I simply must know before I go?" Then, almost as an afterthought, she added, "And once you tell me, will you let me be on my way?"

He sat down beside the young woman again. "I'm a fool." He looked at the young woman. "No offence dear, but I have no interest in waifs nor wenches." The young woman was not giggling now. She slapped his face and stormed down the hall toward the public baths. Gondrial rubbed his cheek with a smirk. "Not the first time and it won't be the last."

Shey was not amused either. "Why don't you go get sober, clean yourself up, and think about how you just treated that young woman?" *What was she saying?* Shey tightened her jaw. "Before you go headfirst into trouble you should first seriously consider how you wish to live your life, and how you wish to be regarded by others." *There! That's better.*

"Well, that's easy. I told you I was a fool. I have loved the same woman for as long as I can remember, and she doesn't give an elf's ear about me. How foolish is that? Live my life? I know exactly how I want to live my life. I want to live it with her. No more lurking about, or sneaking around, but married to the woman I love."

Shey's heart began to pound. "Why don't you just tell her?" She stiffened her jaw again. "And you have a terrifying way of showing your supposed love for one woman."

"Terrifying to whom?"

"Any woman! Carousing is the opposite of stability, I would say."

"You sound just like her."

"Who, this unlucky woman you say you're in love with?"

"Look at you, all young with beautiful yellow hair. You're as pretty as a painting, but you know nothing about love. It helps if the object of your affection loves you back before you go professing your feelings, wouldn't you think? I mean, why not carouse if you know you have no chance and it's completely hopeless."

"Maybe she feels the same and doesn't know how to show it. Maybe you *are* acting like a cad all the time, whether you are one or not, and it has turned her off to you."

"She married a cad. I don't think you have a clue about love at all." He abruptly took a very aloof posture toward her.

Shey felt the heat of anger rising within her, but she also knew she needed to play the ruse. "She is married?"

Gondrial slumped back on the divan, "He's dead."

"A bit callous," Shey said. "And very cad-like!"

"You wouldn't say that if you knew him."

"Why are you telling me this? You should go to her and let her know how you feel. What do you have to lose?" Even as the words left her mouth, she worried about being able to change back into herself. What if he took her advice? She needed to get to Dorenn and change back.

"My dear young woman, so naïve, I have tried that."

"Stop saying that! I am older than you might think."

"Stop saying what? Look at you. You're in the springtime of your young life. You probably have several young men to worry about, or you will shortly. You will come to know what I'm saying to you soon enough."

Shey felt her frustration escalate. "I don't have time for all this. Look you fool headed, half-witted oaf, she feels the same way you do. Go to her and stop lollygagging about, sulking in your drink and carousing, feeling sorry for your witless self. It's the way you live your life that has stunted your love life. Trust me."

Gondrial sat up and eyed the visage of Oria who was really Shey. "Wait a minute. That also sounded just like something Shey would say."

"Well, she would be right to say it."

"Do you know her?"

"How should I know? You never mentioned a name until now." Shey suddenly wanted to hear him say her name again. Shey longed to hear it again. She leaned in toward Gondrial anxiously.

"Shey, err...Lady Shey Namear. Do you know her?"

There it was, she had confirmation. She finally knew how he felt about her without fear, without a doubt. "No, I don't know her, but I know that if it were me, I would want to know how you felt. Take a chance. You can't succeed with wishes and wants; you have to take the chance." She wanted to go to him, but frustratingly, she knew she couldn't. She felt the urgency of changing back to herself more than ever now. "I have to go." She rushed away, holding her robes up off the floor. She turned to look at him once more and she saw his face was curled in a perplexed expression. She looked down at her sloppy manner of dress. *Oh, gods! Did he recognize my robes?*

Dorenn was discussing the peculiar incident with the silver fox with Lourn in the throne room when Morgoran and Ianthill opened the crackling, dangerous portal and came sliding in across the floor. The sword one of them was carrying clanked and banged all the way to the rear of the room. It took him a long moment after the portal dissipated to see the enormous dragon's talon protruding from Ianthill's chest. He wished Seandara had not been busy outside playing with the little fox they had rescued. Her nature magic would come in handy. Vesperin was also absent. Dorenn turned to one of the startled guards running to intercept the intruders. "Guard, it's Morgoran and Ianthill, have someone go fetch the royal healers. The guard hesitated. "Go, I say!" The guard turned and headed for the doorway yelling for someone to get the royal healers.

Morgoran righted himself to his knees clutching Ianthill. He cradled his head. "Don't you die on me, old elf, not now."

Ianthill's eyes were droopy, and blood poured onto the marble floor underneath him in a sticky, dark crimson pool. He feebly reached his hand for Dorenn. Dorenn took it and went down to his knees beside him. "I have the guards getting the royal healers, you just relax."

Ianthill tried to speak, "It's too late."

"No, don't you talk like that," Dorenn said, His eyes welling up with tears. "The royal healers are coming."

"We must be...quick. I...need to make certain my essence...is..."

"Don't speak, Ianthill. Save your strength." Dorenn said.

Ianthill shook his head. "I have to do this." He grasped Dorenn's hand harder than Dorenn thought possible, especially for one so grievously wounded. The old elf's eyes rolled into the back of his head and Dorenn looked up to see Morgoran backing away.

"What are you doing!" Dorenn asked.

Ianthill stiffened and Dorenn felt the essence flowing from Ianthill into his body. Much the same way Toborne's essence had flowed though him. At once, Dorenn knew what Ianthill was doing. He was transferring all he was, all his essence to Dorenn. He was planning on dying. Dorenn tried to pull away, but Ianthill had him literally in a death grip. The healers began to arrive and Ianthill let go of Dorenn's hand and faded into unconsciousness. A man and a woman of Loracia began to prey over him and dress his wound, magically removing the talon from his chest.

Dorenn watched with sadness as the healers moved Ianthill to take him somewhere more comfortable. Dorenn was about to follow when the blonde-headed woman from Lux Amarou appeared in the doorway seconds after the gurney with Ianthill passed.

The young woman looked at Dorenn with watery eyes, "Oh gods, was that Ianthill? What happened?" In the moment, Shey had forgotten what she looked like.

Dorenn's face twisted angrily, "You! What business do you have here?" he motioned to the guards. "Seize her and take her to my chambers. Lock her in under guard."

The guards moved in to take her, "Wait! Dorenn. You never said you were angry with her."

Dorenn was confused. "Her?"

"Didn't Oria help you? Didn't she show you what you must do?" Shey asked.

"What does that have to do with anything? I need answers and you know more than you let on."

"But I'm not Oria, I'm Shey. I need your help. I used dragon magic and..."

Dorenn waved for the guards to take her away.

"But I'm not Oria, Dorenn!" Shey protested as the guards dragged her away. All she could think to do was to draw essence. Immediately she felt Dorenn's control fall over her and his will crush her need to draw essence. For the first time she felt the strength within him, and it was frightening.

Dorenn went to the temple and watched the clerics work on Ianthill for a time. When he was sure the old elf was stable, he roamed around the castle grounds until he found Morgoran sitting on the common balcony outside of the wielder's bedchamber smoking his long-stemmed pipe. The sweet aroma of the tabac made him wish he had brought his own pipe. Morgoran glanced up at him and gestured toward the other chair. Dorenn complied.

"Any word?" Morgoran asked.

"He's stable for the moment. I just left him."

"Good, good."

"Two orders of business. First, I thought it might be a nice idea if you visited Ianthill's bedside and second, where is the sword?"

"Ah, you have Ianthill's essence now. I almost forgot."

"I doubt that very much. I don't think you forget anything, do you?"

Morgoran took his pipe from his mouth long enough to give Dorenn a brief poisonous gaze. "You're right. It has been the foremost thing on my mind, the sword. I have been thinking about what might happen should I give it to you." He took another puff from his pipe. "As far as Ianthill goes, he died the moment he gave you his soul. His shell will eventually wither and die without it. You will need to return it to him if you want him to live."

"Regardless, it's still traditional for you to pay your respects."

Morgoran glared at him. "You will not lecture me on tradition, boy."

Dorenn wanted to be angry, but he remained calm. "What of the sword?"

"I have been thinking about it," Morgoran said.

"And what is your conclusion?"

"I don't know yet."

Dorenn leaned forward and peered over the balcony. "It might be useful in the battles ahead."

"Useful for whom? You realize who you face out there now, don't you? Ianthill knew so I suppose you now know as well. How will this sword help you deal with Shey when she finds out about who her real father is, about who's got Veric in his evil grip?"

"Veric is the least of my worries now. I suppose Shey will adapt as she always does."

"Do you speak of the lich king. Is he the greater of your worries?"

"Are we calling him that now?"

"Well, that's what he is. As a lich, he has access to more dark magical power than any wielder and he is poised on the verge of the Sacred Land, a pool of almost unlimited magic."

"Exactly why Ianthill thought *Cyrodel* and *Dranmalin* should be reunited. To give me an edge. The Sacred Land is far from being a source of unlimited magic."

"It's the closest this world has ever seen."

"Morgoran, are you going to give me *Cyrodel* or not? I must be going. I have matters to tend to."

"Before I hand over the sword to you remember that this is not our plan, these are not our rules. This way is the machinations of the gods, and they don't play by our rules or follow any of our expectations. We play by their rules and are subject to their whims, and therein lies the danger. Are you sure you want me to hand this sword over to you now?"

"You went to Kragodor to get it. Ianthill died retrieving it. Why would you hold it from me?"

Morgoran coughed on a wayward puff of smoke. "Hold on there, I just wanted you to be aware of what you are agreeing to, that's all." He got up from his chair. "It's in here." He led Dorenn to the bed and searched under the straw and cotton mattress. He produced something wrapped in one of the bed sheets and laid it out on the bed. "Take it." He turned and puffed on his pipe as he returned to the balcony.

Dorenn carefully unwrapped the bedsheet to reveal *Cyrodel*. The sword was smaller than *Dranmalin* and had a slightly more feminine appeal to it. The blade had flourishes and vines and the hilt was inlaid with a blue jewel at the pommel. At the end of both guards were dragon heads instead of dragon claws like *Dranmalin*. He wrapped the bed sheet back around it without touching it, picked it up and exited the chamber.

He arrived at his chambers, the door still under guard. He entered. Oria was sitting in a chair positioned toward the balcony. She was staring out into the fields.

"There you are." She said, "I need your help."

Dorenn placed the sword on his bed. "For what?"

"Dorenn, I am Lady Shey, not Oria. I used dragon magic to change my looks and I don't know how to reverse it. Where is the Myradon codex?"

"Nice try. Lady Shey would never change her looks."

"Dorenn Adair! I am Lady Shey."

He did not look convinced. "You realize I can see through disguises. I would know."

"This isn't some illusion, it's dragon magic."

A knock at the chamber door interrupted them. "Enter," Dorenn said.

One of the healers entered. "Forgive the interruption sir, but I am sorry to inform you Master Ianthill has joined the spirit realm."

Shey gasped and clutched her hand to her mouth. Tears streamed down her face. Dorenn looked at her with sympathy. "Very well, healer. Alert the others I will be there shortly." The healer bowed and left. Dorenn went to the north wall of his chamber and recited a rune spell. He glanced at Oria. He could tell by her shocked expression that she didn't know he could speak such a spell. It was an expression he would expect from Lady Shey but not Oria. The wall opened and Dorenn took out the gold laced book known as the Myradon Codex.

"You believe me now?"

Dorenn nodded. "It was something about your reaction to Ianthill's death. His essence is within me now and he knows who you are, who am I to argue?"

“Thank you, Dorenn. Will you stay while I find the right spell? I may need your help.”

“Of course, I will stay. Afterwards I will need your help. I don’t want to plan another funeral alone.”

“I understand. She opened the huge book and began searching.

Seandara scarcely left Dorenn’s side throughout the priests of Loracia’s funeral services for Ianthill or the burial ceremony. Dorenn had come to rely on her more and more. Due to her constant companionship, he could keep his emotions in check, that is, until Morgoran delivered his eulogy at the burial ceremony. Dorenn felt his grip tighten with hers as Morgoran spoke.

“I cannot remember a time without Ianthill. We both came to this world together. He was more than my brother, he was my friend, my mentor, my right arm. For the past one thousand years, he made certain I was safe in my tower, as cursed as I was. His courage never wavered, his heart never strayed, his loyalty remained always vigilant. His death comes from the great evil we have let corrupt our lands. It might not be the totality of the evil we face but it is a facet of it, and I will not rest until I stamp it out.” Morgoran looked directly at Dorenn, and he felt like hiding himself away. “But Ianthill is not gone. His essence lives within the true hope of this land.”

Gondrial was scheduled to speak next but he couldn’t compose himself long enough to honor his mentor and master. His speech was brief. “He was more than my master; he was like a second father to me. I will miss him.” He left the podium and stood next to Lady Shey who was strangely affectionate toward him, Dorenn expected her to comfort Gondrial more than anyone else, but he had never seen her fawn over him so.

Four men each lit a corner of the funeral pyre and the shrouded body of Ianthill burned to ash. When it was done, Dorenn went and placed a single white rose near the ashes but far enough away that it wouldn't wilt due to the heat of the coals that remained. Seandara cupped her hand on his cheek, and he leaned into it. "You know, I was once denying Ianthill, saying destiny is what you make of it or some such impertinent statement. Ianthill looked at me and said do as you will Dorenn but one way or another destiny will have its way with you. I will never forget that."

Seandara's big brown eyes met Dorenn's, and she smiled. His heart fluttered for a moment. It was then that he realized he was in love with her, or maybe the strong emotions of the funeral were just playing tricks on him, and he felt he needed to be near her. Either way, he had never felt closer to a woman before, not even to Tatrice.

"Princess Seandara?" A handmaiden appeared behind them holding a small piece of parchment. "Is there a Princess Seandara here?"

"I am Princess Seandara."

The handmaiden held out the parchment. "I have an urgent message for you from Endil."

Seandara took the parchment and opened it. Her face turned ashen as she read it.

"What does it say?" Dorenn asked.

"It is a summons. There are ships crossing from Darovan full of abominations. A few have made landfall and are amassing at the edge of the Great Sythian Forest near the road to Endil."

Dorenn scoffed, "Why would they land there? I don't see the strategic importance of Endil. The forest is too dense to move troops through."

"There's more. Mother is ill."

"More bad news. Come with me. We will use the one of the portals."

Chapter Twenty

EMPIRES OF DRAGONKIND

Shortly after their arrival in Endil, Foreshome in common speak, Dorenn and Seandara were led directly to the bedchamber of queen Sildariel, while Morgoran opted to first assess the situation with the defenses of the treetop city and disappeared with a few of the elders.

Sildariel was tucked into a white linen bed trimmed with green vines and surrounded by flowers of all kinds.

"Mother!" Seandara said as she went to her bedside.

"My child," Sildariel answered.

"What happened? Elves don't become ill."

"One of the unlife made its way to my chamber and managed to touch me before I could dispatch it. Its corruption has invaded my body, but the clerics say I will recover." She looked at Dorenn. "Where is Morgoran? Did he arrive with you?"

"He's busy checking city defenses. He'll be around to see you."

"I see. Did you bring soldiers?"

"Aye, we have a plan to defend the city. I don't suppose you know why they're attacking, do you? Endil seems so far out of their way."

"It's our nature magic. My scouts say they are attracted to it."

"Attracted to it? how?" Dorenn asked.

"They will attack anyone who attempts to use it immediately. It is as a moth to a flame."

"What of the Archers of Endil?" Dorenn asked the queen.

"They have defended the city well. They have been rotating in shifts for days now. I fear they grow too tired, even with the legendary stamina of my people."

"It's as I thought. As I said, we did bring some soldiers, as many as we could spare, but the bulk of my armies are marching toward the Sacred Land. I worry we're still too few."

Sildariel tried to get up from her sickbed.

"What are you doing mother?" Seandara asked. "Don't get up, there's nothing you can do this minute. Morgoran and Dorenn will take care of everything."

"It is not that, my dear daughter, I feel something is gravely wrong. The forest is calling out to me."

"What's it saying?" Dorenn asked.

Sildariel looked at him as if he were both silly and stupid. She turned to Seandara, "Does he not know anything of your birthright, or of this place?"

"I haven't had the time to school him mother." She put her hand on Dorenn's shoulder. "The forest doesn't talk. It communicates with us in feelings and impressions."

Dorenn nodded, "Still, that's communication. What's wrong with the forest?"

"Something is invading the forest. It isn't the dead, but it is just as sinister."

"Dramyd, Drasmyd Duil?" Dorenn asked, unable to think of anything else that might be hunting them.

"Could it be the Unseen?" Seandara asked. "They seem to accompany the dead wherever they go."

"The Unseen stay near their masters. If Naneden has traveled from the Sacred Land, they will have come with him. I guarantee you would feel him if he were near the forest."

"Aye," Sildariel agreed, "It isn't the Unseen of the lich."

"I had better go investigate." Dorenn said.

"No need," Morgoran said as he entered the chamber. He addressed the queen. "How are you feeling, your majesty?"

"As good as expected. What is it out there? What is in my forest?"

"You *are* ill if you can't pinpoint intruders. You're usually very accurate."

"Morgoran, tell me."

"Very well, but you must promise to stay put and let Dorenn and me handle them."

"I make no such promises, now tell me."

"There are hordes of Dramyd and Drasmyd Duil entering the outskirts of the great forest. I sent out scouts to find out what they are up to, and they should be reporting back shortly. The invaders are still too far out from the city to be a threat as of yet. I have put our soldiers on alert all around Endil with your garrisons of archers. The undead appear to have stopped advancing for now."

"Attack them then and wipe them out," Sildariel commanded.

"Oh no, I wouldn't do that. They still vastly outnumber us, and I fear an attack is precisely what they're waiting for. As soon as I send our men out, they'll swarm and overwhelm them. It's best to dig in, as we have done many times before, and defend Endil."

"Can we send for more soldiers?" Dorenn asked Morgoran.

"We could but I would advise against it just yet. Endil is a very defensible city. I think we can repel any onslaught as long as we keep our wits about us. The men of Trigothia should be marching toward the Sacred Land by now and I think Naneden will call these undead to him when he sees the Trigothians approaching. We simply need to defend Endil and wait him out."

One of the guards at the chamber door lowered his weapon. "Sirs, someone approaches."

Dorenn followed Morgoran out of the chamber onto the high wooden platform. A shadowy figure slinked up around the wooden planks. Both soldiers took defensive positions. Seandara came to stand behind Dorenn. The figure materialized before him. It was a Drasmyd Duil. Dorenn reached for his sword and the two guards lurched forward to defend the princess. The Drasmyd Duil avoided the guards and managed to put them to sleep. They fell to the platform.

"Stop!" The Drasmyd Duil put out his hand in a halting gesture. His voice was not as raspy and gruff as the other Drasmyd Duil Dorenn had encountered. His skin was also different. Instead of jet black, it was a deep blue, almost black. "I am called Indigo, I have come to pledge my fealty to you and offer my legions."

"What was that you just said to me Drasmyd Duil?" Dorenn was dumbfounded. "Do you take me for a fool?"

Indigo let his wings fan out behind him so he could kneel to one knee. "I am of the Duil clan of dragons, supreme leader of what you call the Drasmyd Duil. My clan is also known as the origin clan. Tell them, Morgoran, dreaded thief of our unborn young."

Morgoran straightened his back, “Now wait just one minute. No one has called me that in a very long time and it was Toborne who took your eggs not me!”

“Forgive me.” Indigo bowed. “Vessel of Toborne, the father of Drasmyd Duil and Dramyd alike. I pledge our featly to you.” He bowed before Dorenn.

“Me?” Dorenn was horrified. “I’m not Toborne.”

Indigo looked confused. “You are. He is with you.”

“Aye, of course,” Dorenn said. “You sense his essence.”

Sildariel stumbled out of her bedchamber.” What is the meaning of this?”

“Mother!” Seandara caught the queen as she almost fell from her weakness.

“What is this abomination doing in my city?”

Morgoran hurried to help Seandara and the queen. “Sildariel, this is Indigo, and he is not an abomination. His people are the shapeshifting brood from which all Drasmyd Duil descend.”

“Is your name really Indigo?” Dorenn asked.

“What a strange question,” Indigo said. “The answer is no. However, my dragon name derives from my skin color and there is no common tongue word for it, so I am called Indigo.” He looked thoughtful. “So, I guess the answer is also, aye, it is really Indigo.”

Morgoran coughed and then helped Sildariel to a nearby wooden chair. “If you are quite through with the naming dilemma, I might ask you what you are up to, Indigo.”

Indigo focused on Sildariel. “Oh no, you have been stricken with the fever of the unlife.” He said it in almost child-like tones and Dorenn worried he might be mocking the queen. He stood back upright and let his wings wrap around his body as Dorenn had seen the black Drasmyd Duil do before. His blue skin shimmered and cascades of blue light interwove under the blue hues of his skin until he shifted into the countenance of one of the wood elves. He wore the robes of the priests of Fawlsbane Vex and carried a long wooden staff. "Let me take away the scourge of the mad god Aedreagnon and heal you."

"Absolutely not!" Sildariel protested. "Stay away from me, detestable creature."

"I don't have to touch you." Indigo pointed his staff at Sildariel. Morgoran and Dorenn jumped to subdue him, but he already used his staff on the queen before they could stop him. Sildariel screamed and Seandara held onto her mother. Indigo let his staff rest at his side. He motioned for Dorenn to turn his attention to the queen. She rose from the chair turning her hands over and over as they teemed with energy. Her weakness appeared to be gone.

"Why did you say you were here?" Sildariel asked the Duil clan dragon.

"We have come to honor our pact with Toborne and defend him and his own with our lives." He got down the one knee again before Dorenn. "The Dramyd and Drasmyd Duil are yours to command."

"Get up," Dorenn said. "I don't understand. Your kind is evil. What kind of trick are you playing?"

Indigo stood. "My brother is the Brae Daun Duil, we are not evil. That is unless you wish it of us."

"Wait a moment." Morgoran began. "You have been attacking us and working with Naneden."

Indigo sighed, "I am afraid it is complicated but suffice it to say that we have always served our master, Toborne. Naneden was a mistake and as soon as he became a lich and raised dead Dramyds to serve him, he became our enemy. His army of Unseen have been killing my kind. The lich wants to kill us and raise us as his unliving abominations.

I cannot abide that. We are lost children who long to return to our master, and there he stands." He pointed to Dorenn.

"I am not Toborne," Dorenn reiterated. "I freed him. I freed his essence. I am surprised you still sense any of him within me."

"But you possess all that is left of our master. I can see him within you. Let us serve you."

Dorenn looked to Morgoran for guidance. Morgoran, as if he understood Dorenn's gaze, nodded his approval.

"First, you must prove yourself. I will not blindly trust you who have been so recently attacking us. You say you can fight the undead, or the unliving as it were? Prove it. Send your brood after the legions baring down on this city. Defend us and drive them out of the forest and I will hold your fealty as true and welcome you. This is my word and my bond."

Indigo nodded, "If this is your will, I will carry it out." He shifted back into the bluish Drasmyd Duil and leapt from the platform, wings spreading out and catching the air as he flew away.

"A bit theatrical perhaps," Morgoran said, "But it seems to have gotten the job done. Where did you get those words?"

"They were written on a tapestry hanging on the throne room wall in the castle at Ardenia," Dorenn replied. "I thought they sounded...proper."

"Close enough," Morgoran said.

"Do you believe them?" Seandara asked.

"Not on your life," Dorenn answered. He looked to Morgoran for his answer.

Morgoran noticed, "Time will tell, won't it. I just wouldn't put you or your men in a position of trust. When the time comes, you don't want men relying too heavily on them to do their part."

Sildariel took a deep breath. “Lamiel wants to see the both of you to discuss your Solicanth situation. At first, I was against it but now, in light of what just occurred here, I am inclined to allow it.”

“I will show Dorenn the way,” Seandara said.

“I should oversee the Drasmyd Duil. I don’t have time for diversions.”

Sildariel gave Morgoran a telling gaze.

“Go, boy, I will oversee the battle preparations. It seems important that you see this Lamiel fellow.”

Dorenn let out a long, irritated, sigh. “If we must. Lead on Seandara.”

Seandara took his hand and led him through a series of branches and vine choked, wood-planked rope bridges into what Dorenn thought must be the seedier side of Endil, if there was such a place. The area was darker and not as well kept as what he was used to seeing.

“Where are you taking us?” He asked Seandara. “Is this place safe?”

Seandara stopped. She did not let go of his hand. “Did you think all Endil looked the same as the royal platforms? Do your kings of Symboria live in the houses of peasants?”

“No, but sometimes I think they should.” Seandara’s words had offended him for some odd reason.”

“Why?”

“Because the man in the position of the king should have the strength to rule the people not his place of residence.”

Seandara shrugged, “It’s all one and the same.” She pulled at his arm again and they began to move along the bridge as she spoke. “The pomp and regalia help the subjects identify with their leader, kingdom, and place in the world. It gives them something to take pride in, as sure as the Archers of Endil or the battle flags of the armies.

Imagine the battle you are planning. When the different banners fly over the men joining in the fight together, they will rally."

Dorenn had not thought of how important symbolism could be until that moment. He would certainly feel a swell of pride if he were engaged in battle and saw the banners of Symboria flying over reinforcements. He stumbled over a loose piece of wood and almost fell. Seandara caught his fall. "How much farther?"

"One more bridge and we will be there." She pointed to a heavily foliage covered area across a badly kept wooden bridge.

Dorenn stepped carefully on the bridge as they neared the platform where the elf priest Lamiel, someone Dorenn had never met, lived. The structure built upon the platform was covered with faded, and peeling, white paint. The wood beneath the barren spots appeared grey from being exposed to the weather, some of it peeling back in places. Two sets of windows, both shuttered, one with the left shutters broken and hanging, adorned either side of the entranceway. The faded red front door was slightly ajar.

"Lamiel?" Seandara called, knocking lightly on the red door.

The elf that came to answer the door surprised Dorenn with his physical appearance. He was tall and lean like most of the other elves Dorenn had seen, but he was also old. If he were a human man, Dorenn would have guessed he was in his late sixties or early seventies, but for a Sylvan Elf, he must have been hundreds if not thousands of years old. Other than Ianthill, Dorenn thought that elves never aged beyond the appearance of human thirties. He also knew, from Ianthill, that elves did indeed age but at a much slower rate than their human counterparts, except for the men of the Amar, who outlived many of the elves. Lamiel had kind, greyish eyes with flattering wrinkles accentuating them as he smiled warmly at Seandara. His face was thin, his grey hair was pulled back in a ponytail, he was dressed in the robes of a priest, only they were maroon in color, of a god Dorenn was obviously not familiar with.

"Princess, so good of you to come."

Seandara stepped through the threshold, almost dragging Dorenn with her. "Lamiel, Priest of Xeian, it is pleasing to see you as well."

Lamiel eyed Seandara and Prince Dorenn of Ardenia." He bowed deeply.

Dorenn, still held in Seandara's iron grip, bowed back as best he could. "Priest Lamiel of Xeian." Seandara finally released him from her hold.

"Come, sit." He gestured eagerly at a large wooden table. "I have prepared tea for us as we talk."

"Very kind of you," Seandara said. Dorenn repeated her sentiment, not knowing what else to say. He took a seat opposite Seandara, and she cleared her throat and gestured with the sideways bobbing of her head and the shifting of her eyes that he should sit immediately left of her, across from where Lamiel was probably going to sit. He moved.

Lamiel brought a tray with a large teapot, four cups, and a dish of hard cookies he called biscuits. After the tea was poured, the sugar was stirred and the biscuits were served, Lamiel got down to the business at hand. "I have called you here to discuss with you the Solicanth situation that exists between you."

"Mother says that if we are Solicanths and together we will cause some kind of cataclysm." Seandara blurted out.

"Princess, please. It is impolite to interrupt your elders. I thought you knew better."

Seandara was horrified, Dorenn could see it in the redness of her face." Sorry, I do know better. Please, continue."

Lamiel nodded. "Your mother only heard half of what I told her, apparently. I am the one who foresaw your condition. I told her that on occasion the appearance of Solicanths caused cataclysms, but those rare cases are when Solicanths appeared in times of peace, or where they were not needed. It happens sometimes, perhaps she thought this was such a time." He took a sip of his tea. "However, this is a time when Solicanths are indeed needed, urgently. I am prepared to join you this evening."

Dorenn was drinking his tea and he had to swallow hard to avoid spewing it all over the priest. "What?"

Lamiel gazed at him with a cocked eyebrow. "I do not believe I was unclear. You're Solicanths, the time is now. You are to be joined immediately. The queen agrees with me."

Dorenn could feel his anxiety rise. He looked at Seandara. "What does he mean by joined?" He was thinking of all the essences he had joined with over the past few years."

"Marriage, Dorenn. He means to join us by marriage." Seandara said.

Dorenn sighed his relief before a whole new anxiety began to rise within him. "Why would we need to be married?"

"Allow me." Lamiel began. "Solicanths only appear through heredity. Therefore, any further Solicanths can only be descendants of your union."

"That's disgusting!" Dorenn said. That means both of them will be kin to us!" He eyed Seandara. "That means you and I are kin."

Lamiel chuckled. "No, no. I suppose I wasn't clear after all. There are two pairs of Solicanths. Each of you descended from different lines."

"It would still mean there are common ancestors between both if the two lines married over and over and had children!" Dorenn said.

Lamiel nodded. "That is why you are called Solicanths. Your paths have crossed many times. I thought that part was clear to you. Solicanths are intertwined over many years. If you are worried about common ancestors, just realize that hundreds if not thousands of years pass between appearances. During that time, both lines marry into countless other families. Only the component that makes you Solicanths passes down."

"Then there are two others alive today besides us who are Solicanths?"

Lamiel nodded. His face grave.

"What? What's wrong?" Dorenn asked.

"It's true. There are two others. I fear you will run into them someday. I pray the consequences are negligible."

Dorenn took a deep breath and avoided eye contact with Seandara. "What is the significance of Solicanths? What purpose do they serve in the greater scheme of things? What makes them so important to you? He ventured to look at Seandara and as expected, by her face, she was perplexed at his question.

Solicanths are the product of Xeian and the sole responsibility of Xeian's priests. We are tasked with the preservation of the line so that future Solicanths will come when they are needed. You are a strong man, Dorenn Adair, but you are made stronger with Seandara at your side. Solicanths even separated for a time, can perform feats and tasks impossible otherwise. You have already proven to be different in the way you handled the Hall of Ancients."

"How do you know about that?"

"It is my business to know such things."

"Who are they? Who are the second pair of Solicanths?" Dorenn asked. "Do you know?"

"I couldn't venture a guess as to who they are."

"But it's your business to know these things, right?"

Lamiel took a sip of his tea before answering. He seemed amused. "Clever of you to ask. You truly are a remarkable lad. However, it is my business to know the Solicanths I am responsible for helping, which are the two of you. Another priest of Xeian is responsible for the other line. It isn't my business to know them or their fate until the time comes that you meet them, and I meet their priest. We will both know at the same time, if at all."

Dorenn made it a point to speak directly to Seandara. "Funny how that always seems to be the case, isn't it! Everyone has all the answers until they suddenly don't"

"What are you implying, sir?" Lamiel asked. "That I am lying to you? I assure you that if I were privy to the identity of the others, I would be duty bound to tell you. I am at your service, sir."

Dorenn felt sheepish at Lamiel's scolding. "Forgive me. I have been led to believe otherwise by people before. I shouldn't be so presumptuous."

"There is nothing to forgive. As I said, I am at your service, sir."

"May Seandara and I have time to talk this over?"

"Of course. Queen Sildariel has yet to make the preparations for the wedding. Talk to one another. Oh, and here." He went to a shelf of books and removed one of the heavier, leather bound tomes. "This book contains the marriage ceremonies of the Eridil elves and some of our traditions. Look it over, won't you."

Dorenn took the book. "We will. Now if you will excuse us."

"Of course," Lamiel said.

Two Archers of Endil were waiting just outside when Lamiel opened the door and started out onto the platform.

"Wait!" Dorenn said, "What are you doing?"

Lamiel faced him. "I am excusing myself as you asked."

"I meant for you to excuse us so that we could leave. Isn't this your home?"

"My home? No, this is to be your home until after you are married. Then you will be given quarters on the royal platforms. "This house," he pointed up and around the interior, "is protected and on sacred ground. No magic will allow you to leave it, no spell can harm it. Good day, sir." He bowed and the door was closed and locked behind him.

"You knew about this!" Dorenn asked.

Seandara shrugged. "I suspected."

Chapter Twenty-One

BLOOD AND BONE

The wings of Golvashala, nothing but dull bones, magically keeping the undead dragon and his rider, Naneden, aloft, folded inward to allow the great drake to sail down into the little valley known as the Garden of Bones. The place was neither a garden nor were there any bones visible; it was called the garden of bones because it was a graveyard. This graveyard was the final resting place of countless dragons both great and not so great. Golvashala landed on the hallowed soil and immediately his boney feet began to burn and smoke until the dread lich Naneden set foot on it. The ground withered under the lich's dead touch and the grass turned from green to a sickly brown radiating out from where he stood. He raised his staff with the screaming human skull high above his head; its eye sockets glowed blood red.

"Arise!" he said.

The ground beneath his feet began to crack and it boiled up in great chunks of dirt. The hideous skulls emerged first followed by the bones of the wings and the forelegs reaching out and taking purchase in the undisturbed grass-covered ground. Scores of drakes began to emerge and take flight. Great piles of bones outlining monstrous dragons, held in the air by dark essence. The skies above the Garden of Bones began to cloud up and swell into an unnatural storm.

Naneden cackled as he crawled onto Golvashala's boney spine, and he pointed his staff at the mountain where Draegodor was located. "Onward! Fly to Draegodor and kill every dragon! Kill them all! The flying sea of bones lurched, moving toward Draegodor. "I will not allow the dragons to lend aid to those who would oppose me in the Sacred Land! I will be victorious!" Golvashala roared in response. Naneden lay his hand on the boney head of the former oracle, "You will not be my greatest achievement for long. Perhaps I will resurrect you properly when this is over so you are more than merely a collection of bones," he cackled again, "but I wouldn't count on it."

Naneden's army of dracoliches was met at the gates of Draegodor by King Amarantus and several young drakes who were eager to unleash their terrible fire upon the aberrations. The air was full of intention when the first of the young dragons clashed in a fiery, midair melee with their encroaching undead dragon ancestors. The entirety of the sky seemed to be on fire. Lightning and shards of ice occasionally entered the fray as well.

Not long into the battle, Naneden was ecstatic as his undead dragon minions forced King Amarantus to retreat into the great rocky entrance to the red city of Draegodor. As quickly as he sent in more of his undead drakes, he was just as quickly puzzled as the face of the entrance began to buckle and fall in on itself, crushing many of the undead legions as it fell. The great rock sentinel dragons that guarded Draegodor began to rise from the rocky outcroppings of the mountain. First two and then four sentinels appeared. They turned to the covered entrance and breathed a bluish dragonfire into the stone, sealing the city off from Naneden's attacking army. The rock melted in place as several layers thick of hardening stone. Another two sentinels appeared, moving slowly up the side of the mountain in formation. They swatted the undead dragons out of the air with ease. The frost, fire, and lightning from Naneden's fold had little to no effect on them as they pummeled the attackers to the ground, scattering bones all along the mountainside.

Naneden huffed and then turned the undead Golvashala back toward the Garden of Bones. When he was in place, he raised his staff with fervor. The whole of the valley boiled and coughed up dragon after undead dragon. Vicious, unyielding drakes he bent to his will. Hundreds and thousands of long dead dragonkind bolted from their supposed final resting place to do Naneden's dark bidding. They flew in a frenzy to the gates of Draegodor. Naneden laughed manically so intently he began to cough.

Ganas Nashe raised his goblet to Sylvalora as she flew into the heavens with Jindara on her back. The cousin of princess Seandara and niece of queen Sildariel of Endil had arrived in Denosia on the back of one of the Draegodor dragons sent to rescue the lost army. Now, Jindara would return to the fight for the Sacred Land, having secured the army for transport. Ganas watched as dragon after dragon launched into the sky, some carrying soldiers on their backs and some clutching the ropes of the vessels designed to carry troops home. As a leader, he would be riding on the back of Bladetalon, a blue and white dragon he had gotten to know well.

Ganas waited for the final few dragons to take flight before he crawled up Bladetalon's massive wing to his back. There was a crisp crackle in the air, Ganas now recognized as the sound of the use of a Lora Daine, and a young red drake appeared before him. She crashed to the ground with a fiery thump as if the fire had been expelled at her as she used the Lora Daine.

"What is the meaning of this?" Bladetalon snapped in his low menacing voice. "Who dares chase you, young one?"

The young red dragon regained her composure and got on all fours. "Masters, I have been sent here by King Amarantus." She was still gasping for breath from excitement and apprehension.

"This far by Lora Daine?" Ganas asked.

"King Amarantus has one in the great hall that can reach just about anywhere one way with enough power." Bladetalon answered.

The smaller red dragon caught her breath, "Draegodor is under attack. The dark lich, Naneden, has raised the dead from the Garden of Bones and has used them against us. Hundreds, maybe thousands of our undead ancestors are being forced to attack us in our home."

"Impossible, the sentinels would fight them off," Bladetalon said.

"Aye, they are, but there are so many attacking some have gotten past the great sentinels. The king has sealed off the city, but they keep coming. It's only a matter of time before they break through the defenses. King Amarantus sent me here to hurry you along. Instead of the Sacred Land, you are all needed at Draegodor."

"Clever, the lich is using the dragons to fortify his side. He must know our plans." Ganas said.

"I doubt he knows our plans," Bladetalon said. "He is a cunning strategist. He would surmise the dragons would help regain the Sacred Land against him. He has attacked while most of the dragons of Draegodor are here retrieving the army."

"There is no time to lose," Ganas addressed the young dragon. Fly to all the columns and tell them I have changed their orders. We fly for Draegodor now at top speed. Once you inform the columns of the change, use a Lora Daine and call in all the dragon knights. I have no doubt some of them are already on their way to defend the city, but we need to officially call all of them home." He commanded Bladetalon to take to the air with a whistle. The dragon complied. "Is there an entrance to Draegodor we can slip the men through?"

"The dragon knights know of one, they will enter the city through it no doubt. We can send the men in through the same route."

"Excellent, now fly, my friend, your king needs us!"

"We should fly across the sea and then use our personal Lora Daines when we come in range of land," Bladetalon suggested.

"Wouldn't that put us somewhere in Scarovia?"

"Aye, but we could regroup and use the Lora Daines to get to Draegodor from there. It would be faster than flying the entire way and we would be much more rested for battle."

"Get word to the others." He hesitated. "Do you feel that?"

Bladetalon sniffed the air. "Of what do you speak?"

"Could this be a diversion? A way to divert us from the real battle?"

"Of course, this is possible. But dragons do not lie. The red one says Draegodor is under attack then under attack it is!"

"All right, good enough for me. Get word to all the dragons. We will use the Lora Daines when we get close enough."

Rain beat down relentlessly all the way from the garden of bones to the gates of Draegodor. Naneden had no intention of entering the red city of dragons through the portal. He planned to fight the sentinels and rise up on the undead wings of the dragons to storm the entrance. He was not disappointed; the giant stone guardians of Draegodor materialized out of the rock face of the mountain as soon as the danger of Naneden shadowed them. Legions of the dragons' dead ancestors of Draegodor descended upon the granite behemoths causing more of the guardians to appear from the face of the mountain.

Naneden, riding the lifeless Golvashala, entered the city while the sentinels were occupied. The great hall of the red city was empty except for one dragon knight. Naneden dismounted and floated toward the knight on a cloud of black smoke. The brave knight was visibly shaken by the very presence of the lich. He appeared as if he might bolt but managed to hold his ground. Naneden made it a point to float in close to the knight, taunting him.

"It...is. That is, you are too late, lich. King Amarantus is not here. The dragons of Draegodor have taken all that is sacred from this place. It's an empty, hollow mountain. Useless to the likes of you."

Naneden sent some of the drakes he had with him to search out the city before turning his attention on the knight. "If what you say is true, it is of no matter. Your patrons will perish soon enough, one way or another." His voice was ominous, low, and grating to the ear. He bent down to the granite floor and placed his skeletal fingers gently upon it. The stone beneath his fingers moaned and cracked, not the destructive, gaping cracks, but the miniscule kind that sounded like the snaping of brittle bone. The blight spread along the floor and up the walls. The knight took a step back from the blackened taint as it raced toward him. When it touched him, it climbed up his armored legs and beyond. He let out a muted scream when the rot overtook him. The taint continued on, rotting and destroying any living thing it came in contact with until it overtook the entire city. Satisfied, when the drakes he sent out returned, that he had rendered the city unlivable, he climbed back onto Golvashala. "Fly. Take us back to the tomb in the Sacred Land. I fear the final battle is approaching and we may be at more of a disadvantage than I originally planned."

Golvashala's dead, red glowing eyes, inset in his exposed skull, flashed once as he took flight, beating skeletal wings pushing off the fetted wind of death Naneden brought with him wherever he went. As he flew over the mountain, he could see the crushed rock that used to be the sentinels of Draegodor strown about, the taint he laid upon the place crawled down the face of the mountain like thousands of giant black beetles. The dragons would not be returning to Draegodor anytime soon.

Chapter Twenty-Two

Battlefields of Undead

Tatrice pulled at the ropes tied around her hands. Somewhere in the darkness, she could hear the whimpers of Deylia, she must have had her mouth gagged too. She had been stirred awake by the lumbering, rough ride of the boxed wagon that had brought them to the place she and Deylia now occupied. It smelled dank and moist, like a cellar. She stuck her tongue out as far as she could, trying in vain to loosen the cloth tied around her head and gagging her mouth. She still wasn't sure who Bashir was or why he had kidnapped them. At least Fayne got away. When she concentrated, she could feel Shadesilver flying somewhere in the distance, but she couldn't touch her Lora Daine to contact her. The best she could do was try to guide her dragon friend with the bond forged between them. *The bond!* Tatrice thought. *I can use some of the rudimentary dragon magic Shadesilver showed me.* She stuck her tongue out into the cloth again and concentrated on the image of fire in her mind. A hole burned where her tongue touched. The heat was intense, and she winced as the pain of the burn covered her face. She retracted it but her tongue still got singed by the burning too; the cloth fell away, and her mouth was freed. The dragon magic worked to heal the fire wound, quickly repairing the damage, which was much less than the burns would have been to a normal person. She did the same to the ropes binding her hands, even though a couple of her fingers also got burned then subsequently healed.

She got up and felt along the walls of the room until she found what she was looking for, a sconce. She touched the material inside and it burst into a bright flame. She pulled her fingers away and immediately put the burned ones in her mouth. This time they didn't heal and continued to painfully burn.

Deylia was in the middle of the floor with her mouth gagged and her eyes covered. Tatrice removed her gag and blindfold and then untied her. "Why were your eyes covered?"

"Because I think our friend, Bashir, is not who he seems, and he could only concentrate so long to keep his identity from me. I was already beginning to see through his disguise before he put us in here."

"Who is he then?"

"I don't know. I didn't recognize him, but he seems to believe I might know him from somewhere."

"You think he might be working for someone we know?"

"It's a possibility. All I know is he covered my eyes so I wouldn't see him."

"We need to get out of here before he comes back, no matter who he is."

"How? It's freezing cold out there. Besides, I don't think he's coming back. I don't feel his presence nearby. He's long gone by now. I think he just wanted to delay us from finding Kimala."

"Why?"

"I don't know. Maybe to give him time to be somewhere else, or maybe he did it so he could get us out of the way of another scheme."

"I like you. You are extreme."

"You asked, I answered."

"Shadesilver is flying toward us." Tatrice held her burnt fingers.

"Are you hurt?" Deylia asked, trying to get Tatrice to show her.

"I haven't learned how to use dragon fire well enough not to get myself burned."

"Let me see them."

"It's nothing, just a little burn."

Deylia took Tatrice's hands in hers. "Gods! Your skin is falling away." She closed her hands around Tatrice's. When she opened them, Tatrice was healed. Only a couple of spots of redness remained.

"How did you do that?" Tatrice asked. "I thought you were a mindwielder."

"I am, but I have a few surprises up my sleeve. You can't survive around the city of Trigoth without knowing how to do a little magical healing if you're able. I think all mindwielders can draw small amounts of essence too."

"Lucky for me," Tatrice said. "Now help me get this door open."

Before they could budge it, the door opened, and Bashir entered. Tatrice watched Deylia for confirmation of Bashir's disguise. She nodded back at her. "I don't recognize him. It looks like his disguise is a form of dragon magic, not essence or Drasmyd Duil."

"You can drop the disguise now," Tatrice said. "We know you're not Bashir. Where did he run off to?"

He studied Deylia. “I knew you would see me eventually.” He let the disguise drop and he looked like a young Scarovian with a pale face, dark hair, and brown eyes.

“What are you doing here? Did Bashir force you to keep us here?” Deylia asked.

“It’s complicated. I would never hurt you, but I have a job to complete. I am to slow down Veric’s daughters so Bashir can meet with the king.”

“Daughters?” Tatrice said.

He stared into Tatrice’s eyes for a moment. “In this light, you look just like her.”

Tatrice was taken aback. “Who are you talking about?”

The boy’s soft demeanor turned harsh again. “Help me find your sister.”

Tatrice stuttered. “Who are Veric’s daughters; Lady Shey and who else? Kimala? Who are you and how do you know all this information?”

“I don’t have time for this. My name is Joster. Aye, you are his granddaughter. Lady Shey is your aunt. I am to keep you here for your protection.” He looked nervously out the door directly behind him. “Although I imagine you believe just the opposite.” He took a step back, still looking for something outside the door. “Look, Fayne is in danger, being out there somewhere on her own.”

“Fine, let us go, then.” Tatrice was surprised at the ferocity of her own voice.

“Good, there he is.” Joster began rummaging through one of his waist pouches.

“Who? Who’s out there?” Tatrice asked, feeling a sense of urgency rising within her.

"Bren. He has come for you." He pulled something out of his pouch and tossed it to Tatrice. It was her white dragon stone. "I know Shadesilver is up there somewhere too, and Amadace is not too far away either. I may be punished for this but take your stone and go. Leave this place. Look for your mother no longer. I will find her. She came here looking for something Naneden left behind." He seemed amused by Tatrice's perplexed expression and cracked a smile, confusing her more. "King Naneden, the lich, has tainted her. I work for him, or I did work for him. Kimala knows me. It's the reason for the disguise, but it won't fool her forever. I need to find her before she finds me. I think she will try to kill me on sight."

"*He is lying! He doesn't believe she is here to kill him at all!*" Delia's voice sounded in her head. Joster turned to see if Bren was closer. "Bren has found you. Get your dragons, find Fayne and get out of here!" He tightened his fists around another Lora Daine, and at that moment Tatrice knew he was a Dragon Knight, but not for any of the Draegodor dragons. His Lora Daine was jet black. There was a flash of red light before he was gone. In his place was Bren trudging through the barren brush and blowing snow.

"There you are!" Bren embraced his wife. "I finally found you." Clutched in his hand was his own red Lora Daine. "Take care, Amadace will be here in a moment."

"Wait." Tatrice consulted her own stone. "So will Shadesilver. She is not far."

Bren pushed Tatrice back into the confines of the cabin. "These woods are full of undead and worse. Dramyd and the like were choking the skies only moments ago. Amadace had to fly low to avoid them."

Deylia interrupted. "You two are not planning on leaving, are you? We still need to find Fayne."

"Not if I find you first." Fayne and Trendan appeared at the doorway.

"We have been tracking you since you were in the wagon," Trendan said. "We were formulating a plan to rescue you when we saw Bren."

Tatrice cocked an eyebrow and watched Deylia as the mindwielder scrutinized their friends. After a time, Deylia finally nodded. "It's them, don't worry."

Tatrice shrugged. "All right then. Get ready to get out of here. Shadesilver and Amadace are inbound."

"Won't we freeze riding on dragons in a snowstorm?" Trendan asked.

"You doubt us?" Bren said with a smirk.

"Well..." Trendan began.

"Dragons run hot, and they can heat their scales. Stay bundled and you will be fine." Tatrice answered.

To the north of the cabin, out in the snowy brush, a crash of trees and a tremendous gust of wind almost blew the half-closed door off its hinges.

"I think that's one of them now," Bren said. He headed for the door and then abruptly turned to stop the others. "Get back!" He said in a whispering tone that was entirely too loud.

"What is it?" Tatrice asked.

"A dragon, an *undead* dragon! It's just outside the cabin."

"Did it see you?" Trendan said as he made for one of the windows. "Or hear you?"

Bren grabbed hold of his arm as he passed. "I don't think so but be careful at that window. Don't let it see you." Trendan nodded. Bren let go of his arm and carefully stalked toward the door, slowly trying to get it closed without being detected.

Tatrice studied Bren as he moved. Despite the danger looming just outside, she thought only of him. He came for her. Deep down, she suspected he would hunt for her, but now that he was near her, with her, she realized his devotion was true and she had been taking advantage of him all this time. As she watched him, her eyes cut back through the open door and focused on the threat. The death dragon almost glowed against the white of the snow, the glow of a hideous blackened purple and a black fog emanated from its bare bones giving the illusion of an ethereal body. She realized, by the shift of its glowing red eyes, that it detected Bren at the door, and she took a worried step forward. It roared as it braced itself into an attack position.

"Bren, get out of there! It can see you!"

To her horror, Bren turned to look back at her instead of moving out of the way. She clutched her Lora Daine, which she had never put away, and leaped the distance to Bren, just falling short of him. She reached out and was able to just touch his leg. Sickly, greenish black fire burned toward the door from the maw of the dragon. Since she had been thinking of her marriage, the only thought she could conjure in such a hurry was the name Ni'esa. She knew instantly she had made a mistake and tried to correct it in her mind, but she felt the stone activate and the tug of the magic just as the heat of the dragon fire touched her face. Her breath was taken away, there was a jolt as they traveled through space, and then suddenly she could breathe again.

"My, you two startled me."

Tatrice looked up and brushed her dirty blonde hair out of her face. Ni'esa was sitting in a rocking chair sewing a patch onto something. "But we were told you were dead."

Ni'esa chuckled. "Maybe I am, but it's not very likely."

Bren stirred and opened his eyes. "How far did we travel? We have to help Trendan and the others."

Tatrice turned to Ni'esa. "Where are we?"

"You are in Scarovia, at my home in Wytchmore."

"You are Scarovian? What were you doing in Trigothia marrying couples?"

"I have the right to do so. In fact, I am many things. I have places of residence all over the kingdoms. I am an imprinter, a seamstress, a doll maker, and most important of all, a priestess of Xeian."

Even though they had joined Dorenn as an ally, the decision was made by Queen Sildariel that the Drasmyd Duil and Dramyds were not to be allowed within the city of Endil. They were just barely allowed to be in the Great Sythian Forest. As a result, Dorenn met with one of them outside the city. He had asked to speak to the leader, but the Drasmyd Duil only repeated that he, Dorenn, was their leader. After carefully speaking with one of the creatures, Dorenn found that the only rank designations were Dramyd as soldiers and Drasmyd Duil as lieutenants. He was the supreme leader as Toborne was before him and so on. He also found out there were other Dramyd and Drasmyd Duil commanded by others. Toborne and Morgoran were not the only men experimenting with dragon eggs.

One of the Drasmyd Duil stood before him and reported, in his guttural, vague language, that the undead had changed course, some had boarded their ships and sailed away, the rest were rounded up in the forest and either killed by the Archers of Endil or Dramyd kind.

Seandara joined Dorenn once she saw who he was meeting with. She didn't trust the creatures.

"The legions have been redirected. Something or someone obviously commands them. I don't think they ever wanted Endil." Dorenn said when she approached him.

"Nature magic, like mother said?"

Dorenn nodded. "I think they veered off course, attracted to Endil and they have now been set back on course, probably for the Sacred Land. I think it's time we rejoined the Trigothian army. Your mother is feeling better, and her archers can handle any of the stragglers."

"Where is the army now?"

"I speculate they should be on the docks of Trigoth making ready to sail to Lux Enor. Rennon should have the Adracorian Calvary, lower Sythian footmen, and the Sythian knights crossing the strait to Old Symbor right now, or he will be soon."

"What about Gondrial and Lady Shey?"

"I hope they have rallied the king's men in Symboria, or what's left of them, and are headed west by now. If all goes well, we will surround the legions of Naneden and cut off any hope of retreat." He cleared his throat and faced the Drasmyd Duil. "Listen carefully. The Trigothian army will be sailing across from Trigothia to Lux Enor. You should be able to join them there." The Drasmyd Duil nodded and flew away.

"And what of the other matter? They will be expecting an answer before we leave." Seandara asked.

"Do we have time? Is it that important that we get married right now? If you are by my side, isn't that enough?"

"You don't want to marry me?" She looked hurt.

Dorenn moved to console her. "Oh no, I didn't mean it like that. The past few months I have come to rely on you, and I have strong feelings for you. I realize that now."

"Is it Tatrice?"

"Gods no! She married Bren and despite her telling me over and over it was a mistake or an accident, they never could seem to bring themselves to rectify it. No, I think she is taken now."

"Is there another, then?"

"What? No! When would I have found the time for another?"

"Then we should do as we are told."

Dorenn knew at that moment that he was not going to delay the inevitable. In fact, he was not sure he would ever win an argument with Seandara. "All right. We go through the ceremony before we leave to rejoin the army. How long do you think the ceremony will take?"

Seandara grinned mischievously, "Only an hour or so for the marriage ceremony."

"Oh. Good."

"And three days for the marriage bed."

Chapter Twenty-Three

One Last Plea

Sylvalora and Jindara, Queen Sildariel's niece and Seandara's cousin, arrived at the tomb where Naneden had appropriately set up his Sacred Land headquarters. The tomb used to be part of the Oracle tomb complex where Golvashala hid for centuries, waiting for the right time to reemerge. He should have stayed hidden. The Oracle's gamble for power and conquest over the Sacred Land was met with a swift defeat by the lich Naneden, who promptly put Golvashala into his service as an undead dragon. The Oracle didn't think his gamble through or was too arrogant to realize someone would figure out his plans and have hundreds of years to prepare to defeat them.

Jindara noted the tomb naturally smelled of death and decay. The hastily carved walls of the tunnel leading down into the main chamber were covered with rotting vegetation from a time when the Sacred Land still teemed with plant life. Being one of nature, Jindara hoped the land would once again welcome flora and fauna, once Naneden was dealt with.

"Keep your wits about you and let me do all the speaking. He will try to manipulate you with whatever you feel most passionate about and twist it into hate and anger." Sylvalora said. "Look about for all the exits so if anything goes wrong you can readily escape."

"What about you? Don't you plan to escape if something goes wrong?" Jindara asked.

"I will be doing the same. I only tell you to fend for yourself because there may not be sufficient time to help one another. If negotiations go badly, don't hesitate, and don't wait for me. Get out of there and don't look back."

"Do you think he will agree to your terms?"

Sylvalora chuckled. "I may have given you the wrong impression. He will not turn away from the Sacred Land at my behest. I was around him for quite some time. I managed to learn a few things about him, and I plan to cut off the head of the snake before his venomous bite takes hold."

"Why I am I here then?"

"Two reasons and neither are very good. First, Sildariel insisted she wanted to come along, and I couldn't allow her to, so I managed to talk her out of it. You are the compromise."

"And the second reason?"

"To help me distract Naneden from what I intend to do."

"I wish I had a Lora Daine. I wouldn't need to find an exit if I had one."

"Here," Sylvalora said. "Take one of mine, but you still need to find an exit to give you enough time to activate the stone."

Jindara accepted the silver dragon stone. She sometimes forgot that Sylvalora was the silver drake. "You have another, right?"

"Aye, the one I gave you will only carry a single person. The one I used to bring us here can carry more." She stopped, "Wait." She extended her arm level with Jindara's chest to call a halt. "I hear voices, I believe Naneden is in the next chamber. Follow my lead." Sylvalora boldly walked into the chamber and Jindara followed. The chamber was dim, almost too dim, and a black fog rolled across the floor ominously. Two overly large skeletal men worked on something hanging from the crudely carved walls at either side of Naneden who was seated in a bone laden throne. He glanced up at them as they entered and Jindara had to fight the urge to run with all her might.

"Ah, Sylvalora," Naneden said in a voice as raspy and ominous as a death rattle. "What brings you here to see me. Have you decided to return to me?"

His skeletal face was unreadable, but Jindara thought she caught the hint of sarcasm in his horrible voice.

"I have come to ask you to turn away from your dark ambitions. The Sacred Land has been a point of contention for far too long. The new high king should rule it and use it for the benefit of all the kingdoms."

"So, you have chosen a new high king?"

"No," Sylvalora said. Not yet.

"That is your job, no? I mean, it's up to you to choose a worthy person to become king or possibly the queen, correct? Surely you do not intend for me to keep the throne. You realize I no longer require it? I would prefer to rule over the new high lord rather than look after the throne myself."

"Aye, but if you are hoping for a speedy decision, think again. The process takes time. I must find someone worthy. You're right, that person is not you."

The black smoke around Naneden's skeletal face intensified, "Why not choose me? I would not use the power of the Sacred Land against the surrounding kingdoms, that is, as long as they remain loyal to me."

Sylvalora laughed, "You just said you no longer wanted it. Now, you want it again?"

"I am merely offering my services. I am already the master of the Sacred Land. You are trying to manipulate me, Silver Drake, but I will not fall for your biting words any longer. I would make a fair and just high lord."

"You think you are master of the Sacred Land? You realize the kingdoms will send armies to oust you. If you kept the throne, they would not rest until you were destroyed. Your words are venomous lies. You would betray my trust. No, I shall not choose you."

Naneden stood, more black fog rolled out from under him. "If they come then they will die! I have thought about this day for centuries. I have the only army that matters, a self-replenishing army. As soon as their soldiers fall in battle, I will bring their dead corpses into my army. A couple of days of battle and the whole of their army will be integrated into mine. There is no hope, there is no chance, there is only me. So, find a new high lord, or not. It makes no difference, for I am already the lord of the Sacred Land and you and this pitiful Sylvan Elf cannot stop me or do anything about it!"

"Hey!" Jindara could not help herself. Sylvalora held her hand out again and shook her head. Jindara backed down.

"No, I never made you high lord. You are illegitimate. You took that title yourself and your claim is false. You forget, Naneden, I am the product of the gods. I *can* stop you." She began to transform into the Silver Drake. The two oversized skeletons stopped what they were working on and transformed into giant undead drakes for Naneden's defense.

"Find a spot to hide," Sylvalora said to Jindara.

Jindara nodded and hid behind a large rock formation at the edge of the chamber.

"Naneden, this can all end now. I make one last plea for you to turn from this destructive path or I will be forced to destroy you."

Naneden's voice was steady and clear, "While I appreciate your status as a product of the gods and I understand that you are a being of great power, I cannot allow you to destroy me, as you put it."

The two dragons spit out plums of fire at Sylvalora, but she was not dissuaded. She stood her ground and the fire burned over her and dissipated into nothing. She appeared completely unharmed.

"My turn!" She arched her wings as if to take flight and she blew lightning breath at the dragons in a forward heave. The off-white of their bones charred to black as they shook and shivered from the electric bursts, finally collapsing onto the chamber floor. She rushed to them and stomped the closest one into powder with her powerful clawed feet. The second Dragon tried to get up and attack. She rounded viciously upon it and snapped off its head with a tremendous bite. When the severed, skeletal head hit the floor, she quickly stomped it as well so Naneden wouldn't be able to resurrect it.

From her hiding place, Jindara wondered if either of the dragons had been the remains of Golvashala. Given the ease that Sylvalora defeated them, she concluded that they must be other dragons and not the famous Oracle.

All the while Sylvalora was facing the dragons, Naneden didn't seem particularly worried. Jindara thought he must be preparing something to use on her. As soon as she refocused on him, he brought up his staff, adorned with the screaming human head, to bear on her. In the other hand, he carried a spear that looked like he had picked it up off the ground where it had been subject to rain, snow, and left to weather in the sun for years.

Jindara was horrified at Sylvalora's reaction to the spear. The Silver Drake recoiled and darted her eyes, searching for Jindara's hiding spot. "Go, use the stone, get out of here!"

"What is it?" Jindara could not help herself. She wondered how the great Sylvalora could be frightened of such an old relic as the weathered spear Naneden hefted toward her.

"GO!" Sylvalora said with the thrust of her mighty arm and a claw pointed symbolically to the nearest exit.

Naneden's skulled face shifted to where Jindara ducked out of sight. "Ah, I thought I felt the presence of another...another...an elf! Not much help to you in your present situation, my dear." He said to Sylvalora.

Sylvalora heard his words and realized something. He had already forgotten the elf even though he had addressed her only a few moments before. He had essence sickness! Drawing so much power to become the lich had given him the fever. She saw Jindara lingering, "I told you to get out of here!" Sylvalora pleaded.

Naneden lowered the spear to his side. "No doubt she is curious about this." He bounced the spear in his hand. "It's the spear of Aedreagnon, the god. You see, elf, it has been lost for...well...forever in your eyes, I would assume. It's not so good to be a god-like creature such as Sylvalora, against the weapon of a god forged by a god, you s ee."

Jindara left her crouched position and headed for Sylvalora, her hand over the Lora Daine in her pocket. Naneden hefted the spear again.

Sylvalora held her hand out. "No, stop, you would never make it to me."

Naneden lifted his staff and spoke some awful, guttural words and Sylvalora began to change back to her vulnerable, living, human form.

When she was done changing, Naneden thrust the spear at her. Dark essence surrounded the spear and it disappeared into a black cloud of dust. It struck Sylvalora in the chest, the point continuing through, to exit from her back. The end of the shaft still visible sticking out of her chest. Sylvalora grabbed ahold of the shaft protruding from her chest with both hands.

Jindara immediately took out the Lora Daine, trying to ignore the shock she felt at what she was seeing. It slipped from her fingers and bounced off the rocks at her feet. She got down on her hands and knees frantically trying to find it. She glanced up at Sylvalora who was now propped up backwards by the spear, she looked dead.

Naneden was searching the outlying boulders for Jindara now. She could hear him moving rocks and rasping something. She searched the area at her feet desperately, but the stone looked like all the rest in the haze and darkness of the tomb. At last, the boulder before her moved, exposing her hiding place, and the hideous skull of Naneden appeared. He had another spear from the tomb clutched in his boney fist. He raised it above his head to strike. Fear took its hold, but Jindara was still able to muster enough courage to scoop up a handful of stones and concentrate on the platforms of Endil. There was a whooshing sound and then she was looking at the trees of Foreshome. A sharp pain crippled her chest, and she sank to her knees. She pulled the end of the dark spear from her belly, and it disintegrated as soon as it hit the wooden platform. Only half of the spear had managed to get through before the Lora Daine initiated. She fell over, comforted by the footfalls of her fellow elves running to lend her aid.

Chapter Twenty-Four

Kiss of Fire

The overcast sky aided in keeping Shadesilver hidden. Her own white scales blended in perfectly with both the sky and the snow-covered ground. Not that anyone could see her in the dark anyway, but her coloring would be extremely helpful once the daylight resumed. The white dragon reluctantly followed the trail of her missing dragon knight into the lands of Scarovia. Since Tatrice was in some kind of trouble, the closer Shadesilver flew in relation to her knight the more anxiety the dragon felt. Scarovia was not a place Shadesilver wanted to get caught in. The Kragodor dragons sometimes patrolled the skies, and all dragons have extremely developed night vision. Unlike most they could easily spot her against the white of the snow. As she flew deeper into the kingdom, she couldn't decide whether or not to fly high or stay low. She finally decided to fly low so that she could drop down and hide more quickly if she did spot a dragon patrol.

It wasn't long before her fears came to fruition. She heard the furious beating of wings before she saw what was using them. She instinctively ducked down to the tree line and hide in a copse of four or five enormous trees whose branches stuck out in all directions, obscuring her from above. It came as a bit of shock to her when she saw the creatures. They were not dragons at all but Dramyd and Drasmyd Duil flying west. Now she had another dilemma. Why would that many Dramyd and Drasmyd Duil be flying west? She peered into the direction she knew Tatrice to be and then she looked at the flying menace above, torn between rescuing her dragon knight and following the scourge so she could warn whomever they were flying after. She wished she had a Lora Daine at that moment. If Tatrice still has hers I can find her and warn people too. She took flight as soon as the Dramyds cleared. Of course, if Tatrice had her dragon stone she wouldn't need Shadesilver to come rescue her, potentially. *Stop it, there could be several reasons why Tatrice would be unable to use her stone. I just have to find her.* Shadesilver thought. There was a familiar tingle and an image formed in her mind. Tatrice did have her stone and she was giving her location. Shadesilver adjusted her wing trim and flew in the direction of Tatrice.

The snow and wind blew fiercely as Shadesilver searched. Finally, she saw a sickly green fire below, where Tatrice was located. She circled down to see the washed-out bones of the undead drake attack. She took a deep breath and unleashed lightning breath upon the creature with a high-pitched scream. The lightning cracked, electrifying the air, and striking the exposed bones with deadly force. The spine and skull separated from the rest of the dragon and fell in front of the cabin. It was still able to breathe its fire. Shadesilver landed on the skull and bracing her hind legs she rent the skull from the spine with her front claws. After she was certain the dragon was defeated, she let the illusion of her human form take over her shape. She shook her head to get her platinum blonde hair out of her eyes and ran into the cabin to find Trendan, Fayne, and Deylia behind a makeshift barricade.

"Shadesilver?" Deylia asked.

"Aye, where is Tatrice?"

"She left with Bren," Deylia said.

"She what? She left you all here to fend for yourself?"

Trendan dusted himself off. "No, she was rescuing Bren from the dragon. She didn't mean to leave us here alone."

Shadesilver eyed Fayne. "Forgive me, but do I know you? You smell like Tatrice."

Fayne's eyes narrowed quizzically, "Kind of a strange thing to say. She is my sister, well, half-sister."

"Don't worry, Fayne, she's not who she seems. She is of dragonkin." Deylia said.

Shadesilver smiled. "Tatrice has a sister. That's extraordinary."

A man with black hair, wearing red clothing, appeared behind Shadesilver. She addressed him without even looking at him. "Bren and Tatrice are no longer here, Amadace."

"I sense Bren is still in Scarovia." Amadace began, "But right now, we need to get these folks to safety. You stay here with them while I scout out the area to make sure we are safe to cart them away."

Shadesilver nodded.

Amadace turned, transformed back onto a magnificently beautiful blue dragon, and flew away into the night air.

"Hmm, he wears red but is a blur dragon." Deylia said.

Shadesilver smiled, "Aye, he does that. I think it makes him feel more like he's fooling everyone."

Dorenn could barely contain his excitement when Lamiel bound Seandara's hand to his, even though his gut told him she was equally nervous.

"You may now kiss your bride," Lamiel said.

Dorenn leaned into Seandara as she leaned into him. Their lips were only a short moment from touching when a spark of flame leaped between them. They touched lips with a sharp burning sensation, and both pulled back in pain.

"Ouch!" Seandara said putting her hand up to her mouth. The pain subsided quickly, and Dorenn leaned in for another kiss. This time it went more smoothly. Seandara moved her head sideways to receive his kiss of fire and the spark was quenched.

Dorenn let the kiss linger before pulling back. He opened his eyes to see Seandara smile sweetly at him just before her face began to twist into torment. She began to fall in a faint and Dorenn instantly reached to catch her in mid-fall. Queen Sildariel scarcely beat Morgoran to Seandara's side as Dorenn let her settle to the ground.

"Give her room to breathe," Morgoran said as others began to move to his bride's side.

"Morgoran?" Queen Sildariel asked. "Is it what I feared? The Solicanth curse?"

"Move away woman!" Morgoran snapped.

"I am the queen!" Sildariel said in retaliation.

"Move away queen then!"

Sildariel waved off her guard who was about to come to her aid.

"Of course it isn't some damn fool curse...your majesty." Morgoran said.

"You are a very rude man! I should let the guards take you away."

Morgoran said nothing, but Dorenn knew he didn't care about the queen's threats. "What is it Morgoran?" Dorenn asked, trying to keep his voice even and unwavering.

"Help me get her into your bed, Dorenn. I think she'll be fine. There is no magic present, no illness I can detect, and no poisons. I think it might be nerves."

"When we kissed there was a spark of fire. Could that be the cause?"

Morgoran glared at him as if he should know better. "What do you think?"

"I think not," Dorenn said as he helped his mentor move his bride.

Morgoran pointed to one of the attendants, "You there, go and fetch some cold water." He stopped the attendant by the arm as he was leaving. "You will note I said *cold* water!"

The attendant nodded and ran off to presumably get the water.

Morgoran grunted and groaned as if Seandara were heavy. He and Dorenn moved her across the wooden platform to their new house and into bed.

"Stay with her. I will return in a moment." Morgoran stepped back out onto the platform Dorenn took her hand and waited by her side.

Seandara opened her eyes shortly thereafter, "My, Morgoran can be grumpy." Were her first words.

"I think he's always like that, in reality, I think it just comes out a lot more when he feels pressured or in a crisis," Dorenn said.

Seandara giggled then coughed.

"Easy now, what is all this about?"

"I..." She began to convulse, and Dorenn tried to hold down her shoulders. Morgoran reappeared and pulled him away.

"Give her room. I feel it now. I know what's happening."

"What? What is it?" Dorenn asked. Sildariel was now looking over Morgoran's shoulder.

"If it's what I think it is there is nothing we can do about it. I think it's the silver drake. Did Sylvalora spend any time with her in Ardenia?"

"Some," Dorenn said. "Not any more than the rest of us."

Morgoran bowed his head before looking at Sildariel. "I'm sorry, I think Sylvalora is dead. Seandara is her choice to replace her."

Sildariel was appalled. "What? How can Sylvalora be dead? She was made by the gods."

"No, we made her. She was gifted by the gods. Loracia gave her life and life can be taken away, especially by the embodiment of death. She must have encountered the lich."

"That's wild speculation!" Sildariel said.

"See for yourself." He gestured to Seandara who was taking on a silver pallid skin tone which began to change into the luster of metal.

"I always thought Sheyna would be the next silver drake," Sildariel said. "Why Seandara?"

"Solicanths," Dorenn said without knowing exactly why.

"Preposterous!" Morgoran said. "This Solicanth nonsense has all of you all tied up in knots. It's just silly superstition. If it had any merit at all I would know about it, of all people!"

Dorenn watched with great interest as Seandara regained control and returned to herself. She settled down and began to breathe normally, lulling off to sleep.

"She is sleeping," Dorenn said. "If you wouldn't mind, now that the danger has passed, could we have some privacy?"

"Certainly." Morgoran escorted Sildariel to the door. The attendant came with the cold water. "About time! Someone might die by the time you finish lollygagging about." He took the glass of cold water and downed it. "Not bad; it could be colder. Now, go and get some for the bride."

"He's mean," Seandara said after Morgoran closed the door.

"Nah, he's harmless when you get to know him better," Dorenn smirked. "I thought you were asleep."

"I wanted them to go so I could have my husband all to myself." He reached up and pulled his head down to her and kissed him.

Dorenn pulled back. "Are you all right? All that looked serious earlier."

"I'm fine. If anything, I feel better than I have ever felt."

"But Sylvalora may be dead."

"But I am alive," Seandara said, once again pulling his head down to hers for a kiss.

Dorenn pulled away again. "Wait, I have a wedding gift."

"Now?" Seandara said. "Right now?"

"It's important."

"Are you avoiding me? Are you scared?"

"A little," Dorenn said demurely. "You just had some kind of episode. Wouldn't you be?"

Seandara thought for a moment. "All right, what's your gift?"

Dorenn reached under the bed and produced the sackcloth with *Cyrodel* wrapped within it. Seandara sat up in bed and opened it. She held the sword up. "It's beautiful."

"It's the companion sword to *Dranmalin*."

"Appropriate." She said, "I should learn how to wield it."

"I'll teach you and you can teach me the bow."

Seandara put the sword back in the sackcloth. "I thought you already knew how to use a bow."

"I know a little. I'm sure you could show me more." Dorenn watched out the window as the welcoming sunlight played upon the water of a hanging birdbath before turning his gaze back to Seandara. "Are you certain you're all right?"

"I am." She grabbed a hold of his dress robe and pulled him back to her once more. *Cyrodel*, wrapped in its sackcloth, slid off the side of the bed and clanked loudly on the hardwood floor.

"Wait." Dorenn said. "I'm sorry, but before I can concentrate on my own happiness, I need to find out what happened to Sylvalora."

"What do you plan to do?"

"I will go talk to Morgoran. He will know what to do. I promise I will return right away."

"I suppose I want to know as well. Go to Morgoran. I will be here when you return."

"I love you." Dorenn said.

Seandara just smiled and gave him another kiss this time without the fire. Dorenn disappeared out the door.

"I just hope you are able to show me and stop making excuses to get away," she said as she watched him walk away.

Chapter Twenty-Five

DAMAGED

Lady Shey found Gondrial in one of the three great dining halls of the palace. She had passed King Lourn and two of his king's guards in the hallway and polite conversation led her to Gondrial's whereabouts. She entered the hall to find him sitting over a bowl of soup looking over parchments anchored to the table with heavy, not to mention sizable, salt and pepper shakers. He did not look up when she entered. Shey quickly glanced at her reflection in a clear glass window near the entrance to make sure she still looked like herself and not like Oria. She sat directly across from him.

"What's all this?" She asked.

He looked up from the parchment. "Oh, hello Shey. I'm trying to finalize some of the battle plans for Dorenn. I am off to meet with him tomorrow."

"In Foreshome?"

"Thereabouts, I assume. I haven't heard from him since he left for Endil." He cleared his throat and settled back into his chair. "What are your plans?"

"I thought I might go along with you."

Gondrial suddenly looked as if he swallowed something that didn't agree with him. "All right." He said weakly.

"You don't seem to be very excited about it. You don't want me to come along?"

A courier entered the dining room. "Lady Shey?"

"Oh, thank the gods!" Gondrial said.

"What did you say, Gondrial?" Shey asked.

Gondrial pointed to Lady Shey. "Here! She's right here."

The courier approached. "Lady Shey, forgive my intrusion but I have a communication for you from Endil." He handed her a piece of parchment. She took it and read it while the courier exited without waiting for her reply.

"Well, it seems I will be going along with you regardless of how you feel about it. I have been summoned to Endil by Queen Sildariel. It seems there is a matter I need to tend to with Dorenn and Seandara."

Gondrial's relieved demeanor tightened again.

"You know, that is most unsettling," Shey said. "I could see your relief when the subject changed, and I can see your apprehension now. You aren't even trying to hide it."

Gondrial closed his eyes and slightly shook his head then opened them again. "It's not what you think. Whenever we go somewhere together, there is always some monumental danger looming over us. For once, I would like to travel somewhere and not run into something that promises to try and kill me."

"That's ridiculous! You are in as much trouble without me than you are with me. I'm not buying into this stupid, asinine, explanation."

Gondrial shrugged. "I expected as much. Truth or not, I'm sticking to it. Now, if you will excuse me, I need to make some preparations for the journey to Endil."

"What preparations? You will be traveling by Lora Daine."

Preparations, you know, like provisions. The elves only eat plants and I like a cut of meat occasionally."

"You plan to take cuts of raw meat to Endil?"

"Of course not. They will be dried onto jerky."

"The elves won't allow you to have that in Foreshome much less allow you to eat it in front of them. What are you really up to, Gondrial?"

"Nothing. I just don't want to eat salads the whole time. I will eat it alone in my chambers."

Lady Shey stood, "You go and get your provisions. I will meet you in the throne room. King Lourn will want to send us off personally."

Gondrial nodded, made a curt bow, and left Shey for the exit. She followed him through the door but went in the opposite direction when they reached the hallway. The kitchen wasn't far from the dining hall, so she expected him to join her in the throne room shortly. She walked briskly though the marbled halls of the palace eager to get to Endil. She had a feeling that since the parchment involved both Seandara and Dorenn and Sildariel said it was so important, it might mean they would be joined together. Perhaps they *were* Solicanths, as Queen Sildariel suggested, after all.

When she was granted entrance into the throne room her expectations sank. King Lourn was not preparing to travel to Endil as well, which meant that his only son was probably not getting married after all.

The king was speaking with an advisor when he noticed her entrance. "Ah, my lady, I see the courier found you. Are you ready to travel?"

Shey bowed before the king. "I am."

Gondrial was granted entrance and came to stand beside Shey. He bowed to the king as well.

"Good, you are both ready." King Lourn said. His advisor handed him a large green Lora Daine. "This Lora Daine came by special courier from Draegodor just this afternoon. King Amarantus certainly took his own sweet time fulfilling my request for one, but none the less, here it is." He handed it to Lady Shey, and she heard Gondrial sniff, a sign of his consternation even if the others in the room didn't pick up on it like she did. "Don't let it out of your sight. King Amarantus might not send me another."

"I will, my liege," Shey said.

Lourn smiled at her. "I don't think I will ever get used to that."

"My liege?"

"Exactly, being referred to as such takes some time to get used to."

"I would imagine there are a great many such titles and signs of respect you must relate to."

"Indeed, my lady." He clapped his hands together. "Well, good luck." He looked at Gondrial in particular. "Keep my boy safe."

"Aye, I will my liege."

Lourn nodded and stepped back.

Shey concentrated on the Lora Daine and thought of the wooden platforms of Endil. Gondrial stepped closer to her and took hold of her forearm. There was the familiar whooshing sound of the spell taking effect and then they faded away. But this time it was different. The spell pulled at Shey's body and lasted much longer than it should have. She closed her eyes to better endure the pain of her body being pulled and stretched. At last, the spell ended, and she opened her eyes to the empty, darkened halls of the red city of Draegodor. Gondrial fell in behind her and dropped his pack. The once brilliant wall mural of the great hall was scorched black from dragon's fire.

"What the?" Gondrial said. "Why did you bring us to Draegodor?" He glanced around. "Also, what happened to Draegodor?"

"I didn't bring us here. I concentrated on Endil. We should be in Endil. King Amarantus must have predestined this Lora Daine."

"Or the emergency protocol on Lora Daines has been activated. Anyone of note who tries to use one for the first time since the warning will be transferred here instead.

"Dangerous! Since we were all the way across the map in Ardenia!"

"The halls appear to be empty," Gondrial observed. "Why is Draegodor abandoned." He examined the hallway closer, "Um, Shey!" Gondrial's voice wavered and quaked.

Shey responded to see what Gondrial was alerting her about and instinctively took a step back when she saw the enormous, skeletal dragon lumber into the far end of the empty main hall. It had not seen them yet. She took Gondrial's hand and pulled him along with her to the closest doorway. Their footfalls must have made too much noise because the beast took flight and moved toward them at breakneck speed. They dived into another doorway to avoid being clipped by the undead dragon.

Shey rolled to a stop and got her bearings. "A guardian left behind. Naneden must be behind this. He must have attacked Draegodor."

"Why would he do that?" Gondrial asked. "Of course, strategically, if he took Draegodor he would eliminate them as a potential threat."

"Together the Trigothian army and the dragons would be formidable but if you take them on one at a time instead of together you have a better chance at defeating them both." Shey finished Gondrial's train of thought.

"Where did they go? They weren't killed, were they?" Gondrial asked.

"Hard to say. If they were killed, I'm sure Naneden resurrected them into his army, effectively moving them from threat to ally."

"That's truly a frightening thought."

"King Amarantus sent us the Lora Daine so we would travel here and find out what had happened."

"Unlikely, the stone would have been sent long before this attack. How did he know we would use it?"

"He didn't exactly. He took a gamble. Ardenia is where Dorenn and the Trigothian army is headquartered, He was trying to alert them in general."

"I don't think so. Why not just have the courier tell us?"

Shey looked at Gondrial with amusement. "Sometimes I wonder if there is a brain in your head or some inferior substitute. The courier wouldn't know anything when he left here. Amarantus uses seers. He would have known of the danger, even if he didn't know what the danger was or when it would happen exactly. But, with his seers, he would have known about any pending attacks well ahead of time. By sending a Lora Daine, he could bring someone here without knowing exactly what was going to happen."

"Clever."

"Aye, extremely. Only, it does seem that by knowing the extent of the danger, he could have prepared for it better than he obviously did."

"Dragons can be arrogant. I have heard them boast how no one will ever get past the sentinels should Draegodor be attacked. Besides, look at Morgoran. Seers are not always accurate."

The dragon's fire burned near the doorway and Shey ran with Gondrial as fast and far away from the flames as possible.

"Shey, use the Lora Daine again. Get us out of here. We have seen what we needed to see." Shey held the stone and concentrated on the wooden platforms of Endil. After the whoosh of the spell, they were not standing in Endil but somewhere else, somewhere far away. There were twisted trees and thick underbrush. "Where did you take us now? The Sacred Land?"

"No, I think we are deep in Scarovia."

"Scarovia! Why Scarovia?"

Shey pointed ahead at the light coming from an open door to a wood and stone structure. "Because of him."

Gondrial squinted. "Isn't that..."

"My father? Aye, it is." Lady Shey faltered and almost fell. Gondrial's quick reflexes enabled him to catch her. She looked at him. Her sapphire blue eyes managed to capture the low light.

"What is the matter?" Gondrial asked.

"It's my mother...and something from my past, a memory of my father." She pushed herself upright placing the bottom of her hand on her forehead. "Something horrible has happened." She stared through the open doorway at her father. They shared a moment; he locked eyes with hers and stared back for a long moment before he moved to the door.

"Gondrial!" Shey grabbed hold of his arm. "I see it now. Mother is gone and that is not my father, at least not as he was."

"What in the name of all the gods are you talking about?" Gondrial asked. "I'm confused. How did we even get here?"

Veric stopped at the doorway to the cabin. His eyes narrowed and his brow furrowed with concern. He reached for the door and slowly closed it, closing Shey and Gondrial out.

Shey saw a flood of memories appear before her eyes and she fell to her knees. The pain of the visions pierced her mind like tiny daggers. Gondrial tried to help her, but she pushed his arm away. "It was all kept from me! Father, mother, Rikard." She considered Gondrial's face, "you!"

"Shey?"

"Enowene and my grandmother. They erased my childhood. They erased the truth from me."

"You are beginning to worry me, Shey."

"I'm sorry about this, Gondrial. I really do love you."

"What?"

Shey reached for his head. Her face twisted into a determined grimace. Gondrial's eyes went wide with fear, and he opened his mouth in a silent scream. He tried to fight her off in vain.

"Just a moment more, my love. My true love, I need to make sure I have your essence and that you can't fight him."

Gondrial gasped and Shey finally let him go. He dropped to his knees. He whispered something.

"What? I'm sorry Gondrial." Shey said, not quite hearing what he had whispered. He beckoned her to come closer with his forefinger and Shey leaned down.

"You're insane!" He whispered again.

"Oh, Gondrial. I know I certainly seem that way to you right now. Let me take care of this and I will make it all up to you."

Gondrial shrugged.

Shey looked at the cabin with consternation. It was time to end this. Time to take back everything that was taken from her as a child. She stood and found herself face to face with Veric. She took a startled step back.

"Hello, Sheyna," Veric said. "I thought I told you to stay away from this scoundrel." Veric waved his arm and Gondrial flew back away from her and crashed into a heap. Shey took a step toward him and Veric waved his arm again, sending Gondrial in the opposite direction as if he were a child's rag doll.

"Father, stop it!" Shey cast an impact spell at Veric that knocked him back slightly, but he recovered quickly and did not fall.

"My dear daughter. It's time I put you in your place."

Shey felt her feet betray her as they came out from under her. She toppled to the ground with force, and she thought she felt something snap in the process. She had to get through to him.

"Father, it's mother. I think something horrible has happened to her."

"Nice try, my dear."

"No, here search my thoughts. Am I lying?"

Veric reached and took Shey's head in his hands. She felt a tingle and then he let her go.

"See, father?"

Veric stumbled back. "I must go to her. I can save her. It was the spear of Aedreagnon! I can save her!" He gave Shey a pained look before he used his Lora Daine to disappear right before her eyes.

Chapter Twenty-Six

An Unexpected Encounter

"All right then," Gondrial said. "Shall we try for Endil again?"

Shey took a deep breath and nodded.

"Or do you want to go to your mother? I assume she is in the Sacred Land. It seems that's where we are all headed eventually."

"No, father will go to her. If anyone can handle the situation there with her it will be him. I would just be in the way."

"That's bold of you. I would have predicted you would go."

She confronted him, her face burning, "You would be wrong. She is far from fragile."

"All right. I don't mean to get into your affairs."

"Then don't. Here," She presented the Lora Daine. "Ready to go to Foreshome?"

He nodded and took hold of her arm. The Lora Daine activated. A moment later they were standing in farmland looking at fields of grain.

He turned around to notice a cabin with a smoking chimney behind them.

Shey shivered from the cold, "Where are we now?"

"Did the Lora Daine bring us here on its own?"

"I don't know." She glanced back at the cabin. A large man with dark hair and bulky shoulders came out from behind it. He was whistling until he noticed them standing and watching him. "Oy, who are you two? What are you doing here on my land. Have you come to try to get me to leave again."

"No, we are just passing through. Don't mind us." Gondrial said. "We will be going now."

The man hurried closer, and Shey could now see he was Scarovian. "Gondrial, we're in Scarovia."

"See that you are. I will be right here watching you until you do."

"Okay friend. We are leaving. Do you have the Lora Daine, Shey?"

"Aye, Let me..."

"What is that you have there?" The man had moved at an almost impossible speed and was right next to them now. Oy, that's one of those dragon stones!"

"No, it isn't." Gondrial said.

"Ya, it is."

"No, it isn't. Shey get us out of here."

"Kendric needs one of those. Why don't you hand it over and no one will get hurt."

"I'm sure Kendric can find his own." Gondrial said.

"I'm Kendric," he said pointing to himself.

"Shey, now!"

Shey whispered some words, but nothing happened. "I can't. It isn't working."

Kendric smiled and fangs appeared in his grin, “I will get the stone and have a meal.”

“No, you won’t.” Gondrial said.

“Oh, I will.” He repeated.

“No, I don’t think so.” Gondrial said.

“Stop being so contrary. It’s irritating”

“No, it isn’t. Shey? Now!”

“Dragon magic is unpredictable here. That’s why dragons call it the zone of silence. You have to know where to stand for it to work.

“Kendric knows where to stand.” He reached for the stone and Shey tried to push him away. Angered, he knocked her down flat. “I will take the stone. It is useless to fight.” Gondrial stepped in and the man flung him aside.

“I guess it’s my day to get kicked around. Shey heard him say as he pulled himself to the base of a boulder. The man rushed to him with the speed of the blood feeders who were rumored to live in the Scarovian Nightmare Lands. She watched in horror as he beat Gondrial down and then turned his attention back to her. He flashed his sharp teeth and was next to her in an instant.

Lady Shey rose to her knees. Gondrial was too far away to check on, but he was not moving and Shey took that as a bad sign. She could also see a small blood pool near his head. She looked up at Kendric.

He stood fangs barred, “Why don’t you just accept I will have my way?”

Her anger was nearly insatiable. She began to contemplate how she could kill him? Maybe she could incapacitate him first before delivering the final blow. Shey pushed herself to her feet and stared Kendric down as she carefully walked sideways toward Gondrial. “Stay out of my mind. I can see your true form there, blood feeder.”

“Don’t do it. Don’t go to him. I’ll not allow it.”

Shey took another step and Kendric held up his hands, poised for another attack. “I’ll do it. I’ll destroy him once and for all!”

Shey bowed her head. She knew she could not allow this to go on. She couldn’t let Kendric out alive. She put the stone safely in her pocket and reluctantly drew her daggers.

“Daggers! Are you mad?” Kendric said. “Those cannot hurt me. Didn’t I tell you your weapons can’t hurt me?”

“No, you didn’t. You were too busy marveling after things you cannot have. She leaped to Kendric with the help of essence. Kendric proved to be light on his feet and produced his claws. They had sharp, metal tips on them. He parried her attack. She rounded her leg below him and tripped him to the ground. She was at his neck with her daggers before he knew what she was doing. “I don’t want to hurt you. I’ll give you one more chance to leave us in peace.”

Kendric smiled. “It’s far too late for that.” He kicked her in the gut, sending her over his head to the ground, she recovered and spun around. Onto her feet, she lurched at him, and he blocked again, but this time, Shey used essence and in a whirlwind of blades, she struck Kendric’s forearms while he tried desperately to parry. Sparks flew from the blades as Kendric began matching her blow for blow with his metal tipped claws. She kicked back from him and then flung herself forward again in a blazing attack. Kendric stepped aside and sliced her forearm. She grasped at it to stop the sting and almost lost one of the daggers in the process. Kendric recovered and made his attack. Shey blocked it and made a surprise attack, stabbing him in the gut, just below his ribs. He recoiled back. Shey felt the essence rushing around her and Kendric’s claws began to glow. He could draw essence! Shey decided she had to pull out all the stops and she began to draw in essence too. Before her appeared six daggers, two in her hands and four floating beside them. She attacked, with all six daggers, in a stunning forward heave. Kendric took a step back not sure what to do. Two daggers began carving his gut and two his chest. Shey used her daggers to slice his wrists making his claws fall to his side uselessly.

"Lady I.." He tried to say something, but Shey did not want to hear any more. She commanded all six daggers forward. Two sliced into his neck and two into his chest. One dagger severed his head from his shoulders, the only way to kill a blood feeder. She wiped her blades off as the other daggers disappeared and she put them away.

She ran to Gondrial who was just coming to. "Are you all right?"

Gondrial moaned. He looked at the bleeding Kendric sprawled out on the ground. "Now I remember why I always avoided fighting with you."

She kissed him hard on the lips. All the emotion came flooding forward and she couldn't help herself. "I love you, you fool. I saw you lying here with blood pooling, and I thought the worst. Do you hear me? I love you." She kissed him and hugged him again with tears streaming down her face.

"Shey, I..."

"Don't speak." She said, "If you are going to say something horrible or inappropriate or witty, I don't want to hear it."

"It was you."

"What?" She looked into his face.

"It was you for me. It was always you. Every other woman, every encounter was only a placeholder for you. No one could ever measure up to you."

"Oh Gondrial, you are a fool. But you are my fool." She fell into his arms again.

Gondrial moaned, "Oh, my head. This smiling and kissing hurts."

"Well, get used to it." She said, "Come on, I still have the Lora Daine. We can get out of here. We can go to Endil."

Gondrial nodded. “To Endil then.”

Shey took out the Lora Daine from her pocket. She whispered some words to it, but nothing happened. They kept moving from one place to the next trying it until at last they found a spot where it worked.

Chapter Twenty-Seven

Revenge of the Mindwielders

Dorenn felt the first light of morning on his cheek as he awoke from one of the best night's sleep he had ever had. He reached over and put his hand on Seandara's back and she stirred slightly. He wanted to touch her to confirm she was real, confirm that he was married and his bride was still there next to him. With a satisfied smile on his face, he began to think about the impending battle and how to get back to the Trigothian army. He wondered how they were doing and how far they had gotten toward the Sacred Land. He felt a bit guilty that he was enjoying the comfort of Foreshome while his men marched to their probable deaths in an ugly, barren land by the hands of bloated, stinking corpses. *At least the Drasmyd Duil and Dramyds would be on his side now*. He thought.

He stared at the ceiling. The Dramyds and Drasmyd Duil were on his side now. Something didn't sit right with him about that. He looked over at Seandara again and poked her in the back.

"What, stop it. Go back to sleep. It's too early," She said groggily.

Dorenn left her alone. She felt real enough. He pondered the Dramyds again. Sildariel can detect everything in her realm and the Archers of Endil are deadly accurate with their skills. As long as they guard Endil, nothing would be able to fly in so easily except by sheer excessive numbers. *Wait! Sildariel and the Archers would never allow creatures such as the Drasmyd Duil to just casually fly into the forest. Elves don't get sick and Morgoran was almost too grumpy, even for him. Then Lamiel locked him up in this house just for asking how Sylvalora was and if he should go to her.* He looked around at the room. *Part of Naneden's army was here and they just wandered off!* He felt the panic run up his spine. *Oh, no! None of this is real!* He leaped up from bed. Seandara did not move. He began to draw essence, careful to watch what sources it came from. He let the essence go, and as if a curtain was moved aside, the walls of the room changed. The house was half destroyed by fire. He went to the front door, which was ripped from its hinges, and peered out onto the platforms. Some of them were still burning and thick smoke rose through the trees. Stunned, he leaned against the door jam.

"I sent the Drasmyd Duil and Dramyds straight to the Trigothian army." He muttered. "I gave them the exact position at Lux Enor." He felt sick to his stomach. No one was used to the power of the mindwielders. Every lie they spun and illusion they cast was so vivid and real. If one didn't understand the complexities of people and their personalities, the illusions were nearly impossible to catch. He turned to Seandara again expecting to see someone else there or another illusion but whoever slept there still appeared to be Seandara.

He wondered if the news of Sylvalora had also been a trick, Seandara, if this was Seandara, certainly didn't seem to be that concerned about the silver drake's demise.

I'm sure Morgoran left Ardenia with us. Dorenn concluded before he strapped on *Dranmalin* and started off down the platform toward the royal quarters. He looked back at Seandara. *If that is Seandara, I will come back for her before she wakes up.*

As he walked along the smoldering platforms, Dorenn was careful to avoid places that appeared to be burnt away or dangerously weakened by fire. When he reached the first of the royal quarters, he noticed that most of the palace platform had been burned away. He hesitated before continuing. What if this reality was an illusion? How could the mindwielders be so incredibly accurate with their illusions? Why did he not feel the heat of the fires when he was near the platform before? He made his way through the front, burned away opening to the royal residence. Suspiciously, there were no bodies anywhere. Surely, destruction on this scale would result in casualties. Dorenn plodded on, through the burned-out foyer and beyond. He noticed the royal residence was not smoldering, a sign that the fire that gutted it died out some time ago, or so he assumed. *Was he even married to Seandara or was that part of the illusion?*

Not far into the living space, Dorenn felt the presence of Morgoran. At first, he thought he would round a corner and see the old wielder, but as he got closer to the source, he realized he was sensing Morgoran's essence. Once he came up upon charred remains, he was certain. He braced for what he knew would happen next. Morgoran's essence would join his own just as Toborne had and Ianthill after him. He didn't have to wait long. He bent down to one knee at the remains, a single tear rolling down his face. "You were a grumpy, bitter old man, and I can't imagine the power of the one who killed you this way, but I know it's a waste. No one deserves to burn to death like this."

A sudden noise shook him, and Dorenn regained his senses. At once, he felt the impressions of Morgoran and what had happened. Sildariel had been whisked away while Morgoran fought off...the mindwielder. A reanimation of Naneden that Morgoran was familiar with. Naneden resurrected a mindwielder long dead in the Sacred Land. A friend of Lady Shey's called Marella. Shey had once called her friend the most powerful mindwielder she had ever seen. Dorenn could still feel the fright and respect that Morgoran had for the powerful mindwielder. The harder he thought on it the more the one word kept getting louder in his head...run...RUN!

Perhaps it was a delay in his thinking or his disbelief, but Dorenn only slowly comprehended that he might be in immediate danger. He looked around apprehensively but saw no one. Still, he did not run, but he did move away from where Morgoran fell. He moved with increasing haste back to where he left Seandara. He didn't get far before he saw an ethereal figure move up one of the platforms from the cover of some dense foliage. Remnants of blonde hair flowed from an emaciated head. The apparition was still a good distance away, but not so far away that Dorenn couldn't see she only had one eye remaining. Her clothing was rotting or already rotted away depending on where he looked, and she ambled along as if her joints were all but fused tight.

Realizing that she might not know he was aware of the illusion, he forced himself to fixate on a point ahead as not to look at her and give himself away. He walked forward, trying his best to ignore her when she began to follow him. The stench, even though she was downwind from him, was almost unbearable and he was afraid he might choke on it and alert her. He was fairly certain, by what he had seen, that the woman in his bed was indeed Seandara. He had to get to her as quickly as he could and get her to safety. He again contemplated whether or not his marriage to her had been real but dismissed the thought for later. Right now, he just wanted to get to her. He increased his pace, resisting the urge to look behind to see if Marella was still on his trail. There was no time to mourn Morgoran or Sylvalora if anything had happened to her. The priority of the moment was to get Seandara and get her somewhere safe.

Dorenn rushed into the room of the house where Seandara still slept. "Get up! Wake up Seandara! We are in danger. We must get out of here. He turned his bride over and stared directly into the face of the emaciated Marella. She rose from the bed with malevolent intent, raising her arms and screeching at him. He stumbled back, tripped and landing on his backside, scrambling away by kicking his legs. Marella floated into the air above the bed, her mouth twisted in a skinless grin. Dorenn braced for her attack. There was a rush of air and several thunking sounds as a barrage of magical arrows found their mark in Marella's chest. Dorenn looked back to see Seandara, wielding the bow with endless arrows he had made for her. The apparition fell back on the bed.

"Come on, Dorenn. Didn't you hear me yelling at you?"

"You were the one behind me?"

"Aye, I have been chasing you across two platforms."

He got up and took her outstretched hand. "You can see through the illusion?"

"Not at first. I woke up with you gone and when I went out to look for you the illusion dropped. Then I saw you headed back here, and I followed you. Come on, we have to get to the royal chambers."

Marella began to rise from the bed again. Dorenn pushed forward, clutching Seandara's hand and hurrying back the way he had just come. "Is there a Lora Daine in the royal chambers?"

"No, but my mother can help us."

Dorenn's heart froze. "Seandara, I'm not sure your mother is still in Endil."

"Of course she is. There is a plan in place for emergencies."

They ran up the platform to the royal foyer and passed the spot where Morgoran fell. Dorenn looked at the remains once more. "Poor Morgoran. He held Marella off while your mother escaped."

"He will be honored for his sacrifice," Seandara said.

Dorenn stopped cold. "Wait, I never said he sacrificed himself."

"It's implied."

"Wait, is this real? Is this part of another illusion?"

"We don't have time for this."

He let go of Seandara's hand.

"Oh, for the love of..." Seandara grabbed ahold of Dorenn's head and gave him a deep passionate kiss. She stopped and gazed into his eyes, waiting for his reaction.

"All right, you're real. Lead on."

Gondrial helped Shey to the healer's tent on the outskirts of the Sacred Land battlefield. A pretty young female healer named Verma quickly responded to help Shey with her injuries, but Shey insisted that she help Gondrial first. His wound to the head could be potentially more dangerous. The healer's tent was the first stop for wounded soldiers before being sorted out into the other areas based on the severity of the wounds. Severe wounds went immediately to the clerics of Loracia. Moderate wounds went to the clerics of Fawlsbane, who could actually heal just as well as the clerics of Loracia but had drawn the long straw. The two factions of clerics would trade off when the clerics of Loracia became too tired and fatigued. The only problem was that Loracian clerics would never admit fatigue and would probably heal until they dropped dead on the spot. The lord commander of the clerics of Fawlsbane designated himself to routine checks so he could assess for himself when his faction needed to relief the clerics of Loracia.

Gondrial's head was bandaged, and the healer had moved on to Shey when Rennon threw the tent flap aside. "Gondrial, Shey, what news? What happened to you both?"

Gondrial adjusted the bandages on his head. "We're fine, just a playful romp with a deadly vampire."

"That's good to hear." Rennon reached for Lady Shey's hand to kiss.

"Whoa, easy there with the hand kissing. Didn't you hear what I said, Rennon."

"What happened?"

Gondrial looked to Shey who seemed hesitant to give an answer. "Shey killed a blood feeder."

"Oh, you were serious about that? I thought you were just pulling my leg."

"Nope, she took him on all by herself and won."

"Really? Where were you?"

"Uh, never mind us, what have you been up to here in Dorenn's camp?" He glanced around, "Where is Dorenn anyway?"

"In Foreshome, er Endil. He had some business to attend to there."

"Oh, who did he leave in charge?" Gondrial asked.

"I have no idea. They left suddenly after Seandara got word her mother took ill."

"What? Elves don't get sick." Gondrial said.

Rennon ignored him and grabbed a canvas chair. He pulled it in front of Shey. "My mindwielders have identified others of our kind behind Naneden's lines. I believe he is resurrecting the dead buried from the War of the Oracle."

"Marella," Shey whispered.

"What was that?" Rennon asked.

"I said Marella. I have already seen her. No offense, but I don't think our mindwielders today will stand a chance against our enemies if he uses mindwielders from the War of the Oracle to attack us. They are fully trained."

"Rennon, could I have a word with you?' Gondrial asked.

"Certainly." He left the chair in front of Shey and met Gondrial in the corner of the tent.

"I know what you are getting at and it's a bad idea. You can't ask her to confront her best friend who died a thousand years ago? I'm not sure what that would do to her." He put his arm around Rennon's shoulders, "have you learned how to make people forget things yet?"

"Sorry, no."

"Ahh, well, This is tough on all of us and I'm sure it's going to get tougher for some of us." He indicated Shey.

"This is war, Gondrial. I thought you understood that."

"I'll go," Shey said.

Gondrial looked behind, "Shey? You were listening?"

"Well, you two are hardly whispering at all, in fact, you are whispering so loudly you are almost matching your normal speaking voices." She inspected her bandaged arm. "Rennon's right, this is war, and

I am no more exempt from it than anyone else. I will go see if the mindwielders are Marella and her group."

"I'll go with you," Gondrial said. "Marella's illusions will be tough to spot."

Shey took a deep breath, "I suppose we should report to Dorenn, where did you say he was, Rennon?"

Rennon was busy retying his long hair back and didn't realize Shey was speaking to him.

"Rennon? If you are done playing with your hair, I asked you a question."

Gondrial smirked disapprovingly. "Why don't you get all that hair cut off?"

Rennon finished tying it back, "I don't know, I have always kept it this way."

"It can't be good for battle." Gondrial reached up and tugged on his ponytail. "I could just pull you down with it and slice your neck."

Rennon pulled back and grabbed his ponytail from him. "As if I would let anyone get that close to me."

Gondrial nodded appreciatively.

"Well?" Shey asked.

"I told you. Dorenn went to Foreshome with Seandara. Word is that queen Sildariel is sick or something."

Shey sat up alert. "What? Elves don't get sick."

"That's what I said. You ignored me, though."

"Are you sure the message said she was sick?"

"That's all I know. I was told second hand." Rennon said. "I've received no word from neither Dorenn nor Morgoran." Rennon reacted to a clatter outside the tent. "What was that noise?"

Gondrial opened the tent flap. Men were scrambling, running back and forth with seemingly reckless abandon. "Something is really stirring everyone up out there."

"Here, let me see," Rennon said as Gondrial stepped aside. "Hey, you." He got the attention of one of the soldiers as he ran by.

"Sir?"

"What's going on?"

"We're under attack, sir. On the other side of the camp."

"By unlife?"

"Uh, no sir, by Dramyd. They are flying in from the east and north, more than I have ever seen in my whole life. The skies are black with them."

"Shey, I hope your daggers are still sharp." Gondrial said as he brandished his sword. "Here we go again!"

CHAPTER TWENTY-EIGHT

SOLICANTHS

Seandara led Dorenn to one of the larger trees supporting the royal quarters. It appeared to be like most every other tree support to him, but when Seandara began to use her magic on it, the tree bark rolled to one side revealing a ladder leading down deep into the trunk. She pointed her finger down the shaft indicating she wanted him to go down first. He tested the strength of the ladder and then started down. Seandara stepped out on the ladder and used her skills to make the tree close again. Cascades of pulsing light began to run down the sides of the ladder illuminating the walls inside the tree. The light came from sap-like rivers of liquid flowing up and down beside the edges of the ladder. He was tempted to reach out and touch it.

"What is this light?" Dorenn asked finally.

"It's called liquid light. Incidentally, if you are feeling the need to reach out and touch it, don't. It is cool to the touch, but it will slowly burn away your skin over time."

"Isn't it dangerous to have the stuff around then?"

"I didn't say it would burn my skin. Eridil are immune to it, but we have learned the hard way that visitors tend to be susceptible. It's better to just leave it be."

Dorenn looked down; the liquid light seemed to go on forever. "How far down does this go?"

"Underground."

After what seemed like an hour or more, Dorenn finally set foot on solid earth. His hand cramped from holding onto the ladder, so he rubbed them together, Seandara stepped off the ladder and opened an orifice in the tree as she did up above. Dorenn stepped out into a cavern of color and light. Crystals imbedded in the rough walls glowed blue, red, purple, and white. An illuminated trail led off to another entrance. Rivers of the liquid light flowed on either side of the doorway opposite.

"Come on, Mother will be in the next chamber. This one can be flooded with liquid light if need be."

"Clever," Dorenn said. "It's beautiful in here. I thought it would feel dank and wet like the other caverns I have been in, but it doesn't. It even smells of spring flowers."

Seandara smirked and pointed at her face. "Elves!"

Dorenn chuckled.

Following Seandara into the adjoining chamber, he marveled at the doorway. When they were next to it, he could see that the arch of the doorway was the form of two elves carved in stone reaching toward each other and holding a pot or vase between them as the capstone, which the entire arch depended upon. In the light of the next chamber, a long stone table appeared as if it were a natural extension of the floor. Sitting at the table were several of the Eridil including Queen Sildariel. The queen pushed her chair aside and all but ran to Seandara to embraced her. Dorenn was startled when Morgoran also stood up and made his way to him.

"Oh, my daughter. I had hoped you would snap out of the illusion too." Sildariel said. "I was devastated when we had to come down here without you."

"As I predicted," Morgoran said.

"Aye, It seems you were right, wizard, they were safe as long as they were in the illusion."

"It was Dorenn who broke it, Mother."

Dorenn took Morgoran's outstretched hand and shook it. He knew it was indeed the old wielder's hand he shook because the man had no intention of showing any affection toward him.

"How did you manage it this time, Morgoran," Dorenn asked.

"Manage what?" Morgoran asked.

"I thought you were dead. Who did those remains belong to? How did I feel your essence? It felt just like when Toborne and Ianthill died."

"Oh, that. The remains were probably one of the defenders of the queen. I set up the incident to warn you and you should have known that. And, I have sent more essence than that into the world by passing gas."

"Morgoran!" Queen Sildariel was appalled.

"I apologize for nothing," Morgoran said making his way back to his ale and cheese at the table.

Sildariel focused her attention Seandara. She looked at her wrist where the imprinted mark of marriage was clearly visible. Curious, Dorenn raised his arm and put it next to Seandara's. His imprint was also visible. When the two imprints were side by side, Seandara's glowed slightly silver and Dorenn's gold. "They did join you two, the mindwielders, that much of the illusion was true." She gestured to the table. "Come, sit, You two will want to have something to eat." Dorenn sat beside Seandara opposite Morgoran and Queen Sildariel. Servants brought fruit, cheese, and drink out to them.

"Morgoran." Queen Sildariel did not take her eyes off Seandara. "Why do you think they married them? Doesn't their side of the prophesy say that the Solicanths will destroy them?"

"Not specifically it doesn't. They have documents that imply it as such, but no one takes scrolls and documents of prophecy seriously anymore. Too many of them have proven to be false. However, if I was them and being equally cautious, I would have married them as per doctrine and disposed of them afterward. After all, individually they pose no threat, but together as the prophecy foretells is another matter entirely. Besides, marrying them was the only way they could be certain."

"Certain of what?" Sildariel asked.

"Certain they are the Solicanths to worry about. Thankfully, they are not, or they *would* be dead. There is another pair out there somewhere. You may rest assured of that."

"So, the enemy will be hunting them now," Sildariel said. "Instead of my daughter and her new husband."

"I would say so." Morgoran took a bite of cheese.

Sildariel began to sniffle. "My poor baby, a Solicanth and married."

Morgoran swallowed his cheese. "Get a hold of yourself, your majesty, the world hasn't come crashing down around you or your daughter yet." Morgoran's face suddenly turned ashen.

"Regret those words, did you?" Dorenn asked.

"Aye, almost immediately," Morgoran replied. "I meant the entire world, not just Endil. I'm sure the city up above can be restored. It isn't as bad as all that."

"What do we do now?" Dorenn asked.

"I will use Asheth's grimoire to send us to the nearest Migarath Portal. You must get to the Sacred Land and your Trigothian army."

"I thought Naneden had that grimoire," Dorenn said.

Morgoran scoffed, "There is more than one copy. I happen to have the original. Migarath's personal copy, in fact. The very one he used to invent the Migarath Portals. He left it to me when I was still but a lad."

"Why didn't Shey and Gondrial steal it from you instead of sneaking into the royal library all that time ago back in Symboria?"

"Simple, Sheyna doesn't know I have it and neither does Gondrial." He eyed Dorenn, "And it had better remain that way."

"When did you know we were caught in an illusion?" Dorenn asked.

"I was not aware of it until we were attacked. I knew I had to help get the queen to safety." Morgoran said in his even voice.

"And you didn't send someone after Seandara and me?"

Morgoran's eyes could have burned holes in Dorenn's head. "When do you feel you'll be able or trusted to take care of yourself? I sent you the message clear enough."

"I thought you were dead!"

Sildariel cleared her throat loudly. "Morgoran assured me you would see through the illusion and take care of my daughter. This argument is pointless since you did exactly as Morgoran said and brought my daughter to safety."

Dorenn sat back and relaxed at the queen's words. "Don't get too comfortable. The mindwielders are still up there somewhere. They are wandering around looking for something."

Morgoran fidgeted, "I hadn't thought of that. How could I have been so careless? Gather yourself up now, Dorenn. I need get you out of here for your protection and for the safety of the queen."

The queen stood, "Why? Are we still in danger?"

"Aye," Morgoran said, "I don't know if Shey ever told you, Dorenn, but you are a direct descendant of Marella Arden." He pushed his chair under the table. "What am I saying, I know you must realize it since your father has become king of Ardenia. She, that mindwielder up there, can sense you. Naneden has twisted her with necrotic magic, but even in the state she's in now, she will want to connect with her kin. She'll seek you out."

"I'm coming with you!" Seandara said.

Dorenn helped her up from the table. "Of course." He took her hand as Morgoran revealed the silver bound tome he would use to transport them. "Won't that spell make a terrible racket to wielders? I remember something about it being loud."

"We're not running from Enforcers, Dorenn," Morgoran said condescendingly. "Who gives a flip how loud it is?"

Queen Sildariel went to her daughter and took her hands. "Be well, my daughter."

"Be well, my mother," Seandara replied.

"Good luck to you all," Sildariel said.

Morgoran nodded. "It's time, you ready?"

Dorenn took Seandara's hand and nodded.

Morgoran cast from the book and Dorenn felt the uncomfortable pull of the spell as he traveled through space.

****

Ni'esa pondered Tatrice and Bren for a long moment. Tatrice could think of nothing to say. She should be looking for the woman to dissolve her marriage to Bren, but she couldn't bring herself to ask yet. She also noticed Bren was being very closed mouth as well.

"You seek me out." Ni'esa began to speak at last. "Because you wish to remove the imprints?"

Bren spoke reluctantly, “We did at first.”

“And now?” Ni’esa asked.

Bren looked to Tatrice for an answer.

“I...” Tatrice wanted to say yes, but the words remained elusive.

Ni’esa clasped her hands together, “Well, the way I see it, you have two choices. One, you can remain married and work it out, or two, you can have me remove the imprint and dissolve your marriage. It isn’t all that complicated. However, keep in mind that if you choose to dissolve the marriage the tradition states that you should never be able to marry each other again. You will be free to pursue others but not each other. If anyone tries to imprint you in the future the imprints will not take. It is now your moment of choosing. What will it be?”

Tatrice looked upon her imprint. It was of a lined flower with a rose and heart in the center. She looked at Bren’s and his mirrored hers. She wasn’t sure now, “I don’t know. I..”

Ni’esa laughed, “You see the imprints never lie. In all my days I have only dissolved one marriage and it was truly a mistake. Most of the time the imprints know who they join and do not make mistakes.”

“You speak as though the imprints are alive.” Bren said.

“Don’t be silly. They are just magical, and magic is in everything.” Ni’esa said.

Tatrice held up her arm and looked at her imprint again. When the two imprints were both side by side, the outline of Tatrice’s began to glow slightly silver and Bren’s slightly gold. Ni’esa’s eyes widened, and she grabbed hold of each arm and placed them side by side. They glowed brighter.

“Solicanths! By the gods, you two are Solicanths!”

“What?” Tatrice asked. “What’s a Solicanth?” She pulled her arm away like it was suddenly infected.

"This can't be," Ni'esa said. "There can't be three sets, can there? Not all living at the same time!"

Chapter Twenty-Nine

DRAGONS

After Morgoran had gotten him to a Migarath Portal, it was only a few short hours after and Dorenn was once again riding toward the desolation of the Sacred Land. He would meet up with the Trigothian army soon. He hoped that giving the enemy their location had not come to anything, but Morgoran warned him not to hope the enemy wouldn't immediately act upon the information and exploit it.

Dorenn ordered his party to stop for the night just a half a day's journey from the edges of the Sacred Land. He knew better than to enter it at night. The Sacred Land was bad enough in the daytime, but at night, the things that roamed the bleak land were much more frightening and dangerous. Seandara left earlier and had returned with a bunch of herbs and plants. She said she was brewing him a sleeping draught. He was sure he would hate the horrible taste of it, so he tried his best to fall asleep before she arrived. He was still awake when she turned back the tent flap. He quickly closed his eyes and pretended.

"I know you are still awake," she said.

"I don't need a draught. I will fall asleep soon enough."

"I just said it was a sleeping draught for Morgoran's benefit. It's nature magic, designed to give you some insight into the immediate future. It normally only works with my people very well, but I can't sure how it will affect you." She prepared to give him the draught and he backed away.

"How do you know it won't be dangerous? You said you can't be sure how it works on me."

"Nature magic works differently than yours. Besides, there is nothing in the draught that will hurt you if the magic fails to work. It's just berries, honey, and a few other things."

Dorenn sniffed the draught. Of course, it smelled terrible. "That does not smell like berries and honey. Are there any draughts that smell or taste good?"

"I asked my mother that once. She said if they tasted good people would overuse them." She held the mug to Dorenn's mouth. "Don't taste it, just down it."

Dorenn pinched his nose and drank the thick, black liquid. It slid down his throat with the texture of mud. For a moment, he thought it *was* mud. It stuck in his throat for a moment, and he thought he would choke. After the liquid went down, he closed his eyes and opened them again to the wretchedness of the Sacred Land. He was standing near the crux of the ancient battlefield, where the main fighting occurred all those seasons ago.

He remembered the dreary landscapes and the lack of plant life and the general lack of color. Recently, as the land rejuvenated, plants and color had returned only to be stifled once again by the decay of Naneden and his army of death. The lich had set up his main headquarters very near the spot where the Oracle had built his temple long ago. His dreary presence had sapped the life out of the area. Not even the sun could break through the heavy clouds. The closer one got to the outskirts of the place, the more dread and fear rose within. Dorenn pushed forward, along with Seandara, until the feeling was almost unbearable. Whenever he thought he was close enough to begin drawing essence, he forced himself to move closer anyway. He didn't want to give into the fear and say this was close enough or good enough. They only had one good shot and he had to be close enough to use it.

At one point, Seandara turned again and was about to run off. Dorenn had to grab a hold of her and steady her long enough to press onward. Another time, they both had to turn away and it was Seandara who regained her senses first and turned them back in the correct direction. The fear was almost unbearable.

At last, they were poised close enough where Dorenn thought they had a shot at drawing in the essence of the Sacred Land without alerting Naneden. He stopped and dropped to his knees. Seandara dropped to hers and they touched their foreheads together, still fighting off the agony.

"I don't know if I can do this, Dorenn."

"You have to. We are Solicanths. According to the Tome of Enlightenment and the Myradon Codex, you and I are the only people alive who can do this. We must do this!"

"It takes all of me to stay and not run off. How am I to draw in essence?"

Dorenn unsheathed *Dranmalin*. "You don't think, you just do."

Seandara slowly removed *Cyrodel* from its sheath. "Aye, don't think, just do!"

Dorenn began to draw in all the essence around him and Seandara began to do the same. When the amount became almost unbearable, they crossed the swords, joining them together. It was as if a full man became hungry again as soon as the swords touched. He was uncertain how much power they could help them draw but it must be all of it.

After what seemed like an eternity, Dorenn could feel Seandara slipping. He shored up the amount and squeezed her hand tighter. "Maybe I should call upon the Silver Drake now."

"Aye," Dorenn agreed. "If you feel it's time."

"What will you do?"

Dorenn kept drawing in essence as he thought about it.

"*What is thy heart's will?*" He heard the familiar words in his head. He knew what he had to do. The Myradon codex stated that they were only capable of holding the power of the Sacred Land with the Silver Drake was if they had the aid of a gold dragon, a being created as near to a god as possible. But he also knew that once he allowed the swords to alter him, he might never turn back.

"My heart's will is to be able to draw all of the essence of the Sacred Land."

"*What is thy heart's will?*"

"Damn it, I want to be a gold dragon, I want to be the Gold Drake."

"*Thy will be done.*"

Dorenn closed his eyes and held onto Seandara as they both changed. It felt surprising like being tickled by a thousand tiny hands. When he opened his eyes, he was looking down a golden maw into the face of a great silver dragon, He bowed his head and Seandara touched her head to his again. They began to draw in essence again, this time it felt as if he were pouring a pitcher of water on hot desert sand. The reservoir seemed endless.

He could sense everything around him, He could sense Naneden. But there was someone else. He shuttered as he brushed the dark, menacing mind. Naneden had a secret weapon. Dorenn should have known when Shey told him that he stayed behind. The mind was approaching from the north. It was still far away but it was getting closer. He had to strengthen his resolve. He couldn't let Vesperin, no matter how much he would try, cause him to fail. No, not Vesperin. Someone else! Someone stronger than Naneden.

Dorenn woke up to morning light pouring in through the open tent flap. Seandara was sitting there with a plate of food.

"No, I was about to see something important."

"You have been sleeping all night. You should have already seen all the draught could show you."

"But I haven't. It was silly. It showed me nonsense about turning into a great golden dragon so I could fight as a god. Ridiculous. Why would I need to be a dragon to fight Naneden? It made no sense. I thought you said it would give me insight into the future."

"I didn't say it would do so in a clear and understandable manner. My people find that the truth is often stranger than anything you can imagine. When someone sees something they don't understand, or that they don't want to see, they often dismiss it out of hand." She set his breakfast down in front of him. "At least you got some sleep, look at it that way."

"Some sleep? I dreamt it away." He took the first bite of his breakfast.

After breakfast, Dorenn went to the nearest hill so he could look out towards the Sacred Land. He thought about the vision. Why would he need to be a dragon? He turned back toward the camp and pulled a Lora Daine from his pocket. "I know I told you I would not use these anymore, Amarantus, but I must know. Am I able to breathe life into someone like I did with that silver fox?" He concentrated on the stone and was soon standing on one of the platforms of Endil. The fires had subsided but the mindwielder still roamed nearby. He could see her on one of the opposite platforms. He went to her. When she saw him, she immediately tried to cast some illusion but, knowing what she was attempting, Dorenn saw though it easily. He walked up directly to the woman and stood face to face.

Without wasting another moment, Dorenn grasped Marella's head and trapped her between his forearm and his chest. The stench was almost unbearable. She was writhing and trying to fight him with jabs from her elbows. He extended his free arm just over her mouth. Marella bit into him and he let the essence flow from his arm with his blood. He ignored the pain.

"If I am a part of you, I will restore you with part of me. All that you were is in my head somewhere. If I bring back your body, I can restore all you once were with the essence you left behind."

Marella let out a whimper. Maybe she understood him somehow. He didn't know, but he chose to think that she did. He let the essence flow to her.

Marella went limp and Dorenn let her fall to her knees. She was consumed, bathed, by the bluish red light of the essence Dorenn had released to her. When the light flashed and entered her body totally, she regained her footing and stood up right, looking with confusion at her restored hands. Marella turned to gaze upon Dorenn.

"Wha..what are you?" She looked at her hands again, "What am I?"

"I come from you. I am one of your descendants. You are Marella. Don't you remember?"

Marella still appeared confused.

"You are Marella Arden, mindwielder from Ardenia. I am Dorenn Adair, your descendant. I know Lady Shey, your friend.

"How can you do this? No one can do this. You can't bring back the dead as they were in life."

"I can because I have one thing no one else does. I have your essence, or had your essence, from the Hall of Ancients. I restored it to your body along with part of me. The part of me that came from you. I alone can restore your body and essence."

"You said you know Sheyna, where is She?"

Dorenn extended his hand. "Come with me. I will take you to her. But I will warn you, she doesn't like to be called Sheyna anymore."

Marella chuckled, "You know, I don't think she ever did."

Chapter Thirty

First Battle of the Sacred Land

"How is this possible?" Morgoran asked when he saw Marella. "She is just as I remember her."

"You're speaking about me as if I am some sort of illusion. I'm standing right here, Morgoran," Marella said.

"And she sounds just like her, too!"

"It *is* Marella. Morgoran." Dorenn said. "Hey, Seandara. "Will you help her get cleaned up and give her something to wear?"

"Of course." Seandara took Marella by the hand. "Come with me. I bet you're ready to bathe and get into some different clothes."

"I am," Marella said. "When will Shey arrive? Dorenn said I will get to see her again!"

Seandara nodded, "Aye, you will. Dorenn says she must be in the camp on the edge of the Sacred Land by now. We are headed that way. You will see her tomorrow if all goes well. I bet she will be surprised!"

"Sacred Land? What's that?"

"Oh, it looks like we have a lot to discuss." Seandara said as she led her to the nearby spring to bathe.

Morgoran confronted Dorenn as soon as Marella was out of earshot, "All right, how did you do it? No one has raised the dead and restored life back to a person like that."

"She was brought back by Naneden."

"As undead." Morgoran said. "She was not among the living."

"I thought I might be able to do something about her since I am a descendant, and I had her essence in my head. It just so happens that I could."

"Do you realize what this means? You can bring life back to the dead. You can turn all of Naneden's army."

"Um, no, I can't. I knew even as I brought Marella back that I must use my own blood. I could only bring her back because I am related to her. I don't think it will work on others and to be honest I would be afraid to try. Growing up in Brookhaven and reading the stories in the library and hearing them told by traveling minstrels, every story where someone is brought back from the dead comes back as not themselves or undead. I think this time is a one off."

"So, why did you do it?"

"Shey said she was a great mindwielder. We will need one. Rennon and the others are still learning, but they don't have anyone to teach them, now they do."

Morgoran nodded, "I must admit. That is smart thinking. I hope she has time to teach them enough."

"If I had made the connection earlier, she would have, but as it stands, we do have someone now who knows the ways of old."

"Aye, better late than never," Morgoran said.

"That's what I'm hoping."

When Dorenn and the others arrived at the camp on the front, the skies over the Sacred Land were choked with the dragons of Draegodor as they brought the vessels containing the lost army of the west. They each, in turn, loosed their cargo on the battlefield. Hordes of screaming soldiers poured out of the vessels and engaged the advancing unseen and undead army. The last vestiges of the army of Trigothia rallied behind them as they hacked and cut through Naneden's army. The dragons took back to the sky, taking out multitudes of Dramyd with dragon's fire and dragon's lightning. From the east came the dragons of Kragodor. The exiled dragons attacked the Drasmyd Duil and Unseen reserves, who were trying to make their way into the thick of the battle.

Seandara came to him with another draught. "In days of old, it was traditional for a leader to use a seer to induce a vision before a major battle."

"The battle is already joined. I don't want to drink that nasty concoction."

"Do you want to fail?" Seandara asked.

"I'm beginning to get suspicious you may be making these on purpose just to make me uncomfortable."

"Drink up."

He drank the foul-tasting brew and settled in to see what may come.

Dorenn kept a tight grip on the undead amulet. If he wore the thing, no undead could see him and the fear of the dead could not take him. However, he could neither draw essence nor release it as long as he held onto it. As he walked through the columns of the undead, he wanted to drop the amulet and use all the power inside him to return them to their final rest, but he knew if he did, Naneden would just change them back. He had to kill the head of the snake to set them all free. He reminded himself that if he had the amulet, the undead would not detect him. If he could just get close enough to Naneden without him detecting he was there, he might have a shot. The phylactery was hanging around Naneden's neck. He would have to destroy it by touching it to the amulet.

He was sneaking up behind him when Naneden commanded his legions to attack. Dorenn was not fast enough to reach him before he deployed his army after all. In the distance, he could hear the battle cries and the clashing of steel against steel. He was a few steps from Naneden, the now familiar fear began to invade his body, but he pressed on. As soon as he reached the lich, he held the amulet before him. He was about to win; he was about to kill Naneden.

At once, the lich rounded on Dorenn and the fear within his body felt it would explode, or implode, leaving him helpless and paralyzed. He involuntarily tossed the amulet up and back into the air. The undead immediately avoided the spot where it landed. Dorenn took off running as fast as he could, waves of fear cascading over him in an attack of panic. In desperation, he willed, forced himself to regain control and he rounded to see if Naneden was pursuing him. He was not. Without the amulet, he knew the undead soldiers would come after him, so before they turned on him and thought of Naneden's phylactery and released what he thought was a small amount of essence. The phylactery exploded taking half of Naneden's skull with it. The lich fell to the ground. For a long moment, the undead soldiers just milled around aimlessly.

Dorenn slowly made his way to the body of Naneden. *It couldn't be this easy.* He thought. It wasn't. As soon as he got within a few feet of the lich, he began to rise from the ground. There must have been yet another phylactery somewhere. Dorenn sighed. He couldn't change the soldiers because Naneden would simply turn them back one way or another. He could change into the gold drake using *Dranmalin*, but he was not used to what he could do with the sword yet and it would not add any strategic advantage in this particular situation. Burning Naneden to cinders or breaking all his bones into a million pieces wouldn't matter. As long as Naneden had another phylactery to contain his essence, he would return. He looked at the amulet. It's the only way. I can channel all this essence through that amulet. He started for the amulet when it occurred to him. He couldn't wield essence while it was in his possession and even if he destroyed Naneden with it completely, without destroying the phylactery, he would still return. Naneden had him. he stared into the black eye socket of the half of Naneden's skull that still remained. The undead began to surround him. Soon Naneden would send them after him. Dorenn was resolved to go down fighting. He assumed a defensive posture.

The undead began to perceive him so he thought he might grab hold of the amulet. At least he could avoid them. Dorenn reached for the amulet, but a wispy, feminine hand beat him to it. He looked into the woman's face expecting to see Seandara, Shey, or Tatrice but instead, it was the blackened and slightly emaciated face of Kimala. She bared fangs and growled at him as she passed him. She had something in her hand, and she smashed it with the amulet. Naneden, who had been regenerating his skulled face, shrank back. Kimala leapt to him and began beating his skull in with the amulet. The undead turned and ran to him piling up over Kimala. A purplish glow came out from under the pile and Dorenn turned and ran with all his might. The explosion sent bodies of the undead everywhere and he was knocked to the ground. When he recovered, he could find neither Naneden nor

Kimala. He did see that the armies were still fighting the undead on the outskirts.

Dorenn pulled himself up. His bones ached and his head hurt. Had Kimala done it, had she killed the lich? He staggered over to the spot where Kimala had rescued him. There was an impression in the ground with the jagged bone of a hand covered lightly with the blackened robes of Naneden. Sinewy wisps of smoke began to rise from the spot and the hand twitched and convulsed. Dorenn watched in horror as it clawed and scratched, trying to find a hold on the loose ground in which to pull itself up. Dorenn began to draw in essence. Perhaps he could destroy Naneden in this weakened state. He set himself with his knees slightly apart, ready to brace himself to cast one massive destruction spell. He faltered, however, when the now familiar disembodied laugh of Naneden assailed the air.

"Hah ha ha!" The voice rasped, "You are far too stupid to be in the position of opposing me, Dorenn Adair! I have already won." The ground parted around Naneden's right hand and Naneden rose from the impression with Kimala, pulled aloft by her hair, in his left hand. He floated to the ground before Dorenn and let the unconscious Kimala fall. He straightened, stared at Dorenn, who was once again in the grip of the lich's unnatural aura of fear and placed his boot on the woman's head. He held his screaming skull staff above his head and brought it down on the woman. In a sizzling torrent of purplish lightning, she convulsed and then disintegrated right before Dorenn's eyes.

Dorenn broke through the barrier of fear and pushed his way through the next wave of fear to come. He released the essence within him and leapt into the air, *Dranmalin* first. The sword screamed and spikes twisted through the handle and into Dorenn's hands and then his arms, becoming part of him. He had never seen the sword do something this frightening before. It took over his forearm and Dorenn embraced it, swinging it at the lich, hacking off Naneden's arm and then slicing through his torso, it swung behind him and found purchase through Naneden's waist on the return. He brought a blow down through Naneden's skull and sliced off a leg. Finally, he planted the tip of *Dranmalin* squarely into the dead man's torso, right where his heart should have been. He pulled the sword back and it released him. His bloodied arm where the sword had taken hold healed almost immediately. He began to draw in essence and he released it on the body parts of the lich in waves, and waves of white hot dragon's fire, burning the bones to ash. He fell to his knees afterwards, *Dranmalin* still in hand. *That had to do it!* He thought. He closed his eyes. The sounds of battle still echoed throughout the land surrounding him, and despite the volume of battle, Dorenn could hear the ground began to crawl, to reform beneath him. He felt unclean as if a hoard of bugs scurried across his skin leaving droplets of dirt. He opened his eyes to see Naneden's body outline reform into the hideous lich. He stabbed the point of Dranmalin into the ground and began to pull himself back to his feet. "Stop! How can you do this?"

Naneden's face formed and his cold eye sockets lit up with the dull green light of undeath. Slowly, garbled, and croaky, the lich found his voice. "Fool, I told you I have won. I was a wielder. You can never destroy me." He laughed. "That is unless you are only going to destroy yourself."

"Did you forget. You have a part of me within you. I was a wielder too."

Dorenn cringed, "The Hall of Ancients! His essence is in my head too. Could I be the last phylactery."

"Of course you're not, but you might as well be. As long as my essence is within you, I will never be defeated by you."

Dorenn placed *Dranmalin* point first to his chest. "I will end it now then" He was a little surprised when Naneden made no move to stop him. He took three deep breaths to strengthen his resolve and then he let the sword pass into his chest.

Dranmalin passed through Dorenn and came out the other side leaving him unharmed.

"The dragon hammer is part of you now. You may wish to destroy yourself, but it doesn't want you to and it won't let you do it either. As long as you are part of that sword, I am afraid, you cannot be killed easily either. My dear idiot. What possible reason did I ever have to keep you alive? You, who were supposed to be the one who would defeat me! I would have killed you long ago if I could have." Naneden laughed again. "There is no fool prophecy, there is no chosen one, there is just you and me forever linked. You can't expel the essences within you and as long as a piece of me resides in you, I am here!"

"There has to be a way. I will find it. I will get rid of you."

"You will try."

Naneden began to falter and stumble. "What's happening? What are you doing?"

Dorenn couldn't help but let his face curl up in his most mischievous grin. "You gave me the power. You see. I may not be able to get rid of the essences within me, but I damn well can control them. If your essence within me is the last vestige of you, I have you within my control just as I controlled Toborne."

"No, you can't. I will..."

"Ah, it is the last of you." Dorenn sheathed *Dranmalin* and clenched his fists. He concentrated. Compartmentalizing the essence of the lich. "I think it's time you left this existence." Dorenn pushed hard within himself and reached out for the skull of Naneden. The lich involuntarily leaned into Dorenn's hands. Dorenn's face contorted as he took Naneden's head and squeezed it between his hands. Naneden screamed as Dorenn absorbed him while crushing his bones. Dorenn's head pounded as the lich entered every part of his being. His eyes burned and his body felt as if he had been immersed in hot, scalding water. Dorenn went to his knees. The pain in his head throbbed. He felt disjointed, almost out of control. The sudden realization that this was the end of his life pervaded his mind. He had taken in too much with all the others and now Naneden. He couldn't possibly contain it all. The feeling that he was being watched made him look up. Standing before him, staff in hand was Vesperin, his steely gaze transfixed on Dorenn's face.

"Is this still a vision?" Dorenn said. He looked to the sky and then darted his eyes looking for some sign he was still under the spell of the draught. He couldn't find any.

Chapter Thirty-One

Left Behind

"Vesperin, I thought the worst for you," Dorenn said. "What are you doing in my vision if this is a vision. Have you come to witness my end?"

Vesperin knelt to Dorenn's side. "In some ways, your fear is justified." His voice was different. It was deeper and it had a melancholy lilt to it.

"I stayed behind for you, Dorenn."

"I took in too much essence, Vesperin. Did it work? Did I take the lich out of this world? Is the danger over?"

"It didn't go exactly as you planned," Vesperin said.

"What do you mean?" Dorenn asked.

"The lich did try to corrupt you, but he failed. I am here for you."

"It seems he couldn't kill me outright. How are you even here, Vesperin?"

"Loracia marked me. Remember Signal Hill? I told you then I had a quest, a new purpose, remember?"

"I remember the temple in Signal Hill?" I remember how Kerad said that Vesperin should not have survived the encounter with the Spectre. I don't remember a quest."

"Signal Hill was the crux of it. Loracia did give me life twice. Once when I was born and once again at the time you remember in Signal Hill, but she also gave me another quest, remember? I told you about it in the Vale of Morgoran. I persuaded you to go along with Lady Shey and Gondrial. I said it was important."

"Aye, now I remember."

"Here, that quest comes to an end. I am here after you discovered the final phylactery. I am here on the bequest of Loracia should you subdue Naneden, as you have done."

"I don't understand."

Vesperin sat down on the ground next to Dorenn. "You must realize the consequence of your actions. Everything happens for a reason. I knew I had to stay behind and confront the lich for some reason and now I am clear on why."

Dorenn felt himself rock back and forth with anxiety. "What is this, Vesperin? Are you dead?"

"I wish there was some other way. You are the battleground. No man was ever meant to take on the evils of this world as you have. You can't contain all that resides within you. It will consume you. It will corrupt you, and it will make you the most significant threat to the peoples of these lands."

"I'm not evil. I have control."

"But you were given the answer to your problem long ago. It's the sword, Dorenn, it's *Dranmalin*. Surely you have come to realize the significance of your sword by now?"

"It's just a sword, Vesperin. It does some remarkable things but ultimately it is just steel."

"Slowly, over time, it has been changing you, preparing you. Your communication with it has grown and it beckons you. It has been set it up for you. This ordeal is not over, and you cannot win otherwise. You must use your force of will to command the sword."

Dorenn stared into his friend's sympathetic eyes, "Now I know something's amiss. Why would you try to convince me of such a lie?" He pushed Vesperin back. "You are not Vesperin."

"Listen to reason, Dorenn. What would I gain with a lie?"

"I'm so confused. Are you on my side, Vesperin? Do you aspire to help me? Morgoran may not like me, but he will do whatever he deems necessary to serve the greater good. He will lend me aid no matter his personal feelings."

"I am here for you, Dorenn. You are being consumed from the inside by all those you sought to defeat. This can go one of two ways. You will survive it or you will become something feared throughout all the known lands."

"Will you kill me?"

"What? No, I will not. You have taken on this burden so the rest of us may live in peace. It would be a grievous error to kill you now."

"Why are you here?"

"I told you. I am here for you. Just remember, the secret lies within the sword, within *Dranmalin*." Vesperin reached out and took Dorenn's face within his hands. "What I do, I do willingly. You need one more thing in order to face what comes. I will bring her to you."

Dorenn tried to pull back. "No, you can't!" Vesperin held on to Dorenn tighter. "Stop it Vesperin!" He pleaded. His friend became bathed in a golden light,

Vesperin met Dorenn's gaze, "My prayers have all been for this. I am your redeemer. Someday, you will understand. My pure soul will cleanse your tainted one. If it takes another thousand years, my sacrifice will redeem you."

"No!" Dorenn tried to pull away again and this time he succeeded. When he opened his eyes, Vesperin was gone. Dorenn dropped to his knees. "What have you done? I should have died. I should be dead now!"

"Now, now, don't be so hard on yourself." Dorenn recognized the voice as Veric.

He looked up at Lady Shey's father. "Veric? What are you doing here?"

"I see you defeated the Lich. Not an easy task."

Dorenn got to his feet and looked around. He could hear the sounds of battle still raging nearby. "I had to destroy him. I couldn't let him tap into the power of the Sacred Land."

Veric chuckled condescendingly. "Oh, there was never any danger of that. He couldn't have possibly drawn more essence than he could naturally. At least, not without doing himself deadly harm. I thought you were taught that early on."

"It was mentioned. But I have personally seen it done. He could have used other means, like the jade statuettes."

"Aye, he could have, but it would have taken thousands of them, perhaps tens of thousands."

"He had a plan, I can tell you that," Dorenn said.

"Ah Naneden, he thought he was so wise and powerful. In the end, he only lived up to be the puppet he was."

Dorenn slowly clutched *Dranmalin.* "I wonder whose puppet?"

Dorenn saw Veric eyeing his hand on *Dranmalin* so he went ahead and readied the sword.

"All right, Naneden did have a plan. You see, only a god could take on such power and use it, and he certainly thought of himself as a god."

"But he wasn't."

"That's why he needed Solicanths. Solicanths count together as a god. A pair of them could contain the power and survive." He glanced around mockingly. "Where is your young bride?"

Dorenn answered with his face flushing red with anger.

"It's no matter, I found a pair of Solicanths long ago." He stepped aside revealing Aela and Jot. "Not that I really need them."

The air around Dorenn's head cracked and he saw two glowing, magical arrows wiz by his ears. Veric blocked the arrows from finding their target.

"Seandara!" Dorenn said.

"I was running to camp with Rennon and then I found myself running toward you here," Seandara said.

"Thank you, Vesperin!" Dorenn whispered.

"What's going on here? Is that Veric?"

"Aye, didn't you know when you fired the arrows?"

"I wasn't expecting to see you with sword drawn against an ally."

Dorenn eyed Veric suspiciously, "Are we allies, Veric?"

"As I was saying," Veric continued, "It takes a god to wield the power welling up in the Sacred Land." He drew in essence so fast that Dorenn barely had time to react. He deflected the shards of essence almost too easily.

"It is true then. Fawlsbane Vex was clever to take you under his wing. He has modified you with all those stolen essences and your Solicanth mate." Veric said. "But you are still no god, are you!" Veric reached up and grabbed hold of his own head. "I'm sorry to have to do this, but I need to shed this mortal soul." Veric's eyes went wide with terror. For a moment, Dorenn heard another voice screaming as Veric ripped his own head in half. Black sooty smoke rolled out of the wound and began to coalesce at his feet. The body of Veric fell to the ground. Aela and Jot fell to their knees, bowing deeply. The sooty black smoke hardened, and a horned creature appeared. It had the face and maw of a dragon and a body resembling a Drasmyd Duil, including the bat-like wings. "There." The creature said. "That was so restricting."

"Aedreagnon!" Seandara whispered.

Aedreagnon laughed and began to pull, not merely draw, in essence in great quantities. "I have done it! I managed to get here right under the nose of my father and now nothing can stop me. I will take this power and defeat him as he defeated Fawl and rule this place in his stead. I will be able to reach the flaming sword of the sun at last." He reached over to Aela's head with one hand and Jot with the other. They both screamed as they melted blood, flesh, and bone and absorbed into the god. "I will even take the two pairs of Solicanths so that they cannot oppose me." He moved with frightening speed toward Dorenn and Seandara.

Seandara jumped to Dorenn before the mad god could reach him and they both fell through the ground beneath them. Dorenn felt the pull of rock and earth as he slid along beneath the surface with Seandara's nature magic. They resurfaced far enough away to confuse Aedreagnon. Seandara held *Cyrodel* into the air. Dorenn instinctively grasped *Dranmalin*. "Do you understand now?" Seandara asked. Dorenn nodded as Seandara called forth the silver drake from within and began to change. *Cyrodel* scraped alongside *Dranmalin* as it became part of the silver drake's claw. The claws on *Dranmalin's* hilt once again dug into Dorenn's arm becoming part of his arm.

"It is my will!" Dorenn shouted as he thrust the sword into the air. He thought briefly of Fawlsbane Vex's favorite creation, the golden dragons. *Dranmalin* cried out in a long mournful howl and began to curve. Golden scales began to appear up and down Dorenn's arm as his sword twisted into a claw. Dorenn felt the pain of golden wings protrude forcefully from his back.

Dorenn jolted awake. He glanced around the room in horror.

"What is it?" Seandara asked.

Dorenn met Morgoran's gaze, "Morgoran! I dare not go after the lich. Defeating him will leave me vulnerable to something much worse. We need a new plan. Our enemies have woven a tangled web. Kill one part of it and the rest becomes almost all powerful."

Morgoran nodded, they are weakening us bit by bit with the death of Ianthill and Sylvalora."

"Sylvalora is not dead." Dorenn said, "I have her essence too and I would know. She lives."

"Then we need to find her." Morgoran said.

"Find who?" It was Rennon followed closely by Ganas. "If you are looking for Ganas, I found him."

"Ganas, it's good to see you." Dorenn said as he extended his hand. "Even if you are late."

"We would have arrived sooner, but we went to the defense of Draegodor first, but sadly we were too late."

"Why, what happened to Draegodor?"

"Destroyed by Naneden's undead drakes from the Gardens of Bone." Ganas said.

Dorenn looked to the skies above the battle, "Where are they now then?"

"We did manage to defeat most of them when we intercepted them on the way here. The only danger is the lich now. We crushed the skulls of the fallen drakes. He should not be able to resurrect them again."

Morgoran took a hold of Dorenn's shoulder, "The battle out there is a mere trifle. Most of Naneden's army is in reserve. He will weaken us down before the onslaught. You have no choice but to go after him."

"But I saw what would happen in my vision. The fury of the lich is not the only danger. In fact, killing Naneden makes things worse."

"And how many of my visions came true? Seeing is not a presentation of the truth. It is merely a possibility. If we don't go after the lich, he will hit the Sacred Land with an army so powerful, no one will be able to stop him. We can't do nothing because of a...a dream."

Dorenn thought for a long moment, "We need to split up again. Someone needs to find Sylvalora while the rest of us plan our attack."

"I will stay." Rennon said.

"Aye, You will. Let me introduce you to Marella. She is my ancestor from the War of the Oracle. She is a mindwielder of old." He went to her, "Will you teach me friend your ways? The ways of the mindwielders? He is untrained."

"I will do my best, but you must understand. It takes years of study to master."

"I do. We don't have years. I know you will do what you can."

Marella nodded, "I will."

"I will go find Sylvalora." Morgoran said.

"Gondrial and I will go with you." Shey said as she and Gondrial entered the party.

Marella and Shey locked eyes. "Hello, Sheyna."

"Marella?"

"Aye, it's me."

Shey faced Gondrial, her eye twitched once, and she fell into his arms.

"Well, that's a surprise." Gondrial said, "This is the first time I've seen her faint in the entire time I've known her."

CHAPTER THIRTY-TWO

A NEW DIRECTION

Veric found Sylvalora in the ruins of the city of Endil. She and Jindara were laid out in the infirmary with sheets covering them when the attack of the mindwielders happened. Veric removed the sheet covering Sylvalora and gazed at her face. He put his hand over the wound. It had already healed up. He searched the room and found the spear of Aedreagnon lying on a table.

"She'll wake up shortly."

"I know." Veric said, "Why are you following me, Xeian?"

"Do you plan to take up your spear again?"

"If I must."

"Why are you here? You knew she would resurrect. Neither Vex nor Loracia would let her die. You know this."

"Because my spear is the reason she's hurt, and she can be hurt even if she will not die. I hurt her once again. I had to come."

"What about the elf. Did she deserve to die?"

"Who cares. She was in the wrong place at the wrong time. You are her god; you do something about it."

"Because it is your fault, I will this one time." He floated over to Jindara and flung her sheet back. He breathed life back into her as he healed her wounds. "Sleep little one." He whispered and she went into a deep sleep.

"What now?" Veric asked.

"I am here to take you back to Venifyre. You can't stay in this man's body any longer. We don't want to suffer father's wraith for not intervening. Will you come with me?"

Veric stiffened, "No, brother. I will not come with you. It is my time to shine." He faced Xeian, "You and Breannan made the elves, father made man, mother gives life, Kellegarn made the dwarves, and Ageanna made the dragons. Mother and Father robbed me of the ability to create."

"Not true, you have managed to create Dramyds and Drasmyd Duil. Did you know Mother has forbidden father from destroying them because she considers them a form of life?"

"I didn't create them. They were created by man. My involvement was miniscule."

"So, you want to create something in this world? Is that your plan?"

"Yes, that is my plan."

"And you are hiding in this man to avoid father?"

"No, he knows already. I hide in this man because he is important, and father would not kill him to get to me. Her will manipulate every event otherwise, but he will not risk killing his precious Veric Namear, father of Sheyna and Kimala."

"I see. You want the power of the Sacred Land to make your creation."

"What do you want, Xeian? Do you want me to tell you my whole evil plan so you can run back to father and inform him? He has his human minions running around all over Rennirus doing his bidding, but he can't stand to let me have my time!"

"I want you to come home so we can talk about all this before anyone else gets hurt."

Veric watched as Sylvalora stirred. She was about to wake up. In that moment he realized he needed to hear his brothers and sisters out. Maybe he was going about things all wrong. "All right, I will go with you to Venifyre." He went for his spear.

"You can't take that to the gates of Mount Venifyre brother."

"You want me to leave it here in the hands of man and elf?"

Xeian went to the spear and picked it up himself, "No, but I am going to carry it."

"Naturally," Veric said as he stifled a grin which he knew would give him away. He followed Xeian to his portal, and from there to the godly realm of Venifyre.

The lich, Naneden, entered the graveyard searching for a recent, unmarked grave. He could sense the power of one of the first trine easily, even in death. His staff with the screaming human head glowed ominously as he floated among the tombstones. At last, he came to a fresh grave with no markers, as if not marking it would make it invisible to a lich. He held the staff out over the grave and stopped. Something caught his attention. There was another presence.

"What are you waiting for? Do it!"

The lich turned to face the presence. The man standing in the graveyard with him was clean shaven, handsome, and well dressed. He had dark hair and dark eyes which marked him as eastern Symborian or even Scarovian.

"Why do you hesitate."

Naneden spoke in his raspy, gurgled lich voice, "You have made good on your promise to return I see. How did you do it?"

"Oh, it wasn't hard. I just had to find a mindwielder powerful enough to create a convincing illusion. The killing of all the mindwielders in the first War of the Oracle has proven useful. There is almost no defense against it anymore. It's a good thing I remembered the amulets and talismans made back in the day to see through them or even I might be susceptible."

"So, Marella worked out for you. I want her back now. I have plans for her."

"You can't have her back."

Naneden enraged, "That was the deal, Bashir! I let you live, and you return her to me."

"I realize that, but Dorenn has found a way to resurrect her."

"She was already resurrected."

"Not like you. He restored her back to the way she was before death! She lives and breathes once more."

"What! That's impossible."

"Well, I don't know what to tell you, but he did. She is with him in the Sacred Land now, on his side again."

The lich cursed under his breath then straightened. "It is of no matter. I will find another mindwielder. Ezra Bannon perhaps. Meanwhile, we have a third of the first trine." He raised the staff and it glowed ominously. A moment later a hand came out of the newly churned earth, then another. A moment later a head appeared followed by the rest of the wizard. Ianthill stood in front of the lich and Rodraq.

"I won't be able to contain him long." Naneden said.

Bashir slithered up to elf and put his hand on the undead Ianthill's shoulder, "Don't worry about that. You may not be able to control him for long, but we don't need to hold him for long. What happens after I cast the spell. I mean what do I do with him?"

"How should I know. You will be in Trigothia. Leave him in the streets of Arden to rot the rest of the way for all care. Just make sure you can use him to start the war. It shouldn't be difficult. The kingdoms are already at the brink."

Bashir tightened his grip on Ianthill, "I'm ready. I'll give your regards to the king."

Naneden took out the silver tome with the travel spells he used to send the Army of the West a continent away and began casting one of the spells. As usual, the sound of the incantation was deafening to him, but he sent Bashir and Ianthill off. He turned back toward the graveyard and shrugged, "I may as well." He held the screaming staff aloft. "Get up you useless lot," he rasped. The long dead corpses began to rise from their long slumber. Naneden managed a raspy, dry sound akin to a cackle before he led the newest members of his undead army through the cemetery gates.

Chapter Thirty-Three

All Things Must Pass

King Lourn busied himself in the first morning hours by pouring over reports gathered by the knights he employed into the different sections of his kingdom. He wanted to keep up with such things because he didn't want to feel silly when the noblemen came to court with tribute or to ask favors and he didn't know who they were or where they were from in the kingdom. He had finished his morning bittering tea and was reading over the final piece of news from the Lord Knight's reports from the day before when the doors of his throne room opened into his study and one of his servants burst into the room. He stopped short of the king and bowed on one knee. Lourn tried to place the servant's name but couldn't quite remember.

"Rise, and forgive me but what was your name again? You are one of my ministers, right?"

"Sire, I am your minister of defense. I am loyal to the crown, and I feel it's my duty in this dire hour to advise you."

"Dellah," Lourn called for his wife, "could you join us in here?"

She came in from the adjoining room, "What is it, Lourn?"

"I can read the signs. I am being advised by the minister of defense, but I think I know what this advice will be about."

The minister began to sweat, "forgive me sire, but I am loyal to the crown, and I cannot in good conscious run away without coming to you first."

"Let me save you some time, minister, the other ministers have never accepted me. I am but a simple innkeeper, not a king. They want the other royal families to be in control of Ardenia."

"Sire? You already know?"

"I just finished reading my loyal Lord Knight's reports. It has as much spelled it out for me. How soon? I mean how long do we have before they storm the gates?"

"Sire, your army is loyal to you."

"My army? The one headed for the Sacred Land, that army?"

"You still have your royal guard, sire."

"I am afraid it isn't enough. The Lord Knight's report informs me Adracoria and Sythia have held back discretionary forces to march against Ardenia. Now that I have deployed most of my men, as they should have done, to defend the dangerous Sacred Land from King Naneden there just isn't enough of a force here to repulse the invaders. This Trigothian civil war will unfortunately be very short."

"What are we going to do, Lourn?" Dellah asked.

He bowed his head, "If I thought they would let us go, I would simply abdicate, but I think in this case, we will need to flee and go into hiding. Our line to the throne is clear and I think the families involved would like to see it die out."

"What does that mean for Dorenn and Seandara?" she asked.

"Dorenn will not be able to come back to Ardenia. He is married to the future queen of Endil. I don't think they will do anything to provoke a war with the elves as long as he doesn't try to make a claim to the Ardenian throne." He smacked his fist on the wooden desk before him, "I never wanted to leave the inn. I am no king. It was foolish for them to bring me here. I am not sure why the other Ardenian royal families even allowed it in the first place."

"If I may, sire. It was because of the reign of your ancestor, Marella Arden. She is still revered as one of the greatest leaders for our kingdom. She was taken from us too early in the War of the Oracle."

"Well, I descend from her, but I am clearly not her. She grew up with the knowledge and training to be a ruler. She was a powerful wielder and trained with the fabled First Trine. If I could bring back even a little bit of her through me, I would, but that is quite impossible."

"Obviously, sire, what may I do to help you in your flight from Ardenia?"

Lourn thought for a moment, "Do you know which family has the strongest claim? Is there a way I can hand over power? I do not wish to simply abandon Ardenia. If I can transfer power before I flee, perhaps I can stop this civil war before it begins."

"I will see what I can do to arrange it, sire."

"Very well. Please keep me informed on your progress."

"I will, sire." He bowed and hurried out.

Lourn removed his crown and put it on the desk. He went to the fireplace and took the scepter he had leaning there and also placed it on the desk. He went to Dellah and took her hand, "Come on. It's time to go."

"What? But you just said you wanted to transfer power."

"When the minster brings in my successor, they will see the crown and the scepter and realize what I've done. They will crown the new king or queen and we will be long gone."

"How will we get out of here without being seen."

"Magic, of course. We are going to use the Migarath Portal and go to the Sacred Land or Symboria as quickly as we can. They don't fool me. They will not transfer power peacefully. I am sure as soon as I hand over power to the new king, you and I will lose our heads. No, it's best we go now."

"Lead the way. I am with you."

Lourn kissed Dellah's forehead and they rushed to find the Migarath Portal room.

Chapter Thirty-Four

The Nightmare Lands

Trendan led the two girls to the spot in Wytchmore where he sensed the magic of the Migarath Portal.

"Are you sure Tatrice and Bren will know where to fly?" Deylia asked. "I feel like we are leaving them behind."

"They know." Fayne said. "Wherever they went after the undead dragon attack must have been somewhere they already had in mind, or the Lora Daine wouldn't have worked. They're fine."

Trendan used a wooden plank to pry the door off the portal room. The metal door was flat and flush with the ground like the door to a cellar. It had been stuck and buried under dirt and sand for ages. Shadesilver knew where the portal was, and she could have helped open it, but she was preoccupied with getting to Tatrice and Bren. Amadace and his sister seemed almost obsessed with it, in fact. It was of no matter to him anyway. He knew they would find their own way to the city of Deadeye in due time. The metal door finally gave way and popped open.

"I hope the portal is still intact," Deylia said. "Why does Scarovia have Migarath Portals anyway? Aren't they a western invention?"

Fayne tried to peer down the hole, "I don't see why it wouldn't be intact."

Trendan answered her second question, "They stole the magic and used it for themselves."

"Oh, I guess that makes sense." Deylia said. "I wonder if they have lost the technology too?"

"More than likely, it's been well over a thousand years."

"More like two thousand." Fayne said, "The portal magic is not forgotten at any rate. Wielders like Lady Shey and Morgoran can still do it."

"Then why don't they?" Deylia asked.

Fayne shrugged, "You will have to ask them. If I had to guess, I would say it's dangerous or something."

Trendan joined in, "Sometimes, there're only so many times one can cast a spell before it begins to affect the caster. It's like handling snake venom. I have seen the Darovan elves use leather gloves when milking their snakes for poison. They said handing it for too long makes you get severe hay fever, chills, and itching, even if you don't touch the stuff."

"So, you're saying they don't cast it because the portals might cause harm over time." Deylia said.

"Yes, that's right. They might only use it for emergencies. Come on, follow me and be careful, we don't know what's down here," Trendan said as he took one of his arrows and wrapped a piece of cloth around it. He glanced at both Deylia and Fayne sheepishly, as if he were ashamed of what he was about to do, and then he spoke the Siladil word for flame. The makeshift torch lit up. Sanmir's gift made him feel guilty like he stole something he shouldn't have. He held the torch out in front waving it to and from into the darkness. The portal chamber was dank and dirty. It smelled as if it might have been flooded a few times over the years. Once they entered the final chamber, the portal itself appeared as every Migarath Portal they had ever seen, except this one was covered with a thick layer of dirt.

Trendan handed the torch to Fayne and began wiping the dirt off with his bare hand.

"Hey, you're kicking up dust." Delia said right before she sneezed.

"Sorry, I have to see the crystals." Knocking dust off as he went, he began re-arranging them. He used the magic he was gifted, and the portal came to life, swirling and sparking just as the others had done. "All right Deylia, you want to go first?" Deylia nodded and stepped through the portal. As soon as she had, Trendan grabbed hold of Fayne's free arm and pulled her close to him.

"Gods help me, Lady Shey was right." He pulled in Fayne and kissed her.

Fayne stepped back. "Lady Shey was right! You mean you meant to leave Vesperin behind with Naneden!"

"What? No, of course not. I meant she was right when she said I love you."

Fayne rolled her eyes, "What are you thinking?" She stepped through the portal, taking the torch with her. Trendan stood there for a moment in the darkness, feeling small. "I am beginning to think spontaneity never works as planned!" he said. Luckily the light of the portal allowed him to find his way through.

When Trendan came through the other side of the portal, the Migarath Portal room was in even worse shape than the one they had just left. It was amazing that the portal worked at all. It had lost one of the feet at its base and the door to the surface was breached. Several of the crystals were missing, which meant it could not be used to leave unless they could locate them nearby. Trendan moved ahead of the girls and poked his head out of the broken door.

"Where did you take us?" Deylia asked.

"I thought I set the crystals for Deadeye, but it looks like we skipped passed that portal and connected with this one instead."

"The Deadeye portal could be destroyed so it sent us to the nearest one to it." Fayne said.

Trendan nodded, "That would be my guess." He glanced around the floor with only the light coming in from the damaged door opening to illuminate it. "I don't see any crystals on the floor. We may be on foot now." He poked his head out to look at the landscape, "There is nothing out there, no city, no town. It's the Nightmare Lands but this portal is out in the middle of nowhere. It's out here by itself." He took out the white Lora Daine Shadesilver had given him. "We should be close enough to Deadeye to use this." They huddled together and Trendan concentrated on the city, but nothing happened. "That's strange."

"Have you ever been to Deadeye?" Deylia asked.

"Once, long ago when I came over with some elves from Arillia on a trade mission. I know what the city looks like. The stone should have worked."

They exited the portal room and stood in the open field.

Fayne bent down and felt the soil, "I think we are in the Scar."

"The Scar?" Deylia asked.

"It's like the Sacred Land only worse. According to my people, it was once the capital city of Scarovia. Their science and magic academy magicians were doing experiments with magic and accidentally wiped out the whole city and everyone in it. Nothing has grown here since, and unlike the Sacred Land, it isn't regenerating magic. It's just a big ugly scar on the land."

"Well, we best get to walking then," Trendan said. "Deadeye and Castle Black are east of here. Maybe if we get out of the Scar, we can use the dragon stone."

"Mother was heading for Castle Black. Will we still beat her there?"

"Hmm, not very likely. I guess it depends on how fast we get out of the Scar." Fayne replied.

Trendan took his bow from his back and tested the string, "Be prepared. I have heard tales of the Scar and the surrounding area."

"Me too," Fayne said. "Giant scorpions and other creatures said to be created by the same evil magic that doomed the Scar."

Deylia gulped, "Giant scorpions?"

"Don't worry. I have the far sight of my people and I can't see anything approaching from any direction." He replaced his bow, "I can also use my bow to do a lot of damage if not kill something long before we have to deal with it hand to hand. This open area gives *us* the advantage."

Deylia nodded.

"We will move swiftly out of this barren place. Come, let's go." Fayne said as she secured her weapons and started off east.

Trendan nodded to Deylia as she followed Fayne before he too followed behind.

They had not walked a mile when the eerie fog began to roll in. At first it was a greyish mist flowing ominously along the ground, but then it began to turn black and became difficult to walk through as if it were heavier than air. Trendan felt he was walking through knee high water. He kicked at it, "What is this mist." His voice sounded strange, like it didn't come from his voice. He looked ahead to see Fayne and Deylia were far ahead of him in the distance. "Wait! Come back. How did you get so far ahead of me?" He stumbled and fell. The black took him. He fought against it and finally stood. Fayne was standing within arm's length of him.

"What's the matter, Trendan. Can't an elf keep up with a human and a Noanas?"

"Fayne."

"What's the matter?" She repeated.

He went back down to his knees. "This place is doing something to me. This mist is evil."

"How can mist be evil?"

"Fayne, it's getting difficult to breathe." He met her gaze eye to eye. She smirked.

"Trendan, did you really think there was nothing in this barren land?"

"You are playing with words. Barren means without. Barren means there is nothing."

"I suppose you are right. This land is not barren after all, is it. After all, it's called the Nightmare Lands. Have you ever wondered why?"

"Yes, have you ever wondered why?" Deylia was now beside Fayne. "Do it Fayne. He wants your heart. Give it to him."

She reached out and took his hand. He thought about pulling it back, but she insisted on holding it. Her eyes went wide and warm. He began to feel her love make him feel better. Still on his knees, he closed his eyes and let the mood flow though him. He longed for her touch for so long. He wanted to feel loved for so long and he let go. She moved his hand closer to her chest. Soon, her hand felt smooth and wet. He opened his eyes and was horrified to see his arm was fully inside her chest and wrapped around her heart. It began beating faster. Fayne appeared to be liking the feeling. AS soon as he tried to pull away the heart would flutter and Fayne would writhe in pain. He got the feeling that if he let go of it, she would die.

“Here, let me help you.” Deylia slipped her hands into Fayne’s chest too. She cupped her hands around his and began to pull at his fingers. Fayne would writhe and squirm in pain every time Deylia tried to pry his hands away.

“No, stop it, Deylia, I have got to hold her heart to keep her alive. Stop tugging at my hands.”

“Let her go.” Deylia insisted.

“No, I cannot. My hand is the only reason her heart beats.”

“Trendan, how will you stop the snake?”

“What snake?” He asked.

“The one wrapping around your leg as we speak. It’s crawling up you.”

He looked at his leg to see a hideous snake with a triangular head and diamond patterns on its back slowly crawling up his leg. He was not afraid of snakes. “I am not afraid of snakes.”

“Trendan. Let go!”

“No, I love her. I will not let her die. I can’t let go of her heart. It will stop beating.” He looked into Fayne’s eyes. She was slipping away. “No! Help me save her, Deylia.”

Deylia pushed Fayne aside and she fell to the ground, hidden by the dense, heavy fog on the ground. Trendan still did not open his hand. He still felt Fayne’s heart in the fog. Deylia pulled out a knife and sliced off his hand at the wrist. He lost his hold on Fayne’s heart and he fell back.

“Did you reach his mind?” It was Fayne’s voice.

“I think I have. The venom is powerful. It’s difficult to dispel its effects.”

Trendan regained his senses and pushed away from the snake wrapped around his arm, now with a blade sticking out of its head.

The snake's fangs slipped out of his leg as it lost its grip on him. Deylia retrieved her dagger.

"This place *is* a nightmare." Fayne said.

He looked at his severed hand, but it was not severed. Instead, he held the head of another snake crushed in his hand. He opened it and let it drop into the black mist. What he thought was his hand was Deylia cutting the snake's head away from its body.

Fayne caught him as he lost his footing. The snakes attacking him were dead, but they had injected him with a lot of venom. "How did you know?"

"How did I know what?" Fayne asked.

"How did you know it was in my head?"

She smiled at him, "That's one of the great things about having a mindwielder friend. She could tell.

"Fayne, I'm sorry. I thought I was being strong. I should have told you how I felt earlier. I thought my silence was protecting you."

"Shhh, don't talk. Save your energy." A single tear rolled down her cheek.

Trendan swallowed hard, "Don't grieve. I am content, now that I have told you what was in my heart."

Her face contorted into an ugly cry. "Deyla," she sobbed. Do something." She started rocking back and forth with his head in her arms. He felt comfort and then he felt nothing.

Chapter Thirty-Five

CASTLE BLACK

Deylia's heart ached as she watched Fayne crying over Trendan. She felt helpless.

"I didn't tell him I loved him back," Fayne said in between cries. "I never got the chance to tell him."

"He's not gone yet. He can't be!" Deylia said. She reached down and slapped his face, "We won't let you go, we won't! She slapped him again and he drowsily opened his eyes.

"Oww. Wench."

"I won't let you go." Fayne said.

The black fog began to clear as it was blown away by the beating of powerful wings. Shadesilver landed near them and Tatrice slid off her back. She changed into her platinum blonde form and rushed to Trendan and Fayne.

"What has happened?" The dragon asked. She picked up the carcass of one of the two snakes. "Nightmare Serpents. They bit him?"

Deylia nodded.

"Tatrice, mind your sister. I need to get to him."

Tatrice tried to get Fayne to move but she would not budge, "Fayne, let him go. Silver is going to cleanse him of the poison."

"What? How did you find us. No, I will not let him go ever again."

"She's delirious. Did she get bitten too?" Tatrice asked.

Deylia shook her head, "I don't think so."

"I'm sorry sis. I know we just found out we're siblings, but I have to get you away from him." She reared back and punched her sister in the jaw, using the aid of her dragon magic a touch. Fayne fell back. She pulled Trendan away from her.

"What will Shadesilver do?" Deylia asked."

"Just watch." Tatrice said. "Dragons are serpents too. She can help him."

Shadesilver reverted into her dragon form. She leaned down to Trendan maw first, "From one serpent to another." She said as she let loose a torrent of greenish fire. Deylia was horrified until she realized he was not burning. The fire was dragon's magic.

"She's burning out the poison. It's the only thing the fire will touch." Tatrice told her. "I just hope she's doing it in time to save him."

"I did." Shadesilver said. "He will be just fine. Thank the gods he still had my Lora Daine, or we might not have been able to find him in time to get rid of the venom."

Fayne began to stir. She woke up and bolted upright. She grabbed her head in regret of the sudden movement, "Hey, you hit me!" She hurried to Trendan's side before Tatrice could offer an explanation.

Deylia stifled a happy cry when he opened his eyes and Fayne kissed his forehead. She held his face close to hers.

Trendan made himself stand. Deylia thought he might collapse. "We travel west toward Castle Black. By the time we get there, maybe this groggy feeling I have will have worn off."

Fayne caught him under his arm, “I will help you.”

“Why don’t we put him on Shadesilver’s back?” Deylia inquired.

“No,” Shadesilver said, “He needs to walk off the rest of the poison. It won’t kill him now, but if he doesn’t walk and burn it off, he will not be at his best if we must fight.”

Scarovia was a nasty place in both the visual and in the literal sense. Years of oppression of its people and bad leadership had taken its toll. The road to the capital was unkept, rocky, overgrown, and generally rough. Deylia managed to get several rocks in her shoe. She would stop periodically to fish one out, and then she would have to rush to catch up with the others, who never seemed to get rocks in their shoes, or they just dealt with them and kept going anyway.

It was close to sundown when they passed through the capital city of Blackburn and made their way up to Castle Black on the hill. The black castle of Scarovia loomed ahead. Its defenses were compromised but that didn’t mean the place was not deadly. The winds coming off the ocean to the west were strong and cold, bringing in dense clouds and solid rain. It wasn’t raining at the moment, but the skies were overcast in dark grey clouds. The castle itself had the appearance of being abandoned but it wasn’t. When Naneden left the place, he left behind more than just undead. He had visited the castle at least once since becoming a lich. Trendan knew he had because there was an undead dragon lying in a pile of bones at the entrance, and next to it was an undead man with remnants of blond hair. From their hiding place behind the rocky outcropping, Trendan turned and leaned with his back to the castle.

“What is it?” Deylia asked.

"The dragon and the man. It's all clear to me now. I recognize the one in human form. It's Golvashala. I don't know when Naneden posted the dragon here at his castle, but he did. That dragon is responsible for creating the Sacred Land, and he is guarding the one place where Naneden keeps his most powerful phylactery. A powerful guard for an important item."

"How will Kimala get past him?" Fayne asked.

"She won't." he said, shaking his head. "She'll have to fight him. Just so you know, if she does fight him, she will lose."

"Can we help her?" Fayne asked.

"I don't know. It seems like an impossible task at this point."

Shadesilver peered over the boulder, "If Amadace and Bren get here soon, we might be able to handle the dragons, even Golvashala."

Trendan, who was still feeling the lasting effect of the poison, squeezed the bridge of his nose between his eyes, "So, what's our plan now?"

Fayne put her hand on his shoulder, "You gonna be all right?"

He put his hand over hers, "I will. Don't worry."

"Look!" Deylia pointed at something near the spot where Golvashala patrolled, "is that her?"

Trendan's keen sight zeroed in on the fiendish face of Kimala inching toward the unsuspecting undead dragon in human skeleton form. "It's Kimala. She is making her move toward the castle."

"Should we help her?" Tatrice asked.

Shadesilver assessed the situation. "I don't see how. More than likely, she will rush inside and draw the two dragons in after her, but the fact remains there will be two dragons in the courtyard of the castle to contend with regardless."

"Use your dragon stone to call Amadace and Bren." Deylia suggested.

"We have been. It's a little tricky since we're not using Amadace's stone." Tatrice said.

"He isn't responding in other words," Shadesilver said, "They must have their own issues to contend with at the moment. They will come."

"I think she's about to confront him." Deylia said, "She's about to be seen."

Trendan watched as Kimala stood in Golvashala's sight and the gold dragon did nothing but welcome her. "Something is strange. She is talking to Golvashala. He isn't attacking her and neither is the other dragon."

"They're in league!" Shadesilver said, "We are betrayed."

Trendan focused on Kimala's facial expressions, "I don't think so. She almost seems...sympathetic towards him."

The other dragon saw Kimala and screeched horrifyingly loud and charged her. Tatrice and Fayne moved to run out in to the open, but Shadesilver stopped them both, "Wait, the gold dragon is standing firm."

Now as a full-sized undead dragon, Golvashala launched in front of Kimala and intercepted the attacking dragon. The battle was short lived as the superior gold dragon crushed the smaller one after clawing it into pieces. After he had dispatched the smaller dragon, he again assumed the form of a human skeleton, and together the two of them entered the courtyard of Castle Black leaving the front gates unguarded.

"Is this some kind of trick?" Trendan asked.

"What? What is it, Trendan? We can't see what's happening." Deylia said.

"I can." Shadesilver added.

"So can I." Fayne joined in, "Mother was protected from the smaller dragon by Golvashala and now they are both entering the castle together."

Trendan hefted his pack, bow, and quiver, "Come. Now is our chance." He left their hiding spot without waiting for the others.

Deylia followed first, "What are we going to do?"

"We're going to do what we came here for. Find Kimala and help her get Naneden's phylactery if it exists." Fayne said.

"What about the dragon?"

"I guess we'll find out." Tatrice said.

They ran to the opening of the gates to Castle Black, all the while watching their surroundings for anything that might pop out of the brush after them. They reached the gates and entered the courtyard of blackened stone that led to a twisted walkway though hedges and trees. All the vegetation was dead or dying and did not provide much cover. Golvashala and Kimala waited at the entrance to the plant choked walkway, relaxed, and composed. As soon as they entered the courtyard, they were exposed. There was nowhere to hide and nowhere to take cover. If the two wanted them dead, the small party had been lured into a perfect position for them to do so.

Kimala stepped forward, "Come, we do not have much time to stop Naneden. We will need to fight our way through the castle to the chambers down below. There's not much here. Just a few undead and some of the unseen, but nothing the dragons can't handle on a whim."

"What's all this about?" Trendan asked.

"Ah Trendan, always suspicious. We are here for the phylactery of the lich, the final one, but we cannot access the chamber without sacrificing a dragon. Naneden thought it to be impossible, so he neglected to post many guards here. No one would be able to sacrifice a full-grown dragon."

“Golvashala?”

“Aye, but there is more. He can’t be in his current state. You are going to have to trust me to get him back to something more...alive.”

Chapter Thirty-Six

CONVERGENCE

The foyer of the castle led to two staircases on either side, behind them stairs leading down. Kimala led them to the stairs leading down. Fayne kept close to her mother. She didn't see many changes in the way she looked like she thought she would. That was until they came to the first unseen monster. She turned dark and ugly, complete with fangs. The unseen became visible thanks to something Shadesilver did.

"There are three of them. I will take the one on the left," Trendan said as he shot an arrow into its eye. Kimala jumped on the one in the middle, tearing into the back of its neck. Deylia made the third one veer off and immediately attack a couple of undead who were shambling toward them. The creature tore them apart before she made it run headfirst into Shadesilver's spear.

"Where are we going? Do you know?" Deylia asked.

"Aye, there is a chamber down below. Golvashala is already there." Kimala replied. "There shouldn't be anymore unseen or anything else in our way now. Whatever lurked near the chamber has likely been destroyed by Golvashala."

They continued down a few more stairs to a darkened hall, and finally to two doors with runes scribbled on them. The magical seal had already been breached, presumably by the gold dragon. Deylia ran her hand along the edges, it had been torn from its hinges by a tremendous amount force. Inside the chamber, there was a circle with runes scrawled on the floor. At the center of the circle stood the gold dragon and someone else.

"Vesperin!" Tatrice cried when they got closer to the center of the room. She ran and gave her friend a hug. Fayne joined her although both Vesperin and Fayne both seemed distant from one another now. The hug was awkward.

"What are you doing here?" Tatrice asked. Trendan shook his friend's hand.

Kimala interrupted, "He's here for the dragon just as predicted. He is a major component for the resurrection of Golvashala just as prophesied, but the context was all wrong. It is *this* resurrection he was supposed to be involved in." she held out her hand to Fayne, and I believe you are supposed to be with him for the ritual." Fayne took her mother's hand and joined Vesperin near the undead gold dragon.

Deylia was in awe, "You predicted this all those years ago while still involved in the War of the Oracle? This is why you went into a deep sleep to awaken here in this place a thousand years later?"

The booming, uncomfortably gruff voice of Golvashala sneered, "Of course I didn't. This is a relatively new discovery. I didn't realize what the prophecy was trying to tell me until Naneden made me into one of the undead. This is the resurrection foretold and the one I saw more clearly a few short years before."

"This ritual requires three blood sacrifices," Vesperin said. "A dragon, an enemy, and one of his children. I believe I have found a solution. The problem is that Naneden has taken precautions and he is intelligent. Our sacrifice today may not stop him."

Trendan rubbed his chin, "I don't understand. You're not saying you're going to sacrifice yourself on a longshot, are you?"

Vesperin seemed confused at Trendan's question, "Yes, that is exactly what we're planning."

"That's not sane."

Vesperin smiled, "Oh, I think I understand now. When I say sacrifice, I mean the blood, not the person. No one need die here."

"Ah, well, you should have made that clear upfront." Trendan said.

"Once the final phylactery is procured, the only way it can be destroyed is when it is near the lich. The closer it gets to him the more vulnerable it becomes, which is why it is stored here in the first place. I have been studying this for some time. Ever since I made the choice to stay behind. This is the only way."

Deylia watched as Vesperin prepared for the ritual. The room was situation with three alters where the blood of the three participants would need to be collected but they had a specific order. If the wrong blood when to the wrong alter, it would not open the chamber with the phylactery. The other aspect of the ritual Deylia was worried about was the most difficult and the most important part of the ritual, the resurrection of the oracle Golvashala. The dragon was their enemy. He started a magic war that formed the Sacred Land. He was the reason everyone was fighting now and Vesperin wanted to bring him back to defeat another evil? "Excuse me," she said, "But aren't we just trading one evil for another? If you bring back the oracle, who was already defeated by the lich once, and then you defeat the lich, isn't that just substituting one for the other?" She looked at the undead human form of the oracle, "I mean no offense of course, but you *are* the root cause of all this trouble. Would Sylvalora and Lady Shey allow this if they were here?"

Vesperin gave her an exasperated stare, "I don't know you, but I will answer you. As I have stated, I have studied this plan for quite some time. I have conferred with my goddess, Loracia, about it. I have even died and been resurrected myself so I could gain the knowledge of how to do this ritual. The life being restored is a gift from Loracia herself and she would not allow it if she didn't believe it was for the greater good. Once we get the phylactery, it will be Golvashala who flies Kimala to the battlefield to destroy it with the lich." He kept preparing his sacrificial knife, "Of course you do realize, Golvashala, that should you feel the need to betray us, Fawlsbane Vex himself has vowed to deal with you."

"I do." Golvashala wheezed.

"Good, now, I am ready to preform the ritual." He took the knife and laid it down on one of the altars. He went to the oracle and began filling the undead man with golden light from silky words he spun into ribbons of light. He channeled the life-giving power of the goddess Loracia and used her power to restore life to him.

The oracle looked at his hands and then felt his face. "It's a miracle!"

"Aye, a miracle of the goddess of life," Vesperin said. He led the oracle to one of the altars, "Are you ready?" The oracle nodded. Vesperin took his hand and cut a gash into his palm, the blood dripped onto the altar and began running down a trench carved into the stone extending out from it. Vesperin went to the next altar and cut Kimala's hand to do the same thing. Finally, he went to the third altar and cut his own hand. The blood from the three alters when to the center and intermingled. "Now, for the final component." He stopped to look at each id his friends, "I want to say how much I love each and every one of you." He went to Fayne, "I hope you see it was not me you were looking for but Trendan, the true friend of the Noanas."

"Vesperin, this was not part of the ritual you described. What are you planning to do." Fayne asked.

Trendan stepped up and took his forearm as the circles carved in the stone behind him began to light up and spin, "You said no one need die."

"And I meant it. I am here on borrowed time from the gods, my friend. I have already been to Venifyre. I will now return, forever."

Trendan held on to his arm, "I won't let you."

"Trendan, you would keep me here? In this place of torment and pain rather than let me ascend to the next plane with everlasting life?"

Trendan stared into his eyes for a moment and then released him. He went to the middle of the altars and into the swirling vortex. There was a flash of light then it all went dark and silent. Deylia felt her way to one of the sconces and brought down a torch. She lit it with essence and the warm, dim light filled the room. She went to the center of the altars. A black obsidian statue of a dragon was there on the floor. Kimala rushed to pick it up.

"The phylactery," She proclaimed, "Golvashala, are you ready?"

The man nodded, "We will need to get out of this chamber first and then I will transform.

Trendan took a deep breath, "Shadesilver, see if you can call Bren and Amadace again. Thery need to find us. It's time to join Dorenn in the Sacred Land.

Dorenn took a sip of the searing hot bittering tea. It was so hot, he almost sloshed it out of his cup when he jolted from the unexpected tongue burn. He looked up to see Morgoran with his hand shielding his eyes from the sun. he was peering up at the clouds. Dorenn decided to join him. He hadn't taken two steps when he realized what Morgoran was looking for in the partly cloudy sky. Two specs were coming closer, but one of the specs was a decisive red. When they got a little closer, he could see them better, but he knew Morgoran had probably already surmised who they were.

"Who is it?" Dorenn asked.

"Your friends are converging here at camp. I believe those dragons carry Tatrice, Bren, and the others."

Dorenn smiled, that is good news. Trendan? Is he with them?"

Morgoran looked at him intentionally, "Cast the sight spell and see for yourself."

Dorenn looked at he spec in the sky, "Aye, he is." He pointed to a soldier nearby, "You, please inform the general we can plan our battle strategy now. My friends have arrived." He went to get his sword *Dranmalin,* but it was not where he left it. He searched around his tent and then around camp to no avail. He went to Seandara to see if he had left it with *Cyrodel* and just forgot, but when he got there, he found Seandara searching for *Cyrodel* too.

Morgoran saw him looking behind some water barrels in camp, "Did you lose something?" he said lightheartedly. Dorenn glared at him. His expression turned serious, "Dorenn?"

"Someone has stolen the swords."

"What? I thought maybe you lost the water barrel ladle or something."

"No, I remember where I put the sword and so does Seandara. Someone has stolen *Dranmalin* and *Cyrodel.*"

Morgoran cursed under his breath, “I should have known. I don’t know how they were stolen but I’m sure I know by whom they were stolen.”

“What do we do now?” Dorenn asked.

“There is nothing we can do except move forward with our plans anyway. We can’t let this be a setback.”

Dorenn nodded.

Chapter Thirty-Seven

Wrath of the Solicanths

Dorenn and Seandara met with Morgoran just outside of the spot where Aedreagnon had his workers were constructing his new fortress. The Sacred Land around them was now teeming with life and Dorenn had never felt so much power. He had to hold it away from him because he felt as if it were seeping into him against his will. He knew if he tried to draw in essence the normal way as he always did, he would be flooded with it uncontrollably. "It's like trying to hold back water from spilling out of a full container."

Morgoran chuckled, "Yes, I suppose it does feel that way." He stopped to survey the construction going on. "Whatever you do, should Aedreagnon try to get to Aela and Jot, don't let him. They are also Solicanths."

"Where is our army?" Seandara asked.

"They're just over the next ridge waiting for my orders," Dorenn said. He pointed to the ridge.

"There's a runner coming from that ridge," Seandara said.

Dorenn squinted to get a look. Seandara's elven sight spotted him before he did, "Hmm, I told them to maintain position. I wonder what they're up to."

"They had better not be moving." Morgoran said.

They waited a few minutes until the runner managed to get to them. He straightened once he stood before Dorenn and stuck out a piece of parchment, "A communication from Ardenia, sir."

Dorenn took the parchment and broke the king's seal that told him it was authentic and read it. His face must have given away there was trouble.

"What is it?" Seandara asked, "You just turned white as a corpse."

"My mother and father have fled the capital under threat of death. The remaining Sythian and Adracorian forces have taken Ardenia. My father has been deposed."

"Well, he never liked being king. I think you should keep this secret. You don't want your army falling apart now, right before battle." Morgoran said.

"They waited until we drained all the soldiers from Ardenia and then had their way. Those conniving fools. They must have kept a reserve of men back just for this."

"You can deal with them later. As long as your parents are well, don't let this dissuade you from the task at hand." Morgoran said. "Far worse will happen if Aedreagnon seizes the Sacred Land."

"I have been meaning to ask you. What happens if we defeat him? The balance will be off, right? We let Aedreagnon free by freeing Veric in By'temog but as long as he was captured the balance was secure. If we can't manage to kill him, wouldn't Fawlsbane intervene?""

"Fawlsbane will not kill one of his own so he will not intervene. I don't know what will happen. I just know we need to prevent the mad god from installing himself as the leader with the power of the Sacred Land behind him. I'm sure Fawlsbane has a plan in place to make certain he is still the most powerful god, but he won't intervene directly any more than he already has. His intervention is you, me and whomever else he has put in the path of Aedreagnon. He is depending on us to take care of the threat."

"Do you think he's in there?" He pointed to the massive construction.

"Aye, he's in there. The longer we wait the harder it will be to oust him. Are Bren and Tatrice in position with the dragons?"

"Aye, they are. I am depending on them to wipe out most of the undead army. Now that Naneden is out of the picture, the enemies' numbers should not swell from our fallen."

"The archers are in place?"

Seandara nodded, "Aye, I talked to the commander in person a few hours ago."

Dorenn nodded too, "Rennon and Marella have the mindwielders ready to come down the left flank. Shey and Gondrial have the infantry and the wielders who showed up ready with Trendan and Fayne leading the second wave. I think we're ready."

"Use the Lora Daine and call forth the dragons." Morgoran said.

Dorenn took the dragon stone and turned it in his hand. His nerves were raw, and his heart began to pound. He spoke the words to summon Shadesilver and Amadace.

Gondrial saw the dragons take flight. Wave after wave of them lifted into the air. "That's our sign," he said. He turned to the general at his left, "It's time to move." The general signaled his men, and the columns began to march. Once the men were on the move, he waved to Rennon who was off to the left on top a hill. He used a tiny bit of essence to make his hand a beacon of light so the mindwielder could se it so far away. "Whoa!" he said, feeling lightheaded.

Shey put her hand on his arm, "What's wrong?"

"Nothing, it's just I tried to illuminate my hand and I nearly burnt it off. You don't have to draw any essence in; it's just there waiting to be used. It's almost too much."

"Aye, I feel it too. I shudder to think how our enemies will use it. Will they exercise restraint or use it full force and destroy themselves in the process of destroying us?"

"They probably won't be careful with it; you can bet on that. I think we need to remember our defensive incantations and shields while we are marching. I think they will come in handy when the battle is joined."

"How long until battle?"

"I am thinking as soon as we top the ridge, maybe a little further, but we have the high ground. The dragons will take care of the first columns of undead. We just need to get into the building with Dorenn and Seandara. That's where the real battle for the Sacred Land will take place."

"When we get in there, don't leave me behind no matter what happens. I don't want to repeat the War of the Oracle."

"I won't, Shey."

"Promise me, Gondrial."

"I promise I will stay with you and make sure you are by my side."

She intertwined her arm in his, "You had better keep that promise."

Gondrial looked to the skies, "Brace yourself. Look."

The dragons from Kragodor were flying in to intercept the dragons of Draegodor. Behind them were legions of Dramyd and Drasmyd Duil.

***

Dorenn saw the dark dragons coming in and the Dramyds behind them. Down below him, heading for the construction, Morgoran hurried to find a spot where he and Seandara could slip in without being detected. Dorenn lingered for a specific reason. The dark creatures of Aedreagnon had no idea what was about to hit them. Hidden in the ground away from the prying eyes of anyone working on the construction were the elves, specifically the elves from Darovan. They had made it possible to hide the Dramyd and Drasmyd Duil who had defected to his side. He signaled the lead elf to unleash them and they came from the ground in numbers. The dark creatures were taken by surprise and the first fighting of the new war for the Sacred Land began. Dorenn ran for the spot where Morgoran and Seandara waited for him. They slipped into the interior of the building. The workers were now scattering for cover as dragon fire erupted overhead. The hordes of undead milling around outside the construction began to meander toward the advancing armies closing in from the nearby ridge. He ran until he caught up with Seandara. She was close behind Morgoran as he pushed his way to the inter chamber where the dark and ominous form of Aedreagnon sat on a golden throne. Aela and Jot were not far away sitting on their own.

If Dorenn, Morgoran, or Seandara was expecting him to ramble on about them showing up or the war raging outside they were mistaken. He immediately sent cascades of blackfire at them without so much as uttering a word. They all three dived for cover.

"Remember, don't let him get near the Solicanths!" Morgoran shouted. Aedreagnon attacked him, striking him down. He moved to the wielder and bore down on him until the old man was coughing up blood. Dorenn took Seandara's hand, and they both drew in essence. Seandara dropped them down through the marble floors and they moved at break-neck speeds while Dorenn sent out his own plumbs of blackfire. Jot was knocked back when they emerged from the marble and Aela swung her golden sword at Dorenn's head and missed. He scanned the throne for a view of either *Dranmalin* or *Cyrodel*, but he didn't see them. Perhaps the god was smart enough not to bring them to the chamber. He called out to his sword, but it did not come.

Seandara reached Aela and wrapped her in vines she brought from beneath the stone. The evil Solicanth lost her arm as the vines harshly and forcefully attacked. The power of the Sacred Land made it nearly impossible to hold back. "They are undead!" She shouted to Dorenn.

He sent blackfire at Jot and dodged an attack from the mad god, "He doesn't want us to defeat them. We need a cleric of Loracia."

Seandara smiled wickedly, "No, we don't." She slid to him and embraced him.

"What are you doing?"

"We are also Solicanths," She whispered in his ear. He understood. He embraced her in a tight grip and began to draw in the massive amount of essence the Sacred Land offered. What he couldn't handle flowed into her. The two of them rose into the air. Jot and Aela ran for Aedreagnon. Morgoran tried but he failed to stop them from getting to the mad god. He put a massive hand on each of their heads and began to draw in essence too. Dorenn tried his best to pull the essence away from the god to himself. As he drew it in, he didn't feel the restraint of when he was doing it by himself. Combined with Seandara, he kept drawing it and it seemed endless. Sparks of lightning began to fly from their entwined bodies tearing off large chunks of stone from around the room. Out of the corner of his eye, Dorenn saw Morgoran take cover.

Then before Aedreagnon could rise to full power, Dorenn and Seandara let go of the incredible power within them and struck the god over and over again. In a fit of anger, he crushed both Aela and Jot. They were ineffective compared to the power he wielded now with Seandara anyway. He kept striking the god, tearing out big chucks of flesh as he did. But no matter how many times he hit the mad god, Aedreagnon was able to replenish himself. Dorenn was still drawing essence when suddenly he felt the essence the god was pulling in change direction; he was now on the defensive, using all the power to preserve himself. Dorenn redoubled his efforts and tried harder. He was going to kill the god! He pushed harder and harder. He could barely make out a voice calling his name. At first, he thought he was imagining it until he saw Morgoran waving his arms to get his attention.

"Dorenn, look at Seandara!" Morgoran shouted.

He looked into Seandara's face and realized he was killing her. She was able to supply him a lot of essence but just not enough to kill a god. He let the blackfire fall and they both fell to the floor, their clothes smoking from the dry heat. He was so thirsty. He crawled to a table where a water bowl and pitcher waited. He took the pitcher of water, and even though he was incredibly thirty, he knew Seandara was thirsty too, so he took it to her and made sure she drank from it first. After all, he had almost killed her with essence. After Seandara was done and he took a long drink, he finally focused on Aedreagnon. The god was lying in a pool of thick, black fluid. He did not appear to have breath or movement. With the help of Seandara he had killed the mad god. He watched as Morgoran approached the corpse. Morgoran stumbled back when the mad god's arm began to move. He was extremely weak, but he was not dead.

Dorenn met Morgoran's concerned gaze. The old wielder nodded to him, "This is my destiny. As my brother said. You cannot deny your destiny. Sooner or later, it will have its way with you!"

"No Morgoran! Let us recover and we will attack again."

"You won't recover fast enough. This is the only way." Dorenn felt the essence flowing into Morgoran at an alarming speed. He knew it would not be long before he drew too much. The resulting expulsion of essence from him would finish off Aedreagnon, but unfortunately, it would kill Morgoran too.

Chapter Thirty-Eight

To Defeat a God

Morgoran prepared himself to face Aedreagnon, but Dorenn grabbed his arm so he couldn't go.

"Let me be, Dorenn. Let go of my arm."

"Listen to reason."

"You listen to reason. We almost have him. I can do it. I know what I'm doing." He pulled away from Dorenn. Essence began to flow almost visibly into him. He focused on the mad god who was stirring. He was aware of the bodies of the two dark Solicanths near him. They were already undead, so the god could still use their residual power even though they were no longer living or aware. He released a tiny bit of essence to push them out of the god's reach.

Aedreagnon began to chuckle. It was low laughter at first and then it escalated until it was a cackle, "You have failed, Morgoran. I still live. You are merely a shadow of the first trine. Ianthill is dead and Toborne is long gone. You are the only remaining member. What hope do you have?"

"There never was much hope between my brothers and me. We did our best, but even magic cannot fix the crippling pain that comes from the soul. I could have done things differently, but it is that pain from deep within that makes and breaks us."

"A nice sentiment. I suppose it is appropriate here at your demise, no, the demise of the first trine." He chuckled again. "Years of wisdom dies with a whimper." He sent a torrent of blackfire at Morgoran. The old wielder diverted it and it slammed into a nearby wall, obliterating it. "Why fight now, Morgoran? It's over. Your champion and his Solicanth wench are defeated. By the time they recover, I will have killed you."

"Your power is limited, Aedreagnon. Fawlsbane has abandoned you and your brothers and sisters will not come to your aid. Whatever power you still possess is it, there is no more. I don't have to use all my power. I just have to get you to use up yours."

"You think so?" He manifested a flaming sword and went after Morgoran. The old wielder manifested one as well to parry the god's blows. Now Morgoran was worried, if Aedreagnon planned to fight him hand to hand instead of using magic, that would be in the end of him. He was weak with a sword. He made his way to where Dorenn and Seandara was trying to use the abundant essence to speed in their recuperation. "Dorenn, *Dranmalin* and *Cyrodel* must be here somewhere, see if you can find them. I can't hold him off this way for long."

"Ha! You believe I would bring the weapon foretold to defeat me to a fight? Surely, you don't believe I would be so foolish."

Morgoran blocked another hit and Aedreagnon spun around and knocked him off his feet. He had to use essence to deflect the next blow. The manifested sword in Morgoran's hand dissipated and he backed off barely evading another blow. He threw a magical shield over his head to deflect the next, but even though there was copious amounts of magical essence for him to draw from, he was getting fatigued. He knew the god was about to break the shield and finish him. He met Dorenn's gaze and tried to put on a sympathetic face. He knew that after he fell, the god would then go after Dorenn. The shield dropped and Aedreagnon smirked in triumph. He raised the sword for the final blow.

"To all things come an end." Aedreagnon said. He let the blow fall, but it did not cleave Morgoran into two pieces. Instead, Morgoran opened his eyes to see a very angry Sylvalora holding off the sword. Behind her stood Toborne in his familiar green robes.

"Get up you old fool." Toborne said. "The first trine isn't as dead as he thought."

Morgoran smiled, "A change of heart?"

Toborne looked at Sylvalora, "A change of spirit." He drew in magical power and sent cascades of blackfire over the god. Sylvalora changed into the Silver Drake and attacked furiously.

Toborne cast a spell over Dorenn and a Migarath Portal opened above his head. He flinched trying to get away, unsure what Toborne was doing. A red hewn Drasmyd Duil flew through the portal carrying two swords. It landed before Dorenn and handed *Dranmalin* to him.

"I told you. You would not regret letting me go."

Dorenn held his sword in his hand. It began to claw its way into his forearm, becoming one with him. He leaped at the weakened god and shoved the blade in his chest. *Dranmalin* burned away the god's flesh as it entered. Aedreagnon screamed and fell to his knees. Dorenn removed the blade and let the god fall to his death.

"It's done!" Seandara said running to Dorenn. "The Silver Drake is free to pick a new high lord and the Sacred Land is secure." She gave an exhausted Dorenn a hug.

Morgoran shook Toborne's hand, "I knew you had it in you, brother."

"I'm glad one of us thought so." He pulled Morgoran to him and embraced his brother.

Toborne nodded at a now normal Sylvalora and she gave him a single nod back.

Morgoran knew they had finally come to terms in their long feud just as he had with her when she released him from his curse, "Well, the war isn't over. I can still hear the rumbles of war out there."

Toborne clasped his hands together, "Now that the mad god is dead, let's go have some fun!"

Morgoran followed him out of the great hall with a limp. Every part of his body still ached but he wasn't going to let Toborne know about it. Sylvalora came up behind him and put her hand on his shoulder. He immediately felt better as her healing touch tingled throughout his body.

Dorenn handed Seandara her sword, "Once I can draw essence again, we should go help wrap this thing up."

"I agree. What should we do about the body of Aedreagnon?"

Dorenn glanced back at the dead god, "Let him rot for what he's done and who he's killed. When we get out of here, I will bring this building down on him and it can be his tomb." He took a step and realized Seandara didn't move. He looked into her eyes and saw fear, then he felt it. It was subtle at first but began to build. He recognized the fear he felt when in the presence of the lich, Naneden. Two possibilities ran through his head. First, there was another lich since Naneden was supposed to be dead with the destruction of his phylactery in Scarovia, or second, he had been lying in wait for the right moment to strike. Dorenn let *Dranmalin* sync with him again as he turned to face the danger. Naneden, in his skulled-faced horrific appearance hovered near the mad god's corpse.

"Imagine," he rasped, "the resurrection of a god. A god that must do my bidding."

"Naneden! How?"

"Your kind always underestimates the dead. You see, we are difficult to kill because, and this may come as a shock to you, the living, we are already dead! It's kind of like trying to make water more wet."

"They told me your phylactery was destroyed."

"I had another. I am a lich. I live and die by essence and the power kept in my phylacteries. The knowledge gained by all those years with Morgoran and Toborne experimenting with jade statuettes, and you still do not understand the concept of storing essence, do you."

Dorenn reached into his pocket and grasped the undead amulet. He still had it. But if he put it on to use it, his ability to draw essence would be impaired. He harkened back to his vision with Seandara's draught. Was that playing out for him now. He glanced at Seandara who was completely petrified with fear. She did not have an amulet to take the brunt of the fear Naneden was emanating. He looked around the room as hordes of undead had been slowly entering for the past few minutes, surrounding them both. The vision he had a while back did teach him one thing. The longer he waited the harder this was going to be. *Dranmalin* was the key, it allowed him to not only draw essence, but also to tap into the magic of the dragons. They told him the sword would be the key to defeating the lich. It dug deep into his forearm, consuming it. He heard the familiar words in his head from *Cyrodel, what is thy heart's will*? He observed the sword twisting itself into the stunned Seandara's bare forearm, and the pain of it released her from her fear.

Naneden, quick to see what was coming, raised his screaming human headed staff and began to raise the mad god from his death.

"I will be the Gold Drake." He said reluctantly.

An awful cackle from Naneden made him feel foolish. "That dream is well known. But I must inform you there is no such thing as a Gold Drake. It is a product of that amulet you carry. It isn't real. It is a twisted version of a vision your wench there gave you. That harlot, Kimala will not show up to save you either."

"The sword is the key."

"It's not a very good key, is it. You have failed in every way possible to stop me. There is nothing more you can do. It is time for me to raise this undead god and finally be done with you and your kind." He turned back to the talk of resurrecting the god.

"My heart's will?" He took *Dranmalin* and began to draw essence from it. In turn, the sword drew from the Sacred Land like a bridge of power. "Seandara, bring me your sword." She was still frozen in fear. He moved toward her and clasped *Dranmalin* directly onto *Cyrodel* and the two swords sung out arousing Seandara from her trance. Dorenn pulled essence from Cyrodel too and the sword also began to act as a bridge of power. At first, he was planning to use the power to destroy Naneden, but at the last moment, he realized the lich's words. He could not be killed. He instead took a deep breath and just as he took in the essence of Toborne and other wielders before him, he knew he could do the same with Naneden. After all, as a lich, he was just a very powerful wielder. He used the power the swords afforded him to draw in the essence of the lich just as he was trying to resurrect the mad god.

"What? What are you doing?" Naneden cried out.

"I am getting rid of you." Dorenn stated pouring in the power of the Sacred Land. Seandara was knocked back, but *Cyrodel* remained connected to Dorenn even after she had dropped it. Dorenn felt the essence of Naneden tear way from whatever in this world it was still clinging to and enter him forcefully. His eyes burned and his heart ached, but he did not faulter, he just kept drawing in the lich. Even when Seandara was screaming and crying at his side, he continued to take in the lich until at last the deed was done. The mad god remained dead, and the lich was contained within his soul. But he soon found he could not move. He could not see. He was in darkness with the presence of the lich in his mind. It took all he had to contain him.

CHAPTER THIRTY-NINE

THE SACRED LAND

Seandara watched helplessly as Dorenn stood on the highest point of the Sacred Land. His red eyes glowed and burned with curls of smoke flowing from the corners. He held out his right hand and accepted Morgoran's shackle. Seandara let out a little startled whimper when Dorenn uncontrollably snapped at the archmage. Gondrial took the opportunity and shackled Dorenn's right hand and bound it tight. Dorenn snorted at him, clearly struggling for control now.

Seandara took *Cyrodel* to the stone table where the dragon king Amarantus stood and placed it next to *Dranmalin*. She tried to look up into Dorenn's face, but it was far too painful. But she may never see him, her husband again, so she looked. His face was red and demonic. His eyes were burning red hot. He had the mad god, and countless others fighting for control of him. He was in there somewhere too, but lost, maybe forever. He smiled wickedly at her, and she had to turn aw ay.

King Amarantus covered the two dragon swords and bound them. He stood before the stone alter next to the table and placed them inside it. He slid the stone enclosure to seal them inside forever. "We called this land sacred because of a magic war. We patrolled its borders as if it had significance and weight in our world. We fought over it when it promised great power to whoever controlled its borders. Now that power is used to keep all other threats at bay. No one may use the power of this land. It will forever regenerate to hide and keep our sins from ever plaguing this world again. Once the darkness is bound here, this land truly will be sacred...forever. Dorenn Adair may not hold out all of the evils we have visited on these lands. I am certain evil will still find a way to rear its ugly head in ways unimaginable, but he will contain the evils we made and visited upon ourselves."

Morgoran, Gondrial, and Lady Shey joined hands. Seandara felt a tear fall when she noticed Lady Shey was holding back her own tears. Essence swirled around and Seandara could visibly see it now. The ground that Dorenn stood upon rumbled and contorted. He screamed in torment as the ground sank beneath him and rock and stone folded in over the edges to contain him. Seandara knew that the wielders would bury him deep beneath the Sacred Land. After what seemed hours, they stopped and erected a massive magical seal over the little building made from the stone of the Sacred Land. Almost as soon as they had sealed the new dark one's prison, the land began to purge the Sacred Land. Grass began to grow, and trees, and flowers, as if they were simply just being held back and were now able to grow freely.

Seandara walked to her husband's prison. Shey took her in a hug. "I am so sorry, Seandara. I can't imagine what this must be like."

"No, you really can't," Seandara whispered. She put her hand onto her stomach where Dorenn's child grew inside her.

"You will be in the only one permitted here from this day forward. It will be up to you to take care of him. If you do not want the responsibility, you should tell us now."

"He is my husband. I will take care of him as long as you keep searching for a way to free him from this prison one day."

"You cannot ever let anyone else visit him. You are shielded from the corruption by being his Solicanth."

"I said I would take care of him, and I will. I don't need your warnings. No one will ever come here but me. I promise you that."

Golvashala watched from afar. He had slipped away after the final battle and later found out that he was mistakenly dismissed as missing in battle. The fools thought he was killed in the fight between the dragons. Of course, he did scatter some of his golden scales here and there to feed the rumor, but the reality is he escaped. This is the first time he had been out of hiding in fact. He had to see what they were planning to do with Dorenn. It could affect his future plans. He also stayed out of sight so he could make sure Fawlsbane Vex had not made good on his promise to keep an eye on him. As far as he could tell, the god had completely forgotten him. Maybe he thought he was dead too. At any rate, Dorenn was secure. Golvashala made his way to a spot where he was sure he was ou of sight and took on his dragon form. He flew away into the crisp, winter afternoon skies on his way to Denosia.

Chapter Forty
Aftermath

"Lady Sheyna Namear, do you take Gondrial, son of Gondolar to be your husband?" There was a moment of hesitation and she looked into Gondrial's face for comfort. He cleared his throat nervously. She smiled at him. "I will."

"And do you, Gondrial, take Lady Sheyna Namear to be your wife?"

"Of course I do!" He leaned in and kissed her full on the lips.

"You may now...em...kiss your wife, apparently." the priest of Loracia said.

They both ran down the aisle hand in hand to the reception hall where there would be much feasting.

"So, where's the honeymoon, Gondrial? Morgoran asked.

"Nowhere near the bleedin' Sacred Land. I can tell you that much!" He replied.

Everyone laughed uproariously, but Marella could feel the undercurrent of sadness, and she could see it in the face of Seandara wherever she caught a glimpse of her face. Marella let her eyes fall upon little Cael. He looks so much like his father, even with the addition of pointed ears. He was just over a season old, and he was already tall for his age.

"I thought we might travel to Arillia. The isle is beautiful this time of year and I don't think Shey has been there in quite some time." Gondrial was saying. "I should like to visit home, just to see if it's still there if nothing else."

Sylvalora stepped up and hugged her daughter. "I always knew you would marry, but I never suspected it would be to Gondrial."

"How are you adjusting to your new life, mother?" Shey asked.

"I'm doing fine. There is one issue I must continue to address but other than that I am great. Venifyre is truly my home now. Toborne's penance keeps me busy most days."

Shey put her hand on her shoulder. "I know you have had a tough time adjusting."

"I take comfort in that fact you are still here and happy."

"I will always be here for you, mother."

"And I'm glad you have finally found happiness. Go on your honeymoon and be happy."

"There you are my bride. If you will excuse us, mother, we have a honeymoon to get to."

"I will," Shey said before being carted off by Gondrial to talk to other wedding guests.

Sylvalora noticed Seandara off to herself, so she decided to talk with her. "Hello, Seandara."

"Oh Hello," Seandara said.

"Have you heard anything from Tatrice, Trendan, or Rennon?" She already knew but was still trying to make small talk.

"Tatrice and Bren are still helping to clean up and rebuild Draegodor with the other dragon knights. She was going to come to the wedding, but little Annah took sick."

"Oh, I still love that name, Annah. They named their daughter well. I don't blame her for not coming. Traveling with an infant can be dangerous."

Trendan and Fayne are off somewhere doing something. I can't ever get a straight answer from Morgoran whenever I ask about them. I think they are looking for the lost Noanas race, The remainder of Fayne's people. They are convinced they are still out there somewhere. Rennon and Deylia are in Trigoth. Deylia wants him to learn her way of life. She says it will give him culture. I think they are taking it one day at a time, as far as romance is concerned, I think Rennon has all but won her over now."

"Good, good." Sylvalora leaned in close to Seandara. "Look, I'm not going to beat around the bush. I want to go down there with you the next time you go."

Seandara stepped back. "What? What are you talking about?"

"I know you go to see Dorenn. You travel through the ground. I want to visit him."

"I don't... I mean, you can't. I was told to never let anyone else visit him. The corruption he contains is too dangerous."

"I will not be corrupted. I am the Silver Drake. If I get permission from Morgoran will that convince you?"

"I suppose."

"I will go fetch him. Wait here." She went into the wedding guests and brought the old wielder back to where Seandara stood.

"Sylvalora says she wants to travel with you to Dorenn. It's perfectly all right. She cannot be corrupted by the likes of Naneden."

Seandara sighed, "All right, meet me at my house at dusk. I will have a maiden watch Cael.

"Good, be sure to have your Lora Daine. We could use mine but I would prefer travel with you rather than the other way around."

The air was cool after the sun had gone down, but pleasant as Sylvalora knocked on the door of Seandara's house. A nice, new, well-constructed building near the Tower of Morgoran in Symbor. She could hear Seandara through the door.

"That's my friend, Frieda. We will be back in a couple of hours. Cael is bathed and ready for bed. He will most likely want you to read to him." The maiden said something back that she could not make out. "All right. Go to Morgoran if you have any problems. She opened the door and rushed out.

A moment later they were standing near the building where Dorenn was imprisoned far below. Seandara took hold of Sylvalora's hands, and they sank into the ground. She remembered traveling through the ground wand she also remembered how much she hated it. They entered the chamber and went directly to where Dorenn remained shackled. He was deformed and hideous. He opened his eyes in the light of the luum crystals when Seandara lit them, they were glowing red and smoldering. He began to fight his chains when he saw Sylvalora. He seemed to be instantly soothed by the presence of Seandara when he laid eyes upon her.

Sylvalora took a deep breath. "Sorry Seandara." She used her dragon magic and Seandara fell asleep. Dorenn went wild, pulling at his chains and roaring with anger. She managed to put him to sleep as well. "You have been trying to tell everyone something, but no one was listening," she said, "Fawlsbane is a shameless fool for letting you suffer this long before telling me how to free you." She moved aside the stone covering hiding the two dragon swords *Dranmalin* and *Cyrodel*. She pulled them out of their resting place.

A black mist formed around the floor and then formed into an old man. "Well, that was unexpected. I never thought you would call me foolish."

Sylvalora glanced at him, "What else would it be to let him suffer like this?"

"I had to. Making this containment vessel is hard and it takes a lot of time. I knew as long as the swords were nearby, and he remained in the Sacred Land, he would be able to contain the lich. The swords were the key all right, constantly channeling essence from the Sacred Land above to him. If I could have destroyed the thing within him outright, I would have but it was made by Aedreagnon, and it still contains the last remaining vestiges of him. Dorenn here is not only containing a lich, but he is also keeping a god at bay as well.

He opened his hand and made an obsidian statuette appear out of nowhere. He held it toward Dorenn and drew out Naneden and the vestiges of Aedreagnon into the vessel.

Dorenn stirred awake and looked at the old man, "Fawlsbane?"

"Aye, my boy. I have come to finally free you. You did well." He held up the obsidian vessel, "I have them in here now. They can't escape." He put the vessel on the altar and cast a seal over it so it would stay in place. "Go head and wake her now, Sylvalora."

The Silver Drake waved her hand and Seandara woke up. She took one look at Dorenn and embraced him. "I have come every day," she sobbed.

"I know you have," he said. "I can't wait to meet our son!"

Chapter Forty-One

Legacy

Ganas Nashe stepped off the ship onto a pier in Anisport, Denosia. The city was very different now. The corruption and dingy appearance of the place had gone now since the defeat of Bannon. He was surprised to see the wolf-like people of Verel walking the streets freely. Speaking of Verel, he was waiting at the end of the pier dressed in a fancy coat and nice trousers waiting for him.

"Verel? I don't think I have ever seen you dressed so nicely. Did you dress up for me?"

"Ha, you wish. This is the normal dress of my people. With the evil soldiers gone, my people and the peoples of the city came to a peaceful treaty. Never again will a foreign invader take this city unless they can kill all the Lupinese and humans here first."

"I'm glad to hear it. Sounds like your people can finally live in harmony."

"Aye, it just took a tragedy and an occupation to do it."

"Well, if that's what it takes to open people's eyes..."

"Certainly," He eyed his friend, "But you have not traveled all this way to talk about politics have you."

"No, I suppose I haven't."

"She knew you would come back. I told her not to hold her breath, that she would likely never hear from you again, but still she waited."

"I don't know what to say."

"Don't say anything. There she is."

Ganas looked straight ahead into Azura's big brown eyes. His stomach fluttered. Her mouth curled into a smile. He dropped his bag and went directly into her open arms and kissed her. He was home.

Kimala twirled the black statue containing the phylactery of the lich Naneden between her fingers. No one seemed to notice she didn't destroy it as planned. They had contained the lich in Dorenn and still they did not notice the lich should have been destroyed or weakened enough to be defeated. Her daughters did not seek her out either. The taint the lich had put on her must have done its job and masked her from them. She peered out the window at the cold land known as Scarovia and watched as the people tried to rebuild after the war.

She scoffed at the phylactery, "I have you now. You will not control me."

"Oh, but I already do."

Kimala watched as Naneden paced the floor in front of her. He looked like the madman she was forced to pretend to be her lover. She knew she was seeing things. He wasn't there. He was in her head. He was a figment caused by the taint he had put on her. Every night she was forced to re-live the taint when she went out hunting for food. Here in Scarovia, people were used to her kind, but were too stupid to do anything about it. She felt the pull through the phylactery to go to the Sacred Land where she knew the lich was probably contained somehow, since she found out Dorenn had emerged from the tomb. The lich wanted the phylactery and his freedom no doubt. She put the phylactery away in its little case she had made for it. She put it away because night was coming soon, and she was hungry.

The End of *"Fury of the Lich"* Book 5 of Shadows of the First Trine Epic Fantasy Series.

ALSO BY CLEAVE BOURBON

Tournament of Mages Series:

Red Mage: Ascending Book 1

Blue Mage: Equinox Book 2

Black Mage: Cursed Book 3

Green Mage: Metamorphosis Book 4

Grey Mage: Protector Book 5

White Mage: Rhapsody Book 6

Enter the Arena Book 7

Prequel The Seventh God

Shadows of the First Trine Series:

Book 1 The Harrowing Path

Book 2 Serpent in the Mist

Book 3 Seer of Shadows

Book 4 Undead Inheritance

Book 5 Fury of the Lich

Prequel Shadows of Yesterday

War of the Oracle Series:

Dragon's Blood Book 1

The Cursed Phylactery Book 2

Wizards of War Book 3

Lurker in the Shadows Book 4

GLOSSARY

Adracoria - Southernmost Trigothian kingdom. Ruled by the Adrac family.

Aedreagnon – (a-dray-ag-non) One of the eight gods. First son of Fawlsbane Vex and Loracia. He never did have the creative sense and the drive of purpose like his younger siblings. Instead he was jealous of their creative genius and often used their creations to make followers of his own (Dramyds and Drasmyd Duil out of dragons, etc.) He would also teach his disciples to do the same.His jealously tended to make people misunderstand him and label him as evil.

Ageanna - One of the eight gods. Creator of drakes and dragonkind. Youngest female child of Fawlsbane Vex and Loracia. Fawlsbane loved her creation of dragons so much he made his own (golden and silver dragons) and even created dragons to guard the realm of the gods, Venifyre.

Amadace -Dragon in which Bren serves as First Knight.

Amalease Stone - Stone used to gain entry into the gates of Draegodor. It is located on Mount Urieus.

Amar - Race of high men from Lux Amarou. First creation of Fawlsbane Vex.

Anisport -Largest port city of Denosia, across the Great Sea.

Arasyth/Sythia - Trigothian kingdom between Adracoria and Ardenia, host to the Great Sythian Forest. Ruled by the Arasyth family.

Ardenia - Northernmost Trigothian kingdom. Ruled by the Arden family.

Arillian Elves - High elves from the Isle of Arillia. They migrated to the Isle of Arillia at the end of the first age after their forests became grasslands and the area now known as Ishrak had become cursed. They are the fairest of elves and most elegant.

Are'dune - Race of men who can trace their origins to Lux Amarou and the Amar but are not considered truly high men.

Ascendic Root - A potent root made into a tea and drank. It relieves pain depending on the dose. Higher doses cause euphoria. Weak tea relieves the minor pain of headaches, etc., while strong tea relieves severe pain.

Asheth's Grimoire - An ancient tome containing spells of essence used to travel magically over distances. It is believed that Migarath used spells from the grimoire as a basis to build his famous Migarath Portals. (See Migarath Portals.)

Bannon, Ezra -A powerful mindwielder and ally to Toborne. Also the reeve of Briarwick, Adracoria.

Basillian - One of the great port cities in the kingdom of Symboria. Basillain is located in Northern Symboria, south of Seabrey. Due to disputes and treaties, Basillain is the port city in the north for trade with Adracoria. Seabrey is the northern port city for trade with both Ardenia and Sythia.

Bittering Tea - A strong brew made from the grinding of the bittering bean. It has a distinct aroma and is usually consumed in the morning as a stimulant.

Breannan - One of the eight gods. Oldest daughter of Fawlsbane Vex and Loracia, co-creator of the race of elves, lover of trees, nature and things that grow.

Bren - Dragon knight from Draegodor. First Knight of Amadace.

Brendlewyre - See Theosus Fiderea.

Broodlord - Common name given to a dragon knight with high ranking. (A brood is a family of something. A broodlord would be a high member of a family or lord of the brood.)

Brynna -An Arillian, elf maiden, healer. She is the eldest daughter of Erinthill, and Ianthill's niece. She resides on the Isle of Doom (Rugania).

By'temog -The largest city of Ishrak, it was once the kingdom's capital city. It fell into ruins after the curse of General Sythril. The general is currently trapped as a ghost there, lurking among the ruins.

Chamber of Ancients -An ancient room in the citadel of Rugania (the Isle of Doom) where youthful wielders take part in magical trials. It is also a place to cure essence sickness if necessary.

Darovan - Island continent southwest of the tip of Adracoria where some of the elves of old migrated. Home to the Siladil and Noradil elves.

Delanora/Delanorasylva - Dragon-speak name for Shadesilver.

Dellah – Former Inn mistress of the Tiger's Head Inn in Brookhaven, Symboria. Currently the queen of the Trigothian kingdom of Ardenia, Mother to Dorenn Adair.

Denosia - Mysterious kingdom on the continent across the Great Ocean.

Deylia -A young Trigothian woman who befriends Rennon in the capital of city of Trigoth.

Dorenn Adair - Innkeeper's son from the village of Brookhaven in Southeastern Symboria. Son of Lourn and Dellah Adair.

Draegodor (*Dray-go-door*) - The city of red. Home of the dragons not in exile, nestled deep in the Jagged Mountains.

Dragon Claw - Parrying sword (dagger) of a dragon knight. Not actually a dragon claw but made of metal.

Dragon Fang - Sword of a dragon knight. Not actually a dragon fang but made of metal.

Dragon Knight - Men, elves, dwarves, and Scarovs who have chosen, or have been chosen by the dragons, to serve as knight protectors of the dragon realm.

Drakkius - Symbolic leader of Abaddonia.

Dramyd (*Draw-mid*) - Winged creature created from drake eggs. Designed to kill, they do the bidding of Aedreagnon, Drasmyd Duil, Naneden, and Toborne.

Dranmalin/Draenmaulin - An ancient sword forged by dragons. Its name literally means dragon hammer in ancient dragon-speak. It magically binds to its owner. It is currently Dorenn Adair's sword after leaving Signal Hill.

Drasmyd Duil(*Draws-mid Do-ill*) - Shapeshifters. They are cunning and deadly. They usually lead packs of Dramyds. They are also known as Shadow Lurkers. They answer to Toborne.

Duil Clan -Clan of dragonkind Toborne used to create the Drasmyd Duil. Their specialty is shape-shifting into other beings.

Endil - (Foreshome) Home city of the wood elves (Sylvan, Eridil) located deep in the Great Sythian Forest.

Elanadil - Name of the magical sword of Ianthill. (It is a purely conjured sword.)

Elvander - Name of the magical sword of Seancey Namear.

Enowene (*IN-O-ween*) - Arillian elf and younger sister of Ianthill and Erinthill.

Eridil - Elven name for wood or Sylvan elves. They are the only race of elves that did not migrate; instead, they made their home in Endil (Foreshome), where they still remain. They are shorter than Arillian elves and have slightly darker skin, but are still considered fair and wise.

Erinthill - Arillian elf and fraternal twin sister of Ianthill, mother of Brynna.

Essence Sickness - An illness caused by the unskilled use of drawing essence for magical purposes. It usually occurs to first-time wielders who have yet to be trained. It does not occur, however, if the wielder discovers he can draw essence as a child (before puberty). The illness is characterized by wild mood swings, delusions of grandeur, and eventually insanity. If left untreated, the insanity will be followed by death. Wielders afflicted with essence sickness often speak uncharacteristically of themselves, and say things they would never say otherwise.

Fawlsbane Vex - God, co-creator of the world, and father of the gods. Husband of Loracia, Goddess of Life.

Ganas Nashe(*Gann-is Na-shae*) - Scout from Brookhaven for the king's army of Symboria. Finder of the Lost Army in Denosia.

General Rellagorn -Leader of the army of the North and West. Killed in Denosia by Jac Wills.

General Sythril -General of Sythia who fought in the Ishrakian war. He hired seers to curse the leader of Ishrak so he could win. When the seers cursed Ishrak, they warned him not to follow the beaten army, but he didn't listen. He pursued the opposing army back into Ishrak in order to defeat them unconditionally. Unfortunately, he led his army into a doomed land where he eventually became part of the curse he created.

Golvashala - A golden dragon also known as the Oracle. Golvashala means gold scales in dragon-speak. He is the cause of the War of the Oracle that created the Sacred Land. He is also called Kambor in common tongue.

Gondrial - First apprentice to Ianthill. A longtime friend of Lady Shey.

Hadder -An apothecary in Trigoth who brews potions that affect the mind.

Ianthill (*E-un-thill*) - Member of the holy trine (First Trine) representing elves Xeian, and Breannan. (Favors ruling with compassion, kindness, and a people's majority.)

Imprints/Imprinting - The act of putting matching images, etc., magically into skin. Some cultures do this to signify marriage in which the imprints serve where gold or other precious metals made into rings might serve in other cultures.

Ishrak - Northern kingdom bordering Symboria, the Jagged Mountains, and Ardenia. The kingdom was cursed and remains a forbidding, desolate land full of danger. Only small pockets of man, elf, and civilized folk live there.

Jac - Member of the lost army.

Jungle Elves - See Noradil.

Kambor - Common tongue name used by the Oracle, Golvashala, when in human form.

Kellegarn – One of the eight gods. Creator of the race of Dwarves, he loves all the earth and rocks and gems and taught his creations the ways of stone and mining.

Kerad - Powerful cleric of Loracia currently serving in the Vale of Morgoran and therefore serving Morgoran.

Kimala – Former mistress of Naneden, A spy of Enowene's spy ring.

King Amarantus - Lord and ruler of the dragons of Draegodor.

King Occelot -Thesomewhat sniveling, and sometimes incompetent, ruler of the kingdom of Symboria.

Kragodor -The black city. Nestled in the treacherous Mountains of Madness in Ishrak, Kragodor is home to the exiled dragons who were last known to serve Toborne.

Kyrie -Mysterious, sometimes-companion of Lady Shey. He is a Kylerie elf, which is an elf about half the size of an Arillian Elf. He loves danger and intrigue. His strange habit of showing up when events go wrong drives some people to wonder where his allegiances lie. Dorenn believes Kyrie is more than he seems.

Loracia (*LORE-race-E-uh*) - Goddess of life and mother of the gods.

Lora Daine-(lora dane) (AKA dragon stone) Stone of the dragons and dragon knights used for communication between dragons and their dragon knights over long distances. Depending on the size and magic of the stone, it can send small parties instantly across short distances. It can also sometimes be used to send its user back and forth between stones over greater distances. Dragon stones are rare to normal peasants. Only people of stature (other than the dragons and dragon knights) are allowed to use them.

Lourn – Former Innkeeper and owner of the Tiger's Head Inn in Brookhaven, Symboria. Currently the king of the Trigothian kingdom of Ardenia, Father of Dorenn Adair.

Lux Amarou - Continent in the northwest formerly inhabited by the Amar, (high men). The oldest cities of man are on Lux Amarou, but they are all mostly in ruins now and inhabited by the ghosts of the dead, among other agents of death and destruction for an age past. A few of the living still reside there, but not many.

Lux Enor - Capital of the west. Home city-state of the highlord. The highlord rules over all of Trigothia, Symboria, and what's left of Ishrak. The last highlord, Rastafin Stowe, was assassinated without leaving an heir. To avoid any power vacuums, only the magical Silver Drake can choose one worthy enough to sit on the highest throne in the land. After Rastafin Stowe, she has yet to proclaim a successor, so the throne remains vacant. A warder presides over the day-to-day affairs, but has limited power.

Malantis – One of the eight gods. Third son of Fawlsbane Vex and Loracia. God of the oceans, seas, lakes, rivers, and everything water related.

Melias - Monk of Fawlsbane Vex. Guardian and sworn protector of Dorenn Adair. Now transformed into a creature called the Brae Daun Duil.

Mindwielder/Mindwielding -Sometimes referred to as mentalism, this is what people who can use magic of the mind, with or without drawing essence, are called. One difference between a mindwielder and a wielder is that mindwielders possess the ability to talk to each other mentally (telepathy).

Morgoran- AKA Morgoran Cleareyes. Member of the holy trine (First Trine) representing man and Fawlsbane Vex. He is reputed to be the most powerful wielder who has ever lived. (Favors balance in ruling.)

Mount Aroanian -A mountain peak in the Mountains of Madness of Ishrak.

Mount Urieus -A mountain peak in the Jagged Mountains where people are sent to wait for permission from the dragons to enter into Draegodor.

Myradon - The first and most powerful gold dragon created by Fawlsbane Vex. He guards the ethereal gates of Venifyre.

Myradon Codex - The lost tome written by Myradon that contains the magic of the dragons. It contains a powerful dragon's fire spell, which is executable by potent wielders of essence.

Naneden (*Na-NEED-den*) - Symbolic leader of Scarovia. He is considered to be mad by all who know him.

Nine Cards -A simple card game enjoyed primarily in Symboria as well as parts of the Trigothian kingdoms.

Noanas - Lost race of high dwarf.

Noradil - Elven name for the shadow or jungle elves of Darovan. They migrated along with the Siladil but found the desert too open and sparse. They moved into the dense jungle of Darovan and started harvesting the plant life there to make poisons, medicines, and magical elixirs. Most apothecaries are Noradil.

Oberan (*Oh-ber-ann*) - First dragon knight of King Amarantus.

Rennirus – The name of this realm and everything in it.

Rennon - One of Dorenn's closest friends. Apprentice to Sanmir, the apothecary of Brookhaven, Symboria. He is a powerful mind-wielder and the healer of the mindwielders formerly known as the afflicted.

Rodraq (*Rod-rack*) - Lady Shey's man-of-arms.

Rugania - Island off the coast of Sythia, across the sea from Darovan. Also called the Isle of Doom, this is the place where wielders were once trained by masters in the art of wielding. It is nicknamed the Isle of Doom because anyone trying to sneak on the isle without the wielders' consent and preparation often died before they crossed the beaches.

Sand Elves - See Siladil.

Scarovia - Kingdom east of the Jagged Mountains, home of the Scarovs, or Scarovians as some cultures call them.

Seabrey -Large port city in northern Symboria. Trade city of the north for the kingdoms of Ardenia and Sythia (see Basillain).

Seancey (*SHAWN-see*) - Ranger of Symboria stationed in the Vale of Morgoran, brother of Lady Shey.

Seandara (SHAWN-dar-a) -Princess of Endil (Foreshome). Has a reoccurring dream of Dorenn.

Shadow Elves - See Noradil.

Shadow Lurker - Pertains to a Drasmyd Duil. A nickname.

Shila - Dwarf who helped Lady Shey after she escaped her kidnappers.

Siladil - Elven name for the sand elves of Darovan. They migrated to Darovan and learned to live in the harsh desert conditions. They are notoriously hard to see while traveling across sand, and they can sink down into it as if they were submerging in water. They are fierce fighters and are almost impossible to defeat in the desert. They have darker, sun-kissed skin and light eyes. They are shorter than the Arillian elves and considered to be more primitive.

Sildariel -Stern matron, queen, and leader of the Sylvan elves of Endil.

Solicanth - The joining of two celestial beings through time. They are either a force for great good or a source for great evil. They sometimes live in harmony, but more often than not, they clash. If they live in harmony, they are usually very integral to the peace and prosperity of the kingdoms.

Steban -First dragon knight of Charna (one of King Amarantus' sisters).

Swordmaster Grint - Villager of Brookhaven who taught young village boys (and sometimes girls) the way of weapons. He was an infantry man and good friend of Lourn Adair.

Sylvalora (*SIL-va- lore-a*) - The Silver Drake, sometimes traveling companion and mentor to Lady Shey.

Symbor - Capital city of the kingdom of Symboria. This city was once called Paladine and is not to be confused with Old Symbor, which is now a ruin in the Sacred Land. Old Symbor is the original home of Shey and Seancey.

Symboria - Oldest kingdom of men on the continent proper, home to the race of men known as Are'dune, descendants of the Amar from Lux Amarou.

Tabac -The giant leaf of the tabac plant that is shredded, dried, and cured to fill a pipe.

Tatrice – Former kitchen maiden in the Tiger's Head Inn in Brookhaven, Symboria. Currently she is the first female dragon knight and the first dragon knight of Shadesilver the white dragon.

Toborne - Member of the holy trine (First Trine) representing Aedreagnon and the Scarovs. He tried to steal the Silver Drake but failed. (Favors cut-throat politics and ruling by fear.)

Trendan - Half-elven friend of Dorenn from the realm of the woodland elves. He has lived in Brookhaven most of his life.

Theosus Fiderea - A dragon hidden in Trigothia as an apothecary.

The Archers of Endil - Elven archers from the city of Endil (Foreshome) who have built a reputation as the most feared archers ever known. They are of the Eridil (Sylvan elves) and have never known defeat.

The Defenders - Similar to the Enforcers except that they only patrol the Sacred Land.

The Enforcers - A band of men dedicated to enforcing the law against magic in Symboria and Trigoth the city. The Enforcers are dwindling in numbers and are not actively recruiting. They are considered abominations by those who are left that can wield essence because they are also essence wielders who chose to follow a very different path, which is unforgivable.

The Great Sythian Forest - Huge forest stretching the whole length of the coast of Sythia from north to south. It is the home of the Eridil, among other creatures.

The Isle of Doom - See Rugania.

The Jagged Mountains - Huge mountain range that separates Scarovia and Abaddonia from the West. It is the home of dwarves, Dramyds, and Drasmyd Duil, among others.

The Lost Army - The army of the North and West, lost near a city called Anisport, a whole continent away from where they should be.

The Mountains of Madness - Mountain range in the northern part of Ishrak. Not only are these mountains infested with orcs and foul beasts but it is also home to the black city of Kragodor, city of the fallen (evil) dragons.

The Sacred Land - Huge tract of land once belonging to Symboria that hosted the War of the Oracle and was devastated into a wasteland unable to support life or feed essence for wielders. It is guarded as a reminder of what magic can do to the land and is the reason magic use was outlawed in the southern kingdoms.

The Sea Goddess - A wooden clipper ship captained by Felladane and first officer Edifor.

The Silver Drake - A statuette made of pure silver inset with ruby eyes made by the First Trine to select the one man worthy of leading the kingdoms of the West as overlord or highlord. The gods themselves took up the Silver Drake and each bestowed into it their own gift. It is unknown what many of the gods' gifts were, but the goddess of life, Loracia, gave the Silver Drake the gift of life. Fawlsbane Vex gave it a will and mind of its own.

Tolennor Forest - Forest southwest of the Vale of Morgoran. It is haunted and cursed. The cursed village of Signal Hill was located in this forest.

Tome of Enlightenment - Tome given to man by the god Fawlsbane Vex, laying down the guidelines and ability for man to do magic.

Trigoth - Once the capital city of Trigothia, it was split into three sectors each belonging to the three Trigothian kingdoms of Adracoria, Ardenia, and Sythia.

Trigothia - Ancient kingdom of the three major houses of Are'dune men. In the civil wars, the three families separated the kingdom into the three kingdoms of Ardenia (Arden family), Sythia (Arasyth family), and Adracoria (Adrac family).

Trine – *Definition* - A group of three. The First Trine is the three first disciples: Morgoran, Ianthill, and Toborne.

Tyre -City near Seabrey, Symboria. Last city before advancing to Mount Urieus.

Vale of Morgoran - Vale with the Tower of Morgoran at its center. Once the tower stood there alone, but after Morgoran was cursed to see only the future, a small village cropped up at the tower's base and expanded. People hoped that Morgoran could cure their loved ones or predict their future. Even though Morgoran is no longer cursed, the village still functions and remains.

Venifyre (*Ven-nee-fear*) - Realm and home of the gods. In ancient dragon-speak first created by the gods, *y* is represented as an *ea* sound, so Venifyre is not pronounced *Ven-nee-fire* but *Ven-nee-fear*. So Genidyre would be pronounced *Jin-nee-dear*, not *Jin-nee-dire*.

Veric Namear -An assassin and father of Lady Shey. He was forced against his will to abandon his family when Sheyna was still a toddler. He was possessed by the god Aedreagnon and imprisoned in a library within a cursed city patrolled by undead.

Vesperin - Orphaned cleric of Loracia from Brookhaven, Symboria, and close friend of Dorenn.

Vetell Fex - Monastery located in Symboria, named after the brother of the god Vex. Vetell Fex simply means Fex's home.

War of the Oracle -A war started by Golvashala (the Oracle) to rid the land of magic so he could take over and rule. He was defeated and presumed dead. (This war created The Sacred Land.)

Winterhaven - A festive winter holiday in the Trigothian kingdoms Symboria, Ishrak, Darovan, and Arillia. It is a popular date to get married in the Trigothian kingdoms.

Wielding -The ability to magically draw essence from everything around that contains essence and wield it to accomplish higher functioning magical feats. Drawing too much essence from one area may devoid that area of its ability to replenish essence for a longer period of time. Unless one is a mindwielder, areas devoid of essence are therefore devoid of magic. Areas of devastation come back with greater amounts of essence.

Xeian – One of the eight gods. The middle son and co-creator of the race of elves, lover of trees and green and things that grow.

Printed in the USA
CPSIA information can be obtained
at www.ICGtesting.com
LVHW041017060824
787495LV00009B/38

9 798223 298687